M000289438

AT HOME in the DARK

Edited by
LAWRENCE BLOCK

ISBN -978-1-951939-89-2

This edition design: QA Productions

A LAWRENCE BLOCK PRODUCTION

Table of Contents

IT'S GETTING DARK IN HERE

A FOREWORD BY LAWRENCE BLOCK

AGES AGO, LUCILLE BALL had this exchange on *I Love Lucy* with a snobbish character whose task it was to elevate her culturally:

SNOB: "Now there are two words I never want to hear you say. One is *Swell* and the other is *Lousy*."
LUCY: "Okay. Let's start with the lousy one."

Funny what lingers in the mind . . .

EVERY YEAR OR SO, I stub my toe on a couple of buzzwords and decide I'd just as soon not encounter them again. There are two that I've found increasingly annoying of late, and if Lucy were here I'd tell her that one of them is *Awesome* and the other is *Iconic*.

It is in the nature of the spoken language for words to come and go, and none are more cyclical than those we choose to indicate strong approval or disapproval. *'Swonderful*, Cole Porter told us, that you should care for me. Indeed, *'Smarvelous*, isn't it? *Wonderful, marvelous, terrific, sensational, excellent, brilliant*—each takes its turn as a way of demonstrating great positive enthusiasm.

For quite a few years now, *le mot du jour* has been *awesome.* Now it's a perfectly reasonable word, and means simply that the noun thus modified is likely to inspire awe, even as that which is *wonderful* is clearly full of wonder. If everything thus described is truly awesome, one is left to contemplate a generation of wide-eyed and slack-jawed folk gaping at all that is arrayed in front of them.

Well, okay. Periodically a word of approval swims upstream into the Zeitgeist, resonates with enough of us to have an impact, and becomes the default term for us all—or at least those of us under forty. Before too long its original meaning has been entirely subsumed, and all it means to call something *awesome* is that one likes it.

Deep down where it lives, *awesome* is essentially identical in meaning to *awful*. And there was a time when *awful* and *wonderful* were synonyms—full of awe, full of wonder. Now, as Lucy could tell you, one is swell and the other is lousy.

If anything good is *awesome*, then anything memorable or distinctive is *iconic*. I shouldn't complain, I don't suppose, as several of my own books have had that label applied to them, and perhaps I ought to regard the whole business as awesome. But iconic? Really? No narcissist thinks more highly of his own work than I, but I have trouble picturing any of my books as a literal icon, displayed on the wall of a Russian Orthodox cathedral.

Wait, let me rethink that. Maybe *Eight Million Ways to Die* might make the cut. I mean, dude, that book is *awesome*.

NEVER MIND. I HAVE the honor to present to you seventeen stories, any or all of which you might well describe as awesome or iconic or both. And I want to introduce them by pointing out another buzzword, of one of which I've tired at least as much as I have of the two of them combined.

Noir.

It's a perfectly good word, and particularly useful if you're in Paris and an ominous feline crosses your path. "*Un chat noir!*" you might say—or you might offer a Gallic shrug and pretend you hadn't seen it. Whatever works.

Noir is the French word for black. But when it makes its way across *la mer*, it manages to gain something in translation.

Early on, it became attached to a certain type of motion picture. A French critic named Nino Frank coined the term *Film Noir* in 1946, but it took a couple of decades for the phrase to get any traction. I could tell you what does and doesn't constitute classic film noir, and natter on about its visual style with roots in German Expressionist cinematography, but you can check out Wikipedia as well as I can. (That, after all, is what I did, and how I happen to know about Nino Frank.)

Or you can read a recent novel of mine, *The Girl With the Deep Blue Eyes.* The protagonist, an ex-NYPD cop turned Florida private eye, is addicted to the cinematic genre. When he's not acting out a role in his own real-life Film Noir, he's on the couch with his feet up, watching how Hollywood used to do it.

That's what the French word for black is doing in the English language. It's modifying the word *film*, and describes a specific example thereof.

Now though, it's all over the place.

The credit—or the blame, as you prefer—goes to Johnny Temple of Akashic Books. In 2004 Akashic published *Brooklyn Noir,* Tim McLoughlin's anthology of original crime stories set in that borough. They did very well with it, well enough to prompt McLoughlin to compile and Akashic to publish a sequel, *Brooklyn Noir 2: The Classics,* consisting of reprint. It did well, too, and a lot of publishers would have let it go at that, but Akashic went on to launch a whole cottage industry of darkness.

A look at the publisher's website shows a total of 120 published and forthcoming Noir titles, but the number is sure to be higher by the time you read this. Akashic clearly subscribes to the notion that every city has a dark side, and deserves a chance to tell its own stories.

It is, I must say, a wholly estimable enterprise. I could not begin to estimate the number of writers whose first appearance in print has come in an Akashic anthology. They owe Akashic a debt of gratitude, as does a whole world of readers.

And as do I. I had the pleasure of editing *Manhattan Noir* and *Manhattan Noir 2,* and while neither brought me wealth beyond the dreams of avarice, each was a source of personal and artistic satisfaction. And, after I'd coaxed a couple friends into writing stories for my anthology, I could hardly demur when they turned the tables on me. I'd written one myself for *Manhattan Noir,* and wrote another for S. J. Rozan's *Bronx Noir*, and a third for Sarah Cortez and Bootsie Martinez's *Indian Country Noir.* All three were about the same cheerfully homicidal young woman, and although she didn't yet have a name, she clearly had a purpose in life. I found more stories to write about her, realized they were chapters of a novel in progress, and in time *Getting Off* was published by Hard Case Crime.

So I wish their series continued success. Although their stories have never had much to do with Hollywood's 1940 vision of *noir*, neither are they happy little tales full of kitty cats and bunny rabbits. They are serious stories, taking in the main a hard line on reality, and any gray scale would show them on the dark end of the spectrum.

Noir? Noirish? Okay, fine. I'm happy for them to go on using the word. In fact I'm all for letting them trademark it, just so the rest of the world could quit using it.

That, Gentle Reader, is a rant. And you can relax now. I'm done with it.

So HERE WE HAVE seventeen stories, and you'll note that they cover a lot of ground in terms of genre. Most are crime fiction to a greater or lesser degree, but James Reasoner's is a period Western and Joe Hill's is horror and Joe R. Lansdale's is set in a dystopian future, and what they all have in common, besides their unquestionable excellence, is where they stand on that gray scale.

They are, in a word, *dark*.

And that, I must confess, is the modifier I greatly prefer to *noir.*

It's easy to see I'm partial to it. A few years ago I put together a collection of New York stories for Three Rooms Press, and the title I fastened upon was *Dark City Lights.* (While I was at it I fastened as well upon some of that book's contributors; of the writers in *At Home in the Dark*, six of them—Ed Park, Jim Fusilli, Thomas Pluck, Jill D. Block, Elaine Kagan and Warren Moore—wrote stories for *Dark City Lights.*)

The title came to me early on. Years ago I'd come across O. Henry's last words, spoken on his deathbed, and in case you missed them in the epigraph, you needn't flip pages. "Turn up the lights," said the master of the surprise ending. "I don't want to go home in the dark."

I CAN BUT HOPE you enjoy *At Home in the Dark.* I find it's inspired me, and there's another anthology taking shape in my mind even now. I already have a title in mind, and it's five words long (as my titles tend to be), and it has the word *dark* in it.

Trust me. It'll be awesome.

HOT PANTS

BY ELAINE KAGAN

"DAD?" LUCINDA SAID.

Her father was snoring, relaxed and long in a faded chintz wing chair, legs out in front of him, ankles crossed, size 13 feet in thick white socks on a matching faded chintz ottoman. The chair was permanently placed in front of a large TV screen that was permanently tuned to Turner Classic Movies. The movie playing that morning was something in black-and-white with Jimmy Cagney or maybe it was Mickey Rooney, she wasn't sure which, tapping around a giant movie set that was supposed to look like a street in downtown Manhattan. The guy could really dance.

People shuffled in and out of the long living room. The sound was turned way down on the TV and most of the people pushing their walkers across the ratty rug were silent and smiling. Some sat motionless, like kids playing dead—jaws dropped, heads thrown back, eyes closed—like zombies, Lucinda thought. Twelve white zombies being herded around a big rambling two-story house by two brown women, one brown man, one black woman and two black men rotating hours and days in blue scrubs in Newark, New Jersey.

Mrs. Ventimillia sat at the piano, her hands folded and quiet in her lap. She never played and it wasn't clear if she was looking at the sheet music on the piano table or out the window. Her daughter said she'd been a really terrific jazz pianist—very Bill Evans, her daughter said. Lucinda had to look up Bill Evans. Mrs. Ventimillia had also been a reporter for the New York Post and it was ironic that Mr. Santangelo, who spent most of his time on the cracked leather sofa across from the fireplace that had no logs, was reading a yellowed copy of the New York Post that he carried around in his pocket. It didn't seem to matter that the news wasn't current. Lucinda didn't know if Mrs. Ventimillia and Mr. Santangelo had ever even spoken. Mr. Santangelo was in pretty good shape except for every now and then when he had a screaming fit and threw things. No one so far had figured out what set him off. "He's nuts," her father said.

Lucinda leaned forward, her face closer to her father's. "Daddy?"

His feet jumped a little and the snoring stopped with an abrupt intake of breath as if he'd stopped breathing altogether for maybe twenty seconds, and then started up again. Like a car engine. Not as loud, but still strong. He was still strong, her father. His mind was full of smoke, as he frequently pointed out with a wry laugh when he was "in", as he put it, but his body betrayed his 68 years. He looked maybe 58 tops. He had a character actor face with dark red wavy hair and a solid muscular build. No gut above his belt. He had a splatter of freckles across ruddy cheeks, a thick neck and thick hands. He could probably still jump on and off a fire engine, pull a hose, climb a ladder, chainsaw through a roof, or run into flames looking like the picture poster of how a fire captain should look. Although he just might not be able to remember what a fire engine did—or a hose or a ladder or a chain saw. Or how to brush his teeth or cut his meat or recognize Chief Lang when he came to visit. "I know this guy, right?" he said to Lucinda, tilting his head towards the Fire Chief. Chief Archie Lang and her father had gone through the Academy together, had been best men at each other's weddings and were godfather's to each other's kids. "I'm losing me," her father said in a gruff whisper to Archie Lang, leaning in close and secret. "Don't tell the kid. Okay?" "Okay," Chief Lang said, giving a brave nod to Lucinda and an affectionate punch to her dad's upper arm. Lucinda made a concerted effort to not die right there or throw up. He was "in and out" now, this stalwart father of hers, slipping down the ladder of dementia.

"Hello."

Lucinda looked up. A tiny wiry woman wearing a print dress with pink socks stuffed into white open toed house slippers was standing right next to the arm of her chair. She had several strands of beads slung around her neck, hot pink lipstick with blush to match and she was pushing 90. "Hello, Mrs. Moskowitz."

"Hello, yourself." She looked hard at Lucinda. "Do you know this man?"

"Yes, ma'am," Lucinda said, "he's my father."

"Uh huh. Is he Jewish?"

Lucinda smiled and shook her head. "He's Italian, Mrs. Moskowitz." They'd had this same conversation maybe four times that morning and maybe twenty-seven times in the last month.

"He doesn't look Italian."

"Right," Lucinda said, studying her father, "he actually looks Irish."

Mrs. Moskowitz sighed. "I had an Italian man once," she said, lowering her voice and giving Lucinda a woman-to-woman stare, "he was a no-goodnick, if you know what I mean."

"I do."

"Well, then," she said, pushing her walker forward, "I have to get home," she said, "my mother will kill me. It's a school night, you know."

"Okay," Lucinda said.

Jesus Mary and Joséph. She touched her father's arm; kind of jossled him. "Dad, I have to go to work."

Nicholas John Conte coughed, cleared his throat and opened his eyes. Clear blue; nothing dimmed in the sight area. He stretched a giant's stretch, folding his arms over his face and then extending them out to the sides, spreading his fingers, lifting his legs straight out in front of him, pointing his toes and flexing, and then down again with the appropriate sounds of a big man stretching.

"Hey, Lucy," he said, smiling at his daughter.

"Well, you had a good nap."

"I wasn't asleep."

She laughed. "You weren't?"

"Just checking the inside of my eyelids," he said, and yawned. He'd been saying that since she could remember.

He looked around the room. "Where's your mother?"

"Dad, mom hasn't been here for years. You know that."

He took maybe a minute to ponder it. "Oh, right, the guy with the boat."

"Right."

"Who knew she liked boats?" he said and laughed. He looked around the room. "And here I am at the *big house*."

"Dad."

"When will my house be ready?"

"Soon."

This was his new thing—fixing it in his head that his house was being worked on—plumbing, paint, new floors, etc. He'd tell you. It was Lucinda's choice to let him believe it. The first few months had been endless battles about him getting out of there. "What the hell is going on here, Lucy!" he would shout, "am I a goddamn prisoner?" It came to a near brawl one night with Miguel and Reginald, two of the attendants at the home. It was Reverend Father King's idea to tell him the house was under construction. "You want me to *lie*, Father?" "It's not a lie if you paint the kitchen, Lucinda," he said, leaning back in his chair. So much for being Catholic.

"Damn construction guys," Nick Conte muttered. "This always happens, you know. I told you. *We'll be done by February, we'll be done by March* . . . where's the peanut?"

"In school. I gotta go to work, Dad."

"Oh, right. Sure, kid," he said, pulling his feet back and off the ottoman, stuffing them into his loafers, fixing the front of his shirt, running his hand through his hair and standing up. "How is everything?"

"Good," she said, slipping on her jacket, shrugging her handbag strap over her shoulder and pulling the car keys from her jeans pocket.

"Everything good at the restaurant?"

"Yep."

"They make a great creamed spinach. It's the nutmeg, you know. That's the ticket."

"I know."

He put his hand on her shoulder, steering her to the front door. "Did you bring me my lasagna?"

"Yes, sir, I gave it to Princess. You saw when I got here."

"Right. That's your grandmother's recipe, you know."

"I know."

"Old man Sorrentino had sticky fingers; he could steal your grandma's rosary beads right out of her hand. You know that, right?"

She laughed. "We'll go Sunday."

"Good idea. With the peanut."

She took her father and her six-year old daughter, Maria, to the restaurant every Sunday, every single Sunday since she'd moved him into this wretched place that cost her a small fortune and was supposedly one of the best group houses for people with dementia in all of New Jersey, not just in Belleville or Bloomfield—a big old house smelling faintly of old carpet and Pinesol and burnt onions and Mrs. Moskowitz' Jungle Gardenia and someone's adult Pamper and bad breath and wet dog, which was ridiculous because there was no dog allowed on the premises, not even to visit, which made no sense because it was a known fact that animals helped people with stress and there was enough stress in this place to choke a horse, her mother would have said. Her beautiful mother who had walked out on them when Lucinda was fifteen for a cop named Vinnie who worked in Brooklyn and it was hard to say which was worse—a firefighter's wife leaving him for a cop or the fact that the cop was from Brooklyn. Not even counting the boat. Vinnie had a Criss Craft cabin cruiser, or a Criss Cross cabin cruiser, she wasn't sure which, but it seemed to matter a great deal to her mother.

"She likes the pudding."

"Who?"

"The peanut. She likes the pudding at Serendipity's."

"Sorrentino's, dad."

"At Sorrentino's, right."

"And it's budino. Not pudding."

He shrugged. "Budino . . . pudding . . . what the hell's the difference?"

LUCINDA RESTED HER FOREHEAD against the steering wheel. It was icy. All of New Jersey was icy—the streets, the bare branches of the trees against the pale sky, her heart.

She couldn't take care of him anymore. Not after the thing with the oven. Not after the thing with the car.

"You can't take care of him anymore," her aunt Angie said with defiance, feet planted, arms crossed over her breasts. "It's enough. Soon he won't know how to wipe his own ass," she said.

Lucinda's mouth opened.

"I can say that, he's my brother," Angie said. "What if he takes Maria in the car with him, what if he takes her to Bloomfield Center and loses her? Or drives to Philadelphia?"

Lucinda actually smiled. "Why would dad go to Philadelphia?"

"Oh, I don't know," Angie said, collapsing into a chair, sobbing, "Jesus Mary and Joséph, my Nicky, what a thing."

"It's a good place," Reverend Father King said about the home. "It's enough, Lucinda. This is a good place."

She started the car.

"COMO ESTA, LUCY?" JOSÉ shouted over the din as she walked into Sorrentino's crowded kitchen. Cooks and waiters, busboys and dishwashers jostled for position at sink and stove and counters, moving pots and pans and plates and food with the precision of the New York Yankees or possibly the New York City Ballet Company, she wasn't sure which, and in the middle of the whole commotion stood José, stacking thick white plates on trays. José Conchola had been a busboy at Sorrentino's since Lucinda had been coming there as a little girl. Sixty now, he knew all the regulars and they all knew him, a fixture; as faithful as their recipe for lasagna.

"I'm fine," she said, "good."

"How's the papa?"

"The same."

"The same is good," Enrique said, lifting his eyes from a mountain of tomatoes he was chopping.

"You think?"

"I think, yes," he said emphatically, waving the knife in his hand. "Change is fearful." Enrique was proud of his English and liked to show off his extensive vocabulary, which wasn't always the use of the correct word at the correct time. "With study no one will know I am from Puerto Rico," he would say which brought down the house, or actually the kitchen.

"They will all think you are from Norway!" Simon, one of the dishwashers, shouted and everyone laughed.

If you cooked in Sorrentino's kitchen, you spoke Spanish—Mexico, Puerto Rico, Guatemala—it didn't matter which country—you just couldn't work at Sorrentino's as a chef if you were Italian. It was policy; a proclamation laid down years ago by the old man. "You hire an Italian to cook in your kitchen and they will change your recipe," old man Sorrentino had said with disdain, "you hire a Mexican and they do exactly as you say." The only Italian chef allowed to cook in that kitchen was Sorrentino's nephew, Salvatore, who had gone to the Cordon Bleu of Naples, or whatever the hell was the equivalent and then worked in Manhattan in two restaurants that were supposedly very ladidah but too expensive for Lucinda to try, not even counting trying to get into the city and to the Upper East Side. Enrique told her a plate of gnocchi was $36.00. He'd taken his wife and daughter for her confirmation. "A veal chop cost more than a cheap suit! That is the expression, yes?" "Yes," Lucinda answered, laughing. Carlos, one of Sorrentino's sauté chefs, followed Salvatore around like a puppy but it was Lucinda's take that the other guys in the kitchen thought Salvatore was full of himself. Chu Chu, the grill chef, called him un perro or un cerdo behind his back, which was a dog or a pig, which exasperated José—"you should not be offending the animals." Part of it was jealousy. After all, he had a real education and real experience, although his gnocchi were not cloud pillows of perfection like Carlos made and his veal chop in a balsamic glaze didn't get close to Chu Chu's.

"We got a lot of reservations?"

"Only the old ones," José said, grinning. "They come for the noon whistle," he said smacking the swinging door with his hip and sailing out of the kitchen.

"Que mierda this *noon meliodia*?" Chu Chu asked.

"Speak English!" Enrique shouted.

It was not her intention to end up waiting tables and being pleasant to people who sent back their steak because "this isn't rare, this is mooing," or eating cloud pillows of gnocchi way too late at night, which couldn't be good for her thighs but was good for her purse and her peace of mind. She'd been in line for the general manager position at Armstrong's when they went out of business, in like four hours over some hush-hush crooked money transaction that stunk to high heaven, as her Aunt Angie put it, which happened the week after she'd put her father into "the big house" and Maria into Ridge Street School first grade. She'd been working at Armstrong's for twelve years, from right after she graduated, married Marty, got pregnant, had the peanut Maria, and Marty got sick and then sicker and actually died—*actually* because who dies when they're 36? A schtarker Jewish up-and-coming Immigration lawyer who could dance like Jimmy Cagney or maybe Mickey Rooney, and could actually sew a hem? And tell jokes like a Borscht Belt comic. And had basketball hands? Yes.

So, what the hell was she going to do with no job at Armstrong's? How was she going to pay for everything? She had to call Chief Lang to find out about her dad's pension and insurance. And that Sunday they'd gone to Sorrentino's for early dinner—her dad and Maria and Angie—and like a gift from the Gods, when Marco was cleaning off their table he told her that Rosa had quit that morning with no notice and the Sorrentino's were hysterical looking for someone.

And Angie had come through for her like Justify winning the Triple Crown at Belmont. "I know how to baby sit," she said to Lucinda, eyes narrowing, chin raised. "I baby sat you plenty, didn't I? After your mother ran off into the night."

Lucinda smiled. "It wasn't in the night, Ang." Ah, the age-old story of her mother running away with Vinnie.

"It's a figure of speech, right? Did I step in and take care of you while your father spent days on that fire engine?"

"Yes, ma'am. You did."

"Days, nights . . . all those hours, busting his ass."

"Yes, ma'am."

"So I'll step in again. What's the problem?"

"Well, your time . . . I don't expect you to give up your life to take care of Maria for me while I'm hustling plates of red sauce."

"And what am I supposed to do with my time, Missy? Dust? Play Mahjong?"

Lucinda laughed. "You don't play Mah Jong."

"Well, I could learn," Angie said.

And because Etta and Bruno Sorrentino had known her practically since she'd been born and she'd worked there two summers when she was in high school and they needed somebody fast since Rosa had up and quit with no notice—a *betrayal*, Bruno had said, his lips pulled into a thin line like a guy in *The Godfather*—and because they were more than fair about working out hours with her and the rest of the wait staff so she could see her dad and her kid, she made her peace with it—she bought three white blouses and three pairs of black slacks and black sneakers and learned how to tie the stupid black tie. After all, she didn't need to sing three verses of "I Need This Job" from "A Chorus Line" to know what was up—she would wait tables at Sorrentino's.

* * *

THE FIRST TIME IT happened was last fall. The lovely lull between lunch and dinner. Chu Chu put his feet up. Simon had a cigarette in the alley. They actually locked the front door from 3 to 5. They even turned off the wretched background music which was barely audible when the restaurant was full, but could make your teeth hurt when you could hear it—Italian crooners from the old days—which was okay every now and then but not night and day. Which was one of the songs that played over and over. And, how many times could you listen to Julius LaRosa singing "Eh Compari!"? Bruno was not interested in new music or any of the new devices that could bring music into the restaurant. "I am an old fashioned man, Lucinda; this is an old fashioned restaurant. Lei capisce?"

"I got it," she said.

"Don't make trouble with him," her Aunt Angie said. "He'll have us all bumped off."

"Ang, you're hysterical. The Sorrentino's aren't in the mob."

"What's a mob?" Maria asked.

"A group of people who are up to trouble," Angie answered. "Who wants ice cream?"

It was so slight that she wasn't even sure it had happened. She was outside in back during the lull. Maybe four o'clock, four thirty. It was everything you wanted an autumn afternoon to be—chill in the shade, warm in the dazzling sun, the leaves doing their red and gold thing. She was just standing there watching the sky, actually thinking about Marty running track at Rutgers, coming off the track and hugging her, all sweaty and laughing and she was already all dressed up to go to this tea. "I don't even like tea," she had said. "It's a big deal to get invited to tea at the Dean's," Marty said. "Why?" "Because they're coffee drinkers." "You're all sweaty." "It's sexy, huh?" he said. She closed her eyes.

The car hardly made any noise; Sal's wife's car. It slid up and he got out. If he leaned in to kiss Terry goodbye Lucinda missed it. Terry gave a little wave and Lucinda gave a little wave and the car made a U and took off and Sal walked past her with a "hey," and she had a sweater draped over her shoulders and it had slipped off on one side and as he passed her he kind of propped it back up on her shoulder and his hand barely slid a little down her arm and his fingers moved across her breast. Across her breast. Right? He went in Sorrentino's back door and she stood there.

The second time was the same sort of thing. Right before they unlocked the front door for dinner. The five o'clock whistle, José called it. She was tossing the hot half-sliced bread into the baskets. They sliced them half way through so the people could pull them the rest of the way letting off a tantalizing whiff of hot baked bread. Enrique had sliced the first batch of loaves and was on his way back to the oven. Salvatore was on his way to the stove holding a cupped handful of truffles and as he slid behind her he rubbed the front of his body against her ass. His cock was hard. It wasn't a narrow kitchen. It's not like he didn't have plenty of room to get around her. And it's not like she didn't remember what a hard cock felt like. Son of a bitch. She dropped the bread she was holding and whipped around to look at him but he was already at the stove lecturing Chu Chu on sautéing truffles. She stood there.

"What's up, Lucy?" José said.

"Nothing."

Her heart was racing.

The third time he'd actually cupped her ass. It was in the dining room after they'd closed or at least weren't going to serve anyone else. There were always stragglers. There was a boisterous family falling all over each other after many bottles of Montepulciano struggling to make it to the door. And in the corner booth sat Mr. Ruban with three cronies sipping Remy. Al Ruban was a regular. She wasn't exactly sure who he was but she knew he was somebody. She wasn't exactly sure if people were still connected but if they were, he was. She wasn't interested in knowing. She knew José held him in high regard; he always got in even if he didn't have a reservation, and when Salvatore had gone over to pay his respects he'd practically genuflected in front of the table. It was on Sal's way back. José and Marco had picked up dirty dishes, glasses and silverware and were moving back into the kitchen, trays full. Lucinda bent over to get a tossed napkin they'd missed halfway hidden under the table cloth and as she bent to get it he was behind her cupping her ass. It must have looked as if he was helping her pick up whatever she was going for. His body must have blocked what he was doing with his hand, his fingers sliding to the middle of her ass and pushing. She practically fell getting back up and he made a big deal of saying, "Scuse, scuse," and took off into the kitchen.

She held the crumpled napkin to her chest. She steadied herself. She walked slowly after him.

Simon and Pepe were washing pots and singing. José and Marco were laughing. Chu Chu was on his cell phone. There was no sign of Salvatore who must have been in the little closet office down the hall.

The door was open. He was sitting at the desk scribbling something on a piece of paper.

"What are you doing?" she said.

"I write tomorrow's specials. I think the vongole with tomatoes."

She took a breath. "No. What are you doing with me?"

"What am I doing with you?"

She was clutching the doorframe.

"With me. You had your hand on me."

"What?"

"Don't *what.* You had your hand on my ass."

He stared at her.

"It isn't the first time."

He tilted his head. "Is silly to make a fuss."

"A *fuss*? I'm making a *fuss*? What are you doing, Sal?"

"I want to fuck you."

She could feel her heartbeat in her mouth.

"No one will know."

Her stomach turned.

"Mr. Ruban wants his check, chica," Enrique said from behind her.

She turned. "What?"

Enrique grinned at her. "Mr. Ruban. He wants to pay and leave you a boo coo tip because you are the pinnacle of waitress in all of New Jersey. Yes?"

SHE DIDN'T TELL ANYONE. She didn't go to work for four days feigning a sinus infection. She took a lot of showers. She spent hours in a pew at Sacred Heart Cathedral. "Are you alright, Lucinda?" Reverend Father asked, cornering her in the parking lot by her car. "I'm okay, Father." "Contemplating the sad state of the world, are we?" he said with a wry smile. She didn't answer. "You can always talk to me about things, Lucinda. You know that. Okay?" Oh, sure, Father, she thought. You see, Salvatore wants to fuck me, and I'm not sure what to do because, you know, he's Sorrentino's nephew, and I'm sure it wouldn't sit well with Etta and Bruno, or Sal's wife, but what if they don't believe me, so I've been hitting restaurants all over the hood with my resume, but it's hard to find a job close to Maria's school and to my dad and all . . . so what's your advice, Father?

She read Maria a lot of stories. She ate a lot of cheesecake. She waxed the dining room table countless times. "What's with you and the wax?" Angie said.

They had something for her at Costello's but it was just lunches and they had something for her at the Corner Diner but you needed a place with a bar if you wanted big tips and the best drink in the diner was a chocolate shake.

She worked Thanksgiving. She worked Christmas. She worked in between. She had to. The neighborhood celebrated the holidays big time and Sorrentino's was packed. Big tabs, big tips. The restaurant had a big tree in the front entrance, wrapped empty boxes under the tree, colored lights that flashed on and off strung behind the bar, the works. She stayed away from him. She didn't put herself anywhere near him. He didn't look at her. She didn't look at him. Maybe it would be okay. Maybe it was over. Maybe she had made it up.

And then two days after Christmas when they closed the restaurant so the whole staff could have their big family dinner and she was there with her dad and Maria and Angie because how could she tell her family that they weren't going to the family dinner? And there he was with his wife and their three-year-old Gio and their seven-year old Anthony, telling stories and being charming, and she thought, okay, this is good, it's over. And on her way back from the ladies room he slammed her up against the wall, sliding his wet mouth across her face and eyes, panting "I eat you up, Lucinda," shoving his meaty hand up her skirt and she stomped the high heel of her shoe into his instep.

"EVERYTHING GOOD AT THE restaurant?" her father asked.

"Mmhm."

She'd quit. She'd go in this afternoon and tell them. She'd go into the city and find a goddamn job.

"Did you bring me my lasagna?"

"You saw me, Dad, when I got here."

"Right."

Her father tilted his head towards Mrs. Moskowitz who was across the room. She was head to toe in powder blue, including a piece of tulle wound around her head with a matching piece of tulle wrapped around her walker. "She wanted me to dance with her," Nick Conte said in an irritated whisper, "does that beat all?"

"What?" Lucinda followed his gaze to Mrs. Moskowitz who noticed they were looking at her. She lifted one hand off the walker and gave her father a jaunty wave and a toothy smile.

"I told her maybe eighty-three times I'm married. What the hell would your mother say?"

Nothing, Dad, Lucinda thought. She's probably having a pina colada on Vinnie's boat. Oh for crissakes. Her eyes filled; she couldn't help it. "Dad, do you remember Salvatore?"

"Who?"

Oh, Jesus.

"Salvatore who?" he asked, frowning.

What the hell was she doing?

"Lucinda?"

"Nobody. Really. I was just . . ."

"What the hell is going on?"

She took a breath. "Nothing. I'm sorry, I . . ."

He gave her the stare he gave her when she was sixteen and he'd caught her sneaking through the kitchen after midnight due to the fact she'd been kissing John Turner in his car two doors down the street. His eyes narrowed. "He's the construction guy, right?"

"Daddy, please."

"Goddamn it, Lucinda! Salvatore, my ass! What is it? Plumbing? Electrical? Those sons-a-bitches will take me for all I got. Goddamn it!" he yelled, standing up fast, nearly losing his balance.

Lucinda shot up, grabbed his arm before he fell. He shrugged out of her grasp, straightened his shirt and ran his hand through his hair. "You tell that son-of-a-bitch Salvatore to call *me!* I want to know when my house will be ready! You hear me, Lucinda? You tell him I'm the one who pays the goddamn bills!"

SHE CALLED JOSÉ. SHE met him at Dicky Dee's and watched him eat a hot dog pushed into pizza dough with onions and peppers. It took a half hour to get him to even look her in the eyes after she told him.

"You believe me?"

"It is complicated."

"José . . ."

He shook his head. "You cannot quit without another job."

"I'll go to Etta and Bruno."

"Nothing will happen."

"They'll talk to him."

He laughed. The onions and peppers had left their red-orange grease stain around his mouth. He dabbed paper napkins into a cup of water and wiped at his lips. "We will watch you."

"What do you mean?"

"Enrique and Chu Chu and Simon and me. Even Carlos, we will watch you. Be next to you."

"Etta and Bruno will talk to him."

"No."

"No?"

"No," he said. "And they will be angry."

"At me?"

"He is their family."

She inhaled. *They* will be angry? She hadn't been this angry since Marty up and died. "José, he is a scumbag. Un hijo de puta. Basura."

José visibly flinched.

"I'm sorry," she said. "I know you don't say those things. José . . . please . . ."

He put his hand gently on her arm. "We will watch you."

"You will watch me," Lucinda repeated and felt all the air rush out of her body.

"Like we watched Rosa."

She lifted her head. "Like you watched Rosa," she repeated.

"ME TOO, MY ASS," Rosa said softly, taking a sip of her martini, extending her glass towards Lucinda, "and you can be 'me three', cookie."

She put the glass gently back down on the bar and smoothed her skirt under her legs. "So I see those bitches on TV, you know, those actresses, puta movie stars in their black dresses and their sincere eyes and I listen to how they're going to change the world and bring this sexual harassment thing right to the forefront, you know, like there won't always be some guy trying to get into your pants and I laugh, I gotta tell you, while I'm trying to get a grip on the fact that after seventeen years at Sorrentino's those sons a bitches fired me. I go to Etta and Bruno and Bruno says to me, "Leave your apron," and I think, fuck you, old man, I should take this apron and cut it into little pieces and shove them up your ass, because I ask you, where are we gonna go? Is there a Human Resources Department at Sorrentino's? Are they gonna lock up Salvatore? Ha ha ha. Another girl gets her tit grabbed in Newark. Call the media! Get that chick a black dress, put her on the Golden Gloves!"

"Golden Globes."

"Okay." She sighed. "Do you want to eat something?"

"Sure," Lucinda said.

"They make a really good fried calamari here," Rosa said, "as good as Chu Chu's," she said, lifting her hand and holding her fingers tight against her lips as tears softly covered her face. "I promise," she said, and laughed. "I've gained like maybe twelve pounds."

"You wouldn't know it. You look great."

Rosa cleared her throat and dabbed at the skin under her eyes with the cocktail napkin. "So, you want that? Calamari?"

"Absolutely," Lucinda said. She waved her hand at the bartender.

"My husband wanted to kill him. I said oh, that's good, Jack—then the girls and I can come visit you in prison. Wonderful." She folded and refolded the little damp napkin. Her hands were shaking. "You have a daughter, right?"

"She's six," Lucinda said.

"I have two. Twelve and fifteen." She shook her head. "Don't ask." She smiled at Lucinda. "We shoulda had boys, huh?"

Lucinda smiled back. Jesus.

"Before me he got Denise," Rosa said. Did you know Denise?"

"No, I didn't know Denise."

"She could do six tables of eight without blinking." Rosa took a breath. "Great waitress. Really. She taught me lots of stuff." She lifted her glass and took another sip, "he hurt her," she said in a whisper, "he got her bad in the hallway." She put the glass down. "We could have prosciutto and melon with the calamari," she said, "would you like that?"

"Okay," Lucinda answered. She didn't fall off the stool. She moved her icy glass off the bar. The stem left a perfect wet ring.

THEY WATCHED HER. ESPECIALLY Enrique, as if he were guarding Shakira while she was on tour. She was never alone with Sal. Never. One of them even waited in the hall when she went to the Ladies Room. They never discussed it—whatever José had said to them was enough. And she was calmer; she actually forgot about it every now and then. And when she came to the restaurant with her family on Sundays, because Angie made a big stink when she suggested they go somewhere else—"What do you mean, go somewhere else? Where would we go?" looking at her as she'd lost her mind—if he walked through the dining room while they were there you couldn't possibly imagine he was the man who would do such things—shaking her father's hand, giving Angie the right amount of sweet attention, and when he spoke to Maria he bent down so he was on her level. He even bought her a book about bugs; she'd been fascinated with creepy crawling things since she was maybe eight months old and saw her first rolly-polly bug on the porch.

VALENTINE'S DAY. IT SEEMED like all of New Jersey wanted to be at Sorrentino's for Valentine's Day Dinner. They had stopped taking reservations weeks before. You probably couldn't get in even if you were Al Ruban. José and Marco and Tino were swapping out all the white linens for red, there were red roses going on the tables, red sauce, red velvet cake in the red booths—she was surprised they weren't making the pasta red—thank you, Jesus—and the wait staff was going to wear red ties instead of black which Lucinda thought was truly tacky and totally hysterical. Marty had been the one who went overboard for Valentine's Day—he had actually cut hearts out of red construction paper and thrown them all over the bed and her. "These are itchy," she said to him, paper hearts crackling under her naked butt. "Shut up, Lucinda," he said, laughing, a damp red heart stuck to his chin.

They were ready; everything was humming. Anything that could be cooked ahead of time was cooked, the water was boiling, the garlic was chopped, the tomatoes, the basil, the parsley; the heavenly smell of Bolognese floated from the parking lot out back to the pink neon sign in front.

José and Marco and Tino were bustling dishes and serving pieces to the tables, Simon was stepping in and out of the building to catch a cigarette, Chu Chu and Carlos were pulling filets out of the big freezer, Tino was walking around on his cell phone, having a fight with his wife about when his mother-in-law was finally leaving, and Lucinda was coming back from the ladies room pulling a stray piece of hair back into her pony tail for maybe the sixth time when she realized Salvatore was at the stove. There was no one else in the kitchen.

He was watching her.

She froze.

He smiled.

He had a kitchen towel in his left hand and was reaching for the giant sauté pan behind the huge pots of water.

He didn't take his eyes off her.

She couldn't make her legs move.

The smile became a grin. He put his right hand on the front of his pants and rubbed himself. "I fuck you, Lucinda," he said, in nearly a whisper.

A corner of the towel dipped into the fire under the pot. The flames leaped from his cuff up his shirtsleeve. He yelled and jerked his arm back and his fingers caught the handle of the enormous pot of boiling water that tipped and fell down the front of him—scalding his hand and his pants and his everything. He screamed and fell.

Doors flew open, Carlos and Chu Chu were running, José was shouting but Lucinda didn't move. She just stood there, her hand covering her mouth, and then she smiled.

THE EVE OF INFAMY

BY JIM FUSILLI

THE JUDGE GAVE BILLY Malone a choice: an 18-month stretch in a state prison or the Army. Malone saw the offer as the light of good fortune. His play was drying up and his sinewy, green-eyed charm only went so far. He was thinking he needed a change.

It was coming up on 1941 and the marks had gotten wise. No one in the Bronx, Brooklyn or Manhattan would sit at a poker table with him, so he was reduced to taking down half-wit tourists. On top of that, the precinct cops were aware of his violent record as a juvenile so they were keeping a hard eye on him. They pounced when Billy Malone shattered the jaw of an auto-parts salesman from Akron who accused him of marking the deck with a thumbnail.

"Army," Billy Malone told Judge Steigel in open court.

"I understand you are something of a card sharp," said the judge who, to Billy Malone, looked like a walrus. "Wherever you go, let it be known."

"Yes, your honor," said Billy Malone, a man of few words. He had gotten what he wanted. Why agitate? He figured the Army would give him a free shot at the wide, wide world, a place littered with rubes.

MALONE WAS STATIONED IN Fort Irwin, out in the California desert, north of Barstow and about 150 miles from the nightlife in L.A. He figured his luck had run out, the sandstorms stinging his face, his throat parched from first call until he collapsed in his bunk. A 20-mile run under the scorching sun was a punishment far worse than prison back east.

He heard Los Angeles calling. After a while, he thought he'd go AWOL and lose himself in the big city. Slinging rocks or scrubbing a latrine, he dreamed of a place he'd seen only in the movies: the clubs, the broads, the action, all accompanied by palm trees and orange groves and the cool breeze off the Pacific. He heard the pounding of foamy waves, the seagulls' caw. *Fuck this,* he thought, broiling in the sun, his blond hair trimmed to bristle. *I'm gone.*

Then his unit learned they were shipping out to Oahu.

Suddenly, Billy Malone took to Army life. What the fuck. Do what the screaming sergeant tells you to. Hump, dive, crawl, climb. Shoot, stab. A piece of cake in a climate out of Eden. Free room and board. Lie on the bunk and read the magazines as the scent of ginger and hibiscus wafted into the barracks. Listen to the wind humming through the trees.

On and off the base, the poker action was pitiable. It was theft. He had to bite his cheek to tamp down a smirk. He hung back but within months he'd cleaned out every man in the barracks including a corporal Malone sized up as weak. Next game, Malone threw him cards and the petty prick went to his rack up $600. A three-day pass ensued.

THE CLUB WAS LESS than two miles from the base. The first night, Malone in his floral shirt ran through a December downpour and played the Filipino card sharks straight. He managed to leave up a sawbuck and a half, more than enough for a taxi back to bed. Next night, he won $440, when a rubber trader from Guam dealt him a third jack on the night's last hand.

The hatcheck girl took him home. Her name was Lailani. They spend the next day together too. She knew a secret cove. Someone had been there before: melted candles, discarded rum bottles. She lit the wicks and tossed the empties. Afterwards, she walked naked toward the sunlight at the cove's edge. She returned with a small onyx pipe and a ball of hashish.

He waved her off. He had plans, he told her. He was about to play for real dough.

She nodded discretely when Malone came back to the club. A man sat near him at the bar. A conversation began, the man careful not to come on strong. Malone knew what he was up to, this Hawaiian glad hand, this bullfrog-looking fuck. Malone flashed his bankroll to pay for his drink. The man said no, on the house, and invited him to a private room. Bigger stakes. Saturday night brings in the chumps, he confided.

By midnight, Malone was at the table with a businessman from China; two GIs in blousy civilian clothes, one from Texas, the other was a skinny guy from the Deep South; and a Hawaiian, bloated, full of himself. The GIs counted their money before they anteed up. The Hawaiian, who hassled the hapless help, threw down bills like he owned a mint. Deep South beamed goofy when he won and Hawaiian stared at him with disdain. Malone looked ahead: he'd sit by while Hawaiian slow-played Deep South into poverty. The frog-faced brush had set up the GIs and the Chinaman.

Malone figured he'd been set up too. He had wondered why the rubber trader from Guam threw him the third jack last night, but now he knew. He was there to fatten the pot.

Soon the Chinaman was drained and Texas went in search of a back-alley blowjob. Eight hands in, the Hawaiian showed strong with two kings, but Deep South, who was dealing, raised and re-raised. The Hawaiian called with a boat—kings over sevens. Deep South had four nines. He giggled as he raked in $1,700. The Hawaiian sat stunned, his mouth flapped open.

"YOU WANT TO KEEP on, soldier?" Deep South asked Billy Malone after the Hawaiian limped away.

Malone said, "Why not?" He had 'til dawn.

Deep South dropped his elbows on the table and leaned in with his long, lanky frame. "What do you say to five-card draw? Plain and simple."

"Fine by me," Malone said. He was surprised the Hawaiian had been gutted. Deep South mucked up the house's scam. Deep South, who blew into the palm of his left hand when he was bluffing.

They played even for a while, back and forth. Billy Malone busted up a full house he dealt himself just to see if Deep South was paying attention. Lailani swung by with cocktails, but Malone waved her off. Deep South did too.

Forty minutes in, Deep South raised after dealing himself three fresh cards. Then he blew into his hand. Malone had taken two: He already had three queens. He re-raised, pushing in his last $1,200. Deep South called. Malone showed the ladies. Deep South turned over four sevens, one at a time.

Out $2,600, Malone stood. He dusted his slacks, slipped back into his jacket. Deep South laughed, his Adam's apple bobbing, as he stacked the cash.

Malone pulled himself together and left the back room. The staff was sweeping the floor, chairs were up on the tables. As he walked toward the exit, the lights turned off. Beaten down, he left.

FUCK IT, THOUGHT BILLY Malone as he went along through darkness, palm trees quiet against the crescent moon. Deep South took him down square with the false tell. A legitimate play. As payback, he could take his rival's left thumb or crush his mocking Adam's Apple. But no. Malone would build up another bankroll and locate another game. A lesson learned. Valuable. In the long run, he'd profit from it.

He decided he'd go back to retrieve the girl. Grab a bottle and head to the cove. One last good time before he was due at the base.

The club's front door was locked.

Malone went around back to the screen door to the kitchen.

He entered, passed hanging pots and pans, and there at the bar was everybody but the Chinaman: the rubber salesman from Guam, the Hawaiian who took the beat and the two GIs, Texas and Deep South. They were divvying the pot. The Hawaiian bullfrog came over to pocket his cut. So did Lailani. They moved quickly, efficiently. All business. Good night.

"Next week?" asked the bullfrog.

"You bet," said Deep South. It was easy money, the island full of marks from all over the mainland.

Sunday dawn was maybe an hour off. Malone hid in the parking lot. The remaining cars were settled close to each other. Malone took off his belt. He figured Texas was carrying, Deep South under his protection.

Malone swung the belt and caught Texas in the face with the buckle. Stung, Texas stumbled. Malone kicked his feet out from under him and grabbed the pistol from the GI's waistband. He put the nozzle against the man's sternum and pulled the trigger. On one knee, he turned and shot Deep South in the forehead. In less than a minute, he had the cash and their wallets. He ripped the keys out of Texas's pocket and drove off toward the cove where he and Lailani had spent the afternoon. He'd wait for the rest of them to come. A couple of weeks in the brig for missing curfew would be worth the taste of revenge.

He settled in a crevice, back to the wall, gun drawn.

THEN CAME THE FIRST of more than 300 Jap bombers. Malone heard the earth-rattling explosions. He moved deeper into the cold cave. In the next horrific hours, hundreds of U.S. military personnel were slaughtered. When the raid ended and an eerie tranquility took hold, Malone drove back to the base. In the distance, the island burned, black smoke billowed and the scent of gasoline filling the sky. Dead birds littered the ground.

He discovered the base was in shambles. One of the Jap bombers dropped his payload on the barracks where his unit slept. Most of his outfit was killed, maimed or knocked to their knees. No one remembered Billy Malone had been off-site.

Malone gave a long moment's thought to laying low and heading out. He'd be listed MIA and could start from zero—no record, no history. He'd go to Los Angeles. It was filled with broads like Lailani and with marks like the Chinaman. He knew the big game now. With his blond hair and green eyes, he'd reinvent himself. A Swede. A German who got out before Hitler and the Third Reich. A regular American. He could make it work.

No, he decided, knee-deep in debris. He'd wait out the war and go back to the Bronx. The streets were in his blood. He knew the rooftops and alleyways. Theft came naturally, violence did too. If the next few years broke his way, he could bankroll a future, playing steady amid the turmoil. Then he'd go back home a champion. He'd aim high. The cops wouldn't dare touch him.

About a week after the attack, everybody on high alert, Billy Malone drove a Jeep to the club where he'd been the mark. War or no, he was still out to punish.

But a bomb had leveled the club too, the fire scorching the surrounding property, incinerating the dead and the living. Bodies had been removed. The charred corpses of automobiles remained.

He sent a Christmas card to Judge Steigel, who had shone on him the light of good fortune.

"Thanks for everything," he wrote. He signed it "Very truly yours, Billy Malone. Pearl Harbor, December 1941."

NIGHT ROUNDS

BY JAMES REASONER

DAVE BLAKE GRASPED THE doorknob and tried to twist it, but it didn't turn. He nodded in satisfaction. Trammell's Hardware Store was locked up tight for the night, just like it was supposed to be. Blake moved on down the boardwalk to check the door of the next business.

This was his favorite time of day and favorite part of the job of marshal. Night had fallen over Wagontongue. Most folks were in their homes and had had their supper. Some had turned in already while others sat in parlors, reading by lamplight or singing old songs with the family gathered around the piano. The Lucky Cuss, Wagontongue's only saloon, was still open, but on a week night like this, not many customers would be there and they wouldn't be in any mood to cause a ruckus. Sam Dorn, who owned the place, would likely call it a night and close up soon.

Peace reigned over the settlement . . . just the way Dave Blake liked it.

He'd held down the marshal's job for a little over a year, Wagontongue being the latest in a string of towns where he had worn the badge. Some lawmen settled down in one place and stayed there most of their lives. Dave Blake had never been that way. He'd always felt too many restless stirrings after he'd been somewhere for a while, an urge telling him that he needed to get up and go somewhere else. It was hard on his wife Clarissa, he knew, but he couldn't help it.

The job here in Wagontongue was one of the easiest he'd had. Outlaws didn't have any interest in a sleepy little cowtown like this. The only trouble came when cowboys from the spreads between here and the Prophets rode into town, drank too much busthead at the Lucky Cuss, and got proddy enough to start fights. Blake always managed to break those up without having to resort to gunplay.

He touched his Colt's walnut grips now. Except for target practice, knocking airtights off fence posts, he hadn't fired the gun in five years. As tranquil as Wagontongue was, that streak was likely to continue.

He checked the door of Bennett's saddle shop. Locked. Blake started to move on.

"Marshal, is that you?"

The voice came from behind him, made him pause and half-turn. A man-shaped patch of darkness came along the boardwalk toward him, not really hurrying but moving along pretty briskly. Blake hadn't recognized the voice, so he said, "Yeah, it's me. Who's there?"

"Jack Hargis. I ride for the Circle P."

Blake didn't know the name, but that wasn't surprising. Cowhands moved in and out of the area all the time. Round-up would be coming along soon, so the ranchers were taking on extra hands.

"What can I do for you, Hargis?"

The man waved a hand in the general direction of the Lucky Cuss, at the other end of town and on the opposite side of the street.

"I think some fellas down there are fixin' to cause trouble, Marshal. You might want to go read 'em from the book."

"My rounds will take me that way in a few minutes. I'll look in on the place when I get there. I always do."

Blake didn't mention that Sam Dorn usually treated him to a short beer, and from there he went on home where Clarissa would be waiting for him with a late supper. It was a mighty nice way to finish off the day, which was another reason Blake enjoyed making these rounds. He had something to look forward to.

"I don't know, Marshal," Hargis said as he stepped closer. "It looked kind of serious to me. I'm not sure you should wait."

"I appreciate you speaking up, but I'll get to it." Blake's tone was a little more impatient now. He never had cared for people telling him how to do his job.

"Well, if you're sure . . ." Hargis said as Blake turned to resume his routine.

Blake heard cloth rustle behind him, and then pain hit him in the side like a fist, driving him a step to the right. He gasped, as much surprised as hurt, and tried to turn back and fight, but Hargis crowded into him hard and knocked him to his knees. Hargis's left arm went around Blake's neck and closed tight. He reached down with his right hand and plucked the Colt from its holster.

Hargis put his mouth next to Blake's ear and said, "You feel that, you son of a bitch? Feel that blood running down your side? I could've gutted you, but I didn't. Just one nice clean stab wound . . . for now. Hurts like hell, doesn't it?"

With Hargis's forearm clamped across his throat like an iron bar, Blake couldn't do anything except grunt. Hargis was right, though: the wound hurt clean to Blake's core, bad enough to spread out and fill his mind and body.

"I could cut your throat," Hargis went on. "Still might. But not yet. No, sir, not yet."

He was a strong man. He heaved and lifted Blake back onto his feet. Blake wanted to fight, but his muscles wouldn't do what he told them to. All he could do was stumble along as Hargis dragged him backward along the boardwalk and into an alley.

The man was going to kill him back here and leave him in the dirt and the trash, Blake thought. And he had no idea why.

Hargis didn't stop in the alley to finish the job, though. He kept dragging Blake along, coming into one of the small side streets and then backing toward a large whitewashed building with a number of cottonwood trees around it. Blake was dizzy and disoriented, no doubt because of the blood soaking his shirt on the left side, but he saw enough of his surroundings to realize what Hargis was doing.

Hargis was dragging him toward the Baptist church.

Unlike the businesses in town, the church was never locked. Blake heard his captor fumbling at the door, then Hargis manhandled him into the sanctuary's dark interior. A kick closed the door behind them. Their steps echoed in the big room with its stained-glass windows on the sides.

Hargis wrestled him all the way up the aisle between the rows of pews until they reached the front where the preacher's pulpit stood. There, Hargis dropped him. Blake's legs buckled and he sprawled on the hardwood floor.

The preacher, Timothy Foulger, was going to be mighty annoyed with him for getting blood all over the floor like this. Blake knew that was a crazy thought to be having right now, but he couldn't help it.

A match rasped. Orange flame spurted. Hargis held it to the wick of a lantern, and when the wick caught, he lowered the chimney and set the lantern on the pulpit. Darkness swallowed the wavering yellow glow before it reached the corners, but the light was enough to reveal Blake lying there with Hargis looming over him.

Although, as Blake looked up and tried to focus his fuzzy vision on his attacker, he said, "I . . . I know you. Your name's not Hargis. It's . . . it's . . ."

It couldn't be. The face was a lot thinner, the eyes sunken, the cheekbones sharp against the skin. But the same general lines were there. Blake forced his brain to work, thought about how the man would look twenty pounds heavier and five years younger.

And a crushing burden of grief and hate lighter.

"That's right," the man said. "I'm Wesley Holman."

"I thought . . . you were dead . . . Somebody said . . . you were shot in Pueblo."

"Shot. Not killed. I was laid up for a long time, but that didn't matter. Just gave me more time to think about how I was going to catch up with you one of these days. Or nights, as it turned out."

Holman had stuck Blake's gun behind his belt. He didn't appear to be carrying a gun of his own. He pulled the Colt, pointed it down at Blake, and eased back the hammer. Blake stared at him. Anger, fear, sickness from the pain of the knife wound kept him from doing anything else.

Holman laughed and lowered the hammer.

"Not yet," he said again. "I have to show you something first."

He set the gun on the pulpit beside the lantern. Then he reached under his shirt and took out a small oilcloth-wrapped bundle with string tied around it. He untied the string, put it in his pocket, then laid the bundle on the pulpit, too, and unwrapped it.

Inside was a folded piece of cloth. Holman unfolded it into a section about a foot square and held it up so Blake could see it. The cloth was white silk. In the middle of it was a small round hole, and a dark brown circular stain maybe four inches in diameter surrounded that hole.

"You know what this is, don't you, Marshal? I cut it out of my wife's wedding dress after the undertaker gave it back to me. My first thought was to have her buried in the dress, but later I was glad I didn't. This way, I was able to keep her heart's blood right next to my heart . . . ever since you killed her."

The groan that came from Blake was part pain, part regret.

"It was an accident, Holman, you know that. I never meant for her to be hurt. I . . . I was just trying to stop . . ."

"You were just trying to stop Harv Dailey, I know that. Everybody in town knew that. The brave lawman, just doing his job, going after the man who'd robbed the bank. Running right into the teeth of Dailey's gunfire. You didn't even stop when he shot you. You got off two more rounds of your own. The second one killed Dailey." Holman leaned over and shook the piece of blood-stained silk at Blake. "But the first one killed my wife!"

Blake closed his eyes, unable to stand the sight. He couldn't shut out the memories, though. They were as vivid as they'd ever been. The running gun battle along the street of that Kansas settlement, Harv Dailey unable to get back to his horse because the marshal had reacted too quickly to the sound of shots coming from the bank, the screams as people scattered, the booming gun-thunder, the hammerblow of a bullet striking his left leg and knocking it out from under him . . .

When Blake had gone down, Dailey had paused, a grin stretching across his face. This was his chance to kill the lawman, and then he could steal a horse and there wouldn't be anybody to come after him. Blake had seen death grinning right at him, so he had overcome the pain of his wounded leg and rushed two shots just as Dailey pulled the trigger again.

Blake had had no idea at the time that one of his bullets had missed the bank robber, gone on down the street, and struck Deborah Curtis—Deborah Curtis Holman, as of a few minutes earlier—in the chest just as she and her new husband stepped out the doors of the church where they'd just been married. He didn't find out until hours later, because he had passed out from being shot himself. He didn't even know that his second shot had killed Harv Dailey.

Of course, he was all too aware of everything later. He had spent many nights trying to fall asleep when all he could see was the woman's crumpled, bloody form—even though he hadn't seen it in real life. The vision was plenty real enough for him.

Clarissa tried to help, of course, and so did his friends. It was a terrible tragedy, they said, an accident that nobody could have foreseen, but it wasn't Blake's fault, they all said. There were no charges against him. Nobody blamed him.

But none of that eased the guilt Blake felt. He kept expecting Wes Holman to come to him and confront him, rage at him, even throw a punch at him. Blake wouldn't have blamed him for any of that.

But Holman left town shortly after burying his new bride, and every so often somebody got word of where he was and what he was doing. He got in trouble a lot—he'd always been a hothead of sorts, but everybody thought once he married Deborah Curtis, the storekeeper's girl, he would settle down—and nobody was too surprised when they heard about him getting in gunfights. The news that he'd been shot down in Pueblo came as no shock.

Not long after that, Blake turned in his badge and accepted the marshal's job in another town . . . then another and another . . . until he and Clarissa landed here in Wagontongue. And sometimes days, weeks, even months went by without him thinking about what had happened up there in Kansas. When it did come to mind, he still regretted it, but there was nothing he could do to change the past. He had tried to be a good man, a good marshal, ever since, and that had to be enough.

"You killed her," Holman said again. "Killed my wife."

"I'm . . . sorry," Blake managed to say.

"You reckon that's good enough?" Holman shook his head. "Not hardly, Blake. Sorry never changed a thing."

Blake's mouth was dry. He tried to swallow and couldn't. He closed his eyes and said, "Go ahead . . . Kill me."

"Not yet. You'll bleed to death in a while. I made sure to stick you good and deep. I wish I could take you back up there where it happened . . . drag you in that church where Deborah and I promised we'd be together until . . . until death did us part. But this one will have to do. You just lay right there until my friend gets here."

That confused Blake. He said, "Your . . . friend?"

"Yeah. Fella named Ab Newton. You may have heard of him."

Blake knew the name, all right. He had seen it on reward posters. Newton was a gunman, a hired killer, a vicious outlaw who was wanted across several states and territories. Blake had no idea how Holman had fallen in with him, but it didn't matter.

Holman placed the piece of blood-stained silk on the pulpit and then took out a pocket watch to check the time.

"Ab's going to be bringing somebody else with him. In fact, he ought to be collecting her right about now."

Already, Blake had begun to feel a chill stealing over him. That was from losing so much blood, he thought. But Holman's words made him even colder. Cold right down to the bone.

"Clarissa?" he whispered.

"That's right. She's going to die right in front of you, Blake, the way my wife died in front of me. And then maybe—if you're lucky—I'll cut your throat. Or maybe I'll just leave you here to bleed to death while you're staring into her dead eyes. What do you think? What should I do?"

Blake groaned again. He curled up on himself and began to make gagging sounds as he struggled to breathe.

Holman's eyes widened in alarm. He leaned over, closer to Blake, and said, "Damn it, no! It's not time. She's not here yet. You're not going to die, you son of a—"

Blake had drawn both legs up as he pretended to choke. Now he lifted and straightened them, driving both boot heels into Holman's hip. The desperate kick sent Holman crashing into the pulpit. It overturned as Holman fell to the floor.

The lantern landed right beside him and broke. Kerosene splattered over Holman's clothes, and flames shot up as the fuel caught fire. Holman screamed and rolled but just managed to catch himself on fire even more.

Blake tried to stand up but couldn't make it. He hitched himself along the floor instead as he tried to reach the gun, which had also fallen from the pulpit along with the oilcloth and the piece of wedding dress. He got a hand on the Colt and pulled it toward him. Ragged footsteps made him roll onto his shoulder and look around.

Holman was on his feet again, lurching around as his clothes continued to burn. His hair was on fire, too, and his mouth was wide open but no screams came from it. He tried to rush toward Blake, but he collapsed after only a couple of steps and lay face down, unmoving, as flames continued to leap on and around him.

Blake pushed himself onto his butt and scooted away. He bumped one of the pews, reached up and got hold of it, hauled himself to his feet. Clarissa was all he could think about. Gritting his teeth against the pain and weakness that filled him, he stumbled toward the doors. The floor was on fire and the flames were spreading and smoke already clogged the air. Blake coughed as he fumbled one of the doors open and staggered out into the gloriously cool and clean night.

His house was at the other end of town. Somehow he got one foot in front of the other and made it to the main street again. He thought about firing shots into the air to alert the town that something was wrong, but if he did that, he would warn Ab Newton, too. The man might go ahead and kill Clarissa instead of bringing her to the church as Holman had planned, just so he could make his escape from Wagontongue sooner. Instead, Blake summoned up his fading strength and yelled, "Fire! Fire!" as he stumbled toward his house.

A few cowboys were just going into the Lucky Cuss. They heard Blake's cries and shouted for the other men in the saloon to come help them as they hurried toward the church. The orange glow of the flames was visible now over the roofs of the town. Frontier settlements lived in fear of fire. A crowd would gather in a hurry to stop the blaze from spreading, Blake knew. More than likely, the church would be lost, but it could be rebuilt.

Clarissa. That thought drove him on.

He could have tried to get some of the men to help him, but it never occurred to him. His fear for his wife had crowded out everything else from his mind. The unsteady run up the street seemed to take an eternity, but finally the neat frame house was in front of him and as he started up the walk to the porch, he heard a scream inside.

Like a river turning back on its own course, the pain flowed away from him. He felt nothing except a terrible urgency as he went up the steps onto the porch and hit the door with his shoulder and half-ran, half-fell into the room. The Colt was in his hand as he saw a lean, wolfish man shoving Clarissa away as he turned toward the unexpected threat. Her face was wild with fear and her dress was torn from the struggle. Nearly all of Blake's attention was focused on the man clawing at the gun on his hip, but for a split-second he saw the plates and bowls of food sitting on the table, beyond the killer, waiting for Blake to return from his night rounds and sit down to supper with his wife . . .

The gun in Blake's hand roared and jumped once, twice, three times. Muzzle flame leaped from the barrel of Ab Newton's gun, but Blake didn't feel any fresh shocks. Maybe he was too numb to feel them. Maybe Newton had just drilled him and he didn't know it. But he saw Newton fold up, crumpling in on himself, and hit the floor. The gun skittered out of Newton's hand. He jerked a couple of times and then lay still.

Clarissa screamed and said, "Dave!", then rushed toward him. Blake tried to reach out for her but grasped only a black nothingness instead.

HE MOVED ALONG THE boardwalk, slower than in the past, using a cane now even though he didn't really need it most of the time. But now and then the weakness came back and having something to lean on came in handy. He stopped at the door of each business and rattled the knob.

"If you want to move on again, it's all right with me," Clarissa had said as she stood beside the bed where he was resting. "I understand."

"No, we'll stay," he told her. He reached out, took her hand, squeezed it. "I'm done running."

Because there was no point in it, although he hadn't told her that. No man could escape the past. It was always there, shambling along behind him like a hungry wolf, ready to reach out and rip him with memories. Whether he'd intended it or not, his actions had cost the life of one innocent woman and nearly the life of another. A man who'd never really done anything to deserve it had died consumed by hatred. Nothing in Blake's power could change any of that.

But he could make sure everything was locked up nice and tight, and the town was safe and peaceful around him. He paused for a moment, leaned on the cane, took a deep breath, and moved on to check the next door.

THE FLAGELLANT

BY JOYCE CAROL OATES

Not guilty he'd pleaded. For it was so. *Not guilty* in his soul.

In fact at the pre-trial hearing he'd stood mute. His (young, inexperienced) lawyer had entered the plea for him in a voice sharp like knives rattling in a drawer—*My client pleads not guilty, Your Honor.*

Kiss my ass Your Honor—he'd have liked to say.

Later, the plea was changed to *guilty.* His lawyer explained the deal, he'd shrugged O.K.

Not that he was *guilty* in his own eyes for he knew what had transpired, as no one else did. But Jesus knew his heart and knew that as a man and a father he'd been shamed.

At the *crossing-over time* when daylight ends and dusk begins they approach their Daddy and dare to touch his arm.

He shudders, the child-fingers are hot coals against bare skin.

Hides his face from their terrible eyes. On their small shoulders angel's wings have sprouted sickle-shaped and the feathers of these wings are coarse and of the hue of metal.

Holy Saturday is the day of penitence. Self-discipline is the strategy. He'd promised himself. On his knees he begins his discipline: rod, bare skin.

(Can't see the welts on his back. Awkwardly twists his arm behind his back, tries to feel where the rod has struck. Fingering the shallow wounds. Feeling the blood. Fingers slick with blood.)

(Not so much pain. Numbness. He's disappointed. It has been like this—almost a year. His tongue has become swollen and numb, his heart is shrunken like a wizened prune. What is left of his soul hangs in filthy strips like a torn towel.)

Lifer. He has become a *lifer.*

But *lifer* does not mean *life.* He has learned.

Shaping the word to himself. *Lifer!*

—twenty-five years to life. Which meant—(it has been explained to him more than once)—not that he was sentenced to life in prison but rather that, depending upon his record in the prison, he might be paroled after serving just twenty-five years.

Incomprehensible to him as twenty-five hundred years might be. For he could think only in terms of days, weeks. Enough effort to get through a single day, and through a single night.

But it was told to him, *good behavior* might result in *early parole.*

Though (it was also told to him) it is not likely that a *lifer* would be paroled after his first several appeals to the parole board.

Where would he go, anyway? Back home, they know him and he couldn't bear their knowledge of him, their eyes of disgust and dismay. Anywhere else, no one would know him, he would be lost.

Even his family. His. And hers, scattered through Beechum County.

Who you went to high school with, follows you through your life. You need them, and they need you. Even if you are shamed in their eyes. It is *you.*

Problem was, remorse.

Judge's eyes on him. Courtroom hushed. Waiting.

What the young lawyer tried to explain to him before sentencing—*If you show remorse, Earle. If you seem to regret what you have done . . .*

But he had not done anything!—had not made any decision.

She had been the one. Yet, *she* remained untouched.

WEEKS IN HIS (FREEZING, stinking) cell in men's detention. Segregated unit.

Glancing up nervous as a cat hearing someone approach. Or believed he was hearing someone approach. Thought came to him like heat lightning in the sky—*They are coming to let me out. It was a mistake, no one was hurt.*

Or, thought came to him that he was in the other prison now. State prison. On Death Row. And when they came for him, it was to inject liquid fire into his veins.

You know that you are shit. Ashes to ashes, dust to dust. That's you.

No one came. No one let him out, and no one came to execute him.

He didn't lack remorse but he didn't exude a remorseful air.

A man doesn't cringe. A man doesn't get down onto his knees. A man doesn't *crawl.*

His statement for the judge he'd written carefully on a sheet of white paper provided him by his lawyer.

> *I am sorry for my roll in what became of my children Lucas & Ester. I am sorry that I was temted to anger against the woman who is ther mother for it was this anger she has caused that drove me to that place. I am sorry for that, the woman was ever BORN.*

Pissed him that the smart-ass lawyer wanted to correct his spelling. *Roll* was meant to be *role. Ester* was meant to be *Esther.*

The rest of his statement, the lawyer would not accept and refused to pass on to the judge. As if he had the right.

Took back the paper and crumpled it in his hand. Fuck this!

Anything they could do to you, to break you down, humiliate you, they would. Orange jumpsuit like a clown. Leg-shackles like some animal.

Sneering at you, so ignorant you don't know how to spell your own daughter's name.

Sure, he feels remorse. Wishing to hell he could feel remorse for a whole lot more he'd like to have done when he'd had his freedom. Before he was stopped.

COVERED IN WELTS. BLEEDING.

A good feeling. *Washed in the blood of the Lamb.*

He believes in Jesus not in God. Doesn't give a damn for God.

Pretty sure God doesn't give a damn for him.

When he thinks of God it's the old statue in front of the courthouse. Blind eyes in the frowning face, uplifted sword, mounted on a horse above the walkway. Had to laugh, the General had white bird crap all over him, hat, shoulders. Even the sword.

Why is bird crap *white*?—he'd asked the wise-ass lawyer who'd stared at him.

Just *is.* Some things just *are.*

But when he thinks of Jesus he thinks of a man like himself.

Accusations made against him. Enemies rising against him.

Welts, wounds. Slick swaths of blood.

Striking his back with the rod. Awkward but he can manage. Out of contraband metal, his rod.

It is (maybe) not a "rod" to look at. Your eye seeing what it is would not see "rod."

Yet, pain is inflicted. Such pain, his face contorts in (silent) anguish, agony.

As in the woman's sinewy-snaky body, in the grip of the woman's powerful arms, legs, thighs he'd suffered death, how many times.

Like drowning. Unable to lift his head, lift his mouth out of the black muck to breathe. Sucking him into her. Like sand collapsing, sinking beneath his feet into a water hole and dark water rising to drown him.

The woman's fault from the start when he'd first seen her. Not knowing who she was. Insolent eyes, curve of the body, like a Venus fly trap and him the helpless fly: trapped.

PLENTY OF TIME IN his cell to think and to reconsider. Mistakes he'd made, following the woman who'd been with another man the night he saw her. And her looking at him, allowing him to look at her.

Sex she baited him with. The bait was sex. He hadn't known (then). He has (since) learned.

He'd thought the sex-power was his. Resided in him. Not in the woman but in him as in the past with younger girls, high-school-age girls but with her, he'd been mistaken.

And paying for that mistake ever since.

To be looked at with such disgust. To be sneered-at. That was a punishment in itself but not the kind of punishment that cleansed.

In segregation at the state prison as he'd been at county detention because he'd been designated a special category of inmate because children were involved and this would be known. Because there was no way to keep the charges against him not-known. Because once you are arrested, your life is not your own.

Surrounded by "segregated" inmates like himself. Not all of them white but yes, mostly white.

Yet nothing like himself.

THEY'D COME TO SEARCH his cell. Again.

Because he could not prevent them. Because there were many of them and only one of him.

In his cell there was nowhere to hide anything. (So you would think.) Yet with sneering faces they searched the cell.

And inside his lower body with furious gloved fingers bringing him to his knees.

Yet could not discover contraband. For it was nowhere here.

Where're you hiding it, Earle?—fucker we know you're hiding something.

Their exultation in torturing him. Flushed faces, shining eyes, his screams are joyous to them.

Yet in this place they were confining him, the man who is free in his heart cannot be confined.

No prison, no segregated unit. No cell, no restraints, no straitjacket, no drugs forced down his throat or injected into his arteries to bind him.

Left him where he'd fallen moaning on the filthy floor. A metal instrument (might've been a spoon) they'd shoved up inside him into the most tender part of him had been so forcibly removed, ravaged tissue was carried with it slick with blood.

Thank you Jesus. Washed clean in the blood of the Lamb which is the most shame you can bear on this earth before you are annihilated.

On his knees alone in the night of Holy Saturday observing the seven stations of the cross the flagellant begins his discipline.

Each stroke of the rod against his bare back, bringing expiation.

Crawling on his belly. Tongue extended. Makes himself pencil-thin, slithering like a snake.

Yet: a snake that can control its size.

From the crevice to the concrete.

Scraped raw the skin of his hands, bleeding.

ON STROUTS MILL ROAD where the guardrail has been repaired.

Returning to his (ex)wife's house, his house from which he'd been banished.

Fluidly he moves. He has the power to pass through walls. He has whipped himself into a froth of blood. He has whipped himself invisible.

(It has not happened yet—has it? He sees that it is waiting to happen.) And so this time it will happen differently. Jesus has escaped his enemies and will wander the world free as he wishes like any wild creature without the spell of a wrathful God upon him.

He will take Lucas and Esther with him, in their pajamas. Very quietly he will lift them in his arms. Daddy! Daddy!—the children are smaller than he recalls, this is startling to him, disorienting. The children smell of their bodies, their pajamas are soiled. Halfway he wonders if their mother has drugged them too, to make them sleep.

Seeing it is Daddy they are happy to see him. He will take them to safety. Except they are hungry—whimpering with hunger. The woman has put them to bed without feeding them. Daddy! To Burger King in the pickup. He will take them, he is their daddy. The woman has been left behind, unknowing. The woman is unconscious in her bed, sprawled in nakedness and smelling of liquor.

It will be his error, to think that the woman left behind will not exert her power over him.

Pressing down on the gas pedal. Highway a blur for Daddy too is ravenous with hunger. And thirst. Stops for a six-pack at the 7-Eleven. Pops a can open inside the store, cold beer running down his fingers. This will be observed on the surveillance tape. That Daddy has not eaten, and Daddy has not slept in forty-eight hours. Love for the kids is all Daddy has to nourish him.

Driving through stunted pines. Icy road. Slick pavement, black ice it is called. *Your mother is to blame. The lying whore has sabotaged our family.*

Until now the woman has been pulling the strings. They have been her puppets—the father, the children.

But no longer.

AT THE *CROSSING-OVER TIME*. At home in the dark.

As a boy he'd been taught. He had not wished to know, yet he had been made to know.

The stations of the cross are seven. Christ must bear his cross. Christ must stumble and stand upright again. Christ is bleeding from his wounds: chest, back, head. Soon, spikes will be driven through Christ's hands and feet. It is supposed that Christ was made to lie down upon the roughhewn cross upon which he was nailed. Christ will submit to his crucifixion for it is written. Christ will die as a man, and descend to Hell. And on the third day Christ will rise again to enter the Kingdom of Heaven where he will dwell with the Father for eternity.

He can think of little else. Useless to try to sleep, he must do penance in the darkest hours of the night. Kneels on the filthy floor of the cell. As he has been instructed.

Flagellant is a word no one speaks aloud. Yet many are the *flagellants* seeking penance.

The children's faces! Lucas, Esther. You tend to forget, a child's face is *small.*

The heads of children are small. Fragile as eggshells. Their arms, legs are thin. As if their bones are comprised of a material lighter than adult bones, easily snapped.

Lucas and Esther in their pajamas. Tenderly he lifts them from their beds. The shaking of his hands is steadied somewhat by the weight of the children, it is a good weight, like ballast.

Her fault, the woman's fault, that his hands shake, for it is the woman's fault that he can't sleep, he must self-medicate, the pills leave him dazed and groggy and the other pills spur his heart to palpitations, cause him to break into oozing oily sweat. The woman has cast him from her life, she has made him an exile from his own household. Hadn't he painted the interior of the little house, hadn't he laid the linoleum tile, ash falling from a cigarette in his mouth. He'd stooped, strained his damned back. He'd done a damned good job. Kitchen floor, bathroom floor. He'd got the tiles at a discount and he'd laid them in and she'd said how beautiful they were, how she'd loved him for such care he'd taken to their home.

Tonight he lifts the children in his arms. Lucas first, then Esther. The little boy is three years old, the little girl is one year old. In that year, how much has happened! But he does not blame either of them, it is the mother he blames. Wrong for a mother to love her babies more than she loves their father.

Leaking milk, through her clothes. Disgusted and excited him, the breast-milk smell which is like no other smell.

In his arms against his muscled upper arms he holds the children. He's proud of his body, or was. Working out, lifting weights, no screwing around at the gym, guys he'd known from high school were impressed. And these kids he'd loved more than his own life.

Christ, he has come to hate his own life.

He'd hated the mother more than he'd loved the kids. He did not deny it. Jesus understood. You could not look fully into the face of Jesus for the powerful light in his face but you knew that Jesus understood.

Driving the sleepy children. The little girl in the back, the little boy in the front seat. No child-seat shit. No time to take the child-seats from her car and into the pickup. Lucas could sit in the front seat like an adult. Esther was asleep anyway, let her lie down on the back seat. Lucas was saying *Daddy where are we going?*—worried and confused and didn't know if he liked it. Until Daddy put out his hand to thump the little shoulder to explain.

Anywhere you go with Daddy, you are meant to go.

Daddy will take care of you and your sister. Already, Daddy is doing this.

Driving faster. The woman's voice in his head haranguing. Bitch nagging. Hail striking the windshield pounding against his head.

Lucas is whimpering. *Daddy! Daddy . . .*

The skid. The truck goes into a skid on black ice. Slams into the guard rail and the guard rail crumples like plastic. And now the truck has overturned, the children's screams abruptly cease.

He is crawling out of the truck. All his strength is required. Yelling at the children—*Come on! C'mon! Follow Daddy!*

Yelling for them but can't get back into the fucking truck. Tries, but can't get back. Tugs at the door handle. Thumps the (cracked) window with a fist. A part of him knows it is hopeless.

It's over. No hope. You are fucked.

* * *

SHE'D BEEN THE ONE who'd wanted them. Sober saying, Kids will change us, Earle. Wait and see. Give us something to live for not just us.

She'd begged. She'd pleaded. Licking him up and down with her cool wet tongue he would recall as hot, scalding.

Kids will be like heaven to us, Earle. People like us, we won't get into heaven, they will shut the door on us. But we can peek inside and watch them, see? That's the kids.

He'd never forgiven her for saying such things.

Like the two of them were not enough. The kind of feeling he had for her which was unique in his life, like a river rushing through a desert making the dead land come alive again—that meant nothing to her.

Calling after him. Stumbling in the dark. Half-drunk, or high on pills. Laid down and couldn't lift her head. Ten, twelve hours. Through the morning and into the afternoon and into early evening. How she'd self-medicate, when a migraine came piercing her skull.

Saying, I can't do it any more, Earle. The way you look at me.

There's no oxygen for me to breathe. It's just—I tried—but . . .

The way he'd followed her around when he was supposed to be at work. Checked on her—if her car was parked in the driveway. Called her a dozen times a day on her cell phone. Calling their mutual friends. Guy she'd worked for, he'd suspected her of fucking before they were married and, more he thought about it, possibly after as well.

Sick, he'd felt. Fever in the blood. Infection like hepatitis-C he couldn't shake.

Yet incredulous hearing the woman's words it was sounding like she'd prepared. Or someone had prepared for her. Asking her, what're you saying? Because it had to be a joke. Hadn't he just made a down payment on a Dodge SUV for her? Wanting to see her smile again. Smile at him. And the kids, taking pride in Daddy.

Driving them to school. Picking them up from school. Silver-green vehicle, classy. He'd gotten a bargain on it, pre-used, good as new, joked with the dealer he'd be making payments on it until he was fucking retired or dead.

Important to make the kids proud. Give them something to be proud of in their Daddy.

And then, the woman undermining him. Betraying him. *Injunction*—that was what pushed him over the edge.

Forbidden to approach within one hundred yards of the house and forbidden to approach within one hundred yards of the children and forbidden to approach within one hundred yards of the woman who has requested the *restraining order.*

Wife, she was. *Former wife* it would be written.

Daddy's secret, he'd never wanted kids. Your kids judge you. Your kid are too close-up. Then, they outlive you. They cry because of you, or they disappoint you. In the boy's face a look like shrinking, drawing back from his dad, Christ!—all Earle could do to keep from grabbing the little bastard and shaking him so hard his brains rattled like marbles.

But no. No. He didn't mean it, Christ.

How he'd leaned down and shouted into the kid's (scared-white) face. Opening his mouth wide, feeling his face turn ugly, shouting. *Don't you try to get away from me, you little shit.*

HADN'T MEANT IT. ANY of it. Therapists sympathized. Everyone loses his temper. Parents lose their tempers. Nobody is perfect. A perfect dad does not exist.

Crucial to forgive yourself, the Catholic chaplain said. Between love and hate we may choose hate out of fear of choosing love.

Saying to him, how we don't want forgiveness for our sins when it is our sins we love.

He'd come close to crying, being told such a thing. For it was true, it's his sins he loves, nothing else has meaning to him.

No one but *her.* But *fuck her.*

Driving fast on Strouts Mill Road, and then faster. Eyes steady in their sockets. He was gripping the wheel correctly. He was gripping the wheel as you would grip it if it was alive and trying to get away from you.

He prayed with his eyes open. He had nothing to hide. His eyes took in all things. He did not spare himself. He'd loved his kids more than his own life but he'd hated their mother more than he'd loved them or himself and that was the truth he had to live with.

He was fearful of Jesus. The love in Jesus. The love of Jesus was a pool that could overflow and drown a man.

He could understand meanness. He could see why people were cruel to one another. But forgiveness and love he could not understand.

He was sorry for the crimes he had committed. He believed that Jesus would forgive him but *Jesus would not forgive the crimes his (ex)wife had perpetrated against him and the children.*

She'd told him he would have to leave. They would all be happier if he left she said. He'd said, Happy! We are not on this God-damned earth to be happy.

He had not struck her. He had never struck her. Not head-on, not deliberately. He had struck the air beside her head. He had struck the wall, maimed the wall beside her head but he had never struck her.

Better for us all if we end it now. You, and me, and them. Now.

Shrinking from him, recoiling from the fist swung in the air beside her head the woman had lost her balance, stumbled and fell—how was that his fault? Not his fault. Everyone knew she was a drunk. Junkie. Gained weight since the first pregnancy, thick ankles, aching veins, none of it his fault. Not the good-looking girl he'd fallen in love with and married. She had tricked him. The children were not *hers* to take from him. He was praying with his eyes open. He prayed to them, Lucas and Esther who art in heaven. Innocent children are in heaven looking down upon the rest of us. Our earth is actually Hell—you look down upon it from heaven. In a dream this came to him.

Holy Saturday is the day of liberation. Whipping his back raw with the clumsy rod he has fashioned. Blood streaming, itching, like ants streaming in open wounds.

Thank you, Jesus!—forgive me.

* * *

ANOTHER TIME IT HAPPENS, skidding tires on black ice, the crash.

Another time, there is no way to stop it.

The truck is flung over like a children's toy, tires spinning. Rolling downhill into the creek, and into the litter sunk into the creek, and the children's screams and his own screams mixed together in the stink of oil, gasoline, urine.

Another time, the screams and then the silence.

Well—the children never stopped loving their Daddy, he is sure of that. They have never blamed him. They are in Heaven now, and would not cast the first stone. No child would cast the first stone. The woman, she has cast the first stone. She has cast many stones. She will go to Hell. They will meet in Hell. They will clutch hands in Hell. They will throw their wounded bodies together in Hell. Their eyes will burn dry, sightless, in Hell. Their souls will shrivel like leaves in a pitiless sun and these leaves blown together across a broken pavement.

At the *crossing-over time* such thoughts come to him. Between daytime and night.

For at this time he is not incarcerated in a filthy cell but free to make his way along Strouts Mill Road. He is not driving the pickup. He is on his belly in the wet grass. He has eluded his captors, he is not what they think. The cunning of the snake which has been the female cunning but has now become his.

Strength will come to him, the promise is he will soon stand upright as a man is meant to stand.

Sure he'd heard the term *lifer.* Hadn't known exactly what it meant until it was applied to him in the way he wouldn't have known what *cancer* meant exactly until it was applied to him.

Even then it wasn't an exact knowledge. The charge had not been homicide but manslaughter: vehicular manslaughter. Driving while impaired. Violation of a court-ordered injunction. Breaking-and-entering a residence. The bastards had tried to charge him with abduction of under-age children as well but that charge had been dropped.

To these he'd pleaded *guilty.* Not in his heart but in the courtroom before the judge gazing down upon him in scarcely concealed repugnance as a man might gaze down upon a creature subhuman though standing upright.

Then, his mouth twisted. Furious grin baring ape-teeth, he'd liked to sink into the fucker's neck.

And so he was given the sentence *twenty-five years to life.* Which meant you could not say *I will be out of here in ___ years.* You could not say *This will end for me, I will be released in ___ years.* None of this you could say with certainty. For even dignity is denied you in the orange jump-suit with shackled legs.

He has not seen the young lawyer in a long time. Last time, their exchange had been brief and their consultation had ended abruptly.

Raising his voice, threatening the lawyer provided him by the court.

Fuck the lawyer, what the fuck did he need that asshole for. He did not need him or any lawyer.

Not probation this time but incarceration. One of the other inmates explained to him that when he applied for parole, which would not be for many years, the ex-wife could exert her influence if she wished for she would always be consulted as the ex-wife and the mother of the child-victims. If there had been threats to her, these would be duly recorded in the computer and never deleted.

He foresaw: always the woman would poison them against her.

In this way, always they would be married.

PROBLEM IS, REMORSE.

Heartily sorry for my sins. Now and at the hour of my death Amen.

He did not lack remorse. But he did not exude a remorseful air.

And so, in the courtroom this was perceived. The judge had perceived. Even the asshole lawyer had perceived. If it was remorse it was remorse for not having taken the woman instead of the children and murdering the woman when he'd had the chance. The two of them together in the truck hurtling along Strouts Mill Road.

In her bed upstairs. In her bed that had been his bed. His bed from which she'd exiled him. In this way dooming him and the children and he had not even known it at the time.

Waking in this squalid place and not knowing if the woman was still alive, and if he was still alive. Or both of them dead already.

You are forgiven for the harm you have done yourself. But for the harm you have done the others, you will never be forgiven. Know that, forever you are of the damned.

In the words of Christ this was explained to him. Bloodied face and body of Christ and eyes resembling his own.

In Hell they are together. Grinding against each other's bodies once so beautiful and now no longer but in their memories, in Hell their beautiful smooth young bodies are restored to them. As in a dream in which the most intense yearning is suffused with cold sick horror they are tearing at each other with their teeth, their bodies writhe together like the bodies of coiled snakes. Never will they come to the end of their desire for each other, never will they be freed of each other.

In this, there is a feeling beyond happiness. In this, there is the flagellant's penance.

By now the flagellant has whipped his back raw. He is panting, exhausted.

Bliss of Holy Saturday. And the promise to him, it will never not be Holy Saturday.

THE THINGS I'D DO

BY ED PARK

1.

WHEN I MOVED TO the city, half a lifetime ago, I was excited, scared, confused—everything anyone is when they get here from somewhere else. Still, nothing else would do. What did I know, out in the sticks? My parents hated that I had to move so far away from them to become a cartoonist—at least that was their line. Every day I would sit in their basement, read the sleepy local paper, drive down the same dumb streets, thinking: Get me out of here. I made it into the police blotter, my claim to fame, though no one fingered me as the artist sketching wieners on dirty windshields in the drugstore parking lot.

My dreams were about escape. I was trapped on a submarine, deep under the Atlantic. I was in a library, afterhours. I was in a library in a submarine in the belly of a whale.

I craved the city, or my idea of the city, which turned out to be the same thing: the dense mobs and vertical insanities, skins and tongues unlike my own, mountains of riches and canyons of depravity, the only place where you might be fêted and fetid in the course of a few hours. You can always count on a doodler for a fancy prose style.

2.

THE DAY AFTER I dreamt of a boulder sliding over the mouth of a cave, I called my buddy, Sal, who had moved to the city the winter before. We had known each other basically from birth.

"It's great out here, man," Sal drawled. "Gray skies, broken windows, the works."

"I was thinking of coming out."

"You totally should."

"Can I stay with you?"

"I'd like nothing more." Sal paused. "But the situation has its complexities. Seven living, breathing complexities."

Sal meant roommates. "I thought you lived in a one bedroom."

"Here's an idea. We kind of look alike, right?"

"So it has been said."

"All we need to do is not be in the same part of the apartment at the same time."

"How would that work?"

"Improvisation."

"Thanks," I said. "I owe you one."

"That's the other thing. I'm a little short lately."

"Aren't we the same height?"

"I mean that you'd have to cover my rent. Playwrights don't tend to rake it in until they're in the game for a while."

"How's that going?"

"I've been workshopping it with a bunch of longshoremen. That's not a euphemism." Sal had a gig at the maritime museum. "Are we good on the rental front?"

What did I have to lose, except money I didn't have? So I made a move. I stuffed a small suitcase, borrowed my father's flask. There was a shoebox *behind* the safe, where the bulk of the cash was actually kept. The emergency fund, my mother called it. Wasn't this an emergency, a crisis of the soul? I put the big bills in the lining of my hat, and stuck smaller denominations at random between the pages of the book I was bringing, *Hypnos Wakens*, a manual of mind control. I took some other things as well.

When the house was quiet, I slipped out and caught a bus to the city. I tossed and turned. Was there a patron saint of cartoonists? Would he or she accept my prayer? The fumes were getting to me. There in the darkness I pledged myself to Nyx, goddess of night, mother of Nemesis, Hypnos, and a slew of other deities. I scrawled a manifesto on a flyleaf.

Twelve hours, a million stops, and I was there.

3.

CHEZ SAL WAS INDUSTRIAL space divided by bedsheets tacked to walls, with narrow "corridors" and a huge water stain on the ceiling like a map of ancient China. Light crept in at weird angles, in different colors. It was the middle of summer, and we were on the top floor, but the place stayed weirdly cool. A breeze off the water? We were so far west we could probably jump from the roof into the river if we had to. There was an arcade game, a ripoff of Centipede called Crawlspace. There was a parrot named Crackerjack that belonged to nobody. Maybe it held the lease on the place.

Living in a state of indifference, hostility, and occasional outright anarchy were the seven complexities: Rodney (French but from Montana), Epp (East Texas), Cora (Florida), Yash (from Germany, of Turkish ancestry), Vince (California via Canada), and Lol the Intolerable (Hong Kong, Lima, Pest). It was like a little United Nations in that room. Sal made seven. I was the phantom eighth, the one who wasn't officially there. Put another way: I was Sal.

Sal and I didn't look as similar as we did when we were kids, but close enough. I trimmed my hair in the same style, distorted my gait in imitation. Fortunately, Sal had a girlfriend, and spent weeks at a stretch with her. We didn't see much of Sal.

No one really talked to me, except Crackerjack.

"The things I'd do to that ass," it said, sounding like Groucho Marx.

It was funny, coming from a parrot. "What things? Whose ass?"

"The *things* I'd do to that *ass.*"

Later I wondered what kind of trauma the bird had been through. Crackerjack slept with its eyes open, claws gripping the fire escape. Now and then it would belt out "Copacabana." Yash thought it was the devil incarnate and suggested we poison its food, except there was no food. Nobody fed it, as far as I could tell.

4.

CORA WAS AN ASPIRING photojournalist who toiled in pornography. Vince was a stand-up comedian, who sat down during the day to book cruises at a boutique travel agency. Lol made video art, spent his nights waiting tables at a diner called The Aeneid. Yash, who'd published "unusual" mystery stories in her native Germany, worked the register at a high-end bakery. Epp, mime and aspiring juggler, was a willing subject for psychological studies, while Rodney was a choreographer who bounced at Bulky's, a strip club for those who liked a little excess poundage.

I memorized their bodies. I cast them in my comics, the ones I drew for myself, the panels I thought no one would read. Different pieces got mixed up in the stew of my imagination: Epp's arms on Yash's body, Lol's chin on Vince's face, Crackerjack's beak replacing Cora's nose.

I scanned the want ads, read my hypnosis book. At night, the domain of Nyx, I cast some spells, I guess you could call them. No one heard my ritual, except that crazy bird, who I could swear was muttering along with me. It was all for a laugh, really, but when sleep finally came I was soaring high above the city, my head touching the clouds. As desperate as I was for money, I had left the cave, the submarine, the library far behind. I bathed in the light of the moon.

5.

RODNEY FILLED THE HIGH score board of Crawlspace. Unlike most of us, he didn't spin the trackball incessantly, instead applying quick, nearly imperceptible touches, as though dusting off the bald head of a curate. When he got an extra player at 10,000 points, he would exult, "*Une autre vie!*"

Another life.

6.

THE TV ONLY GOT one channel, reruns of forgotten shows. Yash watched to improve her English. I didn't have the heart to tell her she was picking up speech patterns from thirty years ago, long-lost idioms like "my giddy aunt."

We liked those old anthology shows, each one ending with a twist, the characters disposable. Our favorite was an Australian shocker called *Tales From the Other Side of Sleep*. The episode that stuck with me was the one we never finished, about a famous writer who lives by himself in a clean apartment with green walls. Every day he sits at the kitchen table, staring at his typewriter, the first three buttons of his shirt open. The smallest noises bug him: the rumble of a delivery truck, a neighbor's heavy footfall on the stairs. At last he pecks out a sentence, only to crumple the page in disgust.

"Thinking hard," Yash said, nodding grimly. "Many ideas, genius, think."

After a minute the writer goes to the kitchen for a glass of water. The sink is spick-and-span, save for a small spider in the corner. A blast from the tap washes it down the drain. He goes back to his typewriter, touches the keys with long fingers. But where are the words? He chugs his water, returns the glass to the sink. His eyes widen: There's *another* spider, notably bigger than the first. He turns on the tap until the spider disappears down the hole.

Hours pass. One-thirty. Crumpled paper fills the wastebin. Three forty-five. The light has changed. The green walls look almost yellow. The writer stands by the sink and stares out the window. His face, handsome in the morning, is hollowed out by despair. A drop of water falls from the tap—when he looks down, there's a *tarantula*. The music lashes out. He screams and turns on the water full blast. The spider clings to the edges of the drain. He bangs away at the terrible legs with a long wooden spoon. Finally it returns to the darkness.

"I don't like!" Yash said, eyes wide with panic. "I don't like at all."

"I don't like *it* at all," I corrected. Yash turned off the set and went to the roof for a smoke.

"The things I'd do to that ass," Crackerjack said mournfully.

I never saw the end of that episode. Later that night and for years afterward, I imagined a series of progressively larger arachnids climbing out of the depths, the sink some kind of portal to hell. But what happened at the end? A sort of locked room mystery, maybe: we would find him stiff at the table, wrapped head to toe in silk.

7.

My life in that loft by the river only lasted eight months. I wore out my shoes going to interviews, wore out my hands washing dishes. I got a job as a bike messenger, careening down packed streets on Vince's silver Schwinn. I memorized *Hypnos Wakens*, which had some very practical tips. I looked for illustration work, submitting to all the big places, all the medium places, then to the free rags, published almost solely for fish-wrapping purposes. One of them said yes. I did all their spot art and a weekly political cartoon. The fact that I didn't really know what the mayor looked like proved no hindrance: I drew him as a rat, a tangled python, a decaying gourd covered with flies. (Years later, when I met him at a function, I was surprised at how *clean* he was.)

Like I said, no one read that particular agglomeration of newsprint. No one, it seemed, but Prudence Caliper, a publisher of slick superhero comics: Dartman, Mini-Mega, The Femur. She invited me to "casual coffee" at the top of a skyscraper near the Princeling Comics HQ. We gazed at the clouds, the massive buildings that stretched like a mountain range. A plane crossed the sky with a banner that asked MORTGAGE QUESTIONS?

"Behold, the city," she pronounced.

"I knew you were going to say that."

Prudence smiled. She was about sixty, trying to look twenty-eight. She landed somewhere around fifty-seven. Crackerjack's refrain poked into my head. I felt my horizons broaden. Her uncle had won the company thirty years earlier in a boxing bet, and she'd taken over after his stroke that spring. A bloodless coup, she called it. Her wiry hair was like a massive paintbrush, red with a streak of white. Her eyeglass frames were like goggles from the future. Her skin was good.

"You look like a superhero," I said.

"I knew *you* were going to say that."

We came to terms. She hired me as a B-line retouch specialist, a role she made up. I filled in texture for interiors, partial shadows, anything the old salts—Max, D.P., the legendary Simon Satin—didn't want to bother with or simply forgot. Mostly they would make me get them provisions from the cart on the street. They liked their coffee black with four sugars. Their favorite thing was to make me wait in the sandwich line in ninety-degree heat, then send back orders that had, say, one pickle slice too many.

These were grizzled men. They had worked in the same room for so long that they had started looking alike, bodies like potato sacks. They finished each other's sentences, or more commonly practiced a form of telepathy, finishing them in their heads. Despite it all, they taught me the ropes, little tricks of the trade.

They called me Sally. They were journeymen except for Simon Satin, a legend in the field. Simon Satin liked to slap my ass when I walked by. I protested when he started squeezing. I said, "I have to draw a line."

"Cartoonists generally *do*," Max wheezed. We all laughed and the touching stopped and I earned their respect in the end.

8.

EVENTUALLY I SAVED ENOUGH of the green stuff to leave Chez Sal. It was about time. Rodney was perpetually broke, panhandling by our own front door. Yash had found my sketchbook and was spreading wild rumors about me.

My new digs were cramped and the radiators were demonic but I didn't mind. I offered oaths to Nyx and Nemesis and Hypnos, drank coffee at night, full of ambition. I covered the walls with scenes of battle and lust, strings of words in my fevered chickenscratch.

Five years later I stopped by a bar for a nightcap on my way home from work. The tavern turned out to be a comedy club. The first act went on before I could leave. His jokes had no discernible punchlines. They were more like rambling stories of his impossible roommates. Hecklers brought him to the verge of tears. He mentioned being at war with a parrot, and that's when it clicked: It was Vince, roommate from salad days. His thick head of hair had been reduced to a few oily strands, and his face had gone to fat.

As I left, I caught him outside, smoking and pacing.

"That was great, Vinnie."

He looked up. Then he decked me.

"What was that for?" It hurt to smile. I extended a hand. He slapped it away.

"You stole my bike." Vince shoved me back down with a finger. "You left without paying your share."

"Easy," I said, rubbing my jaw. "So, how's everyone? Lol still making those crazy-ass videos? Epp still juggling up a storm?"

"Ah, hell." He was suddenly subdued. "It's been a rough time. Unreal. Remember Cora?"

"Sure."

"Hit and run, or so they say." He snapped his fingers. "I have my doubts."

"Shit."

"And Lol got some weird infection. No feeling in his elbows. He's under quarantine."

"Poor Lol."

"Epp's arm has been fucked up since that accident at the hatchet rane."

"Oh no." I felt a pang of survivor's guilt.

"Worst of all is Yash. She's lost her mind."

"Maybe it's the language barrier."

"Fuck you, Sal."

"I just mean she wasn't always easy to understand."

He flicked his ash. "She looks like hell. Picks at her skin, pulls out her hair. I can barely walk to the bathroom without her shouting at me to look out. She calls out your name, Sal." He looked me in the eye. "She says they keep coming back."

"Whose *they*?"

"The spiders. They're everywhere now."

Vince had to go back inside for his second set. He wrote down the hospital where Yash had just been taken, earlier that week.

"How's that old bird?" I asked, folding the paper. "How's old Crackerjack doing? I heard you tell that joke."

He shrugged. "Long gone. Flew the coop, right after you did. That's one good thing, I guess. We don't have to hear it say 'Life's a bitch, then you marry one.' I had to jam wax balls in my ears just to hear myself think."

"That's not . . . those weren't the words." I had wondered about that, during his act. "That's not what Crackerjack said."

"Sure it was." Vince looked at me funny. "All day, every day. A broken record with feathers."

He dropped his cigarette, fastidiously grinding it out with his heel. "Take care of yourself, Sal. And visit Yash if you can."

"Of course," I lied.

9.

FLASH BACKWARD FIVE YEARS. At our monthly coffee, Prudence complained about Simon Satin's shaky line, Max's hygiene, D.P.'s B.O. Then she'd drink out of little bottles while I showed her my own drawings, done in a luscious, even decadent line. I had my own cast of characters: Dr. Flood, Angelbot, The Wipe. They weren't based on my former roommates—"flatmates," as Lol would say—but parts bore a resemblance: Rodney's pout, Dave's cornflower eyes.

Prudence smiled and sipped as she flipped through my art.

"There's a way you handle light that I like," she said.

"More like the dark," I said.

"The rest, I don't understand."

"Dr. Flood can make it flood. Frogbot is part robot, part frog. The Wipe wipes people's memories."

"I *get* the powers," she said. But are they heroes or villains?"

"Aren't they one and the same?"

"Don't get postmodern on me."

I worked my way up the ladder. Soon I was writing scripts for the old guard. The characters were young, and their creators were out of touch.

Flash-forward eighteen months. Over skyscraper coffee one day, Prudence announced she was cleaning house.

"The place smells."

"Literally?"

"Literally and figuratively." She looked at her pocket planner. It was a Wednesday. "Go see a movie, Sal."

I caught a doc about the history of dirt. It was the second part of a trilogy and Hypnos paid me a visit there in row eleven. When I came back, at half past four, the office was empty. It was like she had vacuumed up its history, every trace of cigars and graphite, sweat and erasers. A single bifocal lens wobbled on Simon Satin's desk, as though she'd taken a mallet to the side of his snow-white head.

The following week, she hired a squad of young illustrators to work under my command. Then she went out on a bender for three months. It was fine. I was good at delegating. I oversaw the adventures of the New Hazard, the Lightning League, Eve the Reversible Woman, all your other favorites. Eventually I introduced my own creation, The Wipe, and in the third issue I put him up against Cloudman, in a duel that had them careening all over the city.

You all know The Wipe now, thanks to the movie. Maybe your kid has the action figure. The Wipe erases memories. The Wipe helps people forget about the terrible things they'd seen. The Wipe wears a spotless white outfit, just as you'd expect.

The Wipe is a hero, I think. He traps his enemies by digging up their past and presenting it in a way that gives them mental breakdowns. It's very theatrical, like objects in a museum. The psychology's a little black and white, but that just makes it more effective, according to Prudence, who eventually came around. The Wipe had Mommy Issues, Daddy Issues. I could draw from experience.

10.

ONE OF MY ABORTED projects at Princeling was a comic book version of *Hypnos Wakens*. I still had my old copy, a mottled paperback, with pages missing and scads of underlining, but I couldn't quite part with it. Maybe I should have. I had read it cover to cover, several times over, but I dipped in all the time. I caught new angles, fresh wisdom. For example, it wasn't until much later that I paid any attention to the index. It was bonkers. The bulk of the entries were under the letter H, more specifically branching off from the very practical word *How*. I reproduce most of one such page:

How to be popular, 3, 8, 16, 66-69
How to blend in, 210-218
How to distract, 188, 212
How to find inspiration: in art, 76, in life, 107. *See also* Creativity.
How to fool practically everyone: doctors, 173, experts, 173-174,

friends, 166-168, the police, 170-171, yourself, 110, 177
How to gain weight, 75-76
How to get ahead in your career, 55-58, 95, 128-134
How to get things for free, 12, 30-31
How to lose weight, 77-78
How to make a favorable impression: on bosses, 18, 61, on colleagues, 61-62, on strangers, 65
How to make people believe you're someone else, 88-90, 180
How to make someone fall in love with you, 15-19, 25, 33-35, 156-158
How to pass: as another gender, 215, as another race, 216, as someone younger, 218-219, as someone older, 220
How to play dead, 236-239
How to save money, 40-41
How to tame animals: cats, 13, dogs, 15, frogs and toads, 19, serpents, 122, winged creatures, 131-132 *See also* Familiars.
How to wipe out the past: 53, 148-149
How to write persuasively, 6, 76, 156-161

On the bottom of one page someone has scrawled: "How to disappear."

In the end, I couldn't figure out how to adapt the book. I asked one of my assistants to have a go: Goodfellow, someone with real talent. She quit soon after. Graduate school, she said vaguely. I tried to find out where she went, but she must have left the city.

11.

FLASH TO NOW.

I left Princeling nine years ago this August, after a fight with Lee over money. All fights over money are actually over sex, and all fights over sex are actually about power. All fights over sex are probably about whose turn it is to wash the dishes.

Lee was Prudence's cousin, and after Prudence died, she took the reins at Princeling. I'm not saying it should have been me—it just should have been anyone else but her. We were married for approximately forty-five minutes, just enough for her to get the summer house, the cat, the BMW, some Simon Satin originals. I got the movie money and the brownstone and the glassware, plus a nice little case of writer's block.

12.

WHAT I MEAN TO say is, I don't draw comics anymore. I have nothing to prove. I have the movie money and the action figures. Crackerjack sometimes comes calling, its voice crooning obscenities, but mostly I sleep fine.

Une autre vie. How many is it possible to get? I'd ask Rodney, but he lost his last one around seven years ago.

I live on the second floor of the townhouse. The third floor is basically storage, stuff I can't get rid of. I rent out the first. My lodger, a polite researcher from Kazakhstan or Kansas, has asked me to water her plants while she was visiting a cousin in Boston or Austin.

Being on the first floor, my boarder resorts to half a dozen locks, and it takes me a while to find the right keys. I haven't been inside in ages. The room faces an airshaft, but somehow light pours in. I draw the shades. It's a jungle in here, the plants generating their own humidity.

The green is intense. Cascades of aspidistra. Vines like veins. I half-expect Crackerjack to swoop in for a chat.

Trapped in small webs in the herb garden are specimens of *drosophila melanogaster*, the fruit fly, each no bigger than a speck of dirt.

13.

THE TV DRONES AS I spray. It's a show where they use modern methods to solve cold cases. The end is always the same: they track down the killer, now living in Nowheresville, a pillar of the community. At the very least she's someone who waves hello, bakes pies, checks your mail when you're out of town.

Everything's too loud and too bright. I kill the volume and tend to the vigorous plant life. I have the opposite of a green thumb, so chances are everything will be dead soon. The closed captioning mangles whatever it is they're saying. TWISTED HOMEY SIDES, read the stark white letters. Even the simplest phrases turn into word salad. DIET FOLLICLE CRIMES.

My heart goes out to the hearing impaired.

I lock the six locks. I slide the two chains, large and small. There are other pieces of door armor, remnants of this neighborhood's grittier past: A heavy beam I slide through two slats, about six inches north of the knob. A rod that shoots through a series of iron rings, straight down into a three-inch divot drilled into the threshold. In a fit of interior decorating, I push a table against the door and put some planters on top of it.

The silver-haired host describes how, after murdering her parents twenty-five years ago, the killer of the week fled her small town to hide in the big city. A MAIN YAK WALKS AMONG US. Unsolved deaths on the fringes of the city appear unconnected—until now. There's some stupid music. There's a stupid graphic showing a web of connections—a green feather, a page torn from a book, Simon Satin's dismembered hand. Poor old Rodney's left foot. They spell everything out for morons, but what do you expect? (Lee was always on my case because I wouldn't dumb things down at Princeling.)

They're interviewing a slim blonde thing who resembles Goodfellow, my ex-assistant. It's mostly in sillhouette but I know it's her. I can see she's dyed her hair and the voice is garbled but I know it's her.

The host shrugs on a Kevlar vest as a beefy cop blathers about the importance of closure. IT'S THE RETURN OF THE DEPRESSED, one of them proclaims. I try to switch it off but my arm won't move. Nyx have mercy. I just stand there with the mister, drops sliding down the long green blades of mother-in-law's tongue. Host and cop are turning down a street that I know. I think I see my neighbor, walking his beagle. I hate that damn dog.

I switch off the TV as they get to my door.

When the knock comes, I don't jump. You could say I've been waiting for that sound ever since I came to the city. I think of all my diet follicle crimes, my twisted homey sides, the things I'd do, and do, and did.

Another knock, undeniable. Then everything goes quiet for a second. From the kitchen, I can hear a faint scuttling. Something's crawling up the sides of the sink. If Yash were here, I'd ask if anyone has ever written a locked-room mystery from the point of view of the corpse. It could be amazing, if done right. I'm looking up something on page 236, and I laugh when I see that the page is missing.

FAVORED TO DEATH

BY N. J. AYRES

JASON AND ALFIE SAT atop pilings not far from the Laguna Beach pier, the posts cut low enough a tall kid could sling a leg over and not lose grip on a can of beer. The friends sat silent for a moment and focused on the blinking red light of a plane taking its time to forge through a night of flourishing stars.

"Laguna is the greatest place in the world," Jason said. He felt no need to look at Alfie when he said it.

But instead of Alfie saying *Ditto, man*, he answered from deep in his throat, "Laguna sucks."

Jason thought he didn't hear right. He checked the tin-stamped face turned sideways to him and saw it was seriously sour. "You're crazy, man," he said, spreading his arms, teetering a little. "This is paradise."

In honor of Alf's birthday, they'd met with friends for pizza and beer. Now it was just them, waxing on life, politics, what Francie Stevens was wearing, and whether they should quit their dumbass jobs or not.

"So I'm twenty-one," Alfie said. "So what?"

"What, what?" Jason asked.

"What-what? You're more torqued than I thought," Alf said and snuffled once, kind of like a laugh but not a real one.

"Spit it out, doof. What's eating you?"

"I expected . . . I don't know what I expected. Something else."

"We gave you a party, you ingrate." Jason was still nineteen, but he'd pull twenty in six months. He raised his beer high to the chrome moon and shouted, "To turning *one hundred* and twenty-one, the both of us. Yah!"

As he said it, steel-gray clouds overran the moon.

"Damn, Alf. Did you do that?"

"Hey. Special powers."

Jason could hardly see his friend's expression now, just the spectral glow of Alf's sun-tipped hair and the ghost of a "Dave's Waves" tee-shirt he wore so often the letters were fading away.

Soon the menacing clouds slid from the moon, leaving the globe pure as a porch light. It lit up stringers of foam rolling like blown toilet paper on somebody's lawn. The motion made Jason realize he'd folded one too many pepperoni pieces down his gullet. "Dude, I'm sick," he said. "I think I'm dyin'."

He crumpled his can and tossed it into the sea, screw the whales. Well, he cared, but in his mind an aluminum can was something a whale could poop out.

"Get it over with," Alf said, scooping an arm forward as if ushering. He raised his beer to the moon. "A toast: To death. To death, I say. For some, a favor!"

Jason swiveled on his post away from Alf to hurl out all that nasty, three full rolls of the stomach and a couple half-heaves. He twisted away from the puke that was being tidied-up by curls of water, then jumped into the wet on the other side.

Alfie was already off his post and headed for the spot on the sand where they'd left their sandals. Alf's were the expensive kind. He told Jason once what they cost. Jason tried to forget it right away, because the idea just bothered him. How can people spend so much on stuff you wear? But he kept his opinion to himself.

Some days he wondered how he and Alf could even be friends. They'd known each other since middle school. Alf's family was almost-rich, to his family's . . . ordinary. Jason's parents left the state when he was seventeen but out of high school, to open a business in Oregon. Jason didn't mind. He took a room with a cousin and paid hardly anything for rent. The cousins worked different schedules, so they never got in each other's way.

Further: Alf's athletic build to Jason's flab. Alf was born cut and ready, but he wasn't a jock, wasn't a star at school. Something about him held people off except for Jason. A couple of times Alf announced to Jason and a group of kids that he was the type who'd hit the wall young, go out in a blaze. Ride a Harley to heaven, that kind of thing. One time he told Jason the way it would end: somebody would kill him. Drama, thy name is Alf. "Yeah," Jason replied, "and it'll be *me*."

When Alf first met Jason's mother she sang a little of "What's It All About, Alfie?" For some dumb reason Jason had never heard the song before. Alf screwed up his face in pain. Afterward, he kept asking Jason and other people to call him Al, but they'd forget, including Jason.

Lately Alf had been losing his temper over small things, like going past a street they meant to turn on, or store clerks not paying attention to customers the way they should, or tourist families spread out on the sidewalk so a person had to step in the street to get by. He needed a good kick in the butt, Jason vowed, tomorrow maybe, soon as they both got sober.

ALL THAT.

Then, in only a little more than a week, Jason walked the cusp of the beach alone. He stopped at one point, gazed out over the waves, seeing yet not seeing the gliding gulls, the muted orange horizon, the sun as it burned into the bruised skin of ocean.

He whispered, "You sonofabitch, Alfie," and took up a lonesome stone to sidearm it into the sea as far as he could. Then he crouched, sat on his heels, and bawled. For Alfred Burbank Lucian Langdon had taken his life, and in a particularly gruesome way.

*   *   *

WHICH IS MORE WRETCHED? To delete, cancel, erase your own life, or to be murdered? Wait. One plus one equals . . . killer. Suicide is murder, isn't it? God help you if your family's Catholic; no forgiveness there. Alf's family wasn't, but they did go to church sometimes.

Jason told himself he saw it coming.

Jason told himself no way did he see it coming.

He had watched Alfie's moods over the years. Funny one day, pissed the next. Jason hearkened back to the first time he and Alf jerked off together. Alf was fourteen, he still twelve. The act took place in the lee of a big cut-in rock down the beach from Hotel Laguna.

The sky showed barely dark. Before walking there, they had set off a few firecrackers that were almost duds from moisture but good enough to sputter a bit. Three girls down the beach looked over. Alf made some wisecracks to Jason and got the giggles. He pointed at the dim figures of the girls picking up their beach things.

A couple of fireflies flicked around the boys, as if volunteering help with the show. Alf stepped backward and leaned against the rockface. He brought a hand to his groin and massaged himself, said to Jason, "Do this, buddy, mm-m," and half-closed his eyes. "Hey, Jace. Do this." He turned to the rockface, made more sounds, and finished.

When it was over, Jason was surprised: Was this what all the fuss is about? Is that all there is? This wasn't a new sensation. He'd felt it before, since around age seven, but he'd never touched himself like Alfie was doing; he would just press down on his bed while on his stomach, and after he felt it he'd fall off to sleep. That evening on the beach he did laugh himself silly with Alf's jokes and groans. And now, in recollection, he laughed again about it, before he sat on his heels, one finger drilled in the wet sand for balance, and cried like a toddler.

Damn that Alfie. Damn him to a *hundred*-and-twenty-one and way beyond, forevermore. I will never get that close to anyone ever again, Jason told himself.

* * *

THE PARENTS, AS ANYONE might expect, were a mess. Their daughter came down from her job making big bucks in Silicon Valley. But a daughter isn't a son, with all the weight the male gender holds and offers.

The Langdon's pastor and his wife invited them to come stay with them until the service, and they did. That didn't seem odd to Jason because Jason was, as it is called, unaffiliated. He didn't know what was likely in a religious environment.

During the service, Jason sat in the back row of the church, at the deep end of the pew where a shadow was cast by a stained-glass mountain. He rose when the flock rose, sat when obvious, but otherwise did nothing but listen, then scoot out to fresh air afterward.

He overheard someone say the pastor had asked for helpers to clean up the bungalow where Alf's death took place, behind the main house. Alf's parents were leaving for their cabin in the mountains. Jason found the pastor and told him he wanted to help. "Are you sure, son?" the minister asked.

"I have to," Jason answered. *Had* to, because it was there at the bungalow that Jason had slept over with Alfie, built model airplanes with him, eaten stolen candy bars, thumbed through purloined *Playboy* magazines, shared dreams and jokes and generalized bitching. Who could know that one terrible day Jason would be washing a wall with one of Alfie's old "Dave's Waves" tee-shirts, pressing the blood into pores of plaster, paint, and wood?

ONE OF THE CHURCH members by the name of George met Jason at the Langdon address the next early afternoon. Jason led him to the back. A yard-long piece of yellow Keep-out tape that hadn't ripped right dangled from a porch support. Jason yanked it down, bunched it in his fist, and put it in his pocket to toss away later.

George was a semi-retired heating/plumbing man who carried

cleaning supplies even in his personal car. He turned out to be easy to work with, didn't instruct, and treated Jason as an equal.

Once inside, Jason tried not to look for divots in the wood beam where Alf had looped the wire. The first horror was that Alf had done it. The second was: he used barbed wire. Jason shook his head. How could Alf even wrap it? How could anyone at all make a slip-knot that would work if it had barbs? How could . . . ? At the foot of the bed lay the pair of workman gloves shaken off before Alf kicked away the stepstool.

Alf's parents had told Jason he could keep whatever he wanted from the place. The rest could be given away. George had brought cardboard boxes. Jason knew the quirkiness of Alfie's parents, how the mother seemed always busy and nervous and the dad stone quiet unless he had a few drinks.

While Jason worked, he thought about the repugnant way Alf killed himself. The guy he knew would have gone into the hills, done it where he'd have a mystical bonding with the earth, Walt Whitman-style, a "*Look for me under your boot soles!*"-type thing, or weighted himself down with rocks in his pockets like that English writer Virginia Woolf did to let nature's water blanket him to sleep. He wouldn't have done it like a dog defiling his own bed.

And for his parents to come upon. But he forgave him a little, because apparently Alf did it on the day the housekeeper would find him. Jason knew she came once a week on a Tuesday, or after a party. Even at that, though, how cruel toward her, Jason thought. What a smacktard.

True, Alf was given to melodramatic moments, but he also loved the brews and sometimes a toke of weed. Alf should have inhaled more of it. You should've gotten cooled-out, Chief. And Jason cursed him again.

And then there was Heather Reston, how about her? Alf had met her only three months before and seemed pretty hooked. The only reason she wasn't at the pizza birthday celebration was that she had to go to a wedding somewhere.

When the church member left, Jason worked alone gathering up Alf's things. The clothes he took down to a second-hand shop known for helping homeless people. Homeless—in this moneyed city. It's a free country. Why wouldn't they come here? Maybe he'd join them one day.

A small box of Alf's books Jason would leave by a park bench overlooking the ocean—let the tourists or vagrants have a read. There were school texts; a copy of *Moby Dick*; a volume of Whitman skinned up on the spine, and a biography of him called *The Better Angel* detailing his life during the Civil War. Jason was almost going to keep that one, but why? He rarely read. A long time ago, he did, kind of liking a class in European history and one in English Lit, mostly because of the teacher; but those were only two of the four college classes he managed to tug through. He just didn't see a purpose there.

Alf's family, on the other hand, expected a college degree out of their son, after giving him a break to go visit Europe. Alf couldn't dig it, came back before the planned expedition was over. He couldn't supply attention to class work any more than Jason. He did poke at Jason about words misspelled on the chalkboard where Jason had to write the daily specials for the restaurant where he worked as a server. Alf said he wanted to be a poet. An actor. A singer. Musician. But as far as Jason ever saw, his friend might have to go sit in an office in Chicago with an uncle who could use an assistant. For a little income, and for relief of parental jibes, Alf did take on an office job in Costa Mesa as a temp, telling Jason, Wow, do I know how to file stuff in cabinets. Cabinets, like in the old days.

Jason smiled as he recalled the day Alf was outside the café where Jason worked, sitting at one of the tables and watching Jason scrawl with the chalk. "Knock knock," Alf said.

Jason didn't even turn around. "Who's there?"

"Broccoli."

"Broccoli who?"

"Broccoli doesn't have a last name, knucklehead."

And there were two really old computer manuals—who used *them* anymore, now with the Internet? Also, a really old book on how to grow rich, plus three broad handfuls of science fiction monthlies. That was it. The sum of what Alf had in the bungalow for reading material.

A torn slip of paper fell out of one of the magazines. Jason read, in Alf's scrawl and broken out, as in lines of poetry: "*the softened coffin/the ultimate Instead.*" He assumed they were lines from Whitman.

For himself, Jason kept the 2-in-1 tablet he found under the bed, surprised no one had found it; earbuds were coiled on the floor by the lamp table.

The church fellow was gone when another man arrived just before Jason locked up. He introduced himself as Alfie's Uncle Willy. Alf had mentioned an Uncle Willy, sometimes leaving off the "y". Jason imagined him to be the well-off business owner in Chicago, not this stubbled, chestless man wearing a bill cap with a patch so worn away only the gold outline of a fishing pole and the prow of a boat could be seen.

The uncle said, "I knocked up front. I only just heard about Alfie. You know where his folks are?"

"He wanted to be called Al," Jason said.

"Is that right?"

"What I said." Jason wasn't often rude to adults. But this one was so shaggy. Jason then told him they were at Big Bear, above San Bernardino. "Mountains," he said.

Uncle Willy then said he needed to use the toilet. Even the word toilet was ugly, more so because the man who helped Jason with the bungalow took a long time working in the bathroom. When the man caught Jason's look as he exited with the cleaning stuff, he looked down quickly and just said, "Laxative."

It took a moment for Jason to silently guess his friend might've wanted to make sure he wouldn't leave a mess under him. Precautions. Like another thing the idiot did before kicking over the stepstool. Jason overheard that the "young man" had stuffed a long wad of socks in his mouth.

Jason completed locking the door, saying, "You can go in the main house." He just couldn't let Shaggy be in the rooms Alf had used.

In the house, while Jason waited for Willy to come out, he wondered if he should've even let the guy in, told him to relieve himself in the bushes out back. Jason heard water in the sink run and was oddly grateful for that. Willy came out with his cap tucked under an armpit and his hair smoothed down and damp.

He drifted around the main room touching things, as if it had been a long time since he'd been in a house. Above the fireplace, on the mantel, were several miniature sailboats, hobby remnants from Alf's dad.

Finally, as everybody does, he asked the question. "How'd he do it?"

How'd he do it? An agony to explain.

And because it would be, and because Jason was angry with everyone, he walked up to Uncle Willy, looked in his gray-yellow eyes and said, "Slit his throat," and made the motion of a blade across his neck.

Why tell him that? Inserting your head through a loop of barbed-wire and kicking a step-stool away isn't gory enough? He didn't know why. He just said it, did it.

It made Willy step sideways, untuck his hat from under his arm and slap it twice on his thigh. "Now that is just as grody as can be," he said. Grody. A word out of the seventies, Jason assumed.

Willy looked around the room as if for evidence, as if this room were the death place and he wanted to see the stains of red geysers. His beard was a bird's nest begun but never fulfilled. His shirt, a faded black, his tan shorts dappled, and his sandals strung onto his feet by loose leather. When this man who claimed to be an uncle of Alf's was done examining what could not be found, he strode to the front door and out onto the porch. Jason saw him sit on the front step.

The path leading down to the gate was composed of perfect, artfully placed stonework, wig-waggled so as not to be too precise. Jason, seeing the man there and thinking perhaps he misjudged the guy, joined him on the other side of the step because it was built wide, wide as a church pew, although no stained-glass mountain-shadow draped it.

It was then that Jason noticed Uncle Willy's sleeves slightly pulled up, and then when he saw the shiny spatulas of scars on the man's forearms and hands, the webbing of one thumb gone so that the digit looked adhered to the wall of the finger beside it like an odd birth defect.

The two men, youngish and oldish, sat wordless and watched a tan tabby step along the upper railing of the driftwood fence that separated the Langdon property from its neighbor's. The cat slowly wheeled its head around and stared, then sat on its haunches near the juncture of two laced limbs and closed its eyes to the sun.

Jason said, "Alf's folks said if any of his friends came by I could give them something." He almost didn't say it, this strange turkey sitting next to him. But he did. Maybe Jason still wanted to believe in a shred of love.

"How about the guitar?" Willy asked.

"It'll take me a minute," Jason said. As he stood, the feline on the fence turned its head toward them once more. The "M"-marking typical in the fur of a tabby's head made it look like the cat was frowning, or grouchy as hell

Jason walked to the side of the house to his car and got the instrument. It was in a case looking almost as bad as Willy, scraped bald in spots. The man stood when Jason came back to hand it over. He said a scratchy thank you, then turned and stepped down the stone path toward the gate. Jason noticed that a strap on Willy's left sandal had freed itself of its heel anchor.

Willy paused before opening the gate. With a forefinger he gave a stroke to a half-open yellow rose. Released, it bounded up, then dipped again; up, and back again. Willy's fingers stalled it, lightly held it as he inserted his nose in it for a long breathe-in. Then he gave Jason a less excited nod than the one from the rose and said in a voice that sounded scorched, "Tell Grant I came to see him."

That shocked Jason. Brought him out of a fugue. The actual connection. This strange man. Alfie's father's name. He said, "I will."

"Tell him something else."

Jason waited.

"Tell him now we're even."

"I'm sorry?"

"You heard me," Willy said, and thropped the rose again.

Jason wondered from whose side of the Langdon family this derelict had hailed.

* * *

OH, TO HEAR MUSIC, loud music, a means of putting solemn thoughts aside. Jason left the house in Laguna Canyon that he shared with his cousin and headed down to the heart of town. Hotel Laguna was once where movie stars collected to get away from Hollywood. Even Charles Lindbergh lifted shot glasses in the hotel's Pier Nine Bar. Now the premises were shut down except for a hair salon and something else everyone ignored.

But along the sidewalks downtown were mini-art galleries, old record shops, tourist flypaper (cards and postcards), and a bakery whose blueberry muffins were the best in the whole known world. Laguna: boasting the Festival of Arts, the anti-uppity-arts Sawdust Festival, the Playhouse, the frequent occasions for chamber music, surfing competitions, tidepool tours, and once-in-an-alley pubs where fools like Jason and Alfie used to go with fake IDs so they, too, could be called, rightly, Lagunatics.

Jason parked up a hill on Gleneyre and went through the alley behind the library. He headed toward the door of the nightclub with the missing letters that used to spell *White House*. He already knew that inside he'd find Heather Reston, Alf's girlfriend, who had not appeared much affected by any of what had gone on only days before. She'd come to the memorial service, of course, and had cried; but not the way you would if you really loved someone, thought Jason. Before this, Jason sort of liked Heather himself. Everything changes when solid earth becomes a bridge of ropes. Who was the "real" anyone? Who knew anything? Was the world really in-fact, in-truth, flat?

Heather Reston was laughing with two guys and a girl Jason didn't know seated at a crowded table. She spotted Jason and shouted to him through the noise of a rockabilly band whose drummer whipped sticks fiercely to drive the devil down to Georgia. Heather said something to the others, then began making her way toward Jason as he stood near the bar. When she got blocked, she made a motion with her head to Jason that meant, Go out the back door to talk.

And he did start outside, but then he saw a guy urge Heather onto the dance floor. "Wait there," she yelled to Jason. "I'll be right back!" Nothin' like a happy drunk girl.

The dance floor could fit only about twenty people writhing close together. Heather disappeared among them. Jason didn't know why, but he stayed put, still at the bar when the song ended. He liked seeing her have fun, in spite of himself.

But Heather didn't make her way over to him before the next song started. Her dance partner ground to the music in front of her as if she'd already promised the next dance.

Jason glugged half the beer he ordered before wedging out the back door into the alley. He stood for a moment and then hiked the incline toward his car.

"Wait up!" Heather called, coming toward him quickly, chattering about what a cool band it was, pulling her blouse away from her chest to cool off. "Shame on me," she said. "I'm sorry to keep you waiting." She was the type of pretty you see replicated in any beach town, equivalent to a fancy, swirly, narrow-waisted blonde stenciled on a beach towel. Maybe she read it on his face, his condemnation. He kept on walking.

"Jason, I know what you're thinking. Like I don't care what happened to Alfie. That I'm not hurt too. I am. It's awful. But maybe you'll understand when you hear what I have to say." She caught up and put a hand on his arm. He stopped and didn't make it leave.

She glanced down, as if to sort her words, then said, "Things weren't what you think between me and Alf, okay? Alf was my friend. But he wasn't my boyfriend. He couldn't ever be my boyfriend, Jason. He . . . he couldn't be any *girl's* boyfriend."

Jason stood frozen. Her features were deranged by the overhead sulfur streetlight. It could be Halloween.

"Think about it, Jason," she said. "Think about some of the places where he hung out."

"What are you talking about?" He focused on his car ahead. The fog had turned it into what you'd see if algae had grown on it underwater for some time.

He had his car key pointed at the lock, turned it. The locks popped as if that was her cue. "A nightclub named Goldenrod's, Jason? One called The Gay Blades? You didn't know that?"

"You're bonkers."

"It's the truth. You don't want to see it, but it is."

Jason could smell her perfume, or was it the honeysuckle everywhere? Honeysuckle, around his house too, around the Langdon's place, Alf's bedroom window at the bungalow.

He told her, "Yes, he went to Blades once, with two other friends, just to check it out. He said it was hilarious."

"He couldn't tell you, Jason. He said you wouldn't be able to deal with it."

"First off," Jason said, pointing a finger at her, "first off, Alf wasn't gay. Second off, are you saying he would tell you, and not me?"

She just stood there, her eyes searching his. She looked so damned earnest.

He went on, waving his hands. "This is *Laguna*. We had a gay *mayor*, for Christ's sakes."

"I know, Jason."

He jerked the car door open. "Look, it's no big deal anyway today, gay, straight, kangaroo or . . . or, canary. I guarantee, Alf wouldn't have been afraid to tell me. Go back to your buddy in there."

He slid into the car seat but didn't shut the door.

"See?" Heather said. "You made my point. Alfie couldn't talk to you." Her hand clutched the top of the car door. "You're thinking everything's so *out* now. But you're wrong. People still have their prejudices. Even you. Just listen to yourself sometimes, the way you talk."

"The way I talk?"

"I've heard you. Faggot. Worse. I don't even remember. Pinky."

"I've never heard that one, ever. Therefore, I never said it."

She stood away from the door. "Okay, so I'm wrong. It wasn't just you

Alf was scared of. His dad. He told me once his dad would flip *out.* I think it just ate and ate at him until he couldn't take it anymore." Heather clutched her waist, looked down. "We all should have been better friends."

"You don't know what you're talking about," Jason said and started the engine. Heather stepped back, let him shut the door.

He left her there, standing. She'd be safe enough getting back to the club a block down the hill. What the hell did she know? He'd known Alfie—Al—since forever. "I would have seen the signs," he said to himself, even as Heather's words echoed. Didn't Alf also crack wise about queers? Didn't he?

He steamed up the highway, radio loud, other drivers backing off his aggressive driving. Thinking: If Alf—Al—did have a secret and couldn't tell *him*, Jason, why would he go and tell Heather Reston, Miss Cheerleader, who hadn't known Alf but a few months?

Jason said in the cave of his car, "Maybe you did the right thing, Alfie-o," and stepped on the gas.

JASON DIDN'T MEAN TO let the screen door slam shut when Maddy let him in two weeks later. He jumped; she didn't.

"You sure it's okay," Jason said, "me coming?"

"We always like to see you, Jason. Want a soda? I just now put on water for tea if you'd rather." She led him to the kitchen. It was after the dinner hour. The sink was cleaned up.

"No, nothing, thanks," Jason said.

Alf's dad was sitting at the table, carving up a pear over a small plate. His face lit up, just for a second, then fell into a dullness: a wall, no beginning, no end. He told Jason to take a seat, then said, "We want to say thank you for all . . ." His words failed, and he worked the knife again.

At the stove, Maddy was lifting the blue teakettle her son had given her last Christmas. There was no tablecloth, when there had always been a tablecloth. No flowers in a vase, when there had always been flowers everywhere, anywhere. Just Grant eating his pear, one unpeeled, narrow slice at a time, and Maddy pouring water in two cups and asking if he wanted cookies; a pear? ice cream?

He intended to gently ask Al's parents if they thought their son was gay, maybe ask it to help them hang a reason on his suicide. But he still thought the notion was ridiculous. So instead, what he said was, "Uncle Willy stopped by."

Grant laid the knife down, looked at him.

"I gave him Alfie's guitar," Jason said. "That was okay, wasn't it?"

"Willy was here?" Grant said almost inaudibly.

"Did I do wrong? I thought you said . . . I mean, we could probably get it back."

Maddy put a cup in front of Jason and one in front of Grant at the end of the table. "It's not a problem," she said, glancing quickly at her husband, then going for her own cup on the counter.

Jason asked, "Willy, now, is whose brother?" looking for resemblance.

"How's your landscaping business, hon?" Maddy said. "You didn't lose work, did you, being gone those few days? You're not still at the café?"

"None that mattered," Jason said. "That guy *was* his uncle, right?"

Maddy said, "What's done is done. Grant, don't worry about it." She sat too, and before sipping her tea said, "Chamomile," looking toward Jason, then at her cup of tea. "I am so tired," she said to no one.

A soft moan issued from Grant. Jason had never heard a grownup moan. It scared him. Maddy had her head down, blowing on her tea. Jason said, "I'll go ask him for it back. Just tell me how to get in touch with him."

Maddy reached and lightly touched Jason's hand, then withdrew and held the cup with all fingers. "There are things that go back a long way," she said.

Jason persisted, "I can get it back." He wondered what else Grant and Maddy would want back that he'd already disposed of.

"It'll never be over," Grant said. "It will go on and on until we die."

"Shush!" Maddy said. She stood and moved behind her husband's chair and put both hands on the back of it. She said softly to Jason, "Maybe we'll see you later, okay?"

"*Uncle* Willy," Grant said, balling both fists, one with the knife still in it which he was using to cut the pear. "I'll find him. I'm dead already. What does it matter? We're both gone, only he just doesn't know it yet."

Alarmed, Jason said, looking at Maddy, "Is that guy really Alf's uncle?" Maybe . . . maybe he was the one who got Alf to thinking . . . things.

"He was a friend, once," Maddy said. "We called him 'uncle' for Alfie's sake."

Grant asked, "What did he say? What did he *say*?"

Cautiously, Jason answered, "I think he said, 'Tell Grant now we're even.'"

"Oh-h!" Grant stabbed the table with the paring knife. As he did, his hand slid down, the blade made slippery from the fruit. He dropped the knife and opened his hand to look. Barely a little blood seeped out. Grant puffed out a laugh, smiling at his own bright blood, then smacked his hand onto the table.

Transfixed, Jason hoped that when he went to sleep again and awoke the next day the restore point would be the week before.

Maddy darted to the sink and ran water on a kitchen towel, folded it and wrapped the wound as Grant, eyes shut, tipped his head back, his larynx in spasms.

"I should leave," Jason said.

This family was truly falling apart. He wanted nothing more than to be back with his friend Alf, sitting on a pier, laughing at the moon.

But he felt an obligation to stay, and so he remained sitting even before Maddy said, "Wait, hon. You deserve an explanation." She stood behind her husband and stroked his face, covered his eyes with her hands, ran her fingers under his jaw, stroked him like a sculptor forming clay.

"Don't," Grant began, but silenced himself, locked in his own despairing tangle of thoughts.

"It goes back to when Will Evans and Grant were business partners, a long time ago," Maddy said, "in Illinois." She paused to get her breath, drawing a hand over Grant's forehead. "We worked so hard, all of us, on that business. But it didn't do any good. We got into terrible financial trouble. Grant thought . . . Jason, you must never tell anyone this."

"I swear."

"One night, Grant burned down the business. Burned it to the ground. For the insurance." She moved her husband's head upright and took her seat again.

These people were the best people Jason knew. He must have walked into the wrong house, stumbled onto the wrong stage. His own parents had their problems. It's why he didn't miss them. But nothing like this.

Grant's face changed into a loose sandbag. Maddy continued. "What happened has eaten us up every day of our lives. The world is not what you think, Jason. Someday, if you live long enough, you may do something you never thought possible. I'll call it by its name. Violation. We thought the insurance money would allow us a second chance, for Will also. I didn't know about what Grant planned before he did it, but afterward, when he told me, I hid it too, so I'm just as guilty." Now she waved a hand to the walls. "You fail, you err, you sin, whatever you might call it. What I'm telling you, Jason, is that life plays tricks on us all. You just move on. The only thing is—"

And here she stopped, raising her chin as she looked away, eyes pitched in sadness. A light over the sink flickered, like a judgment.

Jason broke in, "Well, gosh, that's not the worst thing I ever heard. I mean, you know."

"Wrong, Jason. You see, the problem was—"

"Maddy, don't!" Grant said. He lifted the towel away from his hand, checked, but didn't stand. "I'm going to bed."

"He's got to know, Grant," she said, stroking her husband's shoulder. "We come to the point we have to share the burden. Jason is strong. He *is*. He's like a son now, in a way. Or do you want to talk to Pastor Davis? I don't."

Her husband bowed his head. He set both hands on the chair as though to rise but still didn't.

"I guess I should go," said Jason.

"I'm not done yet, Jason. Please. Just listen. In the building that burned," Maddy said, "they found Will's son. His name was Tommy. He worked there off and on, doing the books. He was supposed to be at home that night with his wife. But he wasn't. The fire started. Tommy's wife could see it from their apartment. She phoned Will, and he rushed to try to save Tommy. He went into the building three times. He suffered burns on his arms, his hands, his face and scalp."

Grant met Jason's eyes this time, as he said, "I burned down the building his son died in. I knew he'd come. I didn't know when. I thought it would be *me* he'd come after. Me, not Alf! I should have seen it!"

"Oh my God," Jason said quietly. "You've got to do something about this."

Maddy said, "*What*, Jason? What would you recommend? Think about it."

She was there to defend her husband, the one thing she had left, a man torn with unspeakable remorse, grief, shame, and loss.

"It's bad enough to lose our son," Maddy said. "But the real horror, Jason, is that I believe Alfie *knew*. Maybe he heard us talking. Or maybe Will Evans did reach him and told him the ugly secret. We tried to protect Alfie from that knowledge. But now I believe he knew."

"Then, do you think he killed Alf?" Even as he said it, he knew better.

Maddy said, "The coroner told us no. She said definitely suicide. I just wish I could have known he was so sad, so . . ."

"I found something," Jason said. "On Alf's tablet. Poems. Just a few, but kind of dark. Even music he had on there was moody." Jason took half a sheet of paper from his pocket. It had been folded and folded again. "I don't know why I wrote this one down. I guess because it had a recent date. Here, I'll read it. The title is 'Companion'."

Tacks of rain
sprinkle points up.
The wall stain stares:

Yellow-brown outline,
silent,
self-absorbed.
Hag.
Wire lips which kiss not.
Bat-bitten throat.
I'd kiss even that.

Maddy just looked at Jason. "It's the stain in the corner of the bedroom," Maddy said. "The roof needs repair. We meant to do it."

Jason said, unsure if he should tell them more, but he went on. "There was another one, called 'Old Urge'. It talks about a coffin being the 'ultimate Instead'. It was dated five years ago, so maybe he'd been thinking about it for a quite a while. I feel bad I didn't know, didn't maybe listen. I should've known he was that sad." Jason's eyes filled. "I'd better go," he said, and pushed his chair back to rise.

Grant flung himself up, knife in hand again. He came toward Jason, turned the knife to him butt-first, pleading for him to take it. "Kill me!" he said. "I beg you! It won't be punishment enough. It will be a *favor!*"

YEARS LATER, WHEN JASON would fasten his view on the Pacific from his studio where he formed stone fountains and plaster-of-Paris flamingos and garden elves, garden gnomes, smiling turtles, even a couple of mermaids, he would see a wandering figure on the beach at sunset or notice in the incandescent heat of afternoon the shafts of light and planks of shadow play tricks on his mind.

And at night, if Jason happened to be looking out over the ocean from his bedroom window, he might spot those same creosote pilings that he and Alfie sat upon the day of Alf's twenty-first birthday; and, farther up the shoreline, observe the waves shove against the rocks, bubbling at the corners of the world's slack mouth.

Then it would seem a piling would move, obtain legs and walk off slowly down the beach like a man searching for a gleaming thing he could never find. At times, the figure seemed like his lost friend. At times, he thought it was Alf's father, although he knew Grant Langdon was a hollowed-out man who watched endless games of sport on TV and never smiled, never cheered or cursed a team, rarely left the house, while his wife took over all responsibilities.

About six months after that day in the Langdon home, while searching for a peace that would not come, Jason put aside all other activity and went looking for the man called Uncle Willy. By then he knew Willy had not left the beach town, for Jason had glimpsed him downtown as the man was about to board a bus, and another time saw him up closer, eating a sandwich while watching a girls' volleyball game on the beach. That time, the man turned as if feeling Jason's stare. Under the shadow of his bill cap, his blue eyes seemed to lock on Jason's. A calm carried in his expression. To Jason it was as if Will Evans also waited for the next thing, whatever it would be named, challenged it, mocked it . . . waited . . . and maybe willed it.

Jason could not help himself then.

He followed him. He obsessed on the man. He felt himself changing, becoming someone he had never been: stronger, more assured of purpose; wiser, kinder, meaner, closer to his dead friend than ever before. He would haunt this man. He would make him pay. Because, also some things Jason found on Al's computer tablet were five stabs at love letters; five revisions, the first long and the others increasingly short. They were, in their own way, honed poems as well. The file name on the last one was simply YWillyY.

Jason also noted obvious Internet links to erotic websites—porn, if you will, featuring women and men and every combination thereof. The tablet was easy to destroy. The memories from those sites not so much.

WHAT WAS IT MADDY said? We do things, if we live long enough, that we would never imagine. Yet life goes on. For some, anyway.

Death: a punishment to some, to some a favor.

ROUGH MIX

BY WARREN MOORE

I WAS FIRST AT practice, as usual. Okay—as always. But we had played a gig the weekend before, and I hadn't set my kit up since we brought it back to the practice space. So I spread the rug on the concrete floor to keep the bass drum from sliding, unbuckled my cases, and put my kit back together before Gary and Josh showed up. I turned the jam box on—the local dad-rock station was playing "Turn the Page", and the Metallica version is even shittier than the original. So I switched it off and got back to work.

I had already worked up a pretty good sweat by the time I had finished tuning my snare drum. Not surprising. The "practice space" was a corrugated steel self-storage unit at the edge of the county, where an old dragstrip had been. Everything was concrete and metal. Air conditioning wasn't in the picture—we even had power strips and cords plugged into an overhead light fixture, and if a fire broke out while I was behind the set, I was screwed—I'd be crisp before I made it to the door. But it was cheap and far enough from anyone who cared that the cops didn't bother us when we played late. We did have a minifridge, and I got a Gatorade out and stood outside, hoping for a breeze to break the stillness of the South Carolina summer.

But there wasn't a breeze coming, and until the sun moved a bit farther west, I might as well duck back into the space, which at least had places to sit. There were a couple of camp chairs and a love seat by the PA board. I picked my way between Gary's bass amp and Josh's stack to one of the chairs—the thought of the cloth-covered sofa gave me the creeps. There wasn't enough Resolve in the world to clean *that* thing.

It's not like I'm an innocent or anything; Mandy and I had used the space as an impromptu fuckpad ourselves from time to time. But that had been some time back. As had Mandy.

We had gone out a few times the year before, after hooking up at a friend's field party—we weren't even playing it. But I had seen her silhouetted in the headlights, and when I got closer, her hair was between blonde and brown, almost amber. So I grabbed an extra beer, and we talked a while, and she told me about an out-of-the-way tattoo, and well, you know.

And it was good for a while—really good, thinking-about-a-ring good, but then it just seemed to run out of gas. I didn't know why, and she said she didn't either, and it just kind of hung there, and I didn't know what to say or do, so I let her go. And a few months after that, she started showing up at our gigs again, but it wasn't until one night when I saw her between sets with Josh's arm around her waist and her hand in his back pocket that I figured things out.

I was pissed—I mean, it's not like this was some pass-along fuck from a one-nighter at the Brass Ass or something. I thought about quitting, but I liked Gary, and I was the one who started the band in the first place. Then I thought about firing Josh, but then I'd just be the guy who broke up a band over a girl. And even though Josh was an asshole, he could play, and he drew an audience. As I had learned. We had even started to get a little interest from A & R guys at a couple of labels. I wasn't going to just walk away and leave that for him. I tried to shake the thoughts out of my head and got back to work.

The microphone stands were already set up, but I got the mics placed. Each one had colored tape on it so we'd know whose it was. I get blue, Gary gets red, and I was putting Josh's mic with the yellow tape into its cradle when I heard a car roll up. It was Gary's van, and he swung out of the driver's door and banged on the sliding door. "Come on, you guys!"

I heard Josh's voice: "Fuck off." And I heard Mandy's giggle. But they got out of the van and we all went back inside. Josh was working a rock-abilly look today—a black, western-style shirt with fake mother-of-pearl buttons, along with tight jeans and boots. It was gonna be hot as hell when we got going, but I knew he'd make it look good. Some people can just do that. Then there's me. I could drop a grand on wardrobe, but I'm still gonna look like Joe Shit the Rag Man. Mandy was wearing a pale blue tank-top and white denim shorts, and she scrunched herself into a corner of the love seat. Our eyes met for a moment, but then she looked away, back toward Josh.

Josh was talking to Gary about a new pickup he had installed in his Strat—he had changed one that came from the factory for something called a humbucker. I tried to look interested, but that wasn't really my territory. Some guitarists are like custom car guys or mad scientists—they just like to take things apart and monkey with them. Guitars, amps; re-wire this, replace it with that. Drums are easier, and it's just as well—I'm no tech guy. The other guys barely trust me to roll up the cables when we're loading in or out.

In fact, that was why Josh started putting tape on the microphones. I didn't sing enough to need anything fancy, but he had hotrodded his and Gary's mics, and he was really particular about it. I told him once that I couldn't really hear a difference, and he got salty about it, "Oh, the fucking *drummer* doesn't hear the difference." Now I'm pretty sure the issue wasn't me as much as it was that we were playing in a steel shed, but some folks are like that.

Besides, we—drummers, that is—get a lot of that kind of shit. There are a million drummer jokes out there, but they all boil down to this one: "What does it mean when the drummer drools from both corners of his mouth? The stage is level." You get used to it, and you know people don't really mean it, but people kind of take you for granted. "Would all the musicians—and the drummer—report to the stage?" Stuff like that. But you don't want to be an asshole about it, so you just laugh it off.

Had Josh been more like that after he hooked up with Mandy? Maybe I was just noticing it more. Or maybe it was because she was around again, and he had to be Mr. Big Shot, the band leader. Keep the drummer in his place on the back line. Hell, we're a three-piece band. I *am* the back line, along with the amps.

How the hell had that happened? I had started the band, I had booked the gigs at every dive in the Carolinas and a couple in Georgia, and I had always been able to come up with enough to keep the practice space when one of the other guys was short that month. But now Josh was the leader—the front man. And Mandy's man, and I was on the back line.

But even though Josh seemed to have won, it didn't seem to be enough, and he'd still take shots at me—especially in front of Mandy. Really? You took her away from me and you're fucking her and bringing her to practice, and you still have to rag me?

He looked at the mics, and said "Way to go, Barry. You at least got them in the right places. We'll make a gearhead out of you yet."

I shrugged and edged my way behind the drums, and decided to play it as a joke. "Hey, I may not know much about this shit, but I can recognize colors." I grabbed a coiled PA cord and tossed it in his direction for him to get it connected up. Just my luck—the twist tie, like those things you use to keep the bread bag shut came loose, and the cable came partly uncoiled and knocked a box of picks off the top of Gary's amp, scattering some of them on the floor. I started to come back around to help gather them back up, but Josh just shook his head and said, "I think you've done enough." And he cut his eyes toward Mandy with this "why-do-I-put-up-with-this schmuck" look. She smiled at him, patiently, admiringly. I looked down at my stick bag and got a couple out. I felt a bead of sweat trickle down my back.

We ran the cords from the mics to the marked inputs on the board—red to red, blue to blue, yellow to yellow, and then Josh and Gary turned on their amps and tuned up. When they were ready to go, Josh hit an A chord, stepped to the mic, and looked like he was lip-synching. We hadn't turned the board on.

He tugged his wet shirt away from his chest and pointed his chin toward Mandy. "Could you reach behind there and throw that orange switch on the back of the board?" She stretched to do it, and the hem of her shirt rose enough to reveal some of her waist above the belt-loops on her shorts. I remembered how her skin had felt under my fingers, and then under my lips as I had slid the shorts below her hips a long time ago. Josh saw me looking, and gave me a glare.

I suggested that we start with one of our originals, but Gary had been on a reggae kick lately, and there was no way Josh was gonna agree with *me*, so he called for one of our covers—Marley's "Every Little Thing Is Gonna Be All Right." We ran through an 8-bar intro, and then Josh leaned into the mic to start singing.

The guitar shrieked feedback and Josh collapsed, dropping to his knees and slumping sideways, with one leg and his guitar still touching the mic stand. The PA made a popping noise that sounded like a gunshot. Mandy jumped up and was moving toward him. I yelled for her to stay back, but I don't think she heard me. Gary figured out what was going on, though, and body-blocked Mandy back to the sofa.

It smelled like burned wiring, and there was a hint of smoke from the hem of Josh's jeans. The guitar amp kept screaming feedback, but Mandy was almost as loud. It seemed like forever but it was only five or ten seconds before a breaker somewhere must have kicked in, and then there was nothing but the sound of Mandy's screams. I looked around—the lights on the amps were out. The box fan by my drum kit was slowly coming to a stop, but the scorched smell would take much longer to clear the room.

Gary told Mandy not to look as he led her out and I grabbed my cell phone to call 911. And the EMTs got there in a hurry, but all they could do was sedate Mandy. There wasn't anything they could do for Josh. The police and fire people were there a few minutes later, and they took some of our gear, but they figured out it was an accident pretty quickly.

"Josh couldn't fucking leave anything alone," Gary told me a few weeks later, as we were waiting for auditions to start. I nodded. "He must have decided to dick around with the PA. Somehow, he swapped the ground wire for the hot one, and when he touched the stand while he was wearing the guitar, it closed a circuit.

"It's happened before," Gary said. "Back in the 70s, a guitarist got electrocuted on stage like that." I knew that—it was a guy named Les Harvey, from a band called Stone the Crows. But Gary didn't need to know that I knew that, any more than he needed to know that I knew green wires are ground and white ones are live.

I might not know much about this shit, but I can recognize colors.

THIS STRANGE BARGAIN

BY LAURA BENEDICT

THE CHILDREN EMERGE FROM the misting rain on the right shoulder of the road, and I take my foot off the gas, trying to decide if I will stop. Inside the Buick it's warm and dry and smells of cinnamon and chocolate, and the music is Satie, my favorite. I don't want to share the pleasure of this moment with a couple of stringy brats who don't have the sense to carry a flashlight or wear shoes with reflective bands on the heels. But this hesitation is only a game I play with myself. I'll stop. I always do.

A boy and girl, I think, the girl much taller than the boy. Their hair shines platinum in the headlights. They hold hands, which might be touching to some. Sister and younger brother?

Slowing the car, I put the blinker on. I've always been conscientious. A rule follower.

The Buick idles, the Satie plays. I wait for them to reach me. Blondes. Always blondes. I wonder who decided that. I press the button to lower the passenger window.

But the children have abandoned the shoulder for the ostensible safety of the opposite side of the drainage ditch. The girl strides purposefully on. *Stay away from us!* might as well be blinking in lights above her. It's the boy who is curious, and as the girl pulls him along, he stares, open-mouthed, at the car and me. His denim overalls are loose, the legs baggy and too short. He's also barefoot, and the night is chilly, the grass wet. How miserable.

Turning down the Satie, I clear my throat before calling out, "Nice night for ducks!" I smile, assuming they can see me by the soft lighting of the Buick's interior. "Do you need a ride?"

In response, the boy stalls and raises his hand in a tentative wave. Then he looks up at the girl, who jerks him forward.

Damn it. She's going to play hard to get. I ride the brake, letting the car creep forward. The rain picks up.

"Where y'all headed? I hate to see you out in this nasty weather. Won't you let me at least give you an umbrella?" The girl still won't look at me. The boy is not so suspicious of middle-aged women in big cars, bless him. If he has a grandmother, I bet he misses her already. I bet she bakes him cookies and spoils him with presents. Though from the state of his clothing and his shaggy hair, I suspect that the presents—if there are any—are modest. She might even be a heroin addict, or a drunk who beats him. I lean as far as I can toward the passenger window to hold out a cheap folding umbrella.

The girl and I are both surprised when the boy jerks loose of her hand. She shouts as he hurtles down the bank, headed for my car.

"Braylee! Stop!" She sounds more annoyed than panicked. I put the car in park.

The sun-browned face that appears at my window wears a shy smile, revealing a gap where a front tooth should be. Excitement shines in his eyes, and his breath is quick and shallow. *Braylee*? Why do children's names seem to get less dignified with each generation?

"Why hello, Braylee." The words feel foreign in my mouth. I don't want to know their names. "Here you go."

After snatching the umbrella as though he's afraid I'll change my mind, he turns and jogs a few feet. But he stops and looks back.

"Thank you, ma'am." He has an adorable lisp.

"You're welcome!" I dislike adorable.

Turning his attention to the umbrella, he fumbles with the catch. Just as I'm about to offer my advice, the umbrella shoots open. He laughs, but the wind drops from nowhere and plucks the thin sound away. The umbrella is no match for the wind, and its dome fills in an instant, causing the boy to stagger sideways, out of my sight. Has it forced him into the dangerous road?

A curtain of rain crashes against the windshield, enveloping the Buick. Water pours into the passenger window before I can close it. When that's done, I push open my door against the driving rain, and hold onto the car as I make my way to the boy, who lies motionless on the shoulder.

Why tonight? Why not a night filled with the songs of tree frogs, and the whinnying of contented horses in nearby pastures, under a bright moon.

The girl reaches him first, falling to her knees, her voice straining over the clamor of the rain. She flings a worn denim bag on the ground beside her. "You're all right, you're all right. It's okay. I promise it's okay!" Her hands flutter over the boy like moths uncertain where to land. Finally, she slips one hand behind his head and the other beneath his upper back. Rain streams down his face as she gently lifts him to her lap. I wait for him to open his eyes, or make some noise—a scream, or a rattling sigh. I doubt he's mortally injured from such a simple fall, but I watch, just in case. That moment between life and death is so brief, so precious. When he finally opens his mouth, he sputters at the rain.

By some miracle the umbrella still rocks on its head only a few feet from us. I kneel at his side to hold it over the three of us, gravel pressing painfully into my skin.

When the girl pulls her hand from beneath his head, it's smeared with blood, purple in the glow of the Buick's taillights. My breath catches. Maybe it's my imagination, but the blood's sharp tang seems to linger in my nostrils until we get the boy into the car.

THE WINDOWS OF THE Buick are fogged, and the children in the back smell like wet animals. The boy's head is again in the girl's lap, this time with my wool travel blanket between them. Given that he has a head wound, there's little enough blood trickling from it now. I turn on the defroster and swipe my coat sleeve back and forth inside the windshield.

"You're absolutely sure you don't want to take him to the hospital?"

"Can I be in an ambulance?" The boy is groggy, his voice weary. "Why can't I go in an ambulance?" If he's talking he must not be badly injured.

I'm not sure why I feel relieved. For my usual purposes, he might just as well have died on the side of the road. But indecision still nags at me. Twice tonight I could've just driven away. Now that they're in the car I'll just have to make the choice again: to let them live, or let them die.

"You know why we can't go there," the girl whispers.

Pretending I haven't heard, I ask where they were headed before the rain came on. It's lessened some, but the Buick's automatic wipers are still going hard.

"To a friend's house." Her voice is unexpectedly steady. She might be eleven, or at most twelve years old. She has the same wide cheekbones and button chin as the boy, and if they're not brother and sister, they're definitely related. It's too dark to see what color her narrow eyes are, but I think the boy's are blue.

"If you know the address, I can take you there."

She's doesn't answer.

No address. No friend with a house. Liar, liar pants on fire.

"What about home? Your parents must be worried."

"Wait. I have money," she says earnestly. "You can drop us off at a motel."

I confess I didn't see that coming. Flicking on the blinker, I ease the Buick back onto the wet road. "You two hungry? But maybe he shouldn't eat for a while. If he throws up, he really needs to be treated by a doctor. Concussions are dangerous."

"I know what a concussion is." Ah, she's *that* age, where they know everything and every adult is an idiot. For the most part I would agree with her about the adults.

"I want to go to sleep," the boy whines. "I want to go home."

In answer, the girl begins to hum softly, as though she's soothing an infant. *Blacks and bays, dapples and grays, all the pretty little horses.* She doesn't sing the words, but I hear them in my head. If she doesn't stop soon, I *will* put them out of the car, no matter where we are, and the decision will be made.

My answer is to turn up the Satie to shut out the lullaby. *Lullaby.* What blatant sentimentality. A nasty trick to lull a child into a false sense of security. The girl continues humming as though we're already in a contest of wills.

Sorry, sweetie. I will win.

The turn we would take to reach my house approaches on the right, but I don't slow. Ahead, the lights of the next town—such as it is—cast a silver glow on the suffocating clouds. If that was where they were headed, they had a very long walk.

I want to ask who made them leave home. Their parents? A stepmother? There's usually a stepmother involved. It's almost as if stepchildren are of less value than children born within a new marriage. Parent can be selfish, selfish, selfish.

"Almost there," I say.

The humming stops. "Where?"

"The motel." My voice is honey. My voice is innocence. The boy moans softly in his sleep. "You should wake him. He needs to stay awake for at least a few hours."

"I don't believe you."

I glance in the rearview mirror. Unlike the boy's sun-browned face, the girl's is pale in the dim light from the dashboard. Deep lines crease her shallow forehead. "Suit yourself."

"Well, I've never heard that." But after a moment she begins trying to wake him anyway. "Braylee. Braylee, come on."

No response.

"Are you sure you don't want me to drop you both at the hospital—? I'm sorry. I don't know your name." *Oh, why did I ask? So foolish. Making things harder for myself again.*

"Skyla. My brother is Braylee, and I'm Skyla." My brain enjoys an imagined eye roll. *Skyla. What the hell is a Skyla?* It sounds like the name of a women's douche from the 1980s. *Refresh with Skyla!*

"The Red Oak Motel is up ahead. It's not a bad place. Clean, I hear. And the hospital isn't too far away. It's not a big hospital, but it will do the trick if you get worried later."

We're welcomed into town by a badly-lighted car lot hung with sagging ropes of yellow and blue flags. The colors of the local high school. Quaint. Lights blaze from the Taco Bell next to it, but the Hardee's across the road is uncharacteristically dark, given that it's only a bit before ten.

"Do you know how much the motel costs?" There's a satisfying edge of panic in the girl's voice. Not so tough now. (Yes, I'm cruel, but it's an equivocal cruelty.)

"Oh, I don't know. Maybe forty or fifty dollars? Not an expensive one." I don't bother to say that no hotel will let a child her age register, no matter how trashy it is. All I really know about the Red Oak is that it has a bar attached to it called The Shady Acorn, whose parking lot is packed most evenings with pickup trucks and motorcycles, as it is tonight.

I park well away from the bar, and a good forty feet from the tiny motel office. It doesn't matter how far away from it we are, though. She's lying about the money, I'm certain. She'll come around. I'm patient.

Okay. Maybe a little impatient.

In the mirror I see her digging in the denim bag, holding it in such a way that the nearest lamp might help her see inside. Her shoulder-length, tangled hair falls into her face. Finally, she rests her head on the back of the seat.

"I only have nineteen dollars. Will you please give us some money?" She doesn't beg, but she looks as though she might start crying any second.

I turn in my seat, setting my lips in a regretful smile. Shaking my head sympathetically, I tell her that I'd like to help, but that I'm on a fixed income. That I could get them some food, as long as it isn't too expensive. "I'm sorry. Maybe there's some other way I could help?"

She looks down at her sleeping brother. I have to give her credit. She hasn't once indicated that she regrets having him with her.

"Do you have a house?" she asks. "Can we stay until he gets well enough to leave? I don't think it will take very long."

My face warms with . . . pleasure? Anxiety? So many feelings. I'm glad of the shadows. "Oh, of course. I'm sorry I didn't think of it first."

I like the children to ask if they can visit my house. I'm no kidnapper.

As we drive away, my confused feelings harden into disgust. My words and actions contradict all my hopes of changing what I am. I realize I could easily have paid for a room, and given the girl any amount of money. Three times I could have let them go.

UNTIL I WAS SIXTEEN, I was locked in my room just before my mother brought the child—or children—to the house, and not let out until there was no chance I would meet them. When I was allowed to come downstairs, my mother would be all smiles, the ovens cooling, the windows open, and the house sparkling. It would be weeks until she returned to being the disagreeable mother I knew so well. During those weeks, she would spontaneously grab me and hug or tickle me, making me shriek with surprised laughter. In the living room, she swayed to the music of Jean Ritchie and Bob Dylan and Joni Mitchell, her mane of black curls loose about her, her feet encased in lumpy wool socks she or I had knitted, and wearing a long denim dress that brushed her ankles. She baked and cleaned and sat with me and played games or did puzzles. She smiled so much, I would do anything she asked, eat anything she put in front of me, say anything, *be* anything to keep that smile on her face.

Then one morning, I would tap on her door to bring her coffee, and there would be no answer. She'd be lying in bed, her face turned to the wall, and I would know it was over.

I was lonely, living here in the woods with her those other forty-nine weeks of the year. There was school, though, and, four or five times in my life, visits to other girls' houses. I went on day trips to amusement parks and museums, especially once I could drive. I'd still get on a roller coaster if you asked me to. Sometimes, my life outside my home almost felt full. Until I understood what I was, who I would become.

Pariah. Savior. Lucky charm.

I'm the last of my kind, and I'm the only one who knows it.

ONCE I UNLOCK THE kitchen door, I flip on the overhead light, and slip my keys and wallet into their drawer. The children follow, the boy shuffling like an old man. Their heads are bowed as though they're being punished, and not walking into a home where they might be warm and well fed.

My first order of business is to treat the boy's injury. I only have a few squares of medical gauze, so after I've soaped the wound—under his mewling protests and his sister's admonitions about not fussing—I place the gauze and wrap his head in a worn Ace bandage I had used on my mother's tricky knee. When I finish, his head looks cartoonishly large, and his blue eyes enormous. It's hard not to smile. I find him a long-sleeved t-shirt that hangs past his knees, and give the girl a robe to wear while I wash and dry their clothes.

We talk little as they eat. I've stoked one of the ovens and opened the door, which serves to warm the kitchen better than the electric wall heaters. The boy slurps vegetable noodle soup, which dribbles over his bony chin and onto the kitchen towel I've tucked into the neck of the t-shirt. On his feet he wears a pair of my (not at all lumpy) wool socks. Now, he's less drowsy, but I'm making him eat lightly in case he vomits. His blue eyes stray every so often to the plate of my special walnut brownies sitting in the middle of the table. They smell marvelous, if you like that sort of thing. I'm an excellent baker, but more a fan of savory than I am of sweet. When he asks politely for one, I take pity on him, and allow him one brownie, but that is all.

Skyla is all eyes, taking in the big kitchen. It *is* rather grand, with spotless copper pots and pans and colanders hung on a rack suspended from the ceiling. The stove is an ancient eight-burner monstrosity, and the stainless steel refrigerator spits out water and three different shapes of ice on command. The white pine cabinets were taken from a grander French Colonial-style country house some fifty years ago, and the hardware and marble countertops gleam. (Like my mother, I like a clean working area.) But it's the ovens that are truly remarkable. One hundred-year-old Iron Forge ovens built side-by-side into the chimney wall, each with a heavy iron door with a sliding bolt. *Safety first.*

A much slower eater than her brother, Skyla mostly finishes the potato, carrot, and leek stew I set in front of her. She's scooted the sliced carrots to one section of the bowl without comment. Now her eyelids droop and she looks as weary as the boy. But when I try to clear her plate away, she grabs my wrist and gives it a sharp, unpleasant turn. "What if he has a concussion?" she whispers. "Do you think he'll die?"

It's an awful question for a child to ask. What must it be like to worry about someone you love dying? When my mother became ill, I counted the hours until she would be dead.

Across the table, the boy's head tilts onto his outstretched arm, and he makes lazy circles on the wood with one bony finger. The brownies are doing their job. He will be fine.

I pat the girl's hand. "Not tonight, not tomorrow night. The future isn't promised to any of us, but I think he'll live."

THE COTTAGE IS BIG enough that each of the children can have their own upstairs bedroom. Skyla initially resists when I tell her that her brother should be in a room alone, so he can sleep soundly and recover. But when he pushes past us into the room I've assigned him, he gives her a sleepy but rebellious stare and shuts the door in our faces. Again I want to laugh, but I keep it to myself. Skyla gives an adult sigh of resignation and follows me into the adjoining bedroom.

"The baseboard heater is on," I tell her. "You can turn it up to high if you get cold."

She nods, and glances around the room. It's simple, with white walls and a white matelassé spread on the painted iron bed. The braided rug is pale blue and pale green, and I've hung framed posters of Monet's various water lilies on the walls. It's not a bad room, though I never imagined I'd have a guest in it.

"Good night." I turn back to the door and leave, closing it behind me. Skyla didn't eat any of the brownies, but I'm certain she'll sleep through the night.

As I go downstairs to clean up the kitchen and move their clothes to the dryer, my mind makes automatic, ugly calculations: The boy is too thin, his cheeks are hollow, and the skin beneath his eyes is the shade of an early purple plum. His collarbone protrudes, and his fingers look almost skeletal. Remembering his politeness about both the brownies and the umbrella, I imagine he might actually be sweet. The girl is of average height and weight, though she hasn't quite lost her prepubescent baby fat, and has a pleasing, if cautious, temperament. Though the way she twisted my wrist reveals that she has a tough, gristly streak. Metaphorically speaking, of course. We're a long, long way from the medieval belief that how a person acts or appears has something to do with what they're like inside. What a barbaric thought.

I DON'T KNOW WHERE my great-great-grandmother came from, only that she was a widow with a young son, and they'd lived on their own in this place—godforsaken as it was in the nineteenth century—for several years. But then others came, and it turned into a community of sorts, a loose scattering of cabins with a store and a farrier and a meetinghouse nearby, all surrounded by prairie homesteads. Surely the newcomers wondered how she and her child had survived, and even thrived alone in such a wild and hostile place. What they would never know was that the few remaining native people in the area avoided her, claiming that she was evil. That to know her was to invite death. She knew what they said about her, and laughed about it. But to the land's new residents, people who looked like her, she was kind, and they knew she was hardworking. She was a maker and seller of baskets, keeper of a few cows and a sizable garden she and her son tended.

Then a killing winter came in which every family except my great-great-grandmother's lost someone to starvation, sickness, cold. She nursed the sick, shared her food. She was a savior. A survivor. If she'd lived a hundred years earlier, in another place, they might have called her a witch.

Winter far overstayed its welcome, and two days after an early spring blizzard an eight-year-old child disappeared from his family's cabin in the night. His icy footprints led away from the cabin and ended, abruptly, a half-mile later on the snow-covered cow path bordering my family's land. People said he'd gone crazy from starvation. His body was never found. But spring revived into frantic life just a couple of weeks later, as though the earth and sun had finally had enough. The year that followed was one of obscene abundance.

Nature is fickle, and the plenty didn't last, of course. After four years of losses, some superstitious fool remembered how and where the child had disappeared, and imagined he was the sacrificial seed that brought them salvation. It's never been clear to me to what or to whom that person thought the sacrifice was being offered. People who believe in the invisible are dangerous. What they don't understand is that there is always a human there at the beginning who creates that invisible *thing*—a deity or demon or spirit—for their own purposes. Such naïve madness.

It was a bad piece of luck that it seemed to work again, this time at the cost of a young girl's life and, later, the lives of the dozens sacrificed after her.

Thus a terrible tradition was born, with my family secretly at the heart of it.

* * *

I SLEEP BETTER AND longer than I thought I would, and wake to the unfamiliar smell of coffee. Dressing quickly, I hurry downstairs holding onto the handrail because you never know.

In the kitchen the door to the yard is open, and the boy sits on the steps, poking at something with one of my walking sticks. Sleep has caused spikes of blond hair to stick out of the bandage like overnight weeds. He wears only the t-shirt I gave him to sleep in, his childish knobby knees gathered up into it. So, no dire concussion after all.

You might ask why I didn't lock the deadbolts on the doors to keep the children from leaving or even going outside. My mother would have. In the past, I would have.

The year I was twenty-one, the boy offered up to us was too old, too strong, and would not be subdued. Broken furniture, broken dishes, a broken window. So much chaos. It was only chance that he tripped, his face planting in a chair cushion, and I was able to hold his wrists behind his back. I looked away as my mother swung the bat at his head, but I heard his temple cave in with a soft, watery sound I still hear in my dreams. I touch the smooth scar on my chin, the one I cover with makeup. Unlike my mother, who reveled in a quick kill, I believe that the most effective weapons are emotional, and these ejected, rejected children really only want kindness. That's how to win them over to their fate—or at least how to make them more vulnerable. How's that for armchair psychology? There are many ways to devour people.

"Our dad likes coffee before breakfast, and he lets—I mean, *let* us drink it, too." Three identical mugs from the cabinet sit in a line near the coffeemaker. The coffee smells rich and strong and when Skyla picks up a mug and holds it out to me, saliva seeps from the floor of my mouth. What an odd thing for her to do, especially in a stranger's kitchen. Is she trying to manipulate me? Does she already know my plans, when I'm not even sure of them myself? She might not be looking for kindness at all. My theory is only a theory, and there are exceptions.

She says she has no money, but, really, what *is* in that bag she carries? When it's on her shoulder, it sags. Now it occupies the seat of the fourth kitchen chair, slid into its place at the table. So she is unwilling to leave the bag in her room. Interesting.

Maybe she's a thief. There are few things of obvious value in the house, no electronics, jewelry or fine paintings. A child couldn't do anything with a painting! It doesn't matter, though. They won't be leaving here, whatever the circumstances.

"Excellent." I take the mug and sip carefully. The coffee is delicious, and I tell her so. She flushes, obviously pleased. Despite her narrow eyes and sallow skin, she could perhaps grow into a presentable, even pretty girl. "I have cinnamon rolls rising on top of the refrigerator. I'll stir up the fire in the stove and get them baking."

While I'm working, the boy stomps into the kitchen.

"I want some coffee too. Where are all the birds? You don't have any birdfeeders out here or anything. But I found a really big worm. Look!" Beaming, he holds up a foot-long earthworm pinched between his forefinger and thumb. The worm curls and stretches, its head (or tail?) alternately reaching for the boy's hand and the ground.

"Get it outside! What do you mean, bringing that in the house?" Sounding like an angry mother, Skyla slams her own mug on the counter, making both the boy and me wince. He glances uncertainly from me to his sister and back again.

This feels like some kind of test. Which of them to disappoint?

"Let me get a jar, and you can put some dirt in it. If you turn it loose in the house it'll just be confused." My advice sounds remarkably sound and wise to my own ears.

"Yeah. That's right," the boy says. "Worms get confused. Did you know if you cut a worm's tail off, the part with the head gets to grow a new tail? But it doesn't grow a new head on the tail part."

"How fascinating." I get up to take an old Mason jar from a cabinet.

A few minutes later, the boy returns to the kitchen with the jar half-filled with dirt, the worm writhing on its surface. He sets it on the table in front of him, and stares at it, rapt.

"Do you have any pets at home?" I slide the pan of risen rolls into the oven, shut the door and throw the bar across it.

"Why do you lock up the oven like that?" the girl asks.

Why, indeed? "Oh, just habit, I guess. Safety first." Gripping the end of the bar, I slide it back out of place. There's a curious smile on the girl's lips. *Silly old woman*, it says. *We're too old and smart to do something like climb in the oven!*

No. But you're not too big for me to put you in it. My mother's voice. Or is it my own? A sickly sweet taste comes to the back of my throat as though the mucus there holds my worst memories. I've learned that LSD flashbacks happen that way. The drug lives on in some glands and the taste trickles out on and off, sometimes for years.

AFTER THEY DRESS IN their laundered clothes, they tell me they want to explore the house. There's no talk of leaving or motels or pets.

The boy runs ahead of Skyla, skidding down the hall in my socks. He is all energy, and the coffee and cinnamon rolls probably haven't helped. He seems at home, as though he has always lived here. I'm not sure what to do with his happiness, and it bothers me. Was there ever a truly happy child in this house? I certainly wasn't one, except perhaps for those few weeks each year. Every other child who has come here in my lifetime was deathly afraid, and for very good reason.

He tries every door without asking, and strides into rooms, looking like a slightly demented hospital patient in his bandage. Gone is the shy smile from the night before. When he comes to the attic door at the end of the upstairs hall, he finds it locked. "How come?" he asks, looking up at me, his head tipped like a perplexed terrier's.

"A couple of the stairs are wobbly, and sometimes I forget. The lock reminds me. There's nothing up there anyway, except spiders." I give an exaggerated shudder. "Everything I need is down here."

Satisfied, he moves on. Behind me, Skyla is silent, but as she passes by the door I hear the faint movement of its old metal knob as she tests it. I wish she hadn't done that.

They finally settle in the tiny downstairs room my mother hopefully called *the library*, with its piles of *National Geographic* magazines, light mysteries, and romance novels. If you'd known my mother, her taste in books would surprise you. She eschewed horror novels or anything else that described violence or bloody scenes. The same for books in which any harm came to children. If she accidentally purchased a book with any of those elements, she threw it in the garbage can, from which I would rescue it, hide it, and read it. Now I use the library because I get tired of dusting books. Each week I select a stack that perfectly fills my green canvas bag that bears the logo of the local natural foods co-op. They know me at the library.

Skyla discovers the shelf of jigsaw puzzles, and asks if I will do one with her. She looks surprised when I agree. I love puzzles, and I haven't done this one, a Mary Cassatt painting called "Summertime," of a woman and girl in a rowboat, admiring ducks on the water. Even in puzzle form, the dazzling white of the ducks' feathers and the bow on the girl's hat pierce the somber colors of the water like wedges of ice. The mother reclines, resting one elbow on the side of the rowboat. She looks amused. The girl hangs back timidly. Once we have the edge pieces assembled, the boy, who has been looking at magazines, leans over the table, saying he wants to help. But after two or three minutes he wanders off, bored, and takes the worm in the jar to play outside.

What a strange way to spend the day, with these children I don't really know. It's been decades since I've done that. Adults don't make friends the way children can—without agendas, without commitments and worries about the future.

I'm Skyla's future, and the boy's future. My stomach clenches. I think of what's to come, and the work, and the cleaning up, and all the memories that won't die. As I bend over the puzzle, searching for pieces to fill a section of grass, I remember the rich, dark smell of the boy's blood as I doctored his wound and fitted the bandage. My body again floods with a confusion of shame and desire. Hunger for the metallic sweetness of flesh.

Shame.

Fed as a child before I knew what I was eating. The odor of cooking meat and onions and potatoes and tarragon and chervil, with its licorice scent. That day in third grade when I had real licorice for the first time, and the smell of it made me so nervous I vomited on the cloakroom floor.

Shame.

"Are you okay?" I've been staring at the jumbled pieces for too long. Skyla watches me with questioning eyes. Not concerned, just curious.

"I was thinking about dinner."

She drops her gaze to the puzzle and fits in a duck's head. "I used to make dinner a lot. Nobody likes to cook at our house. My dad worked construction and he was never home until late."

"Not your mother? But I guess that's not a very correct thing to assume." I smile. "I mean, maybe your father sometimes cooks on the weekends? You know what I'm saying." My stomach relaxes a bit. It almost feels natural to talk to her. Whatever natural means.

If she really knew me, she would run away. Fast. She should *run away and take the boy with her. But now it's too late.*

"I don't have a mother. We've got a stepmother. My mother died and left us with our dad after Braylee was born. He says he remembers her but he was only a few months old."

"You remember."

Skyla shrugs. "Now our dad's dead. So Braylee and me had to leave."

"How sad." I don't ask for the details. Did she run away of her own accord, taking her brother? If so, then they might be the *wrong children*, and another child—or pair of children—could still be wandering loose on that road. What would happen to them if I didn't retrieve them? The idea is too fantastic to consider.

But I think they *are* the children. It makes sense that they'd been orphaned by their father, and left with the stepmother. There is always an unhappy stepmother involved, like someone planned it from the beginning. (It seems a bit hard on stepmothers. Talk about stereotyping.) The way such things are decided is a mystery to me, as it was to at least my mother and her mother. We are the other side of this strange bargain.

I'm not sure why I feel so uncertain this time. Is it because my mother has only been gone two years? She'd been ill and housebound for a decade, and so I'd mostly dealt with the children alone, anyway. But this time I am completely on my own.

"Do they deliver pizza out here?" Skyla asks. "I know where the Domino's is, but do they come out this far?"

LATER, WE GATHER IN the kitchen to make pizza. Neither of them is good at shaping the dough, but Skyla crumbles dried oregano and basil into the sauce, and slices mushrooms.

"Aren't we going to have pepperoni?" The boy is twisting the dough I gave him to play with into a long, wormlike string. Beside him on the kitchen table is the jar with the real worm. Only an inch of its burrowed body is visible through the glass. "We always have pepperoni. Hey, Skyla. Do you think Daddy eats pizza in heaven? I would eat pizza all the time in heaven. I bet you get whatever you want to eat anytime. Like that place where we went that had fifty pizzas sitting out and you could get any kind you wanted, like pineapple and ham. Pineapple is gross."

"Pepperoni is meat. I don't eat meat, so I don't have any in the house."

"That's so weird," he says. "But how come you have one of those meat hitter things?" He lets the dough drop to the table and goes to the canister that holds spatulas and wooden spoons. Utensils clatter to the counter as he pulls out a steel-headed meat tenderizer. Waving the tenderizer like a club, he says, "Mommy Janelle has one of these. This could really whack somebody. BAM!" The sharp crack of splitting wood shatters the air as the steel head makes contact with the back of a chair. Stunned, the boy stands staring at the destruction, his mouth gaping.

"Give me that!" I'm on him in an instant. One of my flour-covered hands grips his shoulder, and the other wrenches the tenderizer away from him. Without stopping to think, I raise the thing above his head. He looks up at me, his eyes blank with shock.

I've seen those eyes. I see them in my dreams. Sometimes they melt with tears, sometimes fill with disbelief or abject terror. Except those eyes always close just before I bring whatever I'm holding down on the child's head.

Two hands grip my raised arm, pulling at me.

"Stop—Stop it! Don't hurt him! Please!"

I breathe.

I haven't killed him.

The windows are open. Spring peepers chirrup from the woods. A plane passes far overhead.

I breathe.

I haven't killed him.

"I hate you," he screams. "I hate you worse than anybody! You're old and you're mean and you're just like a witch, you're so ugly!" Swiping his arm across the table so the worm jar falls to the floor, he runs from the room. In a split second he is back, leaning on the door frame, his turban bandage sagging to one side. "You're a witch and you're hiding all your secret witch stuff and I'm going to tell everybody and we're going to burn your stupid house down!"

Skyla has let go of my arm. I can't look at her yet. I stare at the tenderizer in my hand. It was my mother's favorite kitchen tool. The boy's footsteps pound up the stairs and along the hallway above our heads, sounding as heavy as a man's.

"He didn't mean it." Her voice shakes. "He does stupid things sometimes, but he's just a little kid."

I feel frozen and empty. The monster living in the shell of my body has retreated to its hiding place. *I know you're a witch!* Witch. Monster. Mother. Stepmother. In a child's eyes, there isn't necessarily a difference.

To my surprise, Skyla doesn't follow Braylee to his room. Without speaking, she kneels by the jar—which, by some miracle, hasn't shattered—and uses the side of her hand to try to brush the spilled dirt back inside. When she's gotten up as much as she can, she picks up the escaped worm without flinching, and drops him back in the jar.

Her eyes evade mine as she asks if there's anything else she can do. I recognize the fragile hesitation in her voice. It's the voice of a girl who doesn't want to make a grownup mad because she's afraid of what will happen.

We have to deal with them quickly, dear. It's best not to know their names so you don't get too attached. Farmers don't name their livestock for a reason.

"Nothing. You don't need to do anything else. Thank you." I notice the over-risen pizza dough. "The dough's full of air bubbles now. It will take a while to get it to where it's ready to shape again."

"That's okay. I'm not hungry." She slides out the broken chair and picks up her bag. Something inside it shifts and I hear the clink of metal on metal. She doesn't seem to notice. "I think I'll go to bed now."

"What about your brother? He hasn't eaten since lunch." Whether he goes hungry or not matters less than the awkwardness between Skyla and me. I don't want her to go upstairs and leave me all alone.

"Don't worry, he's used to it. Our stepmother always makes him go to bed without dinner."

Outside, the sun is almost gone. When I hear the bedroom door shut overhead, I turn off the kitchen light and sit waiting for night to make its way inside.

I WAKE TO THE sound of distant sobs. *The children. Children cry all the time.* But when I open my eyes, I have to wipe tears away to even see the outline of my moonlit window. Fumbling for tissues in my bedside table drawer, I try to remember the last time I cried. There aren't any tissues. It's obviously been a very long time.

What if I had cried in front of the children? Would they have had any sympathy for me? No. Crying would only make me look weak. I don't want to appear weak to them, but they witnessed my breakdown in the kitchen. Yet another reason to do something about them.

Except I don't think I can. If I kill them, I'll become my mother in every way. She's not here to carry the blame. *She made me this way! You have to understand!* If I don't kill them, I'll be a kidnapper. It won't matter that I was only doing what *they* wanted. That I was their sometime priestess, presumed bestower of bounty and success.

I use the bathroom, and return with a roll of toilet paper to keep in my bedside table. Somehow it makes me feel better to imagine that I might cry again, even if it's in my sleep.

Lying down, I wait for sleep to return, but I can only think about the agony of the coming day. Then I hear someone moving through the house.

Quick, light footsteps going down the stairs, then near-silence when they reach the bottom. I want to go to the door to listen, but my bedroom floorboards creak. If it's Skyla, I don't want her to hear me and think I'm spying on her. But what if she's ill? No. There still would be no reason for her to go downstairs. The two of them have their own bathroom. Or perhaps she's hungry, or the boy is hungry. When I think of him, my body warms with anger—at myself. Yes, he's a brat. But thank goodness I didn't kill him. Skyla would have had to be next. I'd still be downstairs, cooking and cleaning into morning. The kitchen would be filled with that wretched, tantalizing odor, even with all the windows open. I push the images from my mind. *I didn't kill him.*

Instead, I imagine them eating a midnight snack from the refrigerator, or stuffing themselves (pun intended, because I haven't completely lost my sense of humor) with leftover cinnamon rolls. I turn on my side to try again to sleep. Perhaps I do, because the next thing I hear is someone walking around in the attic.

MY KEYS, WHICH I had placed in a kitchen drawer the evening before dangle clumsily from the keyhole in the attic door. Amber light from the attic's bare bulbs filters down the stairs. I wish I were dreaming.

Someone stole my keys.

Skyla. She had touched the doorknob as she walked past it, thinking

I wouldn't notice, and she had dared to indulge her curiosity by stealing the keys. Would I have done the same at her age? *Not in my mother's house.* I might have been amused, or maybe even a little pleased at the child's boldness if I didn't know what she would see when she flipped on those lights.

Mommy, don't make me go up there. I don't want to take them by myself. Don't make me. Please, Mommy.

We all have responsibilities, my dear. This is yours now. I have my own. You don't hear me complaining about what I have to do.

Maybe that was the last time I cried. Maybe I stopped crying because it made her so angry.

I creep up the stairs as quietly as I know how. As I get closer, I hear a weak voice, singing. Singing! The words warble, and the tone is pleading and pathetic.

Blacks and bays, dapples and grays, all the pretty little horses.

But it's not Skyla's voice.

"How did you get my keys?"

The song ends abruptly, and the boy turns around. A puddle of urine blossoms at his feet. Behind him, the pile of bones as high as his chin stands silent and still. The oldest bones belong to unknown children who died before that eight-year-old boy from over 150 years ago, and the youngest are those of the last girl I brought home to my mother.

Before I bring a set of bones to the attic, I bleach them to a delicate yellow-white in a warm bath of hydrogen peroxide and water. Later, I set them outside, beneath a kind of protective cage to further bleach them in the sun. Only the skulls turn out truly white. I don't know why.

Seen all together, the bones are magnificent, like an ancient shrine.

The boy screams for Skyla, his tinny screeching filling the attic. He's such a little boy, with such little bones. When he tries to run past me, I grab him. He pushes at me with his hands, and butts me with his unbandaged head.

"Skyla! Skyla!"

I curse myself for feeding this boy, and letting him play and sleep in my house. I curse my mother for making me the way I am.

As he struggles, trying to bite and kick me, it's my rage that makes me strong and keeps me from harm. Finally, I'm able to get my hands around his throat.

I cry out when someone—surely Skyla—hits me with something hard, on my shoulder. The momentum forces me against the boy, but also forces me to let go of him.

Painfully righting myself, I turn to face her. Even in the weak amber light I can see the hate—not fear, but truly hate—in her eyes. I'm so drawn to them, to the newness of this emotion I see, that I almost miss the movement of the claw hammer coming at me again. As I feint left, the blow glances off my ear. I lunge for Skyla, but she's too quick, and I stumble and almost fall as I chase her to the stairs. It's her plan to draw me away from the boy, and I almost stop and return to him in spite, but it's her I have to deal with now. By the time I reach the stairs, she is halfway down, looking over her shoulder to see that I'm following. I pause to reach for the rail because *safety first*. My right foot has just come an inch off the floor when I feel two small hands at my back. It's not a strong shove, but strong enough to pitch me forward so that the stairs rush at me. The skin of my right cheek tears as it meets an exposed nail on a loose tread, and I fold at the waist, my legs and arms jamming against the wall and stairs at impossible angles. When my body finally comes to a tortured kind of rest, I can do nothing. My face and back burn with pain as though I were on fire.

"Witch!" the boy screams down at me.

I close my eyes. I don't want to see.

Skyla's breath comes in low, almost masculine grunts as she brings the hammer down again again again again again. The blows come, each one its own exquisite universe of pain, until I no longer feel anything at all. But I can still hear Skyla's breathing. It rises, louder and louder, until it becomes the breath of hundreds, perhaps thousands, filling my ears with a roar so great that I can finally lose myself inside it.

THE SENIOR GIRLS BAYONET DRILL TEAM

BY JOE R. LANSDALE

THE BUS RIDE CAN be all right, if everyone talks and cuts up, sings the school fight song, and keeps a positive attitude. It keeps your mind off what's to come. Oh, you don't want to not think about it at all, or you won't be ready, you won't have your grit built up. You need that, but you can't think about it all the time, or you start to worry too much.

You got to believe all the training and team preparation will carry you through, even if sometimes it doesn't. I started in Junior High, so I'm an old pro now. This is my last year on the team, and my last event, and if I'm careful, and maybe a little lucky, I'll graduate and move on. It's all about the survivors.

I was thinking about Ronnie. She was full of life and energy and as good as any of us, but she's not with us anymore. She got replaced by a new girl that isn't fit to tie Ronnie's war shoes, which her parents bronzed and keep in their living room on a table next to the ashes of Ronnie's pet shih tzu. I saw the shoes there during the memorial. The dog had been there for at least three years before Ronnie died. It bit me once. Maybe that's why it died. Poisoned. I remembered too that it slept a lot and snored in little stutters, like an old lawn mower starting.

Ronnie has a gold plaque on the wall back at the gym, alongside some others, and if you were to break that plaque apart, behind it you'd find a little slot, and in that slot is her bayonet and her ashes in an urn. I guess that's something. Her name is on the plaque, of course. Her years on the team, and her death year is listed too.

There have been a lot of plaques put in the gym over the years, but it still feels special and sacred to see them. You kind of want to end up there when you're feeling the passion, and the rest of the time that's just what you don't want.

Ronnie also has a nice photo of her in her uniform, holding her bayonet, over in Cumshaw Hall, which is named after the girl they think was the greatest player of all, Margret Cumshaw. Cumshaw Hall is also known as the Hall of Fame.

To be in both spots is unique, so I guess Ronnie has that going for her, though it occurs to me more than now and again, that she hasn't any idea that this is so. I'm not one that believes in the big stadium in the sky. I figure dead is dead, but because of that, I guess you got to look at the honor of it all and know it matters. Without that plaque, photo, ten years from now, who's to know she existed at all?

Sometimes, though, the bus ride can be a pain in the ass, and not just because you might get your mind on what's to come and not be able to lose your thoughts in talk and such, but as of late, we got to put up with Clarisse.

Clarisse thinks she's something swell, but she's not the only one with scars, and she's not the only one who's killed someone. And though she sometimes acts like it, she's not the team captain. Not legitimately, anyway.

It's gotten so it's a chore to ride with her on the bus to a game. She never shuts up, and all she talks about is herself. She acts like we need a blow by blow of her achievements, like the rest of us weren't there to perform as well. Like we didn't see what she did.

She remembers her own deeds perfectly, but the rest of us, well, she finds it hard to remember where we were and what we did, and how there have been a few of us that haven't come back. She scoots over the detail about how our teammates' bodies, as is the rule of the game, become the property of the other team if we aren't able to rescue them before the buzzer. You'd think she saved everyone, to hear her rattle on. She hasn't. We haven't.

We managed a save with Ronnie's body, but we've lost a few. That's tough to think about. The whole ritual when you lose a team member to the other side. The ceremony of the body being hooked up to a harness that the other team takes hold of so they can drag the body around the playing field three or four times, like it's Hector being pulled about the walls of Troy by Achilles in his chariot. And then there's the whole thing of the other team hacking up the body with bayonets when the dragging is done, having to stand there and watch and salute those bastards. That happens, the dead teammate still gets a plaque, but there's nothing behind it but bricks.

When we end up dragging one of theirs and hacking on it, well, I enjoy that part immensely. I put my all into it and think of teammates we've lost. We yell their names as we pull and then hack.

Thing was, Clarisse's bullshit wasn't boosting me up, it was bringing me down, cause all I could think about were the dead comrades and how it could be me, and here it was my last game, and all I had to do was make it through this one and I was graduating and home free.

A number of us were in that position, on the edge of graduation. I think it made half the team solemn. Some of the girls don't want it to end. Me, I can't wait to get out. There's a saying in the squad. First game. Last game. They're the ones that are most likely to get you killed.

First time out you're too full of piss and vinegar to be as cautious as you should be, last time out you're overly cautious, and that could end up just as bad.

Clarisse thinks she's immortal and can do no wrong, but sometimes you go left when you should go right, or the girl on the other team is stronger or swifter than you. Things can change in a heartbeat.

Clarisse, for all her skill, hasn't learned that. For her, every day is Clarisse Day, even though that was just one special day of recognition she got some six months back. It was on account of her having a wonderful moment on the field, so wonderful she was honored with a parade and flowers and one of the boys from the bus repair pool; the usual ritual. Me, I have always played well, and I'm what they call dependable. But I've never had my own day, a parade, flowers, and a boy toy. I've never had that honor. That's okay. I used to think about it, but now the only honor I want is to graduate and not embarrass my team in the process, try to make sure no one gets killed on my side of the field. Especially me.

We may be the state champions, but the position can change in one game. More experienced players you lose on the team, through graduation or death, less likely you'll make State Championship. You can train new girls, bring up the bench team. But it's not the same. They haven't been working together with us the same way. They don't move as one, the way the rest of us do. They're lumps in the gravy. They would need to survive several games before they were like a part of us.

Of course, listening to Clarisse you'd think she was the team all by herself. I've heard of some teams who would leave one of their members to the blades, for whatever reason. Maybe haughty teammates not unlike Clarisse. But no matter how annoying she is, that's not the way we play. That's not team work. We stick with her, like her or not. She's a hell of a player, but she's not the official team captain. But with Janey in the hospital they've given her the team for a while, so I guess, like it or not, she does have that position, but I just can't quite see her that way, as a true leader.

Our coach is around, of course, but she rides in a separate car when we go on a trip to a game. She says us having to deal with one another forces comradery. But I think the coach just likes to ride in a car and not hear our bullshit.

She's had a lot of winning teams, but this year, I figure she's done. She knows we know our stuff, and there's not much she can do. Just have us run our drills and give us a pep talk now and again. She was a great champion before she was a famous coach. She has fifty kills to her credit. Only Margret Cumshaw and Ronnie have more than that. But for all practical purposes, she's out of the picture.

"Thing you got to remember," Clarisse said, turning in the bus seat, looking back at us, "is you can't hesitate. Can't do like Millicent last time out. You have the moment, you take it."

Hearing my name mentioned made my ears burn. I hadn't hesitated. Things went a little wrong is all, and in the end, no one died and we won easily.

"Yeah. We know how it works," Bundy says.

Clarisse gave Bundy a glance, but it wasn't a strong one. We all knew Bundy was vital to our success. Clarisse was too, but nobody liked her the way they liked Bundy, though Bundy can connive a little herself, always wanted to be a team captain, end up a coach.

Bundy was one of our corners. She made things look easy. She wasn't fast like me or some of the other girls, but she was strong and taller than the rest. She had taken on two at a time more than once, and won, leaving them dead in her wake. She had her own parade day, twice, and she also had the scars across her cheeks and chin to prove her moments under the lights. Everyone said it made her look like a warrior, and that's true, but they were still scars. Bundy had been pretty once.

Me, I've done okay in that department. I have a scar on my left side, just below the rib cage, some small ones here and there, but I've come out all right, so far. At least I got both eyes. Bundy has a black pirate patch over her left one.

"I'm merely doing my job," Clarisse says.

"Sounds to me, like you're trying to do all our jobs," I say, and that sets her off a little, but not in words. She just gives me the look. That burning look she usually saves for when we're on the field, the one she has for the girls on the other team. It's the look she wanted to give Bundy but didn't, so I'm getting it double-time.

"As Team Captain," Clarisse says, "I—"

"Temporary Team Captain," I say.

Now that look from her was stronger. Me and her, we've always rubbed each other the wrong way, even back when we were in grade school, when we first started training with wooden bayonets and swatting dummies full of candy at each other's birthday parties.

The dummies were always dressed up in drill team colors from other schools. It was a way of starting to think right about what we wanted to grow up and become. Me and her, we made the team, way we dreamed we would, and though we were a bit at each other all through school, we mostly got along. Guess you could say more than that. That we were close, like competitive sisters. Lately it was nothing but snide remarks and go to hell stares, grins like sharks. Only thing that held us together was the team.

"Just think," says the new girl, Remington, sitting beside me, fidgety, "tonight, all over the country, stadiums will light up, and teams will go inside, and the crowds will grow, and we'll play beneath the lights."

I turn to look at her. "The lights will go up and the teams will march out and look up into the crowd, and you'll be sitting on the bench, maybe getting us some water when we change out."

"Yeah, I guess so," Remington says, turning red, making me feel a bit like an asshole.

Remington was a little thing, just barely made the team, but the roster was thin for new troops this year, so she was the best of the worst. "But I'm on the team. That means something, doesn't it?"

"Sure," I say. "We all start that way, asses on the bench. But eventually you'll get your shot. You'll be all right."

I didn't really think that. I figured first time she was on the field, after she got through the performance, the ritual, she'd hit the turf running and end up with a bayonet through her throat. I'd seen it happen more than once. The real Rah-rahs, as I called them, often didn't make it out of their first game without being badly wounded or dead, sometimes carried away by the other team for that drag and hack business.

I told myself, she got in the game, she went down, I'd do my best to save her body from the other side, but I'd only go so far. I didn't know her like I knew the others. The loss wouldn't be the same. I kind of felt the same way about Clarisse, and we were long time teammates, but at some point, you draw the line on risk. And tonight, I had drawn that line.

If I lived to get on the bus to go home, I would have had all I ever wanted of red, wet grass and cheering crowds. I could probably get an endorsement deal or two if I played my cards right.

But when I, if I, stepped off that field tonight, from that point on I was a happily bored civilian.

"All I ever wanted to be," says Remington, "is on the team, to wear the white and purple."

"You haven't made it yet," I say. "You have on the colors, and you can say you're on the team, but until you're on the field facing those who want to stab you, and you need to stab them, and you've played through, then you can truly say you're one of us. Not before."

She practically glowed there in the thin inner lights of the bus. "I'll get there."

Maybe.

"It's about our school," she says. "It's about our tribe, isn't it? Nothing really matters but our group, right or wrong."

I thought the problem was just that. The way the tribe takes over logic. The way other girls on other teams are the same. Them against us, us against them. But I say what I was expected to say, what I had to say, "Yeah, sure, girl. That's it."

The bus slowed at a light, adjusted with a whining sound which meant it might need some overhaul or something, and then it moved forward again without dying or going to pieces. It just might get us there.

I thought of something my mother said, that they used to have an actual driver up there, in the seat, and it was always a cranky old fart. She said she missed cars and buses that you drove, but me, I can't imagine such a thing. I was cranky enough tonight without having a cranky bus driver. I looked at Clarisse sitting up front, and I'm thinking there was a time when we gave our dolls swords, and each held one and made them fight one another. We got our fingers banged a lot. Lot of girls that wanted to make the team did that, but I didn't know any started as early as we did. We would sleep over at my house, or me at hers, and we'd talk. I couldn't figure it sometimes. How we went from what we were then to what we were now. It's like someone had cast a spell on us. We had a whole new set of friends outside the Team, and now me and her only talked when we had to, when we needed to for the games.

Sometimes it hurt me to think about what had been.

I looked out the window as we passed a field full of corn. There were lights in the field, and you could see the corn standing high, and beyond the field it was as dark as the space between the stars. I remembered once my mother, who had been quite a team champion herself, told me that when people came here, that was the part that was terraformed first. That very spot.

"Once, it was barren, and there was a dome," she said. "Right there is the heart of our beginning."

That was hard to imagine.

"Remington." It was Clarisse's voice cutting through my moment of silence, and I had so been enjoying it. "I think we might pull you off the bench tonight, you know, let you play first, be up front to feel things out."

"What the hell," I say. "She doesn't know her ass from her elbow."

"She's got about three seconds after they blow the whistle," Bundy says. "Then her dead ass will be taking a tour around the arena."

"Two seconds," I say.

"She's been trained," Clarisse says.

"That's right," Remington says. "I'm on the team. I'm honored to have the chance, Captain."

"Temporary Captain," I say.

"Temporary or not," Remington says, "that's the same thing, though. Right?"

Remington's saying that made my face flush. I hoped that didn't show in the poor light. It took me a long moment to say it, but I did. "Right."

I made a point then of deciding not to get to know Remington at all, because tonight would be her last night. I knew what Clarisse was doing. She was going to use someone we weren't close to for probing the team, seeing how good they were, how long it took them to put Remington down. It was a mean sort of gesture, to put her at the front, like she was important to the team, but what she was, was expendable.

I could practically feel Remington vibrate beside me. In a few hours there wouldn't be any more vibrating. It would be over for her, and we might learn something from her death about the other team, which admittedly was a team that changed up their game plans. They had a lot of solid, long term members, and they were without a doubt the toughest we had ever faced. I had seen some of the film made of their games, and it was chilling. They had an amazing defense and an even more amazing offense. When they left the field, it was always wet with the blood of the other team.

"I'm going to make all of you proud," Remington says.

"Of course you are," Bundy says, and all the other girls said something like that out loud. They were supposed to. I didn't say a damn thing. It might cost me some extra laps at the gym, Clarisse wanted to push it, tell the coach, but the thing was, I was done after tonight. I got home I only had one more week on the team, and that was all ceremonial until the graduation honors. I could run a few laps. I could do extra sit-ups or any other exercise that was asked of me. But tonight, I wasn't going to give Clarisse the satisfaction of agreeing with Remington's sacrifice. Poor Remington. She thought she was going to be a hero, not a corpse.

"Should I attack right off?" Remington says.

I didn't answer her. I didn't say anything. She said a few more things out loud, but I wasn't paying any attention any more. I was sitting there looking out at the landscape, flooded white by the moonlight.

WHEN WE GOT TO the café where we always stopped, Clarisse stood by the door of the bus, and as the team came out she reminded us not to eat heavy, the way Jane always did, like we needed to be reminded.

As I started past her, she called my name, says, "I need to speak to you privately."

I took a deep breath and let it out and stood off to the side and let the others pass as they headed into the café.

When it was just me and her, I say, "What?"

"You're supposed to be an example. Keep the new girl up, not try and bring her down."

"She'll go down all right," I say. "She's got about as much chance as a rabbit in a dog's cage."

"She has her training. We were all newbies once, and we all took our chances."

"We were better than her."

"That's how we remember it."

"That's how it was. And why aren't you talking to Bundy? Why didn't you pull her aside?"

"Because you're a Point, like me, like Jane. There has to be a third point, and with Jane out, she's the only one with the jets to play that position."

"Remington's no Jane. She's no anybody. And besides, you don't start the new ones off on Point first game out. Pull Bundy up."

"She's not fast enough. She's better where she is. Remington is fast, I've noticed that at workouts."

"Yeah. All right."

I knew it was a done deal. Clarisse was, much as I hated to admit it, the team captain. Unless the coach decided to override her, Remington would have her two seconds. And then she'd eat dirt.

"You protect the ones who have experience," Clarisse says. "That's how we win, with the regulars."

I quit talking to her then, went inside the café.

There was music playing and I could smell food cooking. I ordered a hamburger, one of the small ones and a side salad. Remington came over and slid into the seat across from me.

"I'm so excited," she says.

"Save some of that," I say. "Tame it, use it."

I don't know why I even bothered. She was a goner.

She chattered on about this and that, about the team, and finally our food came, and still she chattered. I ate slowly, way you need to, and when Remington wasn't chattering, she ate quickly, the way you're not supposed to.

"I know you don't think I'm ready, but I am."

"I know you're not ready."

"I believe in the team."

"That's nice."

"Don't you?"

"Sure," I say, but I wasn't certain. Did I?

Clarisse had already eaten, something small and mostly vegetables, I figured. She always looked great, played great. She came down the aisle of the café, walking between the rows of tables, saying, "Everyone. This is the championship game. This one counts more than any of the others counted. We have to—"

"They all counted," I say, the words jumping out of my mouth. "Ronnie's game counted, didn't it?"

"Of course. That's not what I meant."

"I am so tired of your yacking and trying to act like you're some kind of hot stuff. Why don't you shut up and sit down and just do your part later?"

"You're jealous, aren't you," she says, glaring at me. "You wanted to have a day dedicated to you, and you didn't. Didn't earn one. And you thought you might actually take Jane's place while she was out. Be team captain instead of me."

"You don't know anything," I say, but I was thinking, yep, that's about it. That and the fact that I was tired of the whole thing, tired of dreaming about the final dark, the possible pain. I have nightmares about being dragged around the inner stadium with my dress hiked up and my ass hanging out, flapping along like Clarisse's tongue.

"I'm the team captain," Clarisse says, "like it or not."

"I don't like it much," I say.

Everyone looked from my face to Clarisse's, except Bundy. She says, "This can be settled."

"It can," I say. "The old way it used to be settled."

"We don't do that anymore," Clarisse says.

"You mean you don't want to do it that way," I say.

"You and me, we been friends a long time."

"No, we were friends a long time ago. This whole team captain thing, it can be solved, way Bundy says. It's in the rule book."

Bundy eyed Clarisse, says, "Think she's got you there, Captain."

"Very well," Clarisse says. "This is a bad time for it. Game night. But yeah, I'll give you your satisfaction."

She touched the bayonet strapped to her hip.

That's when Lady Red, owner of the café, her hair dyed red as a beet, drags all three hundred pounds of herself out from behind the counter, wags a finger at us. "You know the rules for any squabbles, fist or bayonets, or just bad language. Take it outside. One of you gets killed, you'll bleed in the parking lot, not on my floor."

"There's no need for this," Remington says. "One for one, and one for all."

"Shut up, Remington," I say.

THE LOT WAS LIT with lights and moonlight. It wasn't as bright as the stadium would be, but it was pretty good. We could see how to kill one another, that was for sure.

We spaced off, ten feet between us, our bayonets drawn, the edges of them winking light. Clarisse stood with her legs a little wider than shoulder width, standing to the side, the bayonet in her forward hand, not the back one, way you should hold it if you knew something. We both knew something, but I got to thinking there might be a reason she was team captain, not me, because earlier she had hit it on the head. I wanted that place, thought I deserved it, and Clarisse had always won out over me, in everything. She got the best body and face to begin with, born that way, and she had better clothes and they fit her the way the same clothes would never have fit me, even if my parents had the money to buy them, and she got all the boys, and twice she got my boyfriends, and all she had to do was walk by and smile, and it was a done deal.

I had dreams where she died, and I never knew how I felt about them. Was I happy or sad? I awoke with tears on my face but a happy heart.

"You've always been jealous of me," Clarisse says, like she's been reading my mind.

"You don't know everything," I say, but right then I'm thinking, yeah, well, she knows a lot, and she probably was a pretty good team captain, and she just might kill me tonight, or wound me bad. I didn't have the team to work with against her. I had me and she had her, and that was it.

Thing was, to save face, I had to do it now, and I thought, maybe I'll wound her good enough, or maybe she'll wound me good enough I won't have to go in with the team tonight. I'll be through.

I swallowed and eased forward and she eased toward me.

"Touch off," she says, and though this isn't a game, just a fight, I do it, reach out and tip my blade against hers. They make a clinking sound, and then we both move back one step, like we would in a game, and start to circle one another.

"This isn't team work," Remington says, stepping out of the circle of girls around us, saying that like it might not occur to us that it wasn't.

It's then, that just beyond Clarisse, as we're circling, I see Bundy's scarred face there in the light, her one eye and her black patch on the other, and she's lit up like she's just had an orgasm, first communion, and a ticket to heaven.

Oh yeah, I'm thinking. We do this, I kill Clarisse, or she kills me, or we just get injured bad, neither of us may be able to be team captain, and next in line is Bundy. Wouldn't be a lot of discussion on that, not tonight, when it's the last game and there's no time to rethink things. Bundy ends up captain tonight, and we win the game, she goes out a hero, gets another parade. Me and Clarisse get some hospital time, and maybe the game's lost because we're not there.

Was that why Bundy was so eager to have us fight?

Was I trying to find excuses to dodge out?

Now Clarisse was easing closer, using the fake step, where you drop your back leg behind you, but your front stays where it was, gives the impression she's moving away, might make you think you can get her on the retreat, but it's just a trick.

I knew all her tricks, and she knew mine.

"We're a team," Remington said. It sounded like her voice had been sent to her via wounded carrier pigeon, like it didn't really want to be there.

"Hush," Bundy says to Remington.

But that's when Remington began to sing our fight song, and damn, her voice was good. It rose up and filled the air and it almost seemed as if the lights got brighter, and if that wasn't enough, some of the other girls started to sing. They tightened the circle around us, and the singing got louder. I could feel tears in my eyes, and then one of those tears escaped and streamed down my face, and the other tears, like lemmings, followed.

"And they called to the crowd, and the crowd called death, and the bayonets came down," they sang, and then the chorus, "Came down, came down, like a mountain, came down."

For whatever reason, that chorus always got me, and it had me then, and I think to myself, get it together, lose the emotion, or Clarisse has got you.

But that's when I see Clarisse's face in the light, and it looks like she's just sucked a lemon. The war paint she wears was running over her cheeks, her face was wet. Her bottom lip was trembling.

All of a sudden, she lowers the bayonet to her side and starts to sing, and then I lower my bayonet, and I start to sing, and coming in late, but clear and strong, Bundy begins to sing.

Everyone of the girls is singing now, and just as loud as they can.

Me and Clarisse spin our bayonets into our sheaths in unison, like one of our drills, and we smile at each other, and we keep singing, and when we come to the end of the song we embrace.

Remington says then, "We got time for a cup of coffee. One cup is good for you in a game, coach told me that, but two, that's too many."

I went over and put my arm around Remington, and then Clarisse did the same thing from the other side, and we walked Remington back into the café, the team following.

* * *

ON THE BUS, ME and Clarisse sat together, up front of everyone else, and were mostly silent in the dark, but when we were maybe like, five miles out, she says, "Do you remember when we were little, how we used to make our dolls fight?"

"Sure," I say. "I remember," not telling her I was thinking just that thing earlier tonight.

"We were close then," she says, "and I always have felt close to you, even when we weren't getting along."

"Me too, I guess."

"I was always jealous of you, Millicent."

"Say you were?"

"You were smart, and could see things quick, and I got to tell you, I maybe overdo a bit when I'm around you, cause I'm thinking whatever I'm doing, you could do as well or better. I don't like to admit that, but I'm admitting it now."

"Yeah, well, you got your stuff too. I never had your looks, your style."

"You say. I mean, you know, you could push your hair back a little more, show your face. You got a good profile, girl."

"Yeah?"

"But mostly you're smart. You're smart, and you'll probably stay smart. No one stays pretty, not in the way they think. My mama told me that."

"She's damn pretty."

"Yeah, but you should see pictures of her when she was younger. She was beyond pretty."

I let that soak in, her compliments, and then I say, "Remington, I don't know. Front lines. I mean, it's your call. She is quick, damn quick, and eager, but I'm thinking maybe you put her in at the back, first round, then move her to the front later, second or third round, third would be best, and by then she's got a feel, isn't quite so eager she's rushing into something she doesn't understand."

Clarisse nodded. "Coach told me, said, you're the Captain, but someone has a suggestion, listen to it, and you like it, do it, you don't, don't do it, but whatever happens it's on your head."

"That's a heavy responsibility."

"Listen here, girl. Let me be completely honest. I wanted Remington up front, because I didn't want you up front. You're great. You can play the spot, you know you can, and you do, but, I figured tonight, we might both go home, and then, we might can, you know, be friends again."

"I'd like that, but I don't want Remington to die for it. And besides, you need me up front with you. Like always."

Well, then we could see the stadium lights, they were pointed out from the stadium toward the sky. A moment later we could see the big open gate that led inside. The bus went in, and then it stopped and we got out.

Clarisse tries to get everyone's attention, but there's too much excitement. Championship game, you know.

"Hey, listen up," I say, and I say it like I mean it. "Captain has something to say."

Everyone goes silent and we huddle around, and Clarisse says, "Remington, you'll play at the back first round, maybe through the second. Then, everything looks good, we'll move you up."

"Yes, Captain," Remington says, and if she looked disappointed, I couldn't tell it.

Clarisse gave us a few more instructions, stuff we already knew, but it's all right to hear it again, to keep sharp.

Then we marched in formation toward the big opening that led onto the field. It was dark in the tunnel and we stopped right at the opening that led onto the field, and looked out. There was some light on the field, but only at the far end, where the other team stood waiting. Being that they were the challenging team, they got to come out first, get hit with their lights.

Clarisse says what we always say before we step onto the field. "We know not what comes."

We chant the same words once, softly, and then Clarisse says, "Remington, lead off with it."

Remington starts to sing our fight song, and then we all start to sing. Bundy slaps Clarisse on the back, and out we go, marching onto the field.

Hearing our voices, our school band starts to play up in the stands, a little heavy on the drums, but good on the horns, and then everyone from our school, parents, students, teachers and so on, they start to sing too, and then the stadium lights flare on us.

We look up and see our supporters standing up, singing, smiling down at us, and we march confidently onto the field, still singing.

IF ONLY YOU WOULD LEAVE ME

BY NANCY PICKARD

THE PROBLEM WITH BEING married to a nice man who adored you was that you couldn't divorce him without looking like a jerk. "Why?" her mother would ask her if Melinda actually did it. "Did he have an affair? Did he hit you? Was he verbally abusive? Did he gamble? Was he addicted to something? Alcohol? Drugs? Leon has always seemed just wonderful to me. I thought you two were doing fine! This is so *sad*. Your dad thinks the world of him. I do, too. Has he done something to deserve this? He's even *improved* since you married him. I've never seen the like of it. I just can't believe you'd leave such a nice man who clearly loves you! Is it because you don't have children yet?"

The incredibly frustrating answer to each of those questions that could be answered by yes or no was, "No," a definitive, wildly irritating, honest, desperate, "No."

He hadn't done anything to deserve it.

He didn't have any goddamn *faults*, he was too good for faults. My God, he even did his own laundry.

Well, there was one major fault that he couldn't correct.

She couldn't *say* it to other people, though. That would be terrible of her to actually confide to anybody, and especially to her parents or to his. His! Oh, my god, they thought she was perfect for their perfect son. How could she say, "He's the world's worst lover." She couldn't. Never, ever. She thought too highly of him to hold him up to that kind of embarrassment. He was far too decent a human being for her to blame a divorce on the Missionary Position.

It wasn't as if she hadn't told him, asked him, encouraged him.

He'd *tried*, kindly person that he was.

But his heart wasn't in it, not any more, not even to please her.

His heart was stuck in slam, bam, thank you ma'am, as if he'd turned into a 1950's advertising salesman with too much "respect" for his wife to bang her like he banged his secretary. Only, there was no secretary, just like there was nothing Melinda would call sex. Once every ten days. In bed. Under the covers. He hated doing it without sheets over them. "I feel so silly," he'd admitted, sweetly, "with my butt stuck up in the air." She'd offered to point her butt to the ceiling, instead, but he'd looked so shocked that she'd let that go, too. Oral sex was out of the question. The mere phrase, "oral sex" made his face go all "Ew." She wondered if he was gay and either didn't know it, or was still hiding it. In this day and age! Good grief. If he was gay, she would gaily support him and set him *free.*

She'd buy the condoms! She'd be their flower girl!

Please figure out you're gay, she thought, often.

Counseling was out, because she didn't actually *want* to save their marriage. She'd given up. Plus, a counselor was sure to ask, "Did you know this before you married him?" No, she could honestly say. But Leon was different then; they'd had sex between the appetizer and the entree back then, between dessert and coffee, to say nothing of between the sheets.

He'd *liked* it.

It was all the fault of the First Community Church of God.

When she thought about how her agnostic husband had suddenly got religion, Melinda wanted to push his face into a Baptismal font. Oh, God—speaking of which—if only he'd have an affair so she could catch him. With a man, with a woman, with a pony, she didn't care, just so long as he cheated and gave her a thank-God, socially acceptable reason to leave him. Maybe she was too caught up in what other people thought, but jeez, why should she have to go through life feeling condemned for leaving a nice man?

LEON HAD HOPED HE could out-sweet her.

His wife loathed ooey-gooey pudding-mouthed people, especially sweet-talking, compliment-throwing men.

"You're always so *nice,* Leon," she'd said recently, in a tone in which she had also said, "Yuk. Our trash bin is *sticky!*"

He thought he was making progress.

Any day now she was supposed to get so fed up with his smarmy efforts to please her that she wouldn't be able to take it any more and would leave him for a ruder, lazier man.

There was only one place he didn't try to please Melinda.

She loved sex.

Before marriage, they'd done it three times a night sometimes. Definitely three times a week, usually more. Surely, she'd go insane any time now with his every-ten-days regimen, soon to drop to every two weeks if she didn't get with his program.

He was surprised she didn't suggest marriage counseling.

"Church?" she asked, dumbfounded when he'd told her he was going.

Church was his excuse for the change in him from loose and thoughtless to zipped up and punctilious. Church wasn't where he'd met the beautiful young choir director, Staci, but it was where he'd followed her, a smitten lamb trotting along after her wagging tail.

There was nothing like naked sex in a bell tower.

Far enough away from the bells not to go deaf; close enough to reverberate like a couple of tuning forks and ring out hallelujah.

He couldn't leave his wife; Melinda had to leave him.

The reason why she had to be driven to abandon a perfect husband was that her parents had given them as a wedding gift a million-dollar house. Leon wanted a For Sale sign on it, and a check made out to him, which he wasn't going to get if she found out who chimed his bells.

* * *

"THERE'S SOMETHING YOU'RE NOT saying," Melinda's mother accused her. "You spend too much time with your dad and me, instead of with your husband. What's going on?"

"Nothing's going on, Mom."

"Well, there. That's your problem. Marriages need something going on, all the time, that third thing."

"What third thing?"

"Any third thing. A shared passion for a sports team. Competitive checkers."

Melinda snickered.

"You laugh."

"I do laugh. Checkers?"

"It doesn't matter what it is, it only has to be something you both love and want to do together! Camping. Fishing. Politics. Crossword puzzles. Building ships in bottles."

"You and Dad don't have a third thing."

"Of course we do."

"What?"

Her mother smirked.

"Stop! Anyway, there's nothing wrong between Leon and me."

"Have you ever gone to that church with him?"

"God, no."

"Well, do it! He'd probably appreciate it."

"He'd think another woman had taken over my body."

But she decided to surprise him. Make one last-ditch effort to save the damn thing. Their marriage. Slip into a pew beside him. See if it turned him on to convert a heathen like her. She supposed that if it made their sex go back to being what it used to be she might not mind staying married to him, even if she had to get her own head baptized to do it. In fact, if she could combine a man who kept gas in her car with a man who never ran out of gas, she might create the perfect spouse.

"You never know," her mother predicted. "Try it."

* * *

MELINDA DIDN'T GO WITH Leon that Sunday to the First Community Church of God. Instead, she slipped into his pew at the last minute to surprise him, which she certainly did, to judge by his double take of a reaction. It nearly made her laugh out loud. She briefly laid her head on his shoulder, to lay claim, so the people behind and beside them wouldn't think a woman he didn't know had moved in for the kill on a handsome man.

Leon was handsome, no question about that.

In his best suit—his Sunday suit? she could hardly believe it—he looked sharp and put-together.

The minister spoke, from down on floor level, in front.

"Good morning!"

"Good morning!" the congregation chirped back at him.

"Welcome friends, and welcome strangers whom we'd love to get to know! For those of you who are here for the first time, let me tell you that in some churches they begin by standing and greeting the people all around them with a handshake. In other churches, they start with hugging each other." Someone in the congregation groaned, and a few people laughed. "But here at FCCG, we start with what we believe everybody needs most desperately in this life. Will you each please stand if you are able and turn to a person near you, and say, 'I forgive you.'"

"What the hell?" Melinda whispered to Leon.

Nevertheless, she stood, turning quickly toward the elderly woman on her other side.

"I forgive you," the woman said, clasping both of Melinda's hands and gazing sincerely into her eyes.

For some reason, that brought a lump to Melinda's chest. "I forgive you, too," she found herself saying. *Oh, why not?* she thought. The woman had lived a long life; surely there was something she couldn't stop regretting. It wouldn't kill a person to try to make her feel better about it.

Everybody then turned to the person on their other side.

"I forgive you," Leon said, looking annoyed, she was startled to see.

"For coming here?" she asked him.

It hadn't occurred to her that maybe Leon wanted this place to himself, alone.

Maybe he wanted some relief from being always at her beck and call, even when she neither becked nor called. If that were the case, then she'd have to keep coming back. Up to this point, she'd merely wished for him to leave her; she hadn't been pro-active. Maybe that was a mistake. Maybe she needed to push him along toward the door. If Leon simply, selfishly refused to give her reasonable grounds for divorce, she'd have to irritate him to death.

She could do that. She sensed she'd be good at that.

"You have to say it, too," he said, testily.

"You don't do anything for me to forgive!"

She tried not to sound pissed off about it, but his slight smirk made her right hand itch to slap him.

She escaped saying she forgave him because by then it was the turn of the people in front and behind them to pardon her. Melinda felt herself getting into the spirit of the thing. "I forgive you!" And you! What had these people ever done in their lives to look so eager to wipe it clean? Did they speed, not the allowable five, but all of six miles an hour over the legal limit? Horrors. Did they blow their autumn leaves onto their neighbors' yards?

It seemed to help, though.

Melinda felt purged of the guilt of desiring to leave a nice man.

She felt inspired by her plan of action: divorce by irritation.

She'd been gritting her teeth and saying, "Thank you!" every time he did a chore for her—pick up anything she dropped, give up the crossword puzzle in the paper to her, hold doors, get her car washed, put the cap on the toothpaste for her, tell her constantly how "lovely" she looked. Now she'd ignore those dozens of "nice" moments every day and night; she'd take them for granted—sweeping the dropped scarf from his hands, doing the Word Jumble first, too, leaving a toothpaste trail on the bathroom counter, skipping the "thank you" to his compliments. When he told her each morning how pretty she looked, she'd lift her chin, smile arrogantly, and say, "I know."

The minister waved everybody back to their seats.

He strode up the three stairs from the floor to the lectern, nodding to the organist and choir. But when he turned to face his congregation, he was a changed man. His friendly smile turned into a ferocious glare. He looked like a preacher instead of a minister.

He slammed down his Bible.

"Damnation!" he thundered, sweeping his gaze from one side of the church to the other.

A number of people, including Leon, jumped in their pews.

Melinda was so startled by his threats of hellfire and brimstone that it took her through half of his sermon to wonder if that's what kept his congregation coming back, desperate for forgiveness the next Sunday. First, he gave them sweetness and light, and then he lowered the Biblical boom.

"Is he always like this?" she whispered to Leon.

He shook his head, seemingly cowed into silence.

The preacher's Cotton Mather oration on the Ten Commandments cemented Melinda's plan of action—six days a week she would wholeheartedly annoy her husband into breaking as many of the Commandments as a busy man could: coveting another man's wife, sliding into adultery, stealing away to a hotel with a lover who appreciated him. On the seventh day, she could return to the pews for a chorus of forgiveness.

At the close of service, the organ player—a very pretty young woman—boomed out a triumphant hymn. It was Bach, so it already had an ominous undertone, but she played it extra loud, as if she were pounding the tips of her fingers into the ivory keys, like a ballerina landing painfully hard on her toes.

THE CUTE LITTLE CHOIR director was in a rage.

"Who was that woman?" she demanded of her lover, via Skype because she wanted to see Leon's face when she interrogated him. "She sat down by you as if she owns you! She put her head on your shoulder! Leon? Are you married? Is she your wife?"

She saw his face.

She heard his hesitation.

Before he could answer, she screamed, "You lying son of a bitch!"

Staci didn't actually belong to the church. She was their hired music director. She had to play their hymns, but she didn't have to play by their rules. "You fucking, lying, Goddamned son of a fucking bitch! I hate you! Don't you ever contact me again!"

HE WAS ALREADY FURIOUS at Melinda for showing up at church.

Now he wanted to kill her. Literally, bloodily kill her.

Forget Mr. Nice Guy. He was so sick of playing perfect husband that he wanted to throw the goddamned vacuum cleaner through the front window. He wanted to strangle Melinda with its cord, and stick its suction to one ear and suck her fucking brains out with it.

Let's not forget the money, his inner self whispered.

Consider that widowers get it all.

"Or, maybe calm down," Leon advised himself, a little unnerved by his own greedy, violent wishes.

He walked around a few blocks before returning to his car.

His phone beeped with Melinda calling, but he didn't answer.

A man could develop beaucoup self-discipline and restraint if a man spent months pretending to be a perfect gentleman, Leon thought, as his blood pressure dropped back down from lethal. Weeks of biding his time. Months of biting his tongue. Washing dishes the minute they got dirty, sweeping a kitchen floor every night, getting up to cook breakfast for two every morning. A man could become quite a domestic soldier armed with intense patience and determination. Smiling through every annoyance.

Never raising his voice or letting his—okay, evil—intent show.

He could get Staci back, he was convinced of that.

She was in love with him, or why would she have been so upset today?

She was a beautiful young woman of refined and expensive taste. Except, perhaps, when she was pissed off at him.

As he pressed "Return Call," to Melinda, he had to laugh at how Staci had cursed him. So cute, so jealous and furious, so sexy.

He *had* to get Melinda to divorce him.

"Hi, Sweetheart," he said in his smarmiest voice when she answered. He could practically feel how it made her skin crawl, and yet she wouldn't complain, because how could a woman complain about a perfect husband? Before she could even ask where he'd been that he hadn't immediately taken her call, he said, "I took a walk to think about what the minister preached this morning, but I'm coming right home now. I'm sorry if I made you worry."

"I forgive you."

He thought she sounded bored, as if she was in the middle of doing her nails.

"What? Oh. Uh, want me to get you some of those pork ribs you love, and corn on the cob? Or would you like something else for lunch? I could run by the grocery store on my way home. Or I could stop by your favorite restaurant and get take out, or I could—"

"Whatever I like," she said, and hung up on him.

"Well, that was rude," Leon remarked to himself. And very annoying. She was supposed to be irritated by how infuriatingly sweet and attentive he was; she wasn't supposed to take him for fucking granted.

"Is this Leon's wife?"

"Leon who?"

"Leon Christopher."

"Yes."

It was a woman's voice that Melinda heard say, "I'm devastated to have to tell you this, but I've been having an affair with your husband. Leon," she said, as if Melinda might have two of them. "I thought I loved him. I didn't know he was married. He's been a bastard to both of us. I'm so sorry—"

"Bless your heart," Melinda purred. "Do you have photos?"

LEON HAD ONLY JUST unclogged a toilet, and made their bed, and pulled her clothes out of the dryer, and she had only just said, "What took you so long?" to the first one, "I hate how you put the top sheet on wrong side up," to the second one, and "I was nearly out of underwear, Leon," without once saying "Thank you," when a man with a gun walked into the kitchen where they stood glaring at each other.

"You slept with the woman I love!" the man screamed at Leon. "Don't deny it, I've seen the naked pictures!"

Melinda looked shocked. "Oh my God, you're the minister!"

The man, tall and dour even without his black robes, shot Leon, dead-on through the heart.

Then he fell to his knees, weeping. With streaming eyes, he looked up at Melinda. "I've committed a terrible sin."

She smiled. "I forgive you."

GIANT'S DESPAIR

BY DUANE SWIERCZYNSKI

1

MIDDLE OF THE NIGHT is when Lonergan's hands hurt the most. A lot of his bedtime routine entails fidgeting and turning and trying not to roll over on them. As a result, Lonergan only ever falls partially asleep. He stares at the ceiling, aware of every creak and pop and moan in the house.

So when the frantic knocking comes at 3 a.m. he's up immediately.

Lonergan glances over at his wife. Jovie, God love her, is still dead to the world, her lips parted a little as she breathes. That is a good thing. They'd had a rough day with the kids. The baby had only gone down a couple of hours ago after much rocking and soothing and lullaby-singing. And the four-year-old continued her giddy mission of destruction throughout the house. It's like living with a pint-sized terrorist who giggles. That said, the kids are the only things that keep them both going these days.

A second round of knocks echoes throughout the house, even louder this time.

Lonergan sits up in bed, trying to keep the bedsprings from making too much noise. His hands throb so hard he can feel his heartbeat in them. He's only wearing skivvies, so he pulls on pajama bottoms and tries to find his slippers in the dark. No luck. Hailee takes a lot of gleeful pleasure in hiding her Pop-Pop's things. The slippers are probably buried somewhere in the backyard under the snow.

People just don't turn up at their house. The main road through Bear Creek is Route 115, which rolls along the top of the mountain. To find the Lonergans' place you have to take a barely-marked gravel road—a glorified driveway actually—and follow it up into the woods. Delivery guys get lost all the time.

Lonergan has a feeling who this might be. A cold little hunch in the bottom of his stomach, even as he hopes he's wrong.

Lonergan hoists himself off the bed and hurries down the hall and into the living room. In the dead silence, each floorboard creak sounds like a scream. He prays the noise won't wake the baby.

Before he reaches the door, Lonergan considers a run down to the basement. When the kids came to live with them, he made a point of locking up his Smith & Wesson SD9 so his granddaughter would never stumble upon it.

But Lonergan figures by the time he finds the keys, goes downstairs, unlocks the closet, unlocks the safe, unlocks the trigger lock, whoever's out front will have woken the entire house, maybe even broken down the damn door. So he continues on.

PEERING THROUGH THE ONE-WAY wide angle viewer, Lonergan sees that he's guessed right. It's the son-in-law.

Son-in-law is wearing shorts, a polo shirt, tennis shoes with no socks. Does he think he's in the Bahamas instead of upstate Pennsylvania in the middle of February? Granted, it's been a relatively mild winter up here in the mountains. But that doesn't mean you should dress to go yachting.

Lonergan hesitates for a minute, hand on the doorknob, steeling himself for whatever bullshit is about to fly out of the boyfriend's mouth—though he is morbidly curious about what the boyfriend might say after all this time. He flips the lock no problem, but his dumb rubber hands have a hard time grasping the doorknob. By the time he finally manages to open the door with both hands he's already annoyed.

Son-in-law looks down at Lonergan like he's anticipating a fight.

"Mr. Lonergan, I want to see my son."

"Isaiah, it's three o'clock in the morning."

"I really need to see him now."

Lonergan spots a late-model Dodge Charger idling in the driveway, light gray exhaust chugging out of the tailpipe. He didn't even turn his car off? What, does the son-in-law assume Lonergan will hurry back into the house, dart into the spare bedroom, scoop up the baby and then just hand him over? With maybe some gas money and a hot coffee for the road?

Son-in-law takes Lonergan's hesitation as an invitation. He steps forward as if to scoot right past him. Lonergan shifts his body to block him.

"Here's what I need," Lonergan says. "I need you to turn around and drive the fuck home."

"You can't keep me from my son."

"Maybe not, but I can kick you off my property."

"I have to see him."

"Not tonight you don't."

Isaiah takes another step forward. Lonergan places a hand on Isaiah's chest and gives him a firm push back. This should tell him: you've gone far enough.

But the son-in-law holds his ground, sensing that maybe he has the advantage. People have underestimated Lonergan since high school—he's only five seven. And Isaiah is a gangly six four.

"Go home, Isaiah," Lonergan says. "Before I call the police."

Lonergan plans on calling the police anyway. As much as Lonergan would like to pound Isaiah Edwards into raw hamburger on the front porch, he knows Isaiah would just hire some fancy lawyer and they'd be in danger of losing the kids.

No, it would be much better if his daughter's widower turned around, climbed back into his expensive car and drove back to Philadelphia.

There's only one route he can take: I-476, the northeast extension of the turnpike. The state troopers will have plenty of time to pick up Isaiah during his two-hour haul back to the city.

"I don't have any problems with the police," Isaiah mutters, but his eyes say the exact opposite.

"Isaiah, don't bullshit me at three in the morning. You've been on the run for two months. You missed your Daria's funeral."

"I couldn't get back home in time. But I'm here now."

"Don't give a shit."

"Just let me hold him."

"Not tonight."

"I was stuck in China on business!"

"Good night," Lonergan says, then pushes on Isaiah's chest with his fingertips.

For a moment Isaiah allows himself to be pushed. But then he plants a foot behind him, grabs Lonergan's hand, and twists.

Fourth of July fireworks blast up Lonergan's arm and down his spine. He falls to his knees in his own doorway, not even aware that he is screaming. Crushing waves of dizziness wash over him.

But Isaiah doesn't let go of his hand. He twists, and twists, and twists.

2

THE PAIN STARTED A couple of years ago, and like a typical guy Lonergan ignored it for as long as possible. But at the start of last summer, it got to the point that he couldn't hold a hammer properly. Diagnosis: carpal tunnel, which meant the thumb and first two fingers of each hand would go numb, tingle, or ache at random intervals.

The doctor whom Lonergan had been seeing as infrequently as possible for the past 20 years said it was simple: he needed surgery. Lonergan told the doc his insurance wouldn't cover it. The doc looked up his plan and agreed: Lonergan's insurance wouldn't cover it. But Lonergan needed surgery nonetheless. They went round and round like this for a while.

Finally the doc agreed to prescribe pain pills, which helped a little. Before, it felt like razor blades were grinding away at the inside of his knuckles. With the pills, it felt like butter knives. The pills did nothing, however, for the bouts of numbness. You need surgery for that, the doctor reminded him. Lonergan reminded the doc that so-called affordable care, in this case, would bankrupt them.

He tried to work through the pain, but the side effects of those pills included exhaustion, dizziness and nausea. These are not symptoms you want to deal with while building someone a full deck off the back of their house.

So Lonergan's only option was to take time off work and pray that his hands would heal themselves. Or at least get him back to the point where he could hold his tools. Jovie still had her job at the Woodlands, even though her feet ached all the time, and Lonergan was convinced she was going to need surgery, too. They were the perfect couple. Between the two of them, they had exactly one set of functional appendages.

Had Daria told her boyfriend about Lonergan's hands? It's very likely. Lonergan made some of the furniture sitting in their house back in Fishtown. At some point Daria must have told him that her father built those bookcases and that entertainment center with his own two hands, and now he couldn't work because of those hands. If Isaiah knew, that means he came up here with a plan in mind.

LONERGAN DOESN'T PASS OUT completely, but for an indeterminate amount of time his brain stops recording. Sad thing is, this is probably the best sleep he's had in months.

When he finally snaps awake he has no idea why he's sprawled out on his own porch in the freezing cold. Then he remembers the knocking. The boyfriend. The baby . . . oh God the baby.

Lonergan makes a pair of fists, not giving a damn about the razor blades in his knuckles. He presses them against the wooden slats of the porch. He pushes himself up. The ground feels like jelly. He leans against the doorway and takes some deep breaths to clear his head. Then he marches back into his house.

Because now Isaiah Edwards is trespassing.

Lonergan's rage gives him all of the strength he needs. He is already relishing the idea of standing at his kitchen sink and washing Isaiah's blood off his knuckles.

The living room is empty. Inside the hearth, the dying embers of last evening's fire wink at him. Isaiah couldn't have come and gone already; the Charger is still humming outside. That means he's in the baby's room. Lonergan charges toward the hallway like a bulldozer, anticipating the worst.

But he only makes it three steps. Isaiah is in the hallway, face-down, arms and legs spread out as if he was attempting a high dive. The back of his head is wet and contorted.

And Jovie, practically naked, is standing over him with a dented can of baby formula in her right hand.

3 TWO MONTHS AGO

Life as they knew it came to an end in mid-December. Lonergan had been clearing the supper dishes when Jovie's cell went off. She hopped up from the kitchen table to find it.

Lonergan had been looking forward to spending the rest of the night with some bourbon. Jovie had been working on a bottle of red since before dinner. He'd taken pain pills with his meal, so he was good on the hands front. Sure, he shouldn't mix pills and bourbon. But it was Tuesday night and he hasn't had to get up for work for seven months, so what difference did it make?

Lonergan was rinsing turkey gravy from a bowl when he heard this horrible choking gasp. He'll never forget the look in her eyes. It was like someone buried a steak knife in her back all the way to the hilt. Lonergan thought she was going to fall over. The plate slipped out of his hands and shattered in the sink.

He ran over to her with dripping hands and held her up with his forearms, still no idea what was going on. Her cell phone slipped away and hit the ground; later they'd discover that the screen had cracked.

It took Lonergan a while to get it out of her, and when she finally told, all the blood drained out of his head. Nothing looked right, nothing sounded right. He didn't know what world he was living in. Pretty sure at that moment Jovie was holding Lonergan up just as much as he was holding her.

They left for Philadelphia not too long after. There wasn't time to cry; no time to think at all, really. The babies were alone with the police. The sun had already set and the drive would take at least two hours. The cops promised someone would stay with the kids until they arrived.

"I'm driving," Jovie said.

Lonergan said, "I really don't think you should be behind the wheel right now."

"You told me it hurts to drive."

It was true. Usually his carpal tunnel meant that clutching a steering wheel was a bit of an ordeal after an hour, but he didn't care about that right now.

"Please, let me do this for you."

"I'm going to go crazy if I don't have something to focus on."

"You had a few glasses of wine."

"Yeah, and right now I don't feel a thing."

So she drove. He knew it was useless to argue when she'd made up her mind about something.

THEY HAD MADE THE trip from Bear Creek to Philly quite a bit over the past two years—Jovie more than Lonergan. It's a leisurely, two-hour descent from bucolic mountains straight into the bowels of urban hell. With every passing mile, everything beautiful about Pennsylvania slowly turns to shit.

Some people love Philadelphia. Some get a flutter in the heart when they see trash and busted-up houses and homeless people eyeing you from every corner. Could be that some people enjoy the thrill of possibly getting mugged at knifepoint. Or they like living with everyone piled on top of them, next to them, under them. But Lonergan hated the city, and couldn't believe Daria had ever moved down there in the first place.

"Did the cops say if the son-in-law is on his way?" Lonergan asked.

"They said the kids were alone," Jovie said. "How could that bastard leave them all alone for so long?"

"Is he on another business trip?"

"That's no excuse."

"I'm not saying that it is. I'm just trying to figure out what's going on."

Lonergan played out the rest of the conversation in his mind like a little chess game and realized that it would inevitably lead them to the part where he asks Jovie about the last time she talked to their daughter. So he shut up and looked off to the horizon.

Lonergan and Jovie made it to Daria's house a little after nine. A bunch of cops were standing outside. One of them broke from the pack.

"You the parents?"

The cop who approached them was about Lonergan's age. Latino, buzz cut, with the nameplate SEGURA. His face tried to project some kind of empathy, but his eyes said that he'd done this dozens of times before.

Jovie suddenly couldn't find the words—something about the question flipped a switch in her brain. Lonergan stepped in.

"We're her parents."

Segura extended his hand for a shake, but Lonergan couldn't do that, so he gave him a fist bump, hoping he'd get it. Cop probably thought Lonergan was a germaphobe. Whatever. Segura led the way into the house.

The first thing to hit Lonergan was the stench—like someone had been sick recently. The startled look on Jovie's face told him she smelled it, too. The weird thing was, the house was spotless. Other than a few toys scattered around the floor, it looked as normal as their own home.

"Come on upstairs. Officer Walczak is there with the kids."

In the master bedroom, a young female cop with full-sleeve tattoos sat on a mattress and rocked the baby. Across from her was Hailee, who was sitting on the floor and was playing a game on an iPhone.

"Hailee, sweetie, can you introduce me to your grandparents?"

Hailee didn't respond at first.

"Hailee, honey?" Jovie said.

The girl looked up at her Nana, and a microsecond later she started bawling. Jovie scooped her up and hugged her tight, trying to keep it together herself. Hailee whispered something to Jovie, who promptly carried her into the bathroom.

At this point the police didn't know the particulars, only that it had happened sometime last night, and it wasn't until the next afternoon that Hailee finally called 911 and told them that her little brother was crying and her mommy wouldn't wake up.

"She tried to do CPR on her mom," Walczak said. "That's what she told me, anyway."

Walczak carefully handed Lonergan the baby.

"I changed him," she said. "I've got a little one at home, so I know the drill. He was a little . . . messy."

Lonergan mumbled his thanks and took little Brandon, trying to keep his hands still as possible. He'd never been comfortable holding babies, even back when his hands worked properly.

He couldn't help but wonder: how long had his daughter and grandchildren been alone in this house?

Brandon was fussing so Lonergan walked around the house a little. From all outward appearances, the place looked okay. Daria was like her mother. Even when things were at their worst and practically spiraling out of control, she kept a tidy place. Lonergan used to joke that Jovie would crawl out of her deathbed to make sure all of the laundry was done before she expired. That joke didn't seem so funny anymore.

Lonergan made his way down to the kitchen because the little guy was amping up his fussing. Maybe he could find a pacifier down here. He opened cabinet doors at random until he found three plastic milk jugs filled with vomit.

4 NOW

LONERGAN AND JOVIE CAN'T quite bring themselves to make eye contact, so they stare down at the corpse. Blood is still dripping out of Isaiah's head and splattering onto the hardwood floor.

"Huh," Lonergan says.

Jovie is wearing what she usually sleeps in, even on the coldest nights: a pair of silk panties. Dark blood is streaked across her arms and décolletage. The same blood that, until very recently, had been pumping through Isaiah's veins.

"The way you screamed, I thought he killed you," Jovie says.

"He surprised me."

"Are you okay?"

Lonergan has been downplaying how badly his hands hurt and now isn't exactly the time to come clean. "Let's worry about me later."

"Is he dead?" Lonergan asks.

"Do you want me to check him for a pulse?"

He isn't sure if she means that as a joke or what. When the tears come, he understands.

"Oh god, Lonny. What are we going to do? I just killed him. I just killed the father of one of our grandbabies."

Lonergan shakes his head. "No, that was self-defense. He trespassed, he was going to hurt the kids, he could have easily hurt you . . ."

But a troubled expression washes over Jovie's face.

"What?" Lonergan asks. "What is it?"

"It wasn't self-defense."

"Of course it was."

"Listen to me. I heard you get out of bed so I followed you. I waited in the living room. I heard you talking. Then I heard you scream."

"Jovie, stop it."

"But it wasn't just the scream. I knew he'd come here for the baby. And there was no way he was taking him. So I grabbed the heaviest thing I could find and I walked up behind him and killed him. I don't even think he heard me coming. So it's my fault. I'll tell the police what happened, I'll confess . . ."

"You're not going to confess to anything."

Lonergan really wishes he had gone down to the basement for his gun. It would have been easy. Isaiah would have opened his big dumb mouth. Lonergan would have showed him the gun. Isaiah would have been on his way. The cops would have scooped him up on the turnpike. *Easy peasy lemon squeezy*, as Hailee likes to say.

But no, Isaiah had to fuck with Lonergan's hands and force his way into the house and put all of them in this predicament.

"Lonny, even if we convince the police that this was self-defense, they're going to take the babies."

Jovie calls her husband "Lonny," short for Lonergan, because he hates his first name and has forbidden anyone to speak it in his presence.

"They won't do that," Lonergan says.

"Oh yes they will. Think about it from their point of view. Why take a chance on leaving two innocent children with a couple of killers?"

Lonergan is no lawyer, but what Jovie is saying makes a lot of sense. The babies have no other living relatives. If Jovie's right, then the kids would be headed straight into the foster system. That is not going to happen. Lonergan is more certain of that than anything else in his life.

"Get cleaned up," Lonergan says, "I'll take care of this."

Jovie starts to open her mouth, but before she can say anything Lonergan steps over the corpse and puts his arms around her. She pulls away at first, nodding down to the blood on her body. Lonergan doesn't care. He holds her tight against him. They're the exact same height; when Jovie wears heels, she definitely has the size advantage.

"I know what I'm doing," Lonergan whispers, and he knew she knew what he meant. Nothing more needed to be said.

Of course that's the moment they hear a sleepy little voice behind them.

"Nana, why are you naked?"

5 TWO MONTHS AGO

AFTER TAKING CUSTODY OF the kids from the police Lonergan and Jovie found a hotel just outside Philadelphia city limits. Lonergan didn't want to stay in Philly proper—as far as he was concerned the city killed their daughter, and he wanted nothing to do with it. Officer Walczak recommended a Radisson, up Route One in nearby Bensalem.

The room was clean, nothing fancy. Two beds. One for Hailee, the other for Lonergan and Jovie with the baby nestled between them. They ordered chicken tenders and fries for Hailee, who ate as if she'd been stranded on a desert island. Which Lonergan supposed she had, in a way. He couldn't imagine what she'd been through today.

Lonergan rubbed his wife's back. "We're going to be all right," he said, mostly because that's the kind of thing you're supposed to say in a situation like this.

Jovie didn't respond, because she's always been the most honest of the two.

Around 3 a.m. the baby started bawling. Jovie sent Lonergan for the bag they'd thrown together at Daria's house to look for a diaper and wipes. Lonergan's fingers didn't work properly and nothing looked familiar. Was this tiny piece of padded plastic really a diaper? Finally he found what Jovie needed and stood by like an idiot as she cleaned up the baby. After a while they settled back in but Lonergan couldn't sleep. He slipped on his shoes and went outside.

LONERGAN DUG THE PACK out of his jacket, tapped out a cigarette, lit it, inhaled, felt the burn in his chest.

Traffic made its way up and down Route One. Across the highway there was a place where you could buy live crabs and cold beer. A little further up you could buy a dirty movie or a sex toy. This was pretty much the last place Lonergan thought he'd find himself on a Wednesday morning in mid-February.

Did Jovie know Daria was using again? They'd been through all of this bullshit when she was with Hailee's junkie father. Daria had gone to rehab. A really expensive rehab. How did Jovie miss the relapse? There were always signs. Did she sound depressed on the phone? Did she borrow more money?

But you don't grill a woman on the same day she lost her daughter.

And really, those questions didn't matter right now. What mattered now was taking care of Hailee and Brandon. Not just watch them for a weekend; they were going to have to *raise* them. The enormity of it all didn't hit him until this moment.

Lonergan had no idea how they were going to afford this.

The last few years had been rough, even before his hands gave up on him. Cable news talking heads called 2008 an "economic downturn;" Lonergan referred to it as "when America shit the bed." His livelihood depended on other families having the money to install a new kitchen or a backyard deck. After Obama took office, work slowed down. A lot. He found himself traveling further away for jobs—even to the northern burb of Philly, sometimes. Which added three, four hours to his work day. By the time Lonergan's hands decided to go AWOL, their savings were down to fumes.

One thing that wasn't going away was the mortgage. When Lonergan bought his house back in 2001, it was a bare-bones shack. He refinanced a few times and built it up into the kind of home Jovie and Daria deserved. And then the housing bubble burst.

The doors behind Lonergan swished open. In his peripheral vision he could see a polo shirt and khakis. Lonergan took another drag.

"Sir, I'm sorry, but you can't smoke that here."

Lonergan turned and stared at him. "I'm outside."

"You can't be within 50 yards of the hotel."

"There's nobody else out here except you. And you're welcome to go back in."

"Please, sir. It's hotel policy. You're going to have to put that out."

Lonergan considered putting it out in his eye. Instead he looked around to see what was fifty yards away. A public park across the street seemed like the best option. He did the frogger thing across the road. Six steps inside, though, he realized the park was actually a cemetery.

He dropped his cigarette to the ground, mashed it with a twist of boot, then crossed the street again and went back upstairs to the room.

Jovie was already awake, showered and dressed. He doubted she slept much, either.

"We have to be at the morgue by 10," she said, as if it were just another errand, like picking up eggs and milk on the way home.

Lonergan nodded, then stretched his fingers as much as he could, which wasn't much at all. He felt a buzzing sensation on the left side of his chest, as if there were a cell phone under his skin.

But he didn't have time to ponder that much because Hailee was already running toward him yelling "Poppa Poppa!" Lonergan had no choice but to pick her up and sit her on his lap, even though his hands were screaming.

Hailee was the love and the nemesis of Lonergan's life. He adored her. But she was also one of the few people on this planet able to catch him off guard. Like she did as she burrowed into his chest like a buzz saw.

"Easy there, honey."

"Nana said we're going to *your* house today."

"Yeah, that's right, sweetie."

"I really like your house."

"I know you do. You like to destroy it!"

But this wouldn't be the usual weekend visit with the grandkids, full of pizza and movies and ice cream and every other treat they could give them. This was forever.

6 NOW

LONERGAN AND JOVIE TENSE up against each other. Both of their minds go to the same place: Can Hailee see the body on the hallway floor? And if so—how the hell are they going to explain it to her?

"Shit," Lonergan whispers.

"Don't worry. I've got her."

Jovie breaks the embrace and runs down the hall toward Hailee, who smiles. Grandma's playing a game! Jovie scoops up granddaughter and carries her the rest of the way down the hall. "What are you doing out of bed you little boldie!" she whisper-yells. Hailee giggles like a loon. "Let's get you tucked back in."

Lonergan turns around and looks down at his son-in-law's body, his mouth twisted up in disgust.

"Better get you tucked away, too."

Lonergan is already thinking about the removal and replacement of the floorboards, since some blood had already soaked down into the wood and cops have those CSI flashlights that can illuminate the tiniest specks of bodily fluids.

But he pushes all that worry aside for the moment and focuses on the task at hand. Dawn will be coming in a few hours, both kids will be awake, and Isaiah's body needs to be out of the house as quickly as possible. Lonergan can worry about the blood splatter and the million other details later.

Then he remembers the Dodge Charger, which is still idling out front.

Lonergan pulls on his jacket, slips on a pair of sneakers, then heads out into the bitter cold.

AT THE DRIVER'S SIDE door, Lonergan reaches in and fumbles around for the keys. There are no keys. The interior of the car reeks of godawful body spray. Lonergan wants to gag, and he isn't even dealing with the corpse yet.

His dumb rubber fingers finally find it: the fat push-button that turns off the ignition. Lonergan pushes it with a knuckle. The mighty engine falls silent.

Fancy as the car is, the interior looks like a stoner's bedroom. Fast food litter, candy wrappers, vape pen stuff, an oversized tablet phone hooked to the dash by umbilical cord.

The backseat is packed tight with stuff from Bullseye. Diapers, baby toys, a bouncy seat, as if Isaiah came straight from a baby shower.

This bothers Lonergan. If Isaiah drove up here with the intention of taking the baby home with him, why isn't all of this stuff back home in Philly?

Lonergan fumbles around a little more until he finds the button that opens the trunk. Sure enough, inside the trunk is a big duffel bag and a smaller carry-on type deal. Goddamnit. Isaiah was planning on taking the baby somewhere else. Another state. Hell, maybe even another country.

Lonergan slams the trunk lid and notices the Charger has a Texas license plate. Is that where Isaiah had been hiding out for the past two months?

Never mind that now. The bigger question is, where's he going to stuff the body? Traditionally, the trunk is the storage space of choice. Lonergan realizes he's going to have to shuffle things around. Haul the baby gear into the house, then put the luggage in the backseat, then put Isaiah in the trunk.

Simple enough, but not for a man with two bad hands.

Lonergan used to be one of those guys who would meet his wife at her car after a shopping trip and stubbornly insist on carrying the entire grocery order at once. He'd loop the handles of the plastic shopping bags around his hands until he was balancing $250 worth of food on each arm. Jovie would try to take one, and he'd tell her no way—I've got this.

And that's what Lonergan thinks now—*I've got this.* He tucks the bouncy seat under his arm and somehow gets a grip on the handles of a plastic bag stuffed to the breaking point with disposable diapers. But halfway back to the house, the bag drops down to the snow and bounces once before rolling down the slight grade of his front lawn. He didn't even feel it slip out of his hand.

"Shit."

Lonergan releases the bouncy seat out from under his arm and guides it down his body with his arm until it rests in the snow. Then he retrieves the bag with the diaper, using his arms like the tines of a forklift truck, before squatting down to pick up the bouncy seat the same way. He may look like an idiot, but it gets the job done.

The next trip out Lonergan uses the same technique; his hands can't be trusted anymore. By the fourth trip, all of the baby gear is out of the backseat and piled up in the living room.

Back out at the car again, Lonergan pops the trunk and tries to do the same thing with the giant duffel bag—picking it up with his arms. But it is heavier than it looks, and doesn't quite have the feel of clothing.

After much fumbling with his useless fingers, Lonergan finally unzips the duffel with his teeth. What he sees confuses him until he stands up straight and takes a step back.

Inside the duffel are two small wrapped presents, along with more cash than he's ever seen gathered in one place.

7 TWO MONTHS AGO

No parent should have to identify the body of their child.

Lonergan didn't know how morgues worked. Would they go in together? And if so, who would watch the kids? What if there was no one available? There was no way he was letting Jovie go in there by herself.

As it turned out there were a couple of staff members who took care of the kids. As the white-coated morgue attendant greeted them, Lonergan thought about the doctor who delivered Daria, some 24 years ago. Might as well been 24 hours ago. The same disinfectant odor hung in the room. The same bleached sheets, now pulled back. *Here's your baby girl . . .*

Lonergan had his arm around Jovie, who was trembling mightily. It took only a second to identify her, but that second went on forever.

The body on the metal tray looked like Daria. But it wasn't her. No more than a clump of hair in the shower was Daria, or a fingernail clipping in the sink. This is the thing she chose to leave behind. She was somewhere else now. That's what Lonergan had to believe, otherwise he was going to lose his mind.

They asked them to stick around. Which made no sense until we were shaking hands with a narcotics detective.

"Valeria Flores," she said. "You can call me Val."

Detective Flores wore a white button-down shirt tucked into dark jeans, badge clipped onto her waistband. She was tall and slender and had an exotic skin tone. Lonergan couldn't tell if she was Latino or Middle Eastern. She also had a massive pair of breasts. Lonergan's eyes were drawn to them and the gold and diamond cross hanging between her cleavage. It was sort of a public announcement that, *I Believe in Jesus Christ*, and oh by the way, *Look What His Father Gave Me.*

"I apologize for making you hang around," Detective Flores said. "And I'm so sorry for your loss."

Lonergan was about to mumble thanks when Jovie interrupted. "What do you want, Detective? Our babies are waiting for us."

"I knew your daughter, Ms. Lonergan. She was a really good mom."

"What do you want?"

Flores nodded; pleasant talk was over. "I'm looking for Isaiah Edwards. He hasn't been in town for a few weeks, and I don't think he knows what happened."

"Well, he should have been here," Jovie said.

"Yes, he should have. Do you know what Isaiah does for a living?"

"Shipping. Something to do with international shipping."

Flores bit back a smile. "Oh yeah, it's definitely international. But shipping something very specific. Do you know what?"

Lonergan was getting annoyed with the cutesy guessing game. "How about you just tell us, Detective?"

"I've been after him for six months. A few weeks ago he dropped off my radar, leaving behind his wife and infant son. Reason I'm telling you folks is, I'm thinking at some point he's going to want to see the baby. Maybe he'll show up to the funeral, maybe not. But at some point he's going to reach out to you, and if he does . . . well, I want to be completely straight with you. Isaiah Edwards is *not* one of the good guys."

"He kind of strikes me as an idiot," Lonergan says.

"He shows up," Flores continued, "I want you to call me right away."

"Can we go now?" Jovie asked.

This seemed to frustrate Flores. "Do you know how your daughter died, Mrs. Lonergan? I mean, specifically?"

"Come on, that's enough, Detective," he says.

"Daria overdosed on fentanyl," Flores says. "Fentanyl is a fake version of heroin, only 50 times more powerful. They're importing it from China, bringing it up through Mexico. It's all over. Do you know what fentanyl does to the human body?"

"Yeah, detective," Lonergan says, "we know."

8 NOW

LONERGAN HOOKS THE HANDLES of the duffle bag over his arms, lugs it inside, drops it on the floor.

Jovie, cleaned up and wearing a robe, is already going through the plastic bags and sorting out the baby items. "What's that?" she asks, nodding at the duffel on the floor.

"Presents for the kids," Lonergan says.

"I don't understand."

"I don't either. How's the little demon?"

"Back to sleep, I think. But just to be sure, I locked the door."

"Good thinking. You don't think she saw anything, do you?"

"I think she was too focused on Nana being naked."

"Right."

They stand there for a moment, staring at each other, because both knew what had to come next.

"Honey, do you have an extra shower curtain and liner? Something you'd use in the guest bathroom?"

"Yeah, I guess you can use that."

"Okay."

"Use the Christmas one in the closet. I can always buy another one."

"The one with the candy canes?"

"No, I use that in our bathroom. I'm thinking of the one with the polar bears."

"Right."

By the time Lonergan returns from fetching the curtain and liner, Jovie has already opened the duffel bag. She is crouched down on her knees in front of it, fingering through the stacks.

"What is this, Lonny?"

"Son-in-law had that in the trunk. I think he was planning on taking the baby and going away for a long time. Possibly forever."

"Is this drug money?"

"Pretty sure he didn't make it giving lap dances."

Jovie shook her head. "No, what I mean is, do you think this money can be traced?"

Lonergan hasn't thought about that. Then again, he is purposefully not considering anything that isn't under the category of corpse disposal.

"Worry about that later. Just stash the money someplace safe while I go take care of the body."

"The body."

Lonergan sees the worry and grief on Jovie's face. He drops the curtain and liner and goes to kneel beside her. He takes her in his arms and pulls her close. The smell of her freshly-washed hair is intoxicating. He wishes they were lying in bed together, instead of out here, doing what they were doing.

"Don't think about it. Pretend he never came here tonight. Pretend this never happened. We can think of a million justifications later, I guarantee you, because this man has done harm to our family and probably hundreds of others. The only thing you have to worry about is hiding that money and hugging those kids when they wake up in a few hours. Because they're all that matter."

Jovie pulls away so she can see his eyes. "Where are you going to put him?"

"Where he belongs."

"Lonny, I'm serious."

"That's something you'll never have to know."

9

THE MOMENT LONERGAN SAW the body he knew *exactly* where he'd be dumping it: an impossibly deep crack high up in the mountains.

Nobody knew about it except a few locals. And even those locals stayed away, because nobody knew how deep it really went.

Lonergan knows about the Crack because of his father. He was a brutal drunk, but once in a while he could be counted on to drop a serious piece of life wisdom.

The Crack is not far from Giant's Despair, the location of an annual motor race that twists 650 feet up along the side of the mountain. Dad was a huge fan of the Giant's Despair Hillclimb, and he'd take Lonergan every year. After getting blasted on beer, he'd wander off to take a piss. Lonergan would always follow him, being a kid and not knowing what else to do. One year, when he was four or five, he wandered over near the Crack. His father yelled and raced over and grabbed him at the last minute, his dick still hanging out of his jeans.

"You can't go near there," he told Lonergan, solemnly (and more than a little drunkenly). "You fall down that crack, there'd be no more you."

It was in that moment, gawking at his father's cock, that Lonergan first understood the concept of death.

No more you.

So of course Lonergan spent a good part of his childhood and adolescence checking out the Crack and running little experiments. He'd throw shit down there and listen for the sound of the object hitting bottom. They never did. For all he knew, those objects were still falling.

Isaiah fits in the trunk okay, after a little folding and shoving and pushing.

But the polar bears on the shower curtain stare up at Lonergan. He feels genuinely bad for them—Hailee thinks they're cute. They are getting a raw deal, having to hang out with a rotting corpse for the rest of eternity. They look up at Lonergan like, what did we ever do to you, asshole?

Jovie approaches from behind as Lonergan slams down the lid. She almost startles him.

"Let me follow you over there," she says.

"You don't even know where I'm going. And that's the whole point."

"How are you going to get back?"

"It's not like I'm driving to Ohio."

The look on Jovie's face tells Lonergan she's going to continue to give him a hard time about this, right up until the minute he's pulling down the driveway.

"Look, you following me doesn't make sense for a lot of reasons. For one, you should be home with the kids."

"We can bring them."

"To watch me dump Brandon's father's body somewhere? Not a good idea. Besides, I really don't want you knowing where I'm going."

"Why?"

"Plausible deniability. And what if someone happens to see us? I'm going to have to disguise myself as it is."

Inside the front closet, Lonergan digs out a ratty old Jack Daniel's cap that came free with a fifth a couple of years ago. Lonergan doesn't like wearing baseball caps. He thinks his bulldog head looks weird in them.

Lonergan squeezes the cap over his head and checks himself out in the closet mirror. Yeah. He looks pretty stupid. Jovie appears in the mirror.

"Why don't you call me and I'll come pick you up?"

"I'm not bringing my cell. Pretty sure the cell towers can track where you're going at all times."

"I don't even know how far you'll be walking."

"My legs work just fine. I won't be gone too long."

"If you're going for a disguise, you're going to need sunglasses."

"I lost my only pair, remember? Last year at the shore?"

"You can borrow mine."

Before Lonergan can get the words *but they're lady sunglasses* out of his mouth Jovie is already across the room and fishing them out of her purse. She puts them on his face. Oversized lenses with faux-gold trim and all.

"How do you even wear these," Lonergan says, looking in the mirror.

"They're stylish."

"I look like a bug."

"As long as you don't look like yourself. Which is all that matters, right?"

Jovie has a point. So with that, Lonergan kisses his wife on the lips and sets out to take care of the final arrangements of Isaiah Edwards.

TO GET TO THE Crack, Lonergan has to drive down the side of one mountain and go up another. Between those two mountains is the city of Wilkes-Barre, where he grew up. It was a city build on coal mining, and it was people like Isaiah who ruined it. Drug dealers, hopping the Martz bus up from Philly, to ply their wares among the hicks.

Lonergan saw the city starting to change back in high school. The town square used to be a place to hang out, watch a movie, go shopping, gorge on Chinese food. Now it was a place to get knifed by people looking for their next fix. Heroin hit this place hard about 10 years ago. Which is why he bought a shack up in the mountains—to get away from this mess. The city was no place for Daria to grow up.

But the heroin found her anyway.

Much as Lonergan would like to take Isaiah's corpse on a little tour of Wilkes-Barre, he doesn't want to be spotted in the Charger. Too many people in town know his face, despite the Jack Daniel's cap and ladies' sunglasses.

So he sticks to I-81, which takes you alongside Wilkes-Barre without actually dipping down into it. Then it's up 309, straight for Giant's Despair.

As cars pass, Lonergan keeps his head low. Sunday morning nosy-bodies would probably notice the fancy car and the Texas plates, but hopefully not him.

Soon, Lonergan is approaching the turn-off to the dirt road that will take him up to the Crack. The Charger's engine screams as it climbs the hill. Lonergan swears he can hear Isaiah's body bounce around, too, as he chugs up the 20 degree incline. But Lonergan is steady and patient. He knows the Charger will clear it, even if it feels like it might flip over backwards and go tumbling down the side of the mountain at any moment.

10

THE POLAR BEARS WON'T even look Lonergan in the eye now; they are resigned to their fate.

Lonergan checks the trunk one last time just to make sure he isn't leaving anything important behind. He doesn't want to send Isaiah into the long hereafter only to later think, shit, *so-and-so* would have really been useful.

On his final sweep through the car Lonergan considers the fancy oversized tablet phone. Shit. He'd remembered to leave his own phone at home, only to forget this one. He presses the home button, but it's password-and-thumb-print protected.

Then Lonergan remembers he has access to Isaiah's thumb. Both of them, in fact.

And for a moment he considers opening up the phone and seeing what Isaiah's been up to. Maybe he has hotel reservations somewhere, or emails from friends who have been hiding his drug-peddling ass for the past two months.

But then Lonergan thinks better of it. This goes against the spirit of their original plan. Namely: pretend Isaiah never came knocking. So better not to open this phone or read anything on it. Because it won't exist after it goes down into the Crack.

Lonergan tosses the phone onto the dirt and then looks around until he finds a decent-sized rock. He crouches down and tries to pick it up, but his fingers refuse to work. *You want us to actually grip something, after what you've put us through tonight?*

He considers stomping the phone with his sneakers. But he could imagine cops someday bagging his shoes and extracting microscopic pieces of glass that could be linked with Isaiah's phone.

So it has to be the rock.

Lonergan crouches down and presses his palms against the sides of the rock. He lifts it, squeezes tight, then gives it a test pound on the dirt. The movement shoots new daggers of pain up his arms. But as long as he can keep the rock between his palms, he can smash Isaiah's phone and the networking components inside of it.

It takes a half-dozen slams until the tablet phone is reduced to electronic junk and shards of glass and twisted metal. Lonergan's arms hurt like hell. But whatever. He'll be able to rest them all day. Whiskey will certain help.

Lonergan scoops up the parts with the sides of his hands and heaves them into the backseat of the Charger, then closes the door with his knee. Isaiah is headed to the afterlife like an Egyptian pharaoh, taking everything he brought up to Bear Creek. Well, minus the diapers and baby stuff.

NOW COMES THE DELICATE part: guiding the Charger to the edge of the Crack and sending it down.

An important part of the process is Lonergan *not* being inside the Charger when it tips over into the Crack. Lonergan sits behind the wheel, fires up the engine, which hesitates a little, as if it knows what's coming.

Lonergan throws it in neutral and engages the emergency brake, both of which hurt his hands more than he anticipated. He climbs out of the car, then reaches in and releases the brake. The Charger reluctantly rolls forward an inch . . . and then stops.

"Shit."

Lonergan eyeballs the terrain in the dim dawn light and realizes there's a bit of an incline leading up to the edge of the Crack, which is something he didn't remember.

Crouching down beside the driver's seat, he places his left hand on the accelerator while hooking his fingers around the bottom of the steering wheel.

Lonergan pushes lightly on the pedal. The Charger jolts forward another inch. He gives it a slightly heavier push, and the Charger jumps a half foot, dragging Lonergan across the dirt a little. Lonergan removes his hand and then takes a deep breath. He stares at the Charger as if it's trying to trick him into hanging on to the steering wheel the moment it tips over the edge. *Ha ha, I'm taking you with me.*

Not in this lifetime.

On the edge of the Crack, a lot of foliage had sprung up since the last time Lonergan had been here. He taps the pedal some more, and the shrubs begin to part in front of the Charger's front fender. The opening of the Crack was close. One more goose to the gas pedal ought to do it . . .

But then Lonergan stops. He looks in the direction of the trunk.

Should he say a few words?

No. Scumbag doesn't deserve them.

Lonergan punches the gas pedal and hops away from the Charger, which roars up over the edge and tips over into the abyss.

And then stops.

The car is nearly vertical, engine still humming, and something is keeping it wedged at the opening of the Crack.

The Charger looks like Winnie the Pooh, ass hanging out of a rabbit hole.

Lonergan doesn't understand it. He's done this before—sent a car up and over the edge and down into the deep dark. That time, twenty odd years ago, things had gone off without a hitch, even though Lonergan was pretty drunk at the time. And he's pretty sure that car was bigger than Isaiah's fancy Charger, too. It was a 1990 Chevy Corsica, and they made cars a little boxier back then.

So what happened in the meantime? Has the Crack narrowed, somehow? A seismic shift over 20 years that made it a poor choice for dumping cars with bodies in the trunk?

Lonergan isn't a geologist any more than he is a detective, but none of that matters now. Somehow, he has to shove the Charger the rest of the way into the Crack. Otherwise, somebody will find the car in a matter of days, they'll find Isaiah's body, they'd do some fancy CSI shit, and then he and Jovie would be writing to each other from their respective prisons.

He walks over to the Charger and gives it good stomp on the rear bumper. Nothing. Stomps again, with the same result.

This is so not good.

Lonergan is tempted to give the Charger a full-on body tackle, or climb on top of the damned trunk and start jumping up and down. But Lonergan is pretty sure that would be too great a temptation for God, and Lonergan would end up like a Looney Tunes cartoon. You'd see his Jack Daniel's cap and lady sunglasses suspended in the air while the rest of him followed the Charger down into the Crack. Only then would they gradually fall, and some rabbit would nibble on a carrot and make a wisecrack.

No more you.

Lonergan has to think of something.

He climbs down onto his belly and pushes through the foliage at the edge, trying to figure out what is hanging things up. Soon, all became clear: it's the goddamned tires. Oversized bastards Isaiah probably had put on custom-style.

"Well shit. You're all about the fancy stuff, aren't you, Izzy."

If Lonergan is going to get this car down into the Crack, he's going to have to deflate both of them.

Back at home, Lonergan has any number of implements that would pop each of these fat tires like bubble wrap. But up here on top of Giant's Despair, Lonergan has nothing but his near-useless hands.

Lonergan knows he has to press down on the spring-loaded poppet inside each tire's Schrader valve. Every 10-year-old with a bike knows how it works. But a 10-year-old has a lot more hand strength than Lonergan does at the moment.

So he begins searching the ground for a nail, a metal pin, something, anything. For a good long time, it is a fruitless search. Lonergan feels like he's on his knees for months. The sun climbs higher in the sky, as if God's focusing a spotlight on him.

"You're a fucking asshole, you know that, Izzy?"

If Isaiah has a response, he doesn't share it with Lonergan.

Lonergan brushes aside wet leaves and finds the metal chassis of a toy car. There is a lot of rust on the damned thing. Some kid probably left it here a couple of decades ago. For all he knows, Lonergan may have been that kid.

Lonergan crawls up next to the Charger, unscrews the plastic cap, then presses the toy car chassis onto the poppet. Air hisses out of the tire like a long, silent fart. Lonergan thinks he's going to be here for a while. But after a few seconds, and completely without warning, the Charger slips into the Crack.

Lonergan's survival instincts kick in and he rolls away quick.

The problem with survival instincts is that they're short-sighted; they don't exactly take in the Big Picture. Lonergan lunges out with both hands and claws his fingers into the dirt. His legs swing out and he feels the sensation of absolutely nothing beneath them. As the dirt starts to fall away from beneath his hands, Lonergan hears his father's voice: *no more you.*

11

LONERGAN IS TOO PANICKED to be aware that the Charger dropped all the way down into the Crack. His eyes don't know how to process what they're seeing, and there's a roar in his ears that blanks out all rational thought.

His hands continue to claw and claw and claw . . .

. . . and then his dumb fingers brush against something that feels like a jagged edge of granite. Oh please. He (thinks) he curls his fingers into tight claws and squeezes the edge the rock as tight as he can. His body weight wants to tug them right off, but he hangs on.

Lonergan thanks whatever preternatural forces conspired to give him a lifeline with this fucking rock. He vows to never let go. He promises to go to bed early, say his prayers, spend the rest of his life comforting the sick and dying.

Spiritual intensions are one thing; physical capability is another. Lonergan maintains his grip on the miracle root for approximately six seconds before his eight trembling fingers slip off the edge of the rock anyway.

He falls.

Sheer instinct causes Lonergan to throw out his arms and legs like a skydiver. As he falls the toes of his boots scrape against the interior wall of the Crack while his useless fingers spread open to catch hold of something, anything, *please don't let this be it.* Something reaches up out of the darkness, twists Lonergan's ankle, then punches him in the face.

THE BLOOD RUSHES TO his head. It takes a long moment to figure out what's happened to him.

He's upside-down, with his boot caught on something. Lonergan has no idea what, but for the moment it doesn't matter. For all he cares God could have reached down into the Crack and caught Lonergan's heel with two fingers, Achilles-style.

He reaches up—or down, he doesn't really know—to touch his face, which is throbbing. His nose and mouth slammed hard against the jagged rock wall. Blood leaks out of his split lip and pulses out of his nostrils. Only Lonergan could manage to have a nosebleed while hanging upside-down.

Lonergan allows himself a small moan of disgust, then spits out some blood. Time to assess the situation.

Under his head there is a yawning void, a darkness that is the most utter black Lonergan has ever seen. The Charger is down there somewhere. Maybe—he was too busy scrambling to survive to listen for the crash. Though did he hear the sound of metal scraping? Or was that the screaming inside his own brain?

Below his boots—or above him, technically—is the opening to the Crack, which appears to be two stories away.

How in the hell is he going to get up there?

Lonergan can't even fake a sense of righteous indignation. If there is such a thing as karma, it is laughing its ass off right now.

IF IT WERE ANY other day, Lonergan would twist around until he pulled his foot loose and let the darkness take him. This is what he deserves.

But this isn't any other day.

Right now, Jovie and the kids are waiting for him to return. What would happen if he never came home? It's not as if Jovie knows where he is. That's the whole point. If he dies down here she'll never know what happened. Maybe she'll think that Isaiah wasn't dead after all, only faking it, and at some point he overpowered Lonergan and dumped *his* body somewhere. And he is just waiting for the right moment to come back and take the baby—and maybe take his revenge on Jovie. How will she be able to live that way?

No, Lonergan refuses to die down in this Crack. He's fine with dying above ground, just as long as Jovie knows about it.

Lonergan snorts up blood, spits it out. The spray is messy. More blood ends up on him than on the wall. Wonderful.

Taking a deep breath, he tries to do a sit-up so he can assess the deal with his foot. The first sit-up reveals nothing, because it's barely a sit-up. God, he's been lazy. Lonergan has worked construction since he was 16, and the physical labor kept him reasonably fit . . . until nine months ago, when he stopped working because of his hands. Puttering around the house, he drank more beer than he should. Ate too many sandwiches, ordered too many pizzas, and did very little to work it off. Karma again. What a bitch.

Lonergan grunts and does another sit-up, his upper-body almost making it to the perpendicular point. He squints but can't see much of his foot. Is it caught on another root? Entirely possible.

It takes as much effort to slowly bring his body back to the starting position. Lonergan doesn't want to just let go and smack the back of his head off the rock wall.

Nausea washes over him. Maybe it's a delayed reaction to everything—the murder, the fall, the face-slam. Or maybe it's because he's done two sit-ups.

Lonergan holds his breath and waits for the feeling to pass. Puking would not be ideal at this very moment.

While he rests, Lonergan considers what he might be able to do *if* he can free his foot. Wouldn't that be a scream, being trapped like this until he passes out and dies. Someday spelunkers would find an upside-down skeleton hanging from the side of the rock wall.

He tells himself to stop it. Solve the problem—don't get morbid.

Lonergan realizes it's not so much the height that's the issue, but the width. He's not sure how wide the Crack is. Wide enough to accommodate a falling Challenger. But was it wider than he was tall?

Because if he can get himself into the right position, he could plant two feet on one side of the Crack, then press his hands against the opposite side. Even if his fingers gave out completely, it wouldn't matter because Lonergan would be using his hands as one end of a wedge.

Inch by inch, he could move his hands and feet and gradually make his way up to the surface.

Possibly.

There is no other option.

Time for one last sit-up.

12

LONERGAN GRUNTS AS HE bends his body in half and grabs hold of his ankle. He laces his fingers together behind his leg, which hurts like hell, but he can complain about it later. Now that he's upright again, Lonergan can see that his foot has indeed been snared by an exposed root. Thank you, Mother Nature.

The next part is going to be the real bitch. He's going to have to force himself to hang on long enough to get himself into position. Which shouldn't take more than a few seconds, but his fingers have been notoriously unreliable today.

Stop the excuses. Jovie and the kids are waiting for you.

Lonergan sees no point in delaying the inevitable. He grunts again and tries to lock his body into this crunched position, then grabs the exposed root and pulls his leg. He's still stuck. Lonergan tries again and realizes, with more than a little horror, that his leg has gone numb. He pumps it a little, trying to get the blood moving again. His plan won't work with a bum leg.

Mid-pump, however, his foot slips free of the root. He screams and tightens his grip as his legs fall out from under him like deadweights. He writhes against the rock wall, knocking it with his knees and trying to get a foothold, any kind of leverage. His hands are numb to the point that Lonergan doesn't even know that he even *has* hands anymore. Are they still holding onto the root? They must be, because he's not falling. Not yet anyway.

Lonergan grunts as pulls himself up then throws his legs out behind him like pistons.

The tips of his shoes scrape rock. The other side of the wall is reachable! But they instantly slip off and all of Lonergan's weight is pulled downward, straining his arms and non-existent hands.

The exhaustion that washes over him is powerful and profound. He would like nothing more than to let go right now, because it's too much, and he's reasonably confident he'll pass out long before his body hits the bottom of the Crack.

But Jovie and the kids are waiting for you.

Screaming now, Lonergan throws out his legs with everything he's got while simultaneously pushing away from the rock. The sound echoes throughout the crevice.

And he doesn't fall.

For the moment.

HE'S MANAGED TO WEDGE his body across the span of the Crack like he'd planned, but his arms and legs are already trembling. And the top is so very far away.

There's also a new problem:

Lonergan has to throw up.

No, for real now. It's coming. There will be no stopping it. Of all childhood maladies, puking is the universally agreed-upon worst. You have zero control over what your body is doing. It's like an alien presence has taken over your brain and decided: *Hey, you know all of this stuff in your stomach? Let's get rid of it! Right now!*

And while you're forcibly ejecting the contents of your stomach, a stubborn animal part of your brain makes you curl up.

Lonergan has never heard of a man being able to remain standing perfectly straight while blowing chunks. It just isn't possible. So if Lonergan pukes, he's going to curl up, and if he curls up, he's going to fall, and from there it'll just be a question of which reaches the bottom first: his body or the contents of his stomach.

Lonergan takes slow, deep breaths, even though they hurt his chest and draw power away from his quivering limbs.

Don't throw up, he tells himself. I'm the brain, which means I'm in charge of the body. So I'm telling you body, don't throw up.

It occurs to him that confessing and going to jail for murder might have been a more pleasurable experience than the one he's enduring right now.

Stop that. The tough part is behind you. Now start climbing. At the very least, it'll take your mind off the nausea.

Lonergan presses his arms forward with strength he's pretty sure he doesn't have and shifts his left foot up a few inches. Then his right. He's tilted forward now, which makes the nausea even worse. He worries his guts will come sliding up his throat and out of his mouth. He pushes out again then moves his left hand up a few inches. And then his right, even though both feel like cold slabs of lunchmeat.

There. Progress.

And still so very far to go.

Don't think about that. Don't think about throwing up. Don't think about your rapidly dwindling reserves of strength.

Just think left, right. Left, right. Left, right. Left right.

All the way up to the top . . .

LONERGAN THROWS AN ARM over the edge of the Crack, hooking the edge with the crook of his arm. The arm trembles. After a long moment his other arm appears.

He is exhausted. His spent legs dangle over the abyss. He twists his body like a worm until his right knee clears the edge, too. He feels like he's on his 99th push-up, and he has to reach one hundred, but all of his muscles are failing at once. Wouldn't God or karma or whoever laugh if he slipped now. He holds his breath and grits his teeth and pushes so hard that he doesn't even remember pulling himself up and over. He remembers vomiting. After that, it's all a white blur.

He's out for a while.

It's not too long, though, because when his eyes pop open it's still morning, and the puke on his shirt is still fresh. Lonergan's entire body burns in an alarming way, like he's already frying in Hell.

And he still has the walk home to look forward to.

Lonergan rolls over and his exhaustion is so complete he's tempted to just stay in that semi-fetal position, for a good long while. Maybe even a few days. But that would be stupid. It was already foolish passing out right next to the scene of the body-and-car dump—though it's not like he had much choice.

Come on. Up and at 'em. Jovie and the kids are waiting.

Anyone watching from nearby would see a broken man rising like a zombie that had just crawled out of that crack in the Earth. Fortunately, nobody is watching. Hopefully nobody is watching.

At any rate it's all downhill from here, both figuratively and literally. Once he's home and has had the chance to recuperate, they can systematically erase all signs of Isaiah Edwards ever visiting their home. Nobody will ever find him, or his car. Lonergan is certain of this because there is another body and another car down there, and no one's disturbed *that* in 20 years. Jovie's first husband was a real prick.

Lonergan makes his way down the mountainside and thinks about the money in that bag. They're going to have to be smart about that, too. Figure out how to hide and invest the lion's share of it for the kids' education someday. See them through college. Give them the shot that Daria threw away.

Maybe this was simply the torture he had to endure to earn this boon for the kids. If that was the case, Lonergan would happily do it all over again.

Though not this very second.

WHISTLING IN THE DARK

BY RICHARD CHIZMAR

"WHAT'S UP WITH YOU?"

Frank Logan, bald head, double-chin, wrinkled suit, looked over at me from the passenger seat of our unmarked sedan. "What do you mean?"

"You were just whistling. You're almost acting like you're . . . happy."

"I wasn't whistling."

"You were whistling, Frank."

"You don't think I would know if I was whistling?"

"That's precisely my point. You've been acting strange all week."

"And you're acting precisely like an asshole."

"You're a child."

"Maybe." He stared out the car window. "But I wasn't whistling."

A FEW MORE MILES of dark highway and I spotted a cluster of patrol cars parked on the grassy shoulder up ahead, both State and County boys, their lights flashing, casting kaleidoscope shadows on the trees and cracked asphalt.

I parked at the end of the line and we walked thirty or so yards to the scene, nodding at the usual cast of uniforms standing around and pretending to be busy.

Trooper Michael Hughes saw us coming and stepped away from the fresh-faced officer he had been lecturing.

"Ben. Frank. Glad they called you guys."

Frank grunted. "Another thirty minutes and we'd have been home in bed." Now that was the Frank Logan I was used to all these years.

"What do you got?" I asked.

Hughes flipped open his notepad, gestured for us to follow, and started walking. "Adolescent female. Caucasian. No ID. Multiple stab wounds in torso and shoulder. Looks like she's been there awhile."

"Who found the body?"

"Two mowers working a road crew. They're both still here waiting to talk to you."

"M.E.?" Frank asked.

"Got here ten minutes before you did."

A pair of spotlights had been set up near the treeline and a tarp stretched out between two patrol cars to block dust from the highway. A commercial riding lawn mower was parked off to the side.

Hughes stopped walking and stepped aside so we could get a better look. The body was tucked under some brush, most of the girl's bare legs hidden beneath the thorny branches. She was wearing tan shorts and a yellow t-shirt. Her hair was long and tangled and brown. Animals had been at her face.

"Evening, gents," Harry Marshall said without looking up at us. He was kneeling next to the body, carefully examining the young girl's fingers.

Marshall had been Baltimore County Medical Examiner for as long as I had been on the job. He wore thin wire glasses, had a full head of wavy grey hair, and was in remarkably good shape for a man in his sixties. The women in the Eastern Precinct called him the Silver Fox behind his back.

"Heard you bowled a two-twenty last week," Frank said.

Harry looked up and smiled. "Two-twenty-six."

"Any witnesses?"

"Just my grandson and his friend. But I took a photo of my score up on the monitor. It was a legit two-twenty-six."

"And I'm the tooth fairy," Frank said under his breath.

"What was that?" Harry asked.

"You get an age on her yet?" I said.

"I'd say nine, maybe ten years old."

"What else?"

"I counted six stab wounds—neat, the weapon was very sharp—but I haven't moved the body yet. There might be more."

"Defensive?"

He nodded. "Both hands and arms. She definitely put up a fight."

"How long you think she's been out here?"

Harry studied the body. "Week. Maybe longer."

"What do you think did that to her face?" Frank asked.

"Could have been anything really. Deer. Raccoons. Groundhogs."

I stared at the smiley-face on the front of her yellow t-shirt. "Sexual?"

"I won't know for sure until I get her back to the office . . ." He leaned closer and reached inside the girl's mouth with two gloved fingers. ". . . but I would answer no as of right now. Doesn't have the look."

"Any idea what—"

"Well, now, this is interesting," Harry interrupted.

"What is?" Frank asked, stepping closer.

Harry looked up. "Someone cut out her tongue."

A FEW MINUTES LATER, I left Frank at Harry Marshall's side and followed Trooper Hughes back to the shoulder of the highway where he introduced me to the road crew. "This is Detective Richards. He has some questions for you." And then Hughes was gone, melting back into the crime scene.

The two men—Ronald Alvarez and Louis Vargas—were both in their late twenties. Faces deeply tan and creased from the sun, arms muscular and smeared with dirt. They were the kind of men who were used to hard work and long hours. Probably without a word of complaint. Right now, they looked nervous.

"This won't take long," I said, pulling out my notepad and a pen.

Both men nodded but didn't say a word.

"Relax. I only have a few questions and then you can go."

"We can go home?" Vargas asked.

"That's right. I'll just need to get your contact info when we're done here in case my partner or I need to talk to you again."

"We both have cell phones," Vargas said.

"So tell me what happened. Which one of you found the body?"

Vargas looked over at his friend.

"I did," Alvarez said, clearing his throat. "Carlos was riding the mower up ahead and I was running the weed-eater."

"We usually take turns," Vargas said. "One day I ride, the next day he rides."

"At first I thought it was a mannequin."

"A mannequin," I said, surprised.

"Yes, sir," Alvarez said. "We find all kinds of strange things along the highway."

"Including a mannequin?"

"Two," Vargas said, holding up a pair of thick fingers.

"No kidding," I said, glancing back at the woods.

"One was dressed as a soldier," Alvarez said. "The other wasn't wearing anything."

"Mostly it's junk," Vargas said. "But sometimes we find things of value."

"What's the strangest thing you've ever come across?" I asked, my curiosity humming.

Vargas thought for a moment. "For me, probably a big velvet framed Elvis Presley. Perfect condition. It's hanging in my living room right now. My wife loves it."

"I found a shoe box full of ashes once. Remember that?"

Vargas nodded. "We couldn't figure out whether it was a person or maybe a dog or cat."

"Would've had to have been a big animal," Alvarez said.

"What did you do with it?" I asked.

"I buried it in a field behind my apartment building," Alvarez said, shrugging his shoulders. "It felt like the right thing to do."

"I found an old Rolex once," Vargas said. "It didn't work, but I sold it to a guy at the pawn shop for fifty bucks. Ronnie and I split the money."

"That's the deal. We always split the money if one of us finds a ditch treasure," Alvarez said.

"Ditch treasure?"

"Yes, sir. That's what we call em. One time I found two brand new fishing rods and reels. Not a scratch on them. Another time, I found a brown paper bag with three hundred and sixty dollars inside."

I whistled and, with my curiosity satisfied, got back to business. "So, Mr. Alvarez, you found the body."

"Yes, sir. Like I said, at first I thought it was a mannequin so I walked right over to it. But once I was close enough and could smell it, I knew I was wrong."

"He came running down the shoulder toward me, waving his arms like a crazy man," Vargas said. "I turned off the mower and hopped down, thinking maybe he'd been bitten by a snake or something."

Alvarez crossed himself at the mention of a snake.

"Ronnie couldn't even talk he was so upset. He dragged me over to the woods and showed me. I called our boss and he told us to wait right here while he called the police."

"Neither of you touched the body?"

"No, sir, we did not," Vargas said.

"Did you disturb the area close to the body in any way? Touch or pick up anything?"

"No, sir. The smell was very bad . . . and we were scared . . . we did not get too close."

"Do the two of you usually mow this area?"

"It depends," Vargas said. "We go where the boss tells us to go. The truck drops us off in the morning and picks us up at the end of the day."

"How about this past summer? How often was this area cut?"

"Again, that's the decision of the boss," Vargas said. "What do you think?" he asked, looking over at Alvarez. "Every two weeks maybe?"

"Less in the summer," he said. "I remember it was almost a month ago that we cut here. Right around my birthday."

"And no sign of the body at that time?" I asked.

"No, sir, I did not see anything," Alvarez said and glanced at his friend. Vargas shook his head.

I flipped the page in my notepad and was just about to ask for their boss's name and contact info when Frank called out from behind me. He was standing halfway up the grassy embankment.

"Need you, partner. Harry found something else." He turned and hurried back to the scene before I could answer.

I waved over a county uniform and instructed him to take down Vargas and Alvarez's phone numbers and addresses, as well as that of their boss.

Then, I was hustling toward the bright lights at the edge of the woods.

"So, WAIT, LET ME get this straight," Trooper Hughes said, as we stood on the side of the highway two hours later and watched Harry Marshall's taillights disappear into the darkness.

"Jesus Christ, Mike, no wonder you never made detective," Frank said. It was almost comforting to have my cranky partner back again.

"Just give me the short version one more time," Hughes said. "So you guys found her tongue stapled to a business card and stuffed in her short's pocket?"

"Well, Harry found it, but that's right," I said.

"And the business card belonged to that hotshot lawyer from the television commercials, and the little girl was his daughter?"

"Hallelujah," Frank said.

"Peter Lotts," I said. "I guess he got mixed up with some bad people and was in the process of flipping on them with the Feds. The bad guys found out and took his daughter."

"And the dumbass didn't tell anyone?" Hughes asked.

I shook my head. "They warned him that if he called the police, his wife would be next. And after that it'd be his turn."

"Poor bastard's downtown right now, blabbing his guts out," Frank said. "Foster said he's a mess. He had no clue they'd already killed his daughter. He thought she was alive all this time. He was trying to come up with enough cash for the ransom."

"But it was never about a pay-off? It was all about him flipping?" Hughes asked.

"Bad guys hate rats," Frank said.

"Hey, speaking of rats, I meant to mention this earlier," Hughes said. "My wife said she saw you with some pretty lady at Giovanni's last Friday night. She was carousing with her book club in the bar. Said you two had a table in the corner and looked awfully chummy."

"Oh, she did, did she," I said, staring at my partner and trying not to smile.

"It's late," Frank grunted and stomped toward the car. "Let's get the hell outta here."

"What's his problem?" Hughes asked.

I shrugged. "Hey, wait up, I have the keys."

Frank swung open the passenger door, looked our way, and flipped us a middle finger, then slammed the door behind him.

"NOT ONE WORD," HE muttered, as I pulled onto the interstate.

"What?"

He took a deep breath. "What Einstein back there said . . . not one damn word about it."

"You mean about you and your . . . date?"

"I mean it, Ben."

I put my hand up. "Okay, okay."

We drove in silence for a while, then:

"It's been three years since the divorce, Frank. It's okay if you've found someone to pass the time with."

He grunted.

"I'm happy for you."

Another grunt. Then:

"We've only gone out on two real dates. But we play Scrabble online and she showed me how to text."

I looked at my partner, at the sudden vulnerability on his face, and wanted to pull over the car and hug him. I thought back to the divorce and how lost he'd been, how he'd started drinking again and with the drinking came the tears and the rage and the bars and the fights in the bars. The two in the morning phone calls to pick him up, the tearful confessions, and bloody fists slamming the walls of his apartment. Three years. It had taken three long years, but here he was playing Scrabble and texting with a woman.

"I met her at the bookstore. She teaches history at the community college. Can you believe that?"

"What's her name?"

"Karen. She's a real nice lady. I don't know what she sees in me."

"Probably the same good things I see in you, Frank."

He laughed in the darkness. "Jesus, don't say that."

I smiled.

"You won't tell anyone, will you, Ben?"

"Nope, I won't say a word, except maybe to Katy."

He nodded. "I guess that's okay."

"You know there's nothing to feel embarrassed or awkward about, right?"

"It's not that," he said, his voice going soft. "I just don't want to . . . I don't want to somehow jinx it."

"I get that," I said, taking the White Marsh exit off the interstate.

"Thanks for not being a jerk about it."

"No need to thank me," I said. "But there is one thing."

"What's that?"

"You *were* whistling."

"Jesus, Ben."

"Admit it."

"I'm not admitting a damn thing."

"Third time this week, too. It just came to me, the tune you were whistling. It was from *Doctor Zhivago*."

"*Doctor Zhivago*? I've never even seen that movie."

"You're a big fat liar, Frank."

"You're a big fat asshole, Ben."

The station house lights glowed in the distance. I slowed and switched on the turn signal.

"You know what, I'm kinda hungry," Frank said.

I turned off the signal and drove on past. "Me too, partner, me too."

For Ed Gorman

O, SWEAR NOT BY THE MOON

BY JILL D. BLOCK

ACT 1 He Said . . .

Rich was sitting at his desk, and Chazz was sprawled across the beanbag chair. They each held a copy of the Ridgely Fells Report.

"Hey, who's this one?" Rich asked. "She's new, right?"

Chazz got up to see which picture Rich was looking at.

"Which one, her? Maggie May Costello. Good God. Who would name their kid Maggie May?"

"It says she's from New York City but doesn't say what school she came from. Tenth grade."

"Oh, yeah. That's right," Chazz said, sitting back down. "I think I heard about her. She's CeeCee's daughter."

"CeeCee Castile?" Rich turned in his chair. "You're so full of shit."

"I'm serious. I heard she was coming here."

"Oh, you *heard*?" Rich asked.

"What, you think you're the only person who hears stuff?"

"So, who exactly did you *hear* from?"

Chazz dropped his copy of the Report on the floor and picked up his phone. "You know that girl with the red hair? The tennis player? You know the one I mean. She hangs out with those girls from San Diego. Anyway, she told me. Her mother is on the board."

"So you're telling me that CeeCee's daughter is a student at Ridgely Fells?" Rich took another look at her picture. "Google it."

"Okay," Chazz said. "Hang on. God, what is with the shit WiFi in this building? Okay. Here it is. We've got CeeCee tour dates. CeeCee's new album. CeeCee at the VMAs. Oh, here. This says she had a daughter in 2003, so she'd be fifteen. That sounds right. Right?"

"Big deal. That doesn't mean—"

"Ok, wait. What about this?" Chazz read from his phone, "Quote, while CeeCee has never confirmed paternity, there have been persistent rumors of a brief affair with Rod Stewart during his marriage to Rachel Hunter, unquote. Uh, hello? Maggie May?"

"None of that proves that she's CeeCee's daughter," Rich said, getting up. "She's in Turner. Let's go meet her."

She Said . . .

"That was so nice," Maggie said. "Don't you think? For them to come by like that?"

"Are you kidding?" Katie replied. "Yeah, it was nice. Seriously. Those guys are seniors. They have never even looked at me before, let alone spoken to me."

"Oh, so that thing about them being from the Welcoming Committee . . . ?"

"Umm, yeah. There's no such thing. I think they just wanted to see you in person."

"Really? That's so . . . did I act like a total dork?"

"You were fine. A little shy, maybe. But people like that. Everyone's just really—"

"That one guy, Rich? He's really cute."

"Oh, totally. He's definitely in the top ten. I would have said he was out of reach, but apparently not." Katie continued, "Chazz, though? Total jerk."

"Yeah. But it's like Rich thinks so too. Do you know what I mean? How he acts like he doesn't even like him?"

"He probably doesn't," Katie said, getting up from her desk and sitting down on her bed. "My guess is that he just hangs out with him for the Blueblood cred."

"What's that?" Maggie asked.

"Okay, so here's how it is." Katie stretched out on her bed, her legs crossed at the ankle, her hands behind her head. "People here are either Misfits or Bluebloods. The Bluebloods are super rich, usually old money, mostly legacy, but also major corporate types. I mean, children of, obviously. But yeah, hedge funds, Fortune 500 companies, like that."

"So, like you," Maggie said.

"Well, yeah. I mean, I'm fourth generation."

"Right."

"And the Misfits are also mostly super rich, but it's different. New money, or shady money. Plus there are the scholarship kids. Oh, and the fuck-ups. You know, like, the kids who got thrown out of other schools."

"Oh, great," Maggie said. "So I'm a Misfit?"

"You? Uhh, no. You're Spawn. Third category: Superstar Spawn. There aren't very many of you. We get maybe one a year, if we're lucky. Maybe not even. There's a girl here, Christina? You'll meet her. Anyway, her father used to be a pro golfer. Like, big time. All the dads were super psyched for parent's weekend last year, like he was going to be helping them with their swings or something. But that guy's nothing like CeeCee."

"Superstar Spawn. Okay. It could be worse."

"Are you kidding? It's the best!" Katie said, sitting up. "I can't believe how lucky I am to have you as my roommate. Seriously. This is going to make my whole year."

"I'm glad I could help. So umm, what makes Rich a Misfit?"

"Shady money. I don't know this for sure, but I think his father is connected." When she saw the look on Maggie's face Katie continued. "Connected. As in, in the mafia."

"Oh. Well, I just thought he was cute."

"He totally is. Plus, it's not like being a Misfit is even a bad thing. The Bluebloods are mostly pretty dull. Except for me, I mean. But seriously, the Misfits are definitely the coolest and the most popular."

"Other than the Spawn?" Maggie asked.

"Right. The Spawn are on their own level. See? You get it. Come on, let's go downstairs. I'll introduce you to everyone."

ACT 2 He Said . . .

Dad, I think I'm in trouble. He closed his eyes, repeating the words in his head, in sync with the on-hold music. *I'm in trouble. I'm in trouble. I'm in trouble.*

"What?" Emphasis on the T. It wasn't a question. It was an order, a command, a countdown clock.

"Oh, hey Dad. Hi." Rich pictured him, hair combed back, double breasted suit, the knife-sharp edge of a white handkerchief just poking out of his breast pocket.

"What is it? She pulled me out of a meeting." He was probably standing at his secretary's desk, Rich imagined, using her phone, stretching the cord across her keyboard, invading her space, while she sat there pretending to be invisible, watching, listening.

"Yeah, I know. JoAnn told me— I mean, I know you're busy. I just—"

"You just what? Richie, I can't do this right now."

Shit, just say it.

"Okay. I umm. I think that I—"

"Speak."

"Okay, yeah," Rich said. "I'm sorry to bother you. I think—" The words he'd practiced were gone.

"You think. You think what? For Christ's sake. Can you understand that I do not have time for this shit today?"

"I know. It's just—" Rich looked up, making sure that he was still alone in the room, that the door was still closed. "There's this, uh, girl," his voice lowering almost to a whisper.

"Jesus Christ. Call your mother."

Wait. Don't hang up. Please don't hang up.

"I would, but I thought— It's just that— I didn't want—"

"Richie, I've got a conference room full of lawyers charging me by the goddamn tenth of an hour. I don't have time for your girl problems."

"Yeah, ok. I know. I'm sorry. It's not really—"

"You're eighteen years old. Whatever it is, deal with it."

"I know. I'm trying, but I really don't— Dad, I don't know what to do."

"You've got ten seconds and I'm hanging up."

"Okay. Sorry." *Say it. Just say it.* "I umm, I think I raped a girl."

"You think—? Jesus, fuck. Call Roland." Click. The call was over.

She Said . . .

"Maggie! Hi, Doll. I'm so glad you called. I was just thinking about you. Are you getting all settled in?" Maggie could hear the muffled street noise in the background, the beep beep beep of a truck backing up.

"Pretty much, yeah. I just, umm, I wanted to thank you for driving me up here. And, like, for helping me unpack and everything." She looked around her room, at the pink throw rug on the floor, the Broadway show posters framed and hung on the walls, the bookcase filled with the books she couldn't bear to leave behind.

"Are you kidding me? I loved it. Besides, isn't that what being an aunt is all about? I get all the glory, and none of the stretch marks."

"Yeah, thanks." Maggie wondered how many times had she said that.

"Hey, so I was just looking at your mom's Instagram. It looks like Tokyo is cuckoo for CeeCee. Have you spoken to her?"

She'd seen all of it. The Instagram stories, the tweets, the TMZ reports.

"Yeah. I mean, no. I haven't heard from her." *Hashtag CeeCee.* "I read about the show. It sounds like it went great. I was going to text her, but then I decided I didn't want to bother her. You know how she is when she's on tour. Like, especially after a big night?"

"Seriously big. Can you believe the Dome holds something like 55,000 people? It's nuts. Anyway, I talked to her right after I dropped you off. And you saw that I sent her those pictures of you and your room. I copied you, didn't I? She really wishes she could have been there to set you up."

"It's okay." *The tour was planned more than a year ago. It would have cost a fortune to cancel. Blah blah blah.* "I get it. The show must go on." *Hashtag Mom.*

"Sweetie, are you ok? Taxi, hey! Sorry, honey, hang on a sec. Hi, thanks. Here, let me just—" The car door closed, muting the background noise. "I'm going to 84th and Riverside. Okay, hon. I'm back. Oof, it's hot out. Anyway, you sound a little, I don't know, homesick maybe?"

"I'm ok. It's weird though, you know? Being new? Everyone here already—"

"Can you just take Madison and then go across on 86th? Sorry. What were you saying?"

"It's nothing. Just that everybody who's my year already knows each other. Pretty much no one ever starts in 10th grade."

"Do they know who your mom is? That should help break the ice."

"Believe me, they know. Everyone keeps pointing and whispering, and then they stop talking when I walk by."

"I'm sorry. That must be annoying. But people will get used to it. I really do think you're going to love it there."

"You're right. It's fine. I mean I think so, too."

"I bet you're going to make some great friends there. Once they stop all the pointing and whispering."

"I know. My roommate's really nice. Katie, who you met? She knows everyone here, and how everything works. I'd be pretty lost without her."

"I'm glad to hear that. It sounds like she's a good friend to have."

"Plus, there's this, umm, this boy."

"Oh yeah? A boy you like? That was fast."

"We just met. Obviously. But he's really nice."

"Tell me more."

ACT 3 He Said . . .

"I SPOKE TO YOUR father. I need you to tell me what happened."

"I thought it doesn't matter what happened," Rich said. "She's fifteen, so it's statutory rape."

"Tell me again where you went to law school?" Roland asked, impatient.

"Sorry. I didn't mean— I googled it."

"Oh, good. You googled it. Next time, google it before you do it. Now tell me what happened."

"So it's not automatic? I thought—"

"Rich, just tell me what happened."

"Okay. We were hanging out, just talking and stuff. And then we were, you know, fooling around. But my asshole friends came looking for me and because they were loud and stupid and it was after curfew, Security followed them into the Tower. And then, all of a—"

"The Tower?"

"It's the building where most of the classrooms are. Other than Sciences which they— Anyway, all of a sudden this guy Walter, he's one of the security guys here, came out onto the roof and—"

"The roof."

"Roof, terrace, whatever. It's like a roofdeck. There's furniture and stuff, like outdoor furniture, but it's just for teachers. Kids aren't supposed to go up there but sometimes we do. There's a door, around the back by the dumpsters? And it's never locked. Anyway, it's called the Tower because it's the tallest building on campus, and from the roof you can see all the way out to the lake."

"Go back. I need you to start at the beginning."

"Oh, okay. I wasn't sure how much— Okay, from the beginning. After dinner, everyone went to Assembly, which started out exactly the same as last year. And every year. The Dean spends forever going through the PSL, even thought it's the—"

"PSL?"

"Policies for Student Life. You know, like the academic honor code, dorm curfews, that kind of thing. But anyway, there's this new thing this year. They've always had a zero tolerance prohibition against smoking, drinking and drugs, but he added this whole other thing, which is new. The Intimate Contact policy statement. You know, about consent and stuff."

Roland didn't say anything, so Rich continued.

"It was pretty awkward, you know? To be sitting there with everyone while he was talking about inappropriate touching, and how no means no? It felt like it went on forever. When it finally ended, there was only about an hour before curfew. Anyway, I saw Maggie while she was walking out and I went and caught up to her. She was with her roommate and some other girls, but they sort of sped up or something, like they were letting us be alone. You know, together. So I figured that meant she liked me. Like, that maybe they had talked about it."

"Right. Then what?"

"We just walked around for a while. People kept coming up to us, kids I know. And at first it was like they were just saying hey, asking about my summer, that kind of thing. But it was pretty obvious people were just trying to get a look at her. It seemed like it made her uncomfortable. So I asked her what it was like, you know, to be CeeCee's daughter."

"CeeCee? The . . . what is she, a singer?"

"Yeah. But she's more than that. She's huge. You know that song, 'Get With You'? That's her."

"I'll have to take your word for it."

"So, yeah. Anyway, we just talked. About how her mom always kept her completely separate from the CeeCee stuff. Like totally sheltered. And how she always felt like she was this distraction, or not even. A burden, or like an old mistake her mom had made. And she told me about how she was home schooled? Like, by teachers who would come to her house. And how she didn't even live with CeeCee."

"What do you mean?"

"I know. It's weird, right? But I guess she was pretty much raised by this nanny. Like, it was the nanny's job to live at Maggie's apartment. And even when CeeCee isn't on tour or anything she lives someplace else. In a completely different building."

"Okay. It sounds like she wasn't appropriately supervised. This is good."

"No. It's not like that. She said it was to protect her, to keep her safe I guess, even though it always made her feel, like, unwanted or something."

"Keep going."

"It's like she was over-supervised. She never hung out with other kids. She said she never had any real friends. It seems like it was always just her and the nanny and her teachers. And books. It seems like she read a million books. Anyway, she was saying how it was her choice to come here, to Ridgely. She said she begged to come, because she was too old for a nanny, but didn't want to be alone, and how she wanted to experience a regular life, to see what it's like to be a normal kid. That's what she said, that she needed to learn how to be normal. Like, to do what normal kids do."

She Said . . .

"I'm telling you," Katie said. "It's a really big deal."

"I don't get it. All we did was have sex. Isn't that what teenagers do?"

"It's a violation of the PSL. They can kick you out. Both of you."

"You've got to be kidding," Maggie said. "You're not kidding? I don't get it. It wasn't anything bad. It was like in a movie. Or a book. Did you ever read—?"

"God, weren't you even listening? Berwin went on and on about the zero tolerance policy. And then an hour later Security totally catches you going at it."

"It wasn't like that," Maggie said.

"Were you, like, in the act?"

"No. I mean, not really. We were . . . we were done. But still, like, cuddling. And the door opened and it was one of the security guys, with a flashlight."

"Jesus. Were you naked?"

"Partly. But he looked away while we got dressed. I really don't get why it's such a big deal."

"Well, it is. You're for sure going to be called before the Disciplinary Committee, and trust me, that's no joke. My brother's friend got caught with beer a couple of years ago and it was this huge thing. You've got to be prepared."

"Prepared how? I don't even—"

"Just tell me what happened," Katie said. "I'm on your side."

"We just, you know, walked around for a long time, talking," Maggie said. "He's really nice. Like, way nicer even than he was when he came by. It was just, I don't know, normal. Regular. Do you know what I mean?"

"So, it was regular. And?"

"And that's it. It was like we really connected. Like, even though our lives are completely different, like how I'm an only child and grew up super sheltered, and he's from this big loud family, and he's the youngest of five, and he went to catholic school, where all his brothers and sisters had gone, but then he had this terrible thing happen—"

"What terrible thing?"

"What? Oh, nothing." Maggie wished she hadn't said anything.

"What? Come on."

"I shouldn't have— Forget it."

"I can't forget it. Tell me."

"It's nothing. I really don't— It was probably private."

"Did he say you couldn't tell anyone?"

"No. But it wasn't like that. I mean, it was just us. It's not really any—"

"Maggie, just tell me. Whatever it is. I'm trying to help you. Let me be your friend."

"God, fine. I was asking why he came here, like why his parents sent him here, when his brothers and sisters all lived at home and went to catholic school. I mean, I get why you came here, how it's this thing in your family. And I know why I came here. But I keep trying to figure out why normal people send their kids away."

"I was right, right? It was it because of that mob thing? I knew it."

"No. It was umm . . . Actually, you know what? Forget it. It wasn't anything."

"Maggie, come on."

"No, really. I don't think I should be talking about this."

"I won't tell anyone."

"There was a priest in his school who, like, you know, messed with him."

"Whoa. Seriously?"

"Yeah, and I guess it went on for a long time. Like, for years. But the thing that was messed up was that he kept it a secret. Even though he didn't like it. And he knew it was wrong. But he was just a little kid when it started. And he knew that for his mother it would be like the most terrible thing that could happen. Because I guess she's super churchy or something. Plus, he said he was afraid his father would kill the guy if he knew. So it was like he was just trying to protect everyone. But no one was protecting him."

"Oh my God."

"I know. Right? But then, when he was in ninth grade, people somehow found out about it and I guess at first he lied about it, like he was still trying to protect the guy. So then it seemed like he was covering it up, like he wasn't a victim at all, even though he totally was."

"Holy crap."

"I know! It made me feel so bad for him. And I guess the whole thing really messed him up for a while, because he ended up taking the rest of that year off from school. And then he came here and started ninth grade over."

"Wow."

"But he's not gay. I mean, I told him it would be fine if he is. Obviously. But he's not. He told me he's had girlfriends. Like, that girl Brenda?"

"Oh, shit. I wasn't even thinking about Brenda."

"What about her? They broke up, didn't they? He said they did. Anyway, listen to this. It was so cute. I asked if he was going to get back together with her and he said no, that he'd met someone he liked better. I was like, yeah? What's she like? And he goes, she's cute and funny and she seems really worldly but she's actually pretty shy. I *thought* he meant me, but I wasn't sure. So I asked if she liked him back and he said he didn't know, so I said he should find out, and he said how. And I said he should try holding her hand."

"Adorable. Then what?"

"He took my hand," Maggie said, smiling.

"Right. I figured. After that."

"It was so nice out, remember? It was a really beautiful night. I thought it was a full moon, but he said not until tonight. Waxing gibbous, he said. Anyway, it was this huge moon, and it looked like it was really low in the sky. So he said let's go up to the Tower. The lock on the service door is broken—he thought they might have fixed it over the summer, but they didn't. So we went up to the roof. It's the tallest building—"

"Yeah. I know."

ACT 4 He Said . . .

"Rich, what the hell did you do?"

"Hey, Susan."

"Dad is freaking out."

"What did he say?" Rich asked.

"He wouldn't tell me what happened. He just said to call you so I can help him figure out what he's going to say to Mom. What happened?"

"I umm, violated the PSL. The Policies for Student Life. I think they might kick me out."

"You fucking moron. It's the third day of school. What did you do? How stupid—?"

"I got caught with a girl. After curfew."

"They'd kick you out for that? They sound worse than the nuns."

"We were, umm . . . we got caught having sex."

"Shit, Richie."

"And she's only fifteen."

"Well, that at least explains why Dad's so freaked out. This is going to kill Mom. No way can she handle another sex scandal."

"It's not a sex scandal. Or, I don't know. I guess maybe it is. Or it could be. It's technically statutory rape. But Roland didn't seem too worried about it."

"Rich, Jesus."

"I know. I messed up."

"Messed up? No. Messed up would be getting caught with weed. This is like you're a goddamn sexual deviant."

He had nothing to say to that.

"I shouldn't have said that."

"Whatever."

"No, really. I'm sorry. It'll be okay. You're fine, right? You'll be okay? We'll figure this out. Just don't do anything stupid. Okay? Rich? Promise me."

"Yeah, okay."

"Okay. I have to call Dad. I'll call you tonight."

She Said . . .

"Are you up?" Maggie asked. "I wasn't sure if it was too late to call."

"We just got to the hotel. I have to change, and then we're going to this club that they say is really wild. The car will be here in a few minutes. Tokyo is insane. Did you see the pictures I posted?"

"Yeah. It looks really cool."

"So quick, tell me. How is it there? Your room looks cute."

"It's okay, I guess."

"Did classes start yet? I don't even know what day it is."

"Not until Monday."

"We fly to Berlin tomorrow. You should see this hotel room, by the way. I'll take some pictures when I get back."

"Okay, yeah. That'll be great."

"So, quick. Tell me everything."

"Well, I was wondering, actually. What would happen if, like, if it doesn't work out here? I mean, if I ummm, if I decide I don't like it."

"What are you talking about? This is what you wanted. Why would you—? Sweetie, you're probably just homesick. Once classes start, you'll be busy, and you'll make lots of friends. That was the point, right?"

"I know, but I was thinking maybe I could move back home. Like, if this doesn't work out."

"Maggie, that would be impossible. I could never make those arrangements from here. You're being silly."

"Or maybe I could come meet you. And just, you know, be with you, on the tour. That would be educational. And I've never been anywhere.

"Sweetie, no way. Don't be ridiculous. You have no idea what this is like. I'm working all the time, and it's nothing but airports and hotels. You would hate it. Listen, I'm getting a call. I have to go. You'll be fine. I promise. Okay?"

"You're right. I was just— I'll be fine. Have fun tonight."

"I love you, Baby. I'll call you soon."

ACT 5

"ARE YOU OK?" HE asked.

"I didn't think you'd come," she said.

"I came as soon as I saw your text."

"It was probably dumb to come back up here," she said. "It's almost curfew."

"It doesn't matter," he said. "The worst thing already happened."

"I know. I'm so sorry. I never should have said anything. I thought she was my friend. Katie, I mean. And she said she wouldn't tell anyone. It was stupid, but I believed her. I never expected that . . . you must hate me."

"It's okay," he said.

"It's not," she said. "I don't care what they say about me. Like, someone wrote SLUT on the dry erase board on my door. Umm, hello? Dry erase, get it? And plus, hearing Rod Stewart blasted on every stereo across campus. Fine, whatever. But I heard what those kids were saying to you. The names they were calling you. I just—"

"It's really okay," he said.

"It's not okay."

"It's like they can't decide if I'm a faggot, a pervert or a rapist. I don't know. Maybe I'm all three."

"You're none of those things. God, I was such an idiot to trust her."

"I don't even know why it was supposed to be such a secret. The thing with Father Joe, I mean. Everyone's been telling me how it's nothing to be ashamed of, my parents, my therapist, and then they come up with this story for me to tell about why I left St. Catherine's, and it's this giant secret for me to keep. I'm supposed to guard it with my life or something. Like the worst thing would be for people to find out. But the worst thing is that it happened, not that people find out about it."

"I shouldn't have said anything. She acted like she was helping me, like if I didn't tell her everything it was going to be worse. Then I find out she has a huge mouth and just wanted me to tell her so she could tell everyone else. I'm really sorry."

"Don't be. I'm glad it's not a secret anymore, the thing with Father Joe. It's like I finally don't have a stomach ache anymore, for the first time since I was nine years old."

"Wow."

"But everything else is my fault. Us getting caught? What I did to you? I never should have even brought you up here. I know the rules, and I know how things work here. I'm really sorry."

"Don't be. I'm not mad at you. This is so dumb. We didn't do anything wrong. So we broke a stupid rule. So what? No one got hurt."

"It's a pretty big deal, actually."

"Do you think they'll really kick us out?"

"Probably not you."

"I don't want to stay here if you're not here. I'm serious. I can't be here without you. Isn't there someone we can talk to? That guy Berwin? I'll tell him I'm fine, that it was my idea."

"I talked to my dad's lawyer today."

"A lawyer? Seriously?"

"He said that there's this thing called the Romeo and Juliet defense. To a statutory rape charge. Because we're close in age, even though you are under sixteen. But only if it was consensual.

"It was. I mean, that's true."

"Are you sure? Because if I hurt you. Or forced you, I would—"

"Are you kidding? You kept asking me if it was okay. You probably asked me at least ten times if I wanted you to stop."

"If you told me to stop, I would have. It's not like I couldn't control myself."

"I know that. I didn't want you to stop. I wanted to do it."

"It just looks bad, you know? Because of how we just met, and that it was just your third day here."

"But it doesn't feel like that. Not to me. I feel like I've known you my whole life. And it's like you know me better than anyone else. I know it seems crazy but I—"

"I really like you. A lot."

"Me too."

"I've never felt like this before."

"Me neither."

"I swear to God. I think I might—"

"Don't."

"What?"

"Don't swear. Just say it. What you were going to say."

"Huh? Sorry. You lost me."

"You said 'I swear to God'. I feel like bad things always happen whenever people say 'I swear'. I know it's dumb. It's like I made up my own superstition. 'O, swear not by the moon.' Do you know that line?"

"I don't— All of a sudden I have no idea what you're talking about."

"It's a line from a play. Never mind. It just popped into my head."

"What play?"

"Did you read *Romeo and Juliet*?"

"Yeah. Well, parts of it."

"Parts of it? How do you not finish *Romeo and Juliet*?"

"I guess I read as much as I needed to write the paper."

"God, I've read it like ten times. Anyway, I just keep thinking— Forget it. This is embarrassing."

"Come on. Tell me."

"Okay, so all day today there is all this bad stuff happening, right? Everyone knows we had sex, we might get kicked out of school, my roommate totally betrayed me and because of my big mouth people are saying all this terrible stuff about you. And I just keep thinking it's like *Romeo and Juliet*. Like we're these star-crossed lovers or something. Like how I was up here looking down from this balcony? And there you were, stepping out of the shadows and looking up at me."

"I was afraid someone would see me, coming here. Roland said I shouldn't even talk to you."

"Do you see what I mean? Then there was that thing you said the lawyer said, about the Romeo and Juliet defense? Plus, the moon is full. It just feels like— Never mind. It's dumb."

"What is it—don't swear by the moon?"

" 'O, swear not by the moon.' I'm not even sure what it really means, but I think it's something like don't make promises about how you feel right now because the moon is always changing, and your feelings might change, too."

"Maybe. But they won't." He took her hand. "I mean, I get it. Things change. And sometimes stuff happens really fast. Like, we literally just met a couple days ago. And I know we don't know what's going to happen. But right now, just you and me? I love you."

"I love you, too. Right now. Just you and me."

They sat in silence.

"Can I ask you something?" Rich asked. "What did you mean in your text?"

"Just that I wanted you to meet me here," she said.

"You said I shouldn't blame myself. And you said goodbye. How come?"

"I was afraid you wouldn't come," said Maggie.

"Were you—? I was afraid you were going to do something. You know, try to do something," Rich said.

"You mean, like, kill myself?"

"Yeah," he answered.

"I don't know. I was only thinking about seeing you. I figured I would wait fifteen minutes. If you didn't come I don't know what I was going to do. It was almost fifteen minutes when I looked down and there you were."

"I saw you sitting on the wall. When I looked up. I was afraid you were going to— Like, right then. You can't do that. Promise me you won't do that."

"You know how you sometimes hear about people who have this huge will to live?" Maggie asked. "I don't think I have that. I never did."

"What do you mean?"

"Like how someone will fight and fight and fight to get away from someone who is attacking them? Or when someone survives for days drinking their own pee after getting lost in the woods? Or cuts off their own arm?"

"Yeah," he said. "Or they lay down really still and flat in the middle of the tracks and the train goes right over them without hurting them?"

"Sort of. Or more like hanging onto a tree for days while a tsunami is wiping out your whole village." Maggie turned to him. "There's no way I would do that. I guess I never felt like my life was really worth fighting for."

"I tried to kill myself once."

"You did?" she asked, surprised.

"The day my mom and dad were called to St. Cat's to first hear about the thing with Father Joe. I didn't think I would be able to face them after they knew. I knew they weren't ever going to look at me the same way as before."

"What did you do? I mean, how?"

"I took all the pills in their medicine chest. And then I got in bed and tried to go to sleep. But then my sister came home and found the empty pill bottles. She drove me to the emergency room and I got my stomach pumped."

"I'm glad," Maggie said. "That it didn't work, I mean. Otherwise we never would have met."

"If you were going to kill yourself, how would you do it?"

"I don't know. Something quick, I guess. Like, jumping off a roof."

"Like from here?" he asked.

"It's high enough, don't you think? Come look."

"Yeah, definitely," he said, leaning across the wide top of the parapet.

She pulled herself up to sit on top of the wall.

"It would be a really big deal," he said, sitting next to her. "I mean, obviously. To your mom and everything. But it would really rock this place, you know? Especially if we both—"

"Really? Would you?" They turned to face out, their legs hanging over the edge.

"I don't know," he said. "I can't stay here."

"There's no place for me to go," she said. "I talked to my mom today. I was thinking maybe I could go be on tour with her or something. Like, if I got kicked out or if I decided to leave? She said no."

"I can't think of a single reason not to."

"The only reason I can think not to is because CeeCee would have to cancel some shows, and someone would lose a shit ton of money. I don't even know who. But that's always her excuse. She can't do this because it will cost someone money. Or she has to do that or it will cost someone money. Whatever."

"And I just keep thinking how my parents are already wrecked by this stuff. At least this would be the end of it." He reaches for her hand. "It really would be like *Romeo and Juliet*."

"It would," she said, looking down onto the path below. "Look, is that the same guy from last night?" she asked. "The security guard who came up here?"

"Yep, Walter."

"Do you think he's looking for us?" she asked.

"Probably. It's past curfew."

"I don't want to get caught again."

"Me neither," he said. "Should we do it?"

"I think so. Don't you?"

"I do," he said. "Are you ready?"

She nodded. "Don't let go of my hand."

They kissed, and together leaned forward into the moonlight.

NIGHTBOUND

BY WALLACE STROBY

"LEAVE HIM," CRISSA SAID. "He's dead."

Adler was face down in the alley, not moving, Martinez kneeling beside him. She could see the entry wound in Adler's back, the blood soaking through his field jacket. From the location of the wound, and the speed he was bleeding out, she knew he was gone already, or would be soon.

They had to keep moving. Back at the stash house, the Dominicans would be recovering from the flashbang she'd thrown on her way out the rear door. The three of them had been halfway down the alley when one of the Dominicans had stumbled out of the vacant brownstone, firing blindly. She'd snapped a shot at him with her Glock, chased him back inside. But Adler had caught a round, gone down hard.

Now Martinez looked up at her, panic in his eyes, all that was visible through the ski mask. She shifted the strap of the gear bag, heavy with money, to her left shoulder, grabbed him by the coat sleeve, pulled him up. "Move!"

Forty feet away was the mouth of the alley, the street beyond. To their left, more empty houses. To the right, a high chain-link fence that bordered a vacant lot. The only way out was ahead.

More shots behind them. She spun, saw two men run out into the alley, guns in their hands. She fired twice without aiming. One round ricocheted off blacktop, the other punched through a plywood-covered window. The men ducked back inside.

She fired another shot to keep them there, shoved Martinez forward. The street ahead was still empty. Where was Lopez? The Dominicans would be going out the front door as well, would try to circle around, block the alley. If they beat Lopez there, she and Martinez would be trapped.

Broken glass and crack vials crunched beneath her feet. She could hear Martinez panting behind her.

A screech of brakes, and the Buick pulled up at the end of the alley, Lopez at the wheel, the rear drivers-side door already open.

She tossed the gear bag into the back seat, threw herself in after it. A shot sounded. Martinez grunted and fell against her.

"Get in!" Lopez said.

She gripped Martinez's field jacket, pulled him to her, and they fell back onto the bag. His legs were still hanging out of the car when Lopez hit the gas. As the Buick lurched forward, she heard rounds strike the left rear fender. She pulled Martinez all the way in just as the Buick made a hard right turn. The momentum swung the door shut.

Martinez moaned. She rolled him off her onto the floor, sat up. They were in a residential area, dark houses on both sides of the street. The transfer car was still a couple of miles away.

"What happened back there?" Lopez said.

She pulled off her ski mask, had to catch her breath before she could speak. "Too many of them. Seven, maybe. At least. More than we thought."

Through the rear window, she saw headlights way back there, coming fast. No other cars around.

"They're on us," she said.

"Shit." Lopez gunned the engine. The Buick swung a left, then another right onto a main thoroughfare, sped by darkened storefronts.

She pushed the mask into a jacket pocket. If she had to do a runner from the car, she didn't want to leave it behind. There would be hair in the material, DNA. Evidence if the cops found it.

Martinez moaned again. She lay a gloved hand atop his. "Steady. You're going to be all right."

They'd scouted this area of East New York for weeks, timed the route, and she knew the chances of running into a squad car were slim. It was midnight shift change, the same reason the Dominicans chose that time for their weekly money pickup. Lopez was an ex-cop, knew the area, the players. Martinez was his brother-in-law. The two of them had found the stash house, gathered the intel, then reached out to her through a middleman. She was the one who'd brought in Adler.

Two blocks ahead was the business district, an intersection controlled at this hour by only a blinking yellow light. She looked back at the street behind. A pair of bright headlights swung out onto it, moving fast.

"They're coming," she said.

Martinez made a slow sign of the cross. His breath was ragged now, wheezing. Collapsed lung, she thought.

Lopez took the left at the yellow light, cut it too close, the drivers' side tires bumping hard over the curb. A red light began to blink on the dash, in time with a soft beep.

"Fuck," he said.

"What?"

"They must have hit the tank. We're losing gas."

Behind them, a dark SUV made the turn, staying on their tail. Highbeams flashed on, lit the inside of the car. The Buick began to sputter and slow. The next turn was still a block ahead.

"Get down!" Lopez said.

The SUV swept into the left lane, came abreast of them. The front passenger side window slid down, and a shotgun barrel came through.

Lopez slammed on the brake. It threw her forward onto Martinez. She heard the roar of the gun, an explosion of glass. The Buick slewed to the right, hit the curb, rolled up on it and came to a stop. The SUV braked just beyond it, then reversed.

She heard the shotgun being ratcheted. Another blast, and safety glass sprayed over her.

She jerked up on the latch of the passenger side door, pushed it open and rolled out onto the sidewalk, the Buick between her and the SUV.

How many men? Two, at least, driver and shooter, but maybe others in back. Likely more on their way from the stash house in another vehicle. She couldn't stay where she was, couldn't run without presenting a target.

A third blast, this time into the rear driver's side. The car rocked with the impact. She heard a door in the SUV open. They were getting out to finish it. Now, she thought.

She raised up, aimed the Glock over the roof of the Buick. The man with the shotgun stood there, lit by the streetlight. Shaven head, facial tattoo. She'd seen him at the stash house. He swung the muzzle toward her, and she fired twice, saw his head snap to the side. He fell back against the SUV, dropped the shotgun and slid to the pavement.

She aimed through the open door of the SUV, but the driver was gone. The rear windows were tinted. She couldn't see inside or through.

She steadied the Glock with both hands, waited. Would he come around the front or back? Were there more men inside, ready to open a side door, start firing?

The driver popped his head over the top of the SUV, pistol resting on the roof. She fired once to get him to duck, then lowered the muzzle and began shooting through the SUV's side windows. The smoked glass exploded and collapsed. She could see the driver on the other side, saw him take the impact of the bullets. She kept firing until he fell out of sight. The rear of the SUV was empty.

Shell casings clinked on the sidewalk behind her. Gunsmoke hung in the air. There'd been fifteen rounds in the Glock—fourteen in the magazine, one in the chamber. How many left?

She went around the front of the Buick. The man with the shotgun lay on his side. A rivulet of blood ran out from below him, shiny on the blacktop, coursed toward the gutter. She kicked the shotgun away, circled the SUV. The driver lay on his back, motionless, eyes open. She put a foot on his pistol, swept it into a storm drain.

In the Buick, Lopez was slumped over onto the passenger seat. He was dead or close to it. There was blood on the dashboard, the steering wheel, and what was left of the windshield. The fuel light still blinked red.

The rear door was pocked with buckshot holes. She pulled it open. Martinez lay still and silent on the floor. His own gun had slid partly out of his jacket pocket, the same model Glock as her own. She took it.

Headlights back at the cross street. She leaned into the car, hauled out the gear bag, swung the strap onto her shoulder.

A block ahead was another intersection, another blinking yellow light. To her right was a wide, unlit alley that ran behind a row of commercial buildings. Their storefronts would face onto that main street. High above, a bright half moon shone through thin clouds.

Headlights lit her, the vehicle coming fast. She took a last look at the Buick, then ran into the darkness of the alley.

Breathe. Think.

Fire escapes here, but their street-level ladders were raised and unreachable. She ran on, the bag thumping against her back. A cat darted from behind a dumpster, crossed her path and disappeared.

She heard a vehicle brake on the street behind her. If it turned into the alley, she'd be caught in its headlights. They'd send someone to the other end too, to cut her off, try to pin her between them.

Ahead on the left was a one-story brick building with a loading dock, a green dumpster and a pile of discarded tires beside it. The metal pull-down gate was covered with graffiti. On the dock was a single, 55-gallon metal drum. She stuck the Glock in her belt, tossed the bag onto the dock and climbed up after it.

There was a heavy padlock at the bottom of the gate. She tugged at it, but there was no give. She looked around, considered the dumpster for a moment. Knew that would be one of the first places they'd look.

No way in, and she couldn't go back. She felt the first sharp edge of panic. She tilted the barrel toward her, heard its contents slosh, smelled motor oil. The drum was half full. She swung and wheeled it closer to the gate, then scrambled atop it. It rocked unsteadily beneath her feet.

The roof was gravel and tarpaper, bordered on all sides by three limp strands of barbed-wire. Broken bottles glinted in the moonlight. There was a silent air conditioning unit in one corner, its grille dark with rust. A few feet away was a closed wooden hatch.

She climbed back down, the barrel shaking. She could hear urgent voices in Spanish on the street back there. They'd be coming this way soon.

Hoisting the gear bag to her shoulder, she climbed carefully back onto the barrel, almost overbalanced. She heaved the bag onto the barbed-wire strands, weighing them down, then crawled onto and over it. Pulling the bag free, she rolled away from the edge, the roof creaking under her.

She backed away farther, out of eyesight from below. Seven men at the stash house. She'd killed two at the SUV. By now they might have called for more men. Likely why they hadn't come down the alley yet. They were waiting for reinforcements.

She crawled toward the air conditioning unit, got her back to it, tried to slow her breathing. The Glock's magazine was empty, with a single round left in the chamber. She took the full clip from Martinez's gun, transferred it to her own, and slapped it home. She pulled the bag toward her, unzipped and opened it. His Glock, her mask and the empty magazine went inside.

She pointed her gun toward the edge of the roof, the butt resting on a thigh. There was nothing she could do about the drum. If they saw it, figured out what she'd done, then it would be all over. But she'd take out as many of them as she could before they got her.

With her left hand, she rifled through the money. Packs of bills, some bank-strapped, some bound with rubber bands. Street money, hundreds, fifties and twenties. She did a rough count in the moonlight. Maybe a hundred thousand altogether. Less than they'd expected. Lopez had said there might be as much as $300,000 at the stash house.

It hadn't been worth it. Lopez, Martinez and Adler all dead, and everything they'd planned gone to hell.

Headlights below. She looked over the edge of the roof, saw a dark SUV come to a stop just inside the alley. Its high-beams lit dumpsters, fire escapes and brick walls. A side door opened and two men got out, both carrying pistols. They'd search the alley on foot. The SUV stayed where it was, engine running.

She could hide here for now, wait them out. But soon they'd know she hadn't come out on any of the neighboring streets, was still somewhere on this block.

How far away was the transfer car? Would she even be able to find it? It was a banged-up Volvo wagon, inconspicuous enough not to draw attention, too old and ugly to invite theft. Lopez had stolen it the day before in Yonkers, cracked the steering column so the ignition could be easily hot-wired again. She'd shown Martinez and Adler how to do it. If something went wrong or they got separated, anyone who could make it to the transfer car would still have a chance of getting clear. But now there was only her.

She gripped the gun, rested the back of her head against the cool metal of the air conditioning unit, looked up at the moon and waited.

WHEN SHE LOOKED AT her watch again, it was one-thirty. A half hour had passed. The SUV was still there. They'd turned off the engine, but left on the headlights.

She crawled toward the front of the roof. The street was lined with dark stores, most with riot gates. No traffic. To the left, past the blinking yellow signal at the intersection, a storefront threw light on the sidewalk. Neon signs in the window read BURGERS PIZZA FRIED CHICKEN 24-HRS. There was a cab parked outside, no one at the wheel.

Stay or go? With the alley blocked, the only way out would be through the front, with the hope she could make it to the cab without being spotted, find the driver. Get away from here.

The other option was to wait until daylight. There would be more cars then, people. The searchers might have given up. But she didn't want to stay here in the meantime, trapped like some animal, her fate being decided by someone or something else.

She took two banded packs of money from the gear bag, stuffed them in her jacket pockets. The bag would be a burden, would slow her down. She'd have to leave it here, come back another time, hope no one found it in the interim.

She zipped the bag back up, wedged it behind the air conditioning unit, covered it with a loose piece of aluminum flashing. It would have to do. If they searched the roof and found it, it would just be her bad luck. There was nothing for it.

The hatch was locked from the inside, but it was old wood. She took out her buck knife, opened the three-inch blade and went to work on the hinges, slicing away wood until the screws were loose. She pulled the hinges free, then pried up that side of the hatch high enough that she could reach in. Her fingers found a bolt. She opened it, then lifted the entire hatch free, set it gently on the roof.

An iron ladder led down into darkness. The familiar smells of motor oil and rubber drifted up. She closed the knife, put it away, took out her penlight. She shone the beam inside, saw an oil-stained concrete floor, a lift pit with no lift. More tires. She switched off the light, put it away.

Go on, she thought. You can't stay here and wait for whatever's coming.

She tucked the Glock in her waistband, sat on the edge of the opening, swung her legs in, felt for the rungs with her feet. She let herself down slowly. Five rungs. Six. Her feet touched concrete.

To the front was a bay door, a single window set high in its center letting in streetlight. On the other side of the lift pit, an open doorway led to an office.

She circled the pit, staying out of the light. Inside the office was a battered metal desk and filing cabinet. The cabinet's drawers were open and empty. The desktop was filmed with dust. On the floor was an auto parts calendar from 2015.

She took out the Glock, held it at her side. A wide-gridded riot gate covered the front window, faint streetlight coming through. To the right of it was a glass door in a recessed doorway, with cardboard taped over a missing panel. From here, she had a clear view of the street in both directions. There was only one pole light working on the block, maybe twenty feet to her left. Beyond that, across the intersection, was the bright storefront. The cab was still there.

Headlights from the right. She stepped away from the door, back into the shadows, watched a dark Navigator approach and slow.

She took steady breaths. *Don't panic*, she thought. *Watch. Wait.*

Another pair of lights came from the opposite direction. It was a low-slung two-door Acura. The vehicles stopped abreast of each other, window to window, the drivers talking. The car drove off.

The Navigator crossed the intersection, pulled up behind the taxi. Three men she hadn't seen before got out and went inside the restaurant. After a few minutes they emerged, and got back in the Navigator. She watched it pull away.

They might be doing circles, grids, looking for her. The Acura too. One or more of them might be coming back this way before long. It was time to move.

With her left hand, she unlocked the door. It had swollen in its frame, wouldn't open. She pulled hard, shook it. It rattled and creaked as it came free. Cool night air flowed in. She put the Glock in her pocket, kept her hand on it.

Outside, she cut left up the sidewalk, walking fast, but not running. She crossed the street, stayed close to the storefronts on the other side. Ahead, the yellow light blinked, lit the blacktop.

On the other side of the intersection, she stopped short of the restaurant, looked through a side window. It was bright and stark inside. Plastic tables and chairs, a counter window with thick bulletproof glass. Behind it, a young black man in a white t-shirt and apron was texting on a phone, thumbs busy.

A single table was occupied. A thin, dark-skinned man with glasses and graying hair was reading a newspaper.

She tried the rear door of the cab, wanting to get in, out of sight. It was locked. She went up to the window near where the man sat, tapped a knuckle on the glass. The second time she did it, he looked up from his paper. The counter man had put down his phone, was watching her.

She pointed at the cab. The thin man nodded briskly, took off his glasses and stowed them in a jacket pocket. He got up, left the newspaper on the table.

She waited beside the taxi, looking in both directions. No headlights, no police cruisers, no sirens.

The thin man came outside. "Miss, may I help you?"

He had an accent she couldn't place, West Africa or somewhere in the Caribbean.

"I need a ride," she said. "To somewhere not far from here."

He looked around, then back at her. "Are you alone?"

"Yes." Her breathing grew faster. She wanted to get in the cab, off the street.

"Where are you coming from?" he said.

"Queens. My car broke down. Can we go?"

With her left hand, she worked loose a bill from the pack. Her other hand stayed on the gun.

She folded the bill, held it out. It was a hundred.

"Just a few blocks," she said. "But we need to leave now."

He looked in the direction the Navigator had gone, then at her, the hand still in her pocket.

"Now," she said. "Let's go. Please."

He took out keys, hit the remote button, unlocked the cab. The headlights blipped.

"Of course," he said. "Anywhere you want."

* * *

SHE WATCHED THE SIGNS on the deserted streets they passed, giving him directions through the grid in the Plexiglass divider. When they came to a block that looked familiar, she said, "Slow down."

She recognized the neighborhood now. Warehouses, muffler shops and garages. Ahead was the side street where they'd left the Volvo. A dark White Castle on the corner had been their landmark.

"Turn left up there," she said.

From a wide alley on the right, an SUV charged out, blocked the street. The Navigator. The taxi driver braked hard, sounded the horn, stopped when he saw the men spilling out of the Navigator into the cab's headlights.

She threw herself across the back seat, clawed at the passenger door handle, just as the first shots came through the cab's windshield. She got the door open, tumbled out onto the ground. The cab was still rolling. It thumped solidly into the side of the Navigator.

She pulled out the Glock, brought it up. Three men were still shooting into the cab, glass and upholstery exploding. They'd hadn't seen her get out.

She stood, took one of them down with a center-mass chest shot, swung her muzzle toward the next one, fired and missed. The round blew out a side window in the Navigator. The two men dropped down behind the cover of the cab.

Farther down the street behind her, another vehicle was coming fast. The Acura. She ran into the alley the Navigator had come out of, heard the pop of guns behind her. A bullet ricocheted off the pavement to her right. She cut across the alley into a vacant lot, ran through thigh-high weeds. More shots. Something tugged at the tail of her jacket.

The Acura turned down the alley after her. There were men on foot as well, coming through the weeds. But she was away from the street lamps now, and they had no clear target. She hurdled an overturned shopping cart, and then she was back on cracked sidewalk, another empty street, this one wider. There was an elevated roadway ahead, cars speeding along it, a dark underpass below. She heard the men behind her, didn't look back.

She crossed the street, ran for the shadows of the underpass, cars humming above. The Acura turned left, caught her in its headlights. She made the underpass, lungs burning, came out on the other side. There on the right was a lot full of tractor trailers, surrounded by a high fence topped with razor wire. Parked in front of the closed gate, facing away from her, was a police cruiser.

She stumbled onto the weedy shoulder at the fence's far corner, about thirty feet behind the cruiser. She couldn't breathe. To her right, a dirt access road ran parallel to the overpass.

The cruiser's interior light was on. A uniformed cop sat behind the wheel, drinking from a styrofoam cup.

The Acura emerged from the underpass, the front passenger window gliding down. The car slowed and came to a stop, headlamps illuminating the cruiser. The uniform turned to look back at it. Traffic rumbled by above.

The Acura didn't move. After a minute, the window slid closed again, and the car made a long, slow u-turn away from the cruiser. Giving up.

She raised the Glock above her head and squeezed the trigger three times. The sharp cracks split the night. The Acura's tires squealed as it pulled away fast. The cruiser's rollers flashed into life, and the cop swung it into a hard U-turn, headed after the car, siren rising and falling.

Across the street, the lot was empty.

She sat down in the dirt of the access road, couldn't seem to get enough air. Head between her knees, she resisted the urge to be sick. She put the Glock away, felt the right side of her jacket, the rent where a bullet had passed through the material without touching her. Pure luck, she thought. The only reason you're alive.

From the access road, an embankment led up to the overpass. She started up it, heard another siren. A second cruiser sped past below, lights rolling, following the first. Backup.

Once on the elevated roadway, there was a shoulder wide enough to walk on. A car flew past, so close she felt its slipstream. Another slowed, beeped its horn, came abreast of her. She put a hand on the Glock in her pocket. A man yelled something at her from the passenger side window, then the car sped up and passed her.

She walked on. There was a major intersection ahead, where the highway dropped down to cross another main road. On one side of the road was a dark strip mall. On the other, a three-story building with a bright lobby, and a sign above it that read PARKWAY MOTOR INN.

She let two cars pass, then sprinted across the road toward the motel. The parking lot was less than half full. She stopped to get her breath back, brushed grit and dirt from her clothes as best she could.

She gripped the big silver handle of the glass door, pulled. It wouldn't open. Inside the lobby, a turbaned clerk stood behind thick glass at the front desk. He frowned at her.

Wearily, she took out the hundred she'd offered the cab driver, unfolded it and pressed it against the glass. She held it there, waited. The door buzzed.

She opened it and went in. She was done running.

THE CLERK TOOK THE two hundreds she gave him without a word, offered no change and asked for no ID. A key card attached to a diamond-shaped piece of green plastic came back in the pass-through slot. Room 110.

The lobby smelled of stale cigarette smoke and disinfectant. There was a skinny ATM near the front desk counter, a couple of worn chairs, and planters full of dusty plastic flowers.

She went down the orange-carpeted hallway. An ice machine rattled in an alcove at the end of the corridor. She heard grunting from behind a door she passed.

The room was as she'd expected. Mirror on the ceiling over the bed. Dresser and night stand, a single chair, and no windows. White shag carpet, and a TV bolted to a brace on the wall. The cigarette smell was strong in here as well.

A door led to an adjoining room. The connecting door was locked. She put an ear to it. No sound inside. She closed her door again, bolted it.

The bathroom was small, the sink mineral-stained. She realized then how thirsty she was, ran water, cupped some and drank, then spit it out. It tasted of metal.

The chair went against the hall door, the top rail wedged under the knob. It would give her warning at least, if the clerk or someone else with a key tried to come in. Then she took the Glock into the bathroom, set it on the toilet tank, undressed and showered, let the spray wash the last bits of safety glass from her hair, the tension from her shoulders. She would be sore and aching tomorrow.

When she was done, she dried off with a towel that smelled like burnt hair, dressed again. She checked the doors a final time, then sat on the edge of the bed. She thought about the cab driver. He was dead, almost certainly, and for no other reason than he had tried to help her.

She stretched out atop the comforter, not trusting the sheets, looked at her watch. Three a.m. Only three hours since they'd gone in the back door of the stash house. You're alive, she thought, and a lot of people aren't.

She needed sleep. Tomorrow she'd get a cab to take her into Manhattan. From Penn Station, she'd catch a train south to New Jersey and home. It wouldn't be safe to go back for the money tomorrow. They'd still be looking for her. She'd have to wait, return another time, hope it was still there when she did.

She moved the Glock to the bed, in easy reach. She was too tired to turn out the lights, too tired to do anything. She looked up at her reflection, and closed her eyes.

SHE WOKE IN SILENCE, not sure why, raised her watch. Four-thirty.

Muscles stiff, she slid off the bed, picked up the Glock, went to the hall door and listened. Outside, the hum of the ice machine. Then, from the direction of the lobby, the quiet voices of men, too low for her to make out the words. After a moment, she realized they were speaking Spanish. Her stomach tightened.

She slipped on the jacket and gloves, pocketed the Glock, got out her knife. She went to the adjoining door. Still no sound from the other side. She worked the blade into the jamb of the inner door, pried at the deadbolt. The wood there was soft. The door opened easily.

This room was the mirror image of hers. She went in, closed both connecting doors behind her. On the far side of the room was another door. She used the knife again. The next room had the same setup, but this time no connecting door. It was the last room in the hall.

She closed the knife, went to the hall door, looked through the spyhole, got a distorted, fisheye view of the hallway, the vending alcove with the ice machine. Next to it a stairwell door.

She took out the Glock, held her breath. The voices down the hall had quieted. Easing the door open, she looked back toward 110. Three Dominicans stood outside the door. One of them held a gun to the back of the turbaned clerk's head. The clerk slid a keycard into the reader, and when the door unlocked, they tried to push him inside, met the resistance of the chair. One of them hit the door with his shoulder, knocked it open. She heard the chair fall. They shoved the clerk inside, crowded in behind him. The third man stayed in the hall.

"Hey," she said, and raised the Glock.

He turned toward her, gun coming up, and she fired, hit him in the shoulder. It spun him around and dropped him. She ran to the fire door, slammed her hip into the panic bar, found herself in a dim concrete stairwell. To the left, stairs ran up. Straight ahead, another fire door, this one leading outside, with a sign that read EMERGENCY EXIT ONLY! ALARM WILL SOUND!

Shots from down the hall. A round hit the door frame behind her. She kicked the bar with the sole of her foot, jolted it open. An alarm began to bleat loudly. Outside was the rear parking lot. The way they'd expect her to go.

She took the stairs two at a time. At the third landing was a shorter flight that led to the roof. The alarm kept on, echoed through the stairwell.

Another door, another panic bar. Then she was out on a blacktop roof. She could see the lights of the highway, the overpass. Far to the west, the glow of Manhattan.

In the front lot, three dark SUVs were idling near the entrance, headlights on. One of them was the Navigator. She could see the missing window, the collision damage. Another car pulled into the lot behind them. The Acura.

People were stumbling out of the lobby doors into the lot now, some half dressed, unsure what to do, where to go. There were sirens in the distance.

From the side of the roof, a fire escape ran down, its last level a hinged ladder. Flashing lights came down the highway and across the overpass, a fire engine and a police cruiser. They pulled into the lot.

She put away the Glock, swung out onto the fire escape, went down quickly. On the bottom rungs, her weight carried the hinged section down. She dropped the last couple feet to the pavement, landed wrong. Her ankle twisted under her, and she fell hard. A surge of pain ran up her leg.

Now the night was filled with sirens, people shouting, and the steady blare of the fire alarm. She got to her feet, braced herself against the wall, tested the ankle. It hurt, but would bear her weight. She limped to the front corner of the building. Two fire trucks in the lot now, another cruiser. Red and blue lights bathed the vehicles, the people milling around.

The Acura and two of the SUVs were blocked in by the trucks. The third one, a dark Chevy Tahoe, was about fifteen feet from her, parked away from the others, engine running. The passenger door was ajar, the seat there empty. She could see the man at the wheel.

Pain flashing in her foot, she limped across the distance. When she reached the Tahoe, she pulled the door wider, pointed the Glock inside.

The driver turned, saw the gun. Before he could react, she swung up and into the seat, pulled the door shut behind her. "Drive."

It was one of the men from the stash house, who'd fired at them as they ran in the alley. He was younger than the others, with long hair slicked back. When he didn't respond, she aimed the gun at his groin. "Your call."

The interior of the Tahoe was washed in emergency lights, red, blue, and red again.

"You gonna pull that trigger?" he said, "All these cops around? I don't think so."

"I'm betting in all this confusion, no one notices. You want to find out?"

An automatic was wedged between the driver's seat and the console, a 9 mm Steyr. She pulled it out, put it in her left coat pocket.

"You the one we been chasing, eh?" he said. "Didn't think it would be a woman."

She cocked the Glock's hammer for effect. "Go."

He looked at her, then reversed, swung the Tahoe around clear of the emergency vehicles, pointed it out of the lot. Through the motel doors, she could see the lobby was full of firefighters and cops. There were horns blowing as people were trying to leave, their cars blocked in.

The Tahoe bumped onto the highway, turned right. Another cruiser, lights and siren going, passed them from the opposite direction, turned into the lot.

"Where?" he said. Staying cool.

"Just drive."

She tried to calm herself, figure out her next move. They were headed east, deeper into Brooklyn, the streets empty, the sirens fading behind them. Ahead on the right was the empty lot of a darkened pancake house.

She pointed. "Pull over in there."

He slowed, glided into the lot.

"Kill the lights," she said. "And get out."

He turned off the headlights, looked at her. "You the one got the money?"

She didn't answer.

"If you didn't, you know where it is, right?"

"Why?"

"Maybe I make you a deal."

She lowered the hammer on the Glock. "Like what?"

"You take me to it. You give me half. Then I take you wherever you want to go."

"What about your bosses?"

"Fuck 'em."

She looked at him, weighing it. "Why should I trust you?"

"You got the guns. What do I have?"

"A lot of balls, rip off your own people that way."

"Money's money."

"Half is too much for just a ride."

"A ride and a lie. You held a gun on me, was nothing I could do. I let you out somewhere up the road, don't know where you went. Part of it's true, right?"

"You think they'll believe that?"

"They'll have to, won't they?"

"Or I could just shoot you and take your ride. Not give you anything."

"You could do that. But I don't think you will."

In the console compartment, a cellphone began to buzz.

"They're looking for me already," he said. "Soon they're gonna know what happened."

He was right. It would only be a matter of time before someone found them.

"Put it in Park," she said.

He did, turned to her. "What do you say?"

"Get out."

"You're making a mistake."

"Out."

He opened the door, stepped down. With the Glock still on him, she climbed over the console and into the drivers seat.

"They'll never stop looking for you," he said. "And when they find you . . . You'll be begging them to kill you. But first you'll give up the money. And then you'll have nothing, *puta*. Not even your life."

She thought about Adler and Martinez and Lopez. The cab driver. Everything she'd been through tonight.

"It'll be bad for you," he said. "And it'll go on for a long time."

"I believe you," she said, and shot him.

SHE LEFT THE TAHOE on a dark street in Bay Ridge, two blocks from the Verrazano, keys still in the ignition. She walked down to the bayfront, squeezed through a hole in a chain-link fence, reached the cracked seawall. She tossed the two guns out into the water. The sky to the east had lightened to a pale blue.

She walked until she found a subway station, took the R train into Manhattan. Three hours later, she was home.

"SLOW DOWN UP HERE," she said. "But don't stop."

She powered the Towncar's rear window halfway down. The tire shop was ahead on the right. More people around now, more traffic, but a lot of the storefronts were still dark, riot gates in place, businesses that were gone for good.

Luis, the driver, looked at her in the rearview. "This isn't a good area. Even in the daytime. I know. I used to live here."

"Go around the block again."

She looked at the shop's recessed entrance as they passed. No one inside she could see, the door still closed.

She'd waited two days to come back, taken the train up from home. At Penn Station in Manhattan, she'd called a car service from a burner cell, used a fake name.

They circled the block, came back around.

"Pull up here," she said.

He steered the Towncar to the curb. She looked at the shop door, the darkness beyond it, wondered what waited for her there.

Three possibilities. The money was still here, hadn't been found. Or the Dominicans had searched the building and roof, taken it. Or they were there in the tire shop now, or somewhere close by, watching, waiting for someone to come back.

The Towncar stuck out here. It would look wrong to have it standing outside the shop too long.

"Wait five minutes," she said. "Then come back to get me." She opened her door.

"Maybe you should tell me what this is all about."

"Five minutes," she said. "That's all it will take. One way or the other."

She shut the door behind her. Her gloved right hand went to the .32 Beretta Tomcat in the pocket of her leather car coat. She limped into the doorway of the tire shop. Behind her, the Towncar pulled back into traffic.

She tried the knob. It was still unlocked. Inside, she eased the door shut behind her, drew the Tomcat.

The office was as she'd left it. In the bay, a shaft of light came through the roof hatch, lit dust motes. She went to the ladder, listened. No voices, no footsteps.

Up the ladder to the roof. It was empty. To the west, an airliner traced a white line across the sky.

She made her way to the air conditioning unit, pulled back the flashing, and there was the gear bag. She knelt, unzipped it. The money was inside, along with Martinez's gun, and the empty magazine. Her mask. Everything there.

She zipped the bag back up, slung it over her shoulder, stuck the Tomcat in her belt, climbed down the ladder.

Back in the office, she stood just inside the door, watched the street, the cars going by, feeling exposed. She glanced at her watch. Five minutes since Luis had dropped her off.

A dark SUV with smoked windows pulled up outside. She backed farther into the office shadows, took out the Tomcat. The SUV stayed there. She waited for someone to get out, come inside. She raised the gun.

Horns blew. The SUV drove on. Two minutes later, the Towncar slid to the curb.

Deep breath. She put the gun away, opened the door. The front passenger window came down. Luis leaned over. "Sorry. Traffic. Everything okay?"

She went out quickly, ignoring the pain in her ankle. There was no sign of the SUV. She opened the rear door of the Towncar, tossed in the gear bag, climbed in after it, and pulled the door shut.

She met his eyes in the rearview.

"Just something that belonged to me," she said. "Something I had to leave behind."

"And now?"

"Let's go back to Penn."

He waited for a break in traffic, then made a U-turn across both lanes, headed back the way they'd come. She looked out the rear window. No SUV, no one following them.

They passed the all-night restaurant, crowded now, a line at the counter. She'd ask Rathka, her lawyer, to find out the cab driver's name, if he had family. If so, she'd figure out a way to get part of the money to them. It was all she could do, but it wasn't enough. No amount would ever be enough.

"Luis, do me a favor?"

"Sure. What?"

She took four hundreds from her pocket, leaned over the seat and held them out. "Tell your dispatcher when you got the call to pick me up, there was no one there."

He looked at the bills.

"You never brought me out here. You never saw me at all," she said. "Can you deal with that?"

"That's a lot of money."

"Can you?"

He hesitated. "I think so."

"Then that's good for both of us. Take it."

He did.

She sat back, looked out the window at the streets passing by, kept one hand on the gear bag.

"Glad you didn't hang around too long back there," he said. "That's a rough neighborhood."

"I know," she said.

THE CUCUZZA CURSE

BY THOMAS PLUCK

THE FLAMES DANCED IN Vito Ferro's rheumy eyes as the intense heat blistered the skin black. The brick beehive of the Neapolitan pizza oven at full fire was as hot as a crematorium, and cooked a pie to perfection in under seven minutes. This gave the crust a crispness on the teeth but left chew in the dough, and melted the sliced rounds of bone-white mozzarella without boiling the bright acidity out of the tomato sauce, like a steel oven would.

"Looks about done, right Uncle Veet?" His grandnephew Peter worked runnels into his soft knuckles with his thumbs, kneading invisible worry beads.

Peter was smart, a college boy—unlike Vito's *stronzo* sons—but he chattered when outside of his element.

Vito snapped callused fingers, and Peter slid the wooden paddle, the pizza peel, beneath the pie and brought it to the work counter, where he cut it into uneven eighths with jerky, hesitant thrusts of the roller.

Vito studied the pie solemnly.

His family proudly called themselves Catholics, but their true religion was food. Pizza, in particular. Vito had made a covenant with the god of the oven paid for in toil. In the oven he had built with his own hands, a transfiguration occurred, turning a little flour and water topped with tomato sauce and cheese into a meal that made customers line down the block for hours, and his family lived like barons had in the old country.

Vito slapped Peter on the shoulder. "*Bene. Mangia.*"

The kid pulled off a slice and bit into it with pride. "It's good!"

Vito remembered when he'd made his first pie back in Napoli, and felt a little twinge in his chest. He took a slice and noted the droop of the the triangle. The center was the hardest to get right. Too often they were soft and watery. He closed his eyes and chewed slow.

The burning began as a small pill of pain at the back of his throat, then blossomed into fiery agony, as if he'd eaten a spoonful of hot coals from the oven. He ran for the galvanized sink and drank from the faucet like a dog to quench the grease fire in his mouth. Sweat ran down his face and he collapsed to the floor.

HE WOKE TO PETER fanning him with an apron. When he could talk without agony, he dialed the phone. Hoping he would get no answer. Vito didn't know what frightened him more—the curse or Aldo Quattrocchi, the mafiosi who'd lent him thirty thousand dollars to open the restaurant, even though he was of an age where he shouldn't buy green bananas.

"CALM DOWN," THE VOICE chilled his ear like he'd opened the deep freeze. "I'll send the *Gagootza*."

Stately, tanned Joey Cucuzza, resplendent in a tailored slate suit, pink shirt with its collar open to frame a red Italian horn pendant shaped like a dog dick, listened while the ancient pizza-man beseeched him.

Vito scratched his sunken, gray-haired chest through a sweat-soaked white undershirt.

"You burnt your tongue on a slice of pizza?" Joey fixed things for Aldo Quattrocchi, a captain in the broken family of northern Jersey crime. He had come directly from his no-work job at Port Newark, where he read the newspapers and day-traded when he wasn't at the gym, out to lunch with the dock boss, or enjoying a nooner in the apartment he kept in Ironbound.

Or visiting Aldo's Newark subjects, who expected protection for their payments of street tax.

"I explain." Vito took a grayed rag from the pocket of his chinos and mopped his face.

Vito Ferro was a northern New Jersey institution, the first to make Neapolitan style pies, and had paid street tax on his first shop in Hoboken long before Joey and Aldo were born. Aldo could be sentimental when he wasn't telling you to tack someone's fingertips to a table with finishing nails.

He wouldn't send Joey for that kind of job. They had apes for that. Joey was here because he knew people, and he knew *people.* Now touching forty, he had come up as a runner for an uncle who ran gay bars for the Jewish mob in Manhattan. He had a reputation as a reasonable if foppish good earner with an even temper, respected by men of violence and friendly enough to be a face with the citizens.

"Got any coffee?" Joey nodded toward the shiny pipeworks of the espresso machine.

"It's not hooked up yet." The nephew swallowed spit. College boy had locks of brown curls like a Greek shepherd, no ring, and a nice physique. Eyebrows tweezed, with intelligent eyes above a slack jaw. Hands too soft for labor.

Joey wondered how the kid wound up here.

"How exactly are you spending Mister Quattrocchi's money?" They'd had the thirty grand for six weeks. You paid your first month on receipt, but they would be late for the next unless business picked up soon.

"I had the oven brought brick by brick from Napoli," Peter said. "It's the same one Uncle Veet used in his first pizzeria. It took me a week to find the place. They don't speak the Italian I learned in school."

Vito winced and sipped milk like he was nursing an ulcer.

Joey had visited Napoli to broker a deal with the *Camorra* for containers half-filled with fake Gucci handbags and half with young Slovenian women, and the mangled street Italian he'd learned growing up served him well. He'd also picked up a snobbery for classic Neapolitan pizza, and after Vito retired, no one else came close. His sons were clowns in comparison.

"They put up a wall around the oven, turned the place into some Irish pub."

"My sons, they do this," Vito sneered. "I retire, give them my business, and they do this to me. *Disgraciata!*" He drew into himself with shame, then curled back two fingers of his right hand and spat between the horns of pointer and pinky finger. "It is the *mal occhio*."

The evil eye.

Joey touched the *cornuto,* the Italian horn at his throat.

His family was only three generations from the old country, where people were still killed over such things.

"I tell Aldo that, and he's gonna say 'Old Vito is *pazzo*,' and you know what they do to mad dogs, Mister Vito."

Vito spread the dollop of saliva into the black and white tiles with the sole of his black loafer. "I bite into the pizza from that oven, it burns me. Tell him, Pietro."

Peter shrugged helplessly. "He looked like he was dying, Mister Cucuzza."

Joey buffed manicured nails on his slacks. "Why don't you make me a pie while you tell me the history of the world part one."

Vito took a risen ball of dough from a tray in the refrigerator. The short old man was bent and his skin was crepe paper, but his forearms flexed as he tossed the dough. He made quick work of it, then sat to tell the story in the seven minutes of baking.

He wrung his apron in his hands. Embarrassed and afraid, sure of his fate.

Joey listened to the story, even though he'd read it in the newspaper. One son had sued the other over use of the name Original Vito's Neapolitan Pizza. A reality show was pitched. It became a joke. Vito had enough, coming out of retirement to save his good name.

Except he didn't have any money.

Like many who came over, Vito had no papers, never applied for a social security number. Everything legit was in his wife's name, and when she succumbed to cancer, it went to their sons, Sal and Nunzio. When he retired, his boys took everything but the house he lived in, left him squeaking by on his wife's social security check. No more new Cadillacs every year for Vito.

"*Scumbari*," the old man said.

So he went to Aldo, who like most guys his age from Hoboken, loved Frank Sinatra, Fiore's mozzarella, and Vito Ferro's Neapolitan pizza.

Vito slid out the pie and cut it with quick swipes of the roller.

Joey folded a slice and took a bite. No fires of hell. Only fresh marinara, the tart milky taste of Fiore's handmade mozzarella cheese, and Vito's perfect crust. He grunted in appreciation.

"Have one, Mister Vito."

Vito looked at the pie as if it were a rattlesnake coiled on the wooden pizza peel. "No, Giuseppe. I have the *mal occhio* on me. And it comes from my own sons." He gripped his chest to remove the invisible knife from his heart.

Protection was protection. "We'll help you, Mister Vito."

IN THE AIR CONDITIONED LEATHER confines of his red Alfa Romeo sedan, Joey called his mother.

"Joseph." Kitchen sounds and Animal Planet in the background. "To what do I owe the honor?"

He'd missed two Sundays in a row. She was probably getting ready to put a *mal occhio* on him. "Ma. I told you, the port's open Sundays this month."

It was, but Joey had been in Provincetown, eating littleneck clams and working on his tan.

"You could come Wednesdays. Your uncle comes over for pasta."

They were both at the age where old stories played on repeat. Once a week more than enough. "Hey Ma, you remember the crier at great-grandpa Nick's funeral? Witch Nose."

His great-grandfather had raised goats. All Joey remembered besides the funeral was that he both looked and smelled like a billy goat, and from the family gossip, he was hornier than one.

"Angelina. She always liked you."

"She still crying, or did she shuffle off to Buffalo?" Their family euphemism for death.

"No one uses criers any more."

True. They'd hired them for her grandfather because he'd been a nasty old prick who gelded billy goats with knife and a pair of pliers, and beat his sons for growing bigger than him.

The criers had been unnecessary. All his mistresses showed up, a half dozen of the heftiest Italian widows of Nutley, crying like six operas going on at once. His mother had been mortified.

"She made the best *pignoli* until she got the arthritis. She's still on the old street. Next to where Raffiola lived." Old person directions. He knew the house.

"You got her number?"

"No, but where's she gonna go? She's all alone. Like how I'm gonna be when a crane falls on you."

"Thanks, Ma. I'll be there Sunday. Unless a crane falls on me."

"Don't talk like that." She clucked her tongue. He could see her make the sign of the cross.

JOEY'S OLD NEIGHBORHOOD OF Avondale had been handed down by the Italians to the next generation of immigrants. The two-story, green or white siding homes were so close together that you could climb out one window into your neighbor's for surreptitious infidelity. After his old man copped a croak, his mother sold the creaky hand-built house and bought a condo.

Instead of Bon Jovi blaring from the stereo of an IROC Camaro,

"Despacito" warbled from an open window, but little else had changed. The men were away at work, the kids were in school, and the women worked side hustles in the kitchens, watched toddlers, ran a sewing machine. He parked on the sidewalk in front of a house with ancient grapevines strangling a trellis over the backyard.

The wooden front door was painted shut and dead-bolted. It had probably never been opened except to move in furniture generations ago. The skinny driveway held a lemon-colored K-car on four flat tires, cardboard boxes stuffed to the windows. Behind it, three cracked concrete steps with a railing made of lead plumbing pipe led to a storm door that left white powder on his knuckles when he rapped on it. He heard a voice, then steps.

He studied Angelina's yard while he waited. A rotting wine press, a wooden barrel topped with greasy rainwater. Ivy covered the chainlink fence, and pale green baseball bats of Italian squash dangled nearly four feet to the ground.

Cucuzza.

His phallic namesake squash, which had led to the playground taunts that tempered his mettle. The early battles taught him into a peacemaker until a growth spurt turned him into a rangy bloodier of noses.

A hunched form opened the inside door, and a wizened face jabbed a pointy chin his way.

"*Buongiorn* Guiseppe," she said, and shuffled back into the kitchen. "Your mother say you come."

So Ma had her number, but wanted him to visit the old broad.

With arthritic fingers like the tangled white roots of a pulled root, she stirred the heady contents of a pot with a wooden spoon. A translucent crescent of squash rose to the top.

Cucuzza. Of course.

His father had loved it cooked with potatoes, hot peppers, and tomato sauce in a peasant stew called *giambotta*. Joey would sop up the sauce with bread, ignoring the watery squash until he took a cuff to the ear.

"Sit, eat."

He dusted a vinyl chair with his pocket square and sat while she poured black coffee from a glass percolator and set out a plate of *pizzelle*, delicate waffle-shaped cookies snow-dusted with confectioner's sugar.

He went through the rituals of politeness, asked of family, listened to her aches and troubles. Her hand was cold when she touched his wrist, her eyes bright.

"Angelina, I need you to tell me how to free somebody from the evil eye."

Her eyes turned steely serious. "I show you."

He left with a Corning-ware dish of stewed cucuzza and half of a long Italian loaf from Vitiello's bakery.

Back in the kitchen of Vito's Original Classic Neapolitan Pizza Pies, Vito stared at a steel mixing bowl filled with water. The kid was up front working the sparse lunch crowd, stumbling occasionally but eager to prove himself. Joey set a green bottle of olive oil next to the bowl.

"Three drops in the water. One at a time."

Angelina had told him that someone unburdened by the *fascina*, the hold of the evil eye, would create three separate drops. He tried it himself in her kitchen.

Vito scratched at his belly, then tilted the bottle over the water.

One drop. Then two, three golden pearls floated atop the water in a lazy spin.

They leaned in close.

Slowly, the drops found each other and made a single orb that resembled nothing less than the yellow eye of the devil himself.

They hadn't waited for the water to settle, Joey thought. But it didn't matter. Vito thought he was cursed, and the olive oil affirmed his belief.

And he'd believe in the cure.

Joey handed him a can of Morton's salt.

"Shake some in, say an Our Father. Do that three times."

Vito beseeched him with his pouchy eyes. Joey prayed with him in Italian, silently hoping that he wouldn't burst into flames.

"Now we do the test again?"

"Don't tempt fate, Vito." He gripped the old man's shoulder, still strong. "Angelina says you are free of the *fascina*."

Vito winced at the word, then hugged him.

Joey wished such wards worked, but in his experience human nature was stronger than magic. He dropped his flour-speckled suit coat off at the dry cleaner, and brought Angelina's dish to the office at the port, where the boys scarfed it down.

"It's Cucuzza's cucuzza!" one *gavone* bellowed around a mouthful.

Joey grabbed the crotch of his summer suit. "Eat *this* cucuzza."

They laughed as he told them the story. One asked him to put the *mal occhio* on his mother in-law. He went to his office to finish reading the papers and trade stocks before closing.

ALDO CALLED HIM THE next morning, crabbier than usual. Joey talked him down. They hadn't met this week, and Aldo had a sit-down that afternoon, which always gave him the *agita*.

"I feel like *I* got hit with the *mal occhio*. You wanna drizzle some olive oil and find out?"

"After the meet. You got this. You're a golden god."

"I don't feel like one."

"You will tonight."

"Speaking of evil eyes, you gotta see Vito again. He's busting my balls. Why'd I give that old fuck my number? He should be calling you."

"You wanted the quick vig on thirty gees. Doing street work, when you're the big *capita cazzo*."

"It's easy money. That vig paid for your new coat."

"When do I see this coat?"

"The apartment. Wear it today. *Ciao*."

* * *

Joey wore the two-button pale blue silk Isaia sport coat over faded gray jeans and a matching snug shirt.

Peter stoked the oven, raking the coals with a shovel.

Vito stared into a bowl of oil-dotted water. "I can't cook anymore. Tell Mister Quattrocchi to take my business. I die soon."

"Talk to me."

The old man flicked his eyes toward his grandnephew.

"Wait outside kid," Joey said. "Go play on your phone."

He flinched, but left under the withering stare.

Vito told him, in stuttering broken English. "Today, I see the face of the dead."

Joey held back the look that said he was *pazzo.*

"My family is from Bari. My uncles, they were fisherman who go to America, but my mother and father run a little restaurant by the water."

Joey prepared for more ancient history.

"We fed the soldiers. Italian, then English and American. Then the Germans raid the harbor with screaming bomber planes. One ship was full of mustard gas. The Americans say no, but the gas rolled in and kill my family."

He looked down. "My mother put a wet towel over my face, but she breathe in too much."

"*Condoglianze.*"

"I am orphan. The Americans put me on a train to Napoli. I apprentice in a pizzeria, make good money. So I come here."

That morning, he came to make dough and sauce, and was met with a blast of heat and a glow from the oven.

"The oven was flaming like the fires of hell. A young girl stirring the coals. She screams at me, tears gold chains from her neck and throws them in the fire." His eyes went away, like he was talking about the past.

"She scoop up the coals in her hand and throws them at me."

He held up his apron. It was scorched with a black mark, burned with a scatter of pinholes like a shotgun blast.

"I drive home, pray the rosary. Peter calls me, asks why I leave the door unlocked. I come back, everything is clean. The oven is empty."

"Who was she?"

Vito pulled a gold chain from his shirt and kissed the large pendant of Jesus wearing the crown of thorns. "The evil eye, showing me my family in hell. Lies, to hurt me."

Joey looked into the bowl. The gleaming oil stared back as one big eye.

"Make your pies, Mister Vito. I'll fix this."

Outside, he found the kid leaning on the bricks, one knee bent like a flamingo as he thumbed his phone. He looked too much of a chooch to be pulling one over on anybody. And what motive? He was partners with the crazy old bastard. If they couldn't pay the vig, one of Aldo's apes would break his clean-shaven arms.

"You like slinging pizza dough for a living?"

Peter shrugged. "Uncle Veet put me through college after my father died from 9/11. He was a fireman. Took a ferry over to help dig for weeks. It got into his lungs."

Joey nodded. They had watched the towers go down from Newark harbor, helpless.

"You see anything when you got here this morning?"

The kid shook his head, eyes rattling like dice. "The oven was empty."

"Think maybe your uncle's got oldtimer's disease?" Joey switched gears to dockworker talk. He liked smart people thinking he was ignorant and easily fooled.

"You mean Alzheimer's? He doesn't forget a thing, Mister C. He's as good with numbers as I am, and I have a degree in Finance. I took a little psych, too. He's got a lot guilt. My uncles broke his heart."

Family shit. The only think Joey hated more than eating cucuzza was dealing with other people's family shit.

He thought about it in the privacy of the Alfa Romeo as the Beastie Boys rapped about Shadrach, Meshach, and Abednego on the stereo.

Guilt meant lies. He could lean on the old man, but *vecchioni* could be stubborn. What scared people of that age was more frightening than pain or death.

The sons would talk. They couldn't want Vito's competition. There were a thousand pizza joints in Jersey, but one more Original Vito's Neapolitan Pizzas diluted the brand. And the old man had public sympathy.

JOEY KILLED A FEW hours at the port listening to the dock boss complain, then drove over the black steel dinosaur skeleton of the Pulaski skyway into the lesser hell of late morning traffic. An hour later he emerged in the labyrinth of huddled four-story brick buildings that was Hoboken. The neighborhood had gentrified into a sixth borough of New York, a haven for frat boys and trust fund kids who skipped Williamsburg after draining it dry of cool.

He parked in front of a hydrant next to a beauty spa and walked the block. Four old men held court at a card table next to a stoop and watched the neighborhood. Ground down by life, sandpaper stubble chins defying their morning shaves. Two of them tightened up at his approach, another puffed a black cigar that smelled like feet.

"Joey C," the last one said, with a respectful nod. A retired shipping man. "Good to see you."

"*Buon dia*, Skippy."

"What brings you here? Can't be the *ah'pizz*."

"That bad?" Joey nodded toward Vito's first pizzeria, rechristened *Gavones*.

The smoker laughed. "Fiore won't even sell him *mozzarella* no more."

"He sells this thing called a Garbage Pie," Skippy said. "The kids line up for it. Puffing the *marijuan* right on the corner with those vape pens, clouds like someone oughtta be playing 'Harlem Nocturne.'"

The men shook their heads.

"I'll talk to him."

The new sign depicted a spike-haired guido caricature straight out of *Jersey Shore*, gripping a slice in a pumped fist dripping grease onto a muscle shirt. Joey pushed open the door, and heard the smoker mutter *finocchio* before it closed behind him.

Inside, the place did a brisk early lunch business, mostly young people on phones yammering over pies smothered with everything from chicken fingers and mozzarella sticks to pineapple rings and bacon slices. The menu on the wall listed myriad combinations that made Joey's head hurt.

Worse, Lou Monte sang "Dominic the Italian Christmas Donkey" on the speakers. In September.

A spray-tanned guy with stretch marked shoulders worked the oven, a beehive of checkered ceramic tiles with the color baked out of them. Vito's first.

Joey skipped the line. "Nunzio here?"

"In the back, bro."

Past another kid working a deep fryer was an open door. Inside was a big refrigerator and a flour-scattered work table where the presumed Nunzio worked the dough. He flicked his eyes at Joey but kept rolling, setting softballs of pizza dough on wax paper-lined trays.

Joey watched for a minute. "How you doing, Nunzi?"

"You mind? Some of us gotta work for a living." They were off Aldo's turf, but the attitude took some balls. He admired it over the ass-kissing he usually got.

"You seem to be doing all right. But your father, something's got him upset."

Nunzio rolled his eyes. "When's he not upset? He retired ten years ago. My mother, all she wanted was a vacation in the old country. She had to go alone on a Mario Perillo cruise. He wouldn't leave the business alone for that long."

He paused for a quick sign of the cross, dabbing himself with flour. "May she rest in peace, sixty years with that stubborn *vecchione*."

Joey could smell the spite. A cheap, perfectionist father who hewed to tradition. He knew the sting well.

"So Vito's cheap. He took care of you and your kids."

"He's tighter than a crab's ass, and that's waterproof." He slapped a dough ball down.

"You gotta bust his balls with this stoner shit? Calling it a garbage pie? He thinks you put the evil eye on him."

Nunzio laughed and started on a new bowl, mixing flour and water. "He's always been superstitious. I heard he had the new place blessed by a priest. He cries the blues, but he wants for nothing. His problem is he's got to run everything, and it's not like the old days. We tried staying traditional, and almost sank like the Titanic. The *'merigons* want gluten-free crust, vegan cheese. Crazy toppings.

"He wanted money to open his own place, but it isn't there. It all went into my brother's fancy-ass place in Millburn and the grandkids' college. My daughter and her husband make good money, but they can't make that nut alone. Vito got to retire. Me, I'm gonna keel over in front of that oven before my day comes."

Once the steam settled, Joey went in. "He owes Aldo thirty large. One of you is either playing games with him or he's losing his marbles. Either way, when he can't pay, you know who we hit up." You inherited street debt from your parents, your children. It was a curse you couldn't dispel using salt and olive oil.

"My little cousin couldn't lend it to him?" He punched down the dough. "That's who you should hit up. His partner?"

"The kid can't even afford to dress right."

"That's how they all dress these days, like bums. He's got cush, believe me. How you think he's got time to make pizzas with Cheapo Vito?" He wiped flour off his hands, and Joey stepped back to avoid getting the dust on his new coat.

"Kid thinks his shit don't stink, just like my brother with his villa out in the 'burbs." Nunzio carried a tray of dough to the icebox. "My son saw him with a hot broad all over him at the club. Me, I'm working seven days a week, I haven't had my ashes hauled in a month."

Joey left Nunzio to his dough. If was too busy to get laid, he wouldn't have time to prank his father over old grudges.

* * *

ON THE WALK BACK to the car, he let the past creep in.

Joey's uncle on his mother's side came for coffee every morning once his father left for work. Weary-eyed after the New York bars closed, he walked Joey to school before heading home to sleep. Taught him to laugh at life, introduced him to Mel Brooks movies, gave them a VCR when they cost a grand and weighed fifty pounds.

After a bottle of red at Sunday dinner, his father would jab young Joey in the chest.

You turn into a finocchio *like your uncle, and I'll put a bullet in your head.*

Joey thought the word had something to do with Pinocchio. His uncle *did* walk like he was on strings. When Joey grew older and his disinterest in girls became obvious, he took a beating from the old man. His uncle gave him the couch at his flat and a job as a runner. By then he learned that *finocchio* was Italian for fennel. The root looked like a man's genitals, so the word served double duty as a slur toward gay men.

At the card table, the smoker grinned at him around the stub of his cigar. Joey slapped it out of his mouth and sprayed him with embers. The other men cringed and shouted in surprise. "Next time the lit end goes up your ass."

Joey wiped the ashes off his jacket and squealed the Alfa's tires up the street. He felt like hitting a heavy bag, taking a cold shower and a nooner. He headed towards the highway to brace the other son.

What Nunzio said about Peter bothered him. If the kid was loaded, why did Vito go to the street for money? Maybe he spent the loan on tail, and this was his way out of it.

The stereo played Boz Scaggs, and Joey smiled. His uncle called him Scuzz Baggs. He had a funny name for everybody. Barry Manilow was Barry Cantaloupe. He loved wordplay and old euphemisms, like *getting your ashes hauled.*

He called Aldo on the bluetooth. Before the sit-down, he would hit the sauna to steam himself of the poisons he drank to sleep. Alcoholism galloped Aldo's family like a mudder at Monmouth racetrack.

Aldo picked up without a word. Just heavy breath.

"Babe. I'm sorry. I'm handling the Vito Ferro bullshit. Tell me who handles his trash?"

"Off the top of my head?"

"Save me a trip back."

"Maybe you should be back at the apartment in an hour. Bring me a prosciutto and *mozz* from Fiore's."

"Love to, but I'm stuck on 280." He wasn't on the highway yet, but he was following a scent, however faint, and didn't want to leave the trail.

Besides, he wanted Aldo hungry and sharp for the sit-down, not sated and logy.

"Tonight we'll celebrate with a steak at Arthur's on the water. I made reservations." Joey touched the *cornuto* at his throat. It was the anniversary of their trip to Capri, where Aldo bought him the pendant made from the local coral.

A low grumble as Aldo's gears turned. He was no good with dates, but he'd know who hauled trash for the people who owed him money.

"Exo carting. Terry Peru's thing."

"Thanks babe. Pick you up at eight."

He looked the number up on his phone, weaving a little on the road.

They had spent two weeks in Italy, including a trip to Sicily to find Aldo's family village, where they learned Sicilian stiletto fighting from a *'Ndrangheta* knife master. Joey had bought them matching handmade stilettos as an anniversary present. Eleventh was steel. He fingered the abalone handle of the stiletto in the pocket of his new coat. Silk was twelfth. Aldo miscounted.

Joey smiled and tried to convince the gravelly-voiced receptionist of Exo Carting to put him through to her boss.

She said he'd call back.

* * *

INTERSTATE 280 TURNED INTO a parking lot in the hills. He made his way to the shoulder and rode it a half a mile, ignoring the horns of cars in the right lane that he sprayed with kicked-up debris.

Angelina would be home. He wasn't angry that her evil eye cure hadn't worked, but he needed her to come up with a spell or something to keep Vito from giving himself a heart attack over globs of olive oil in a bowl.

He tailgated a bus in the afternoon idiot traffic, the road clogged with harried mothers in minivans and Q-tip-headed old fucks with boxes of tissues in their rear windows. He kneaded the wheel. His even temper took work.

His phone buzzed.

"Terry. Thank you for getting back so quickly." His overly polite tone begged for discourtesy, so that he could retort.

"Anything for Joey C. What you need?"

"What days you pick up on Mulberry, down by the Rock?"

"Uhh . . ." Paper flipping. "This morning."

Fuck. It was his own fault for not checking the trash after Vito said the oven was empty.

"I need to look in whatever truck picked up Vito Ferro's dumpster this morning. They still out?"

Terry huffed, a laugh cut short. "No, they get done by noon."

"I need you to get them on the radio before they dump." Newark had a trash incinerator. Not everything got burned, but once it was in the system to be sorted, he'd have no way of finding their trash.

"I could try, but . . ."

"You think I'm asking 'cause I like rooting through other people's shit?"

A pause while Terry swallowed the response in his mouth.

"I'll radio them right now. What you want them to do?"

"Have them meet me in the Meadowlands where you dump your hazmat trash when you're short on the vig."

Terry didn't chuckle at that one. He was into Aldo for six figures for fantasy sports bets. "Can they just dump and go?"

A Lexus truck stopped to double park. Joey stomped the brake and the Alfa Romeo shuddered. "Your sister's ass!"

"I'm sorry Joey. They're on the clock."

"Not you. Some *bucciacca* cut me off." He swerved into the oncoming lane and gunned past. "Tell your guys to wait. You think I'm sifting through that shit?"

In the silence, he saw Terry lick his fat lips.

"Make 'em punch out. They'll get paid."

"Gimme an hour."

"Make it two."

JOEY HIT THE GYM and took a hot shower before he rapped on Angelina's door. She didn't come. He flicked open his stiletto and popped the storm door's lock. He found her sprawled on an easy chair, mouth open, eyes closed. Chest not rising.

He leaned in to listen for breath. She smelled like sharp provolone. He squinted at the fine gold chain below the marbled wattle of her neck.

A Star of David dangled on it.

Joey didn't know until high school that it was possible to be both Italian and Jewish. He thought his *paísans* were all Catholics until his English teacher, Ms. Stolfi, mentioned celebrating Passover. He had been incredulous, insisting she couldn't be both. She made him read *Survival in Auschwitz* by Primo Levi, and give an oral report to the class. He'd been so nervous.

The snort of a warthog interrupted his reverie.

Joey jumped back from Angelina, knocking an African violet from the window sill. He caught the pot before it hit the floor.

She squinted at him. "Joey? I fall asleep. I make coffee." She heaved herself out of the chair and shuffled to the kitchen.

Over fresh coffee, he told her about Vito and the olive oil.

"That one? He cursed himself." She sneered, her face a white prune. "How you think he come here with money?"

Joey sipped espresso from a tiny cup and let her talk.

"No one has money. Mussolini, he suck the land dry, *sfachim!*" She raised a bony fist. "My family, they make Aliyah to the Holy land after the war. Who want to live with *ratti* who sell you out to *fascisti*? Nothing to eat, but Vito Ferro, he come to America, build a pizzeria."

"Maybe the *mala vita*?" The bad life.

Angelina pursed her lips and poked him with a finger. "You ask me?"

Joey shrugged, sheepish. She was right. Vito paid his street tax, but never bought the olive oil the port boys jacked and sold by the truckload. He stayed clean.

"The *mala vita* make money from the war too," she said. "Blood money. You no come to America with money. You come to *make* money. You have money, why you leave?" She pointed a gnarled finger and nodded over it, as if answering her own question.

JOEY TOOK THE BRIDGE over the dirty Passaic and weaved into the Meadowlands, a swamp so clogged with bodies and pollution that if zombies existed they would have risen from its poisoned muck. He passed a tall radio tower with three blinking red lights, then cut down a rutted road hedged by reeds on both sides.

The Alfa bounced along, scraping on the grass, and stopped nose to nose with a Mack garbage truck. He stepped around the truck and found two men in sooty worksuits spreading the truck's dumped load over the flattened reeds using long poles.

"We're looking for ashes," he said, and stood back to watch.

"That's over here," the squat bald one said, and jabbed at pile of trash bags that had melted and torn.

Between the reeds, he caught the afternoon sun sparkling on the water, and the SuperFund site looked beautiful if you ignored the fish and bird-shit smell of the flats bared by low tide. The white underbelly of a dead crab raised its claws from the mud like a pair of praying hands.

His thoughts turned to his father.

After the beating ruined his Roman nose, Joey had learned to pass among straight men. They weren't that different, but many would only freely express themselves through anger or desire. If you wanted something from them, you translated your needs into their pidgin.

He didn't need to explain himself to the garbage men, they would dig because they feared him. But they would work harder if they imagined he was the devil-may-care, unfaithful piece of shit they wished they could be.

"We're looking for my *goomar's* chain," Joey said. "Dumb broad threw it in the fireplace because I'm taking my wife to Punta Cana. Now she wants it back." He rolled his eyes for the convincer.

They muttered about girlfriends and wives as they kicked through the ashes, and marsh birds cried and swooped overhead.

"I got something," the tall one said, and bent to thrust his gloved hand into the ashes.

Joey walked closer. The worker brushed soot off the coil in his palm.

"Thought gold would melt into nothing." He held up a blackened mess of burn spaghetti.

Joey took it in his handkerchief. "You think that *bucciacca* is worth gold?" He snickered.

The necklaces had melted. Any gold coating was long gone and the amulets were unrecognizable. Gimcrack for a parlor trick to scare an old man. He wrapped the mess into his pocket.

"Thank you fellas." He gave them each a hundred.

HE PULLED INTO THE radio station's driveway and stared at the dead neon letters of the white WMCA hut and thought about who would want to torment Vito Ferro to death.

He had killed for business, and for personal reasons. Personal got messy. You wanted them to know *why*.

Do things like cut their hands off with bolt cutters and throw them, still zip-tied together, for the crabs to eat in the swamp. Hands that could never hit you again.

He called the pizza joint in Millburn that the other son had opened.

"Vito's Neapolitan Pizza and Italian Specialties," a young woman answered.

"Sal please. Tell him it's Joey Cucuzza."

He spent a minute listening to Mario Lanza. No corny Lou Monte for the rich *'merigons.*

"Sal here. Who is this?"

"Joe Cucuzza. I'm a business associate of your father's. I need to find his partner, your nephew Peter. He still at home?"

"Why don't you call him then?" Cocky.

"It would be a lot easier if you told me where he lives, Sal. I'm calling as a courtesy. If I drive out there, maybe those imports you sell get held up in customs until they rot."

"Whoa, easy. I'm just protecting my family."

"I understand, Sal. He's not in trouble. He's the finance wiz, right? He's hooking me up with some hedge funds."

"He's got a condo in Jersey City," Sal said. "With his fiancée."

Joey committed the address to memory.

VITO'S ORIGINAL CLASSIC NEAPOLITAN Pizza Pies was nearly abandoned by five o'clock, after the downtown Newark commuters fled and before the gentrifiers came out for dinner. Peter leaned on the counter, playing on his phone.

The scent of tomato sauce filled the restaurant like a siren song. Joey followed it, snapping his fingers for the kid to follow.

Vito stirred a huge pot of sauce, a bubbling blood red witch's brew.

"Mister Vito," Joey said, and spun a chair backwards to sit facing the old man. "I've found who's giving you the evil eye. And they won't be bothering you any more."

Before Vito could talk, Joey said, "You have a ghost. And my *strega* says the only way to exorcise a ghost is to set them to rest. So tell me the real story of how you came to America."

The kid put his phone down.

Vito frowned. "I tell you. I made money in Napoli, everyone know my pizza."

"If you were flush, why'd you come here?"

"It is America. My family was dead."

"The country was in ruins, but you were selling pies? Why don't you tell me where you got the money."

"I do not have to explain myself to mafiosi. You bleed us dry!" Vito stood and made a fist. The scarred skin of his forearms stretched over old muscle.

"Easy, Uncle Veet," Peter said.

"I spoke to my *strega*, Vito. She's Jewish, you know? We had a lot more Jewish Italians before the war than after it. Their neighbors ratted them out. Took everything they owned. And when the war was over and Mussolini was strung up by his balls, people took revenge on those no-good rat fucks. That ring any bells?"

Vito shuddered, fists at his sides. "They do not belong there!"

Peter gasped. "Uncle Vito."

Joey shrugged. "Your uncle's not the nice guy you thought. But you know that already, don't you kid?"

Peter let his jaw go slack.

"Don't play dumb. Make us a pie. Margherita. And no hot sauce this time." Joey took a bottle from his pocket and set it on the table.

Peter stammered. "I don't know what you're talking about."

"Houshmand's NastyVicious Hot Sauce. They make this at Rowan college." Joey turned the bottle around. "You went to Rowan, didn't you?"

"Pietro?" Vito stared.

"Uncle Veet, he wants to turn us against each other. Take over your business."

"Aldo owns the building. It's in his interest for you to make lots of money, so he can jack up your rent. Try again, kid."

"I didn't do anything."

"You two talk this out. That pie had better make me lie back and think of Napoli." Joey walked to his car and returned holding a young lady by the nape of her neck. "Good of you not to run, *bella donna*."

"I wouldn't miss it for the world."

The pie was in the oven, Peter cowering as Uncle Vito jabbed his finger and swore. "*Vaffanculo!* You do this to me?"

Vito screamed and grabbed his chest when he saw the girl.

"Meet Peter's wife-to-be," Joey said. "I found her in the Jersey City condo she shares with your nephew."

Vito scrunched his face. "Peter, you said you live at home, you have no money."

"She's a stage manager. She used Peter's father's fireman gloves to scoop the coals. They're rated for twelve hundred degrees." A fireman told Joey that once on a date. He nudged her forward. "Give him your best vengeful ghost act, honey."

She grabbed a pizza slicer. "I don't need to act, this Nazi motherfucker robbed my family and sent them to the camps! My *nonna* remembers you."

Vito held up his hands in shock.

The girl was a ringer for her grandmother. She'd shown Joey the photo while she begged for her life at stiletto point.

Peter exchanged his dumbstruck act for a sneer of loathing. "Valeria's grandmother told me everything. How could you *do* that?"

"You don't know what it's like to starve!" Vito snarled. "None of you."

"My *nonna* does," Valeria said. "You took her gold necklace. From a little girl! You made them hide in your oven from the secret police. Was that some sick joke? Then you turned them in. She saw a picture in the paper of you arguing with your sons, and she nearly had a heart attack."

Joey rapped the hot sauce bottle on the counter. "My pizza is burning."

Peter quickly scooped it onto the peel. The cheese bubbled, the edges of the crust were a little dark.

"It's all right, I like it blistery," Joey said, and turned to Peter and

Valeria. "Now, what do I do with you? You tried to kill a man under our protection."

Joey flicked open his stiletto. The seven inch blade gleamed with the oven's fire. He waved the tip at Valeria, who set down the pizza slicer.

Peter held up his hands. "Technically, we're the ones under your protection, Mister Cucuzza."

"How so?"

"We've been paying the street tax," Valeria said. "Our money. Not his. He's broke as fuck."

Joey slowly closed his stiletto. "This is between you, then." He took the roller and cut the pizza, folding a slice, taking a bite. "Not bad, kid."

Vito growled, "Kill them. He is not my blood, marrying a Jew. We are Italian, Guiseppe!"

"This is for my *nonna!*" Valeria snatched the pizza slicer and lunged at Vito.

He stumbled back. Valeria gave chase, with Peter trying hold her back in vain.

Joey ate his slice while the three of them disappeared into the kitchen. A loud crash gonged and a scream gargled out.

More screams. Then the crying gave Angelina a run for her money.

His phone buzzed. Aldo.

"How's my Apollo?" he answered.

"I hope you liked Napoli," Aldo huffed. Excited. "You're going back. They asked for you, said you're *ingamba* . . ."

Ingambatissimo, probably. It meant he knew his shit. Which he did.

"In *Gabbadone!*" Aldo laughed.

Hung like a horse. That was correct, too.

"Can't wait. See you for dinner, babe." Joey finished his slice to the crust and walked into the kitchen.

Sauce covered the floor, the stove, and Vito. He twitched and bubbled, mouth open and filled with his famous sauce, face unrecognizable with the skin boiled off.

"We should have stuffed him in the oven," Valeria cried, hugged to her fiancé's chest. Peter looked relieved and exhausted, now that the man he'd once idolized had paid for his crimes.

Joey felt a pang, recalling the feeling.

"*Ciao* for now," he said, and boxed the pizza, took it to his car. The port boys would be grateful. On the drive back, he wondered if the kids could make it work with a death between them.

Joey patted the gift box with the matching stiletto, and thought of his man using it to cut into a juicy rare steak.

It took a strong love, but you could do it.

COLD COMFORT

BY HILARY DAVIDSON

THE ARTISTS AT THE Humphrey Funeral Home were miracle workers, but even they couldn't piece Abby Killingsworth's face back together. In life, she had a curious charisma that was immediately striking in spite of her flaws. It was powerful yet puzzling: her eyes were wide-set and her nose had a bump and her lips were so plump and ripe that they lent her a faintly cartoonish appearance. Yet, when observed together in their heart-shaped frame, a peculiar alchemy occurred that could render complete strangers mute.

Abby had been a great beauty in life. In death, she was a broken statue, mere fragments of cold marble. My own heart had cracked in sadness when I first laid eyes on her lifeless body. In the oasis of false comfort that was the Humphrey Funeral Home, with its piped-in violin music, I kept up my unperturbed façade by imagining that Abby was elsewhere.

"The casket will stay closed," her mother announced. It was the day before Abby's funeral, and we stood together in a viewing room at the Humphrey. It was preposterously grand, with a domed ceiling that spoke of aspirations to royal chapelhood. Janet Killingsworth had asked me to accompany her to provide moral support, since her husband had refused to leave the house since his daughter's death. "I don't want anyone seeing what that bastard did to her." She bit her lip. "I'm sorry, Father, I didn't mean to swear."

"Please don't worry about that." I struggled to come up with something meaningful to say, anything that could blunt the pain. "Abby is at peace now, you must concentrate on that."

"Oh, Father, I try to. But when I think of what that monster did to my baby . . ." Janet's voice cracked. I put my hand on her shoulder, and she rested her head on my chest.

"Why would God take my baby?" Janet sobbed.

Of all the questions asked of me since I'd joined the priesthood, this was the most perplexing. I had no answers, only the same platitudes I'd heard since I was a boy growing up in County Cork. "All I can promise is that there is meaning in everything. It is invisible to us, so we must trust the Lord in all things."

Janet inhaled sharply and shuddered. "There's one other thing," she said, pulling away. "I want you to perform an Absolution for Abby."

I stared at her. Absolution had been removed from the Funeral Mass before I was born. I'd only performed it a handful of times, in unusual circumstances.

"My daughter may have been . . . involved with a man," Janet said quietly.

"What?"

Janet read the shock in my face, and quickly added. "Abby was such a good girl, and I don't know if it really counts as an affair, because she was separated from her husband, but . . ."

"Why would you suspect such a thing?"

Janet wiped her eyes. "Abby was pregnant."

"What? Abby told you that?"

"No, Father. The police did. It came up in the autopsy." She choked on that last word.

"The child might've been her husband's," I pointed out.

"No. Abby didn't see Frank at all. She told me she didn't." Janet gazed at me. "What did Abby say to you?"

"It wasn't anything she said outright," I explained. "It was her attitude. Whenever I visited her in the past few weeks, she was in a much more forgiving frame of mind about Frank. She believed he was capable of change, I think." I was silent for a moment. "I saw vases of daisies in her suite a couple of times. I suppose I simply assumed that they were from Frank. That was the flower they used at their wedding."

"She seemed so happy, before she died," Janet said softly. "Glowing. Almost as if she were in love. That wasn't because of Frank. She didn't love him anymore. A mother knows these things."

"You haven't said anything about this, have you?" I asked. "It's not anyone's business, but of course people might wonder . . ."

"No. I don't want her good name ruined. There are people who might think what that bastard—her husband, I mean—did to her was justified."

"No one would ever think that."

"Some people are cruel, Father. Abby was a good girl, but she . . . she had her flaws."

"We all do," I told her, speaking softly but with a firmness I hoped would comfort her. "We are all flawed creatures, yet the Lord loves us nonetheless."

THE VISITATION STARTED AT three that afternoon. I stayed for the first two hours, offering comfort when I could. Abby had been an only child, but she had relatives on three continents, so her parents planned two days of visitation before her funeral to allow everyone to arrive in time. I left at five o'clock, stopping by my office at the church, as it was only six blocks from the funeral home. To my surprise, my secretary, Millie Tamliss, was still at her desk. She was seventy-two years old, with white hair and faded blue eyes. Her bones were only slightly larger than a sparrow's, and she seemed to live on air. In the years since I'd come to the parish, I'd never observed her eating or drinking.

"Good evening, Father. How was it?"

"Very sad. So many people came by to pay their respects. No one can quite believe it."

"I still can't, myself. Poor girl. It's heartbreaking." She clicked open her black patent purse, extracted a tissue, and blew her nose. "Just so you know, Father, there's something wrong with the phone line. It's been ringing off the hook for the past hour, but no one's there when I answer."

"Technology. Never reliable when you need it to be." I resisted the urge to glance at my watch. Mildred normally left the office by four, or four-thirty at the latest. Whoever was calling wasn't expecting her to answer. "Thank you for staying so late. You didn't have to do that."

"I thought it would be best. On account of the gentleman."

"What gentleman?"

"He's in your office."

I glanced at my door, which was closed all but an inch. My stomach churned slightly. Before I could ask her anything else, Mildred was up on her spindly legs. "I'm off to pay my respects to the Killingsworths," she announced. "Good night, Father."

"Good night," I murmured, and turned to my office. It was six steps from Mildred's desk. When I opened the door, I found a tall man in a suit studying my bookcase. His head swiveled in my direction. His thin face was narrowed to such a sharp point, it looked as if it had once been caught in a door.

"Good evening, Father Byrne," he said. "I'm Detective Reed. We talked on the phone a couple times."

"Yes, of course," I said, recognizing his voice. "Have you brought Frank DeSilva into custody?"

Frank was Abby's estranged husband, the man who went to the small hotel where Abby was renting a room and beat her to death. There had never been any doubt about who had murdered Abby. Frank was on camera entering the hotel, then departing with blood on his weathered hands and white shirt.

Reed shook his head. "He's still in the wind. I need to ask you a few more questions."

He was alone, which surprised me. I'd thought police officers did everything in pairs, like creatures bound for Noah's Ark.

"Of course. Would you care for some tea?"

"No, thanks."

I sat at my desk, surreptitiously checking to see if anything had been moved. The screen of my computer was on, which meant he'd touched it, though it was stuck on the password screen. "How can I help you?" I asked.

Reed stayed on his feet. "We're having trouble getting a bead on Frank DeSilva. His parents are dead, and he's got no family in the area."

"I'm sorry, but I don't know his friends."

"That's okay. I'd like you to tell me about Abby's relationship with her husband."

"I'm the priest who married them." I took a breath. "I've known Abby since I came to this parish seven years ago. She was a teenager then, fifteen or sixteen. Frank, I only met two years ago, when they became engaged and came to me for pre-marital counselling." I stared at my hands. "I didn't know that he was abusive towards her, not back then. I'm not even sure that he *was* abusive at that time. From what Abby told me, he started beating her after they came home from their honeymoon." I frowned, remembering exactly what Abby had told me about it. "There was a sporting event on television, a rugby match or something like it. Frank wanted to watch it and Abby had promised they would have dinner with her parents. That was the first time he hit her."

"Football," the detective corrected me. "It was football."

"That's it. But since you already know the story, why ask me?"

"It's often helpful to get different perspectives on the same event," Reed said.

"I see. Well, I didn't know what had transpired at the time. Abby came to church on a regular basis, but Frank rarely showed up. Christmas and Easter, those were the only times I saw him the year after they married. Then Abby suddenly left him. Her family was upset. They're very conservative."

"Yes, I've met them, Father."

His mouth twisted on that last word, and he frowned. I knew he was raised a Catholic from the way he addressed me. Perhaps he'd been an altar boy once.

"Abby's parents asked me to speak with her," I continued. "'Talk sense into her,' that was how they put it. I did, but then . . ."

My mouth was suddenly dry. I could still remember Abby, standing in my office in the exact spot the detective stood now, pulling off the cardigan she wore despite the summer heat, revealing an angry pattern of tangled red scars on her shoulder. *Frank shoved me against a hot stove because he lost money on a poker game,* Abby had cried out to me. *You're telling me that I should go back to the man who did this to me?*

"What is it?" Reed prompted me.

"When I counseled Abby, she told me about her husband's abuse. She told me things that still make me feel sick inside." I exhaled sharply. "It is my duty to love all of God's children, but I was horrified by what Frank had done."

"Did she show you any evidence?"

"Excuse me?"

"Did she show you any evidence? Photographs, video, anything like that?"

I blinked at him. "I took Abby's word for the truth, Detective. She was deeply shaken by what her husband had done."

"I didn't mean to suggest that we don't believe she was abused," Reed clarified. "But Abby only reported the abuse to you and to her parents. We've been interviewing her friends, and none of them knew anything about it. She admitted to her best friend that Frank had problems with drinking and gambling. Nothing about the violence."

"Abby was an intensely private young woman," I said. "Honestly, I think she had trouble believing the violence happened. That sort of thing wasn't supposed to occur in her world."

"Her parents were glad that she could confide in you."

"When she told me, I suddenly understood why she'd had so many inexplicable accidents. I remember her coming to church with a cast on one wrist, and later, on crutches one time. It all made sense when she told me the truth."

"What happened after Abby left Frank?"

"She moved back into her parents' home. She wanted to finish her university degree, since she hadn't graduated. Unfortunately, Frank would show up on their doorstep, demanding to see Abby. I know he sent her flowers. He tried to win her back. Their courtship had been a whirlwind, and he tried to re-create that."

"Did Abby call it a whirlwind?"

"No. Janet—Abby's mother—used that word. She talked to me when the pre-marital counselling started. She was concerned about Abby getting involved too quickly."

"She had doubts about Frank?"

"Yes. She never liked him, but her primary concern was that the relationship was moving too fast, and that Abby always leapt before she looked. She made snap decisions, sometimes to her detriment." I sighed. "Abby chose to leave her parents' home because Frank wouldn't let her alone there. Her parents supported her. They didn't want Abby to be harassed."

"And that's how Abby ended up at the Griffin Hotel. Nice place, maybe on the old-fashioned side. How far is it from here, maybe a fifteen-minute walk?"

The phone on my desk started to ring. I gave it a sidelong glance, then turned my attention back to the detective.

"Aren't you going to get that?" he asked.

"Mildred said there was a problem with the phone," I murmured, but I picked it up. "Hello?" I said.

"Father, I'm so glad you answered," said the voice on the other end. "I need . . ."

"Hello?" I said again. "Detective, I believe there is a problem with this phone line." I hung up. "I'm sorry, where were we?"

"Why don't you tell me about Frank DeSilva. The Killingsworths told me that he came to see you."

"Yes. When Frank couldn't find Abby at her parents' home any longer, he decided to come here." I took a breath, remembering the first time Frank had shown up solo at my office. He wore a well-cut dark suit and an expensive watch and cufflinks, but he reeked of desperation, and his eyes were dark and hollow. *Please, Father, help me get my wife back. Help her come to her senses,* he had begged me. "I offered him my counsel."

"Meaning what, exactly?"

"I told him he needed anger-management counselling and help with his gambling and his drinking," I said. "I told him flatly that his wife would never come back if he couldn't be a proper husband."

"You believed Abby should go back to him?" Reed asked.

"I believe in forgiveness," I told him. "I believe in redemption."

"You thought Abby should forgive her husband?"

"Yes, for her own peace of mind. But I didn't believe they could live together again unless Frank changed."

"Tell me about Frank's visit to your office the day that Abby died," he said.

"We spoke about this on the phone already."

"True, but even the smallest detail might help."

I steepled my fingers together, conjuring up the memory. Frank had looked well the last time I'd laid eyes on him. He'd lost some weight when he stopped drinking, and he had an aura of fragile, almost boyish, hope. "Frank cared a tremendous deal about appearances," I said. "He came in, dressed in his best, hair neatly cut and such. He believed he was ready to be reconciled with Abby. It had been six months since she left him. I counselled him on patience." I paused again, remembering how I'd congratulated Frank, only my words had made his face pale. I pushed the thought away. "Frank didn't like to be told he couldn't have something he wanted, right when he wanted it."

"Your secretary, Mildred Tamliss, told me you left Frank in your office for a few minutes, and then Frank came running out like the devil was after him."

I rocked back in my chair, genuinely startled that Millie would be so indiscreet. "I had some literature I wanted to give him about anger-management therapy. I asked him to pray while I went to retrieve it. When I came back, Frank was gone."

"Here's what I'm struggling with," Reed said. "After Frank DeSilva left your office, he went to his estranged wife's place and beat her to death. I want to understand *how* that happened. Something in your conversation must've set him off."

I frowned at that. "You want to blame me for what Frank did?"

"Of course not. But something happened."

I shook my head. "I understand that my telling Frank he couldn't have what he wanted upset him. I take responsibility for that. Perhaps I could have . . . said something different. Perhaps I should have been kinder. Frank believed that he had done enough work on himself and he was entitled to his reward, which was Abby. I attempted to explain to him that the world didn't work that way."

"Did you tell him where he could find Abby?"

"Of course not." I rose to my feet. "You're leaving out part of the story. Frank left my office and went to a bar. At least, that's what you said on the phone."

He ignored that. "Did you know that Abby Killingsworth was pregnant when she died?"

"Yes."

"She told you?"

"Her mother did, this morning."

Reed's jaw tightened. It was obvious that he was disappointed. He had hoped to shake me with the news, and he had failed.

Still, he didn't give up. "Who was the father of the child?"

"How could I possibly know that?"

"Well, Father, Abby was living at a hotel for the past four months, so she didn't have neighbors who could identify you, but the hotel staff certainly does."

I'd been well aware, from the way he watched me and his abrupt manner, that he disliked me. There it was, suddenly, the real reason for his poisonous suspicion. It rocked me inside, though I was determined not to show it on my face. How dare he make such an assumption about me? What possible grounds could he have for it?

"I visited Abby every week," I said. "I listened to her confession. I gave her communion. She was afraid to come to church, in case her husband might surprise her there."

"Surely there are other churches she could've gone to, Father. Yours wasn't the only one."

"Abby needed support at a difficult time in her life. I am a longtime friend of her family. I wasn't about to abandon her in her time of need."

"How devoted of you. Didn't you comfort her?"

"Not in the way you're suggesting."

Reed's mouth twitched up in a rough facsimile of a smile. "I wouldn't blame you, Father. This isn't like those sicko priests molesting children. It's not a crime if you had a relationship with Abby. You're a good-looking guy. What are you, thirty-nine? Forty?"

"It's time for you to leave," I said, as calmly as I could manage. "Have a good evening, Detective."

THE NEXT MORNING, I went to see Bishop Calton. He was a man I knew well, one with a fondness for dachshunds and Tolstoy and gin, but this wasn't a social call. He kept me waiting for half an hour in his library, a grand wood-paneled room with a vaulted ceiling and a ladder stretching two stories up. I was so engrossed I didn't hear him enter.

"Every time you come here, I feel like you're measuring the curtains, Michael." Calton was a red-cheeked elf of a man with a cap of wild white hair that appeared impervious to combing.

"Good morning, Your Excellency. Thank you for seeing me on short notice."

"I have an appointment at noon, so let's keep this brief."

"We have a problem. His name is Detective William Reed."

"I don't know the name."

"He's investigating the murder of one of my parishioners," I explained. "A woman named Abby Killingsworth, who was murdered by her husband. It should be an open-and-shut case. She was murdered in a hotel. There's video evidence. DNA evidence."

"What a sad circumstance," the bishop murmured.

"He came to see me last night. In the course of our interview, he made some odious statements about priests. Or rather, *sicko priests,* as he called them."

The bishop's white eyebrows shot heavenwards in alarm. "What does child abuse have to do with this case?"

"Absolutely nothing. But his hatred of the Church was palpable," I said. "Abby and her family are very involved in the church. I have the sense that he's trying to blame the Church for what happened."

"That won't do," the bishop said. "Not at all. What did you say his name was again?"

"Detective William Reed."

"We don't have the pull we used to," the bishop said. "However, if this detective is making statements against the Church and clergy in the course of his investigation, he must be removed."

"I agree heartily," I said. It was always important to allow the bishop to claim credit for whatever idea you came to him with. I'd learned that some years earlier.

We spoke only briefly after that. I drove back to the parish house and parked the car. I retrieved the mail and noticed, amid the advertisements, a hand-addressed envelope with no return address. I tore it open and found a note on plain white paper, written in a childish block print and replete with misspellings.

I'm desparate, Father. I don't know who else to turn to. Call me.

There was a telephone number I didn't recognize underneath. I stared at it, then went into the house and burned the missive and its cover. I didn't want to speak with Frank again. I didn't want to listen to his confession and hear him sob. I didn't want to have him describe the gory details of what he'd done to his wife, and how it hadn't really been his fault, because the alcohol always clouded his judgment and made him lose control. He would find a way to blame everyone else for the terrible choices he'd made, and for committing a horrific act of murder. Now that Abby was gone, I wished that he would vanish as well. There was no comfort I could offer him. I dropped the little ash-heap into the kitchen garbage, wiped my eyes, and headed to the funeral home for the second day of Abby's visitation.

THAT EVENING, I FOUND Detective Reed waiting at my doorstep of the parish house. He gave me his sardonic smile. "Evening, Father Byrne. I'm here to offer you an apology."

"I don't believe we have anything further to discuss."

"I'm sorry our conversation yesterday upset you so much that you ran to your bishop," he said.

"I hope you might reflect on what you said to me. Your efforts should be concentrated on finding Frank."

"I have been reflecting, Father. More than you can imagine."

His words were mild, but there was an undercurrent of a threat in them, lurking like a worm in an apple.

"Well, then, I hope that you'll reconsider your animus toward the Church," I said.

"My animus is towards people who abuse positions of trust," Reed said. "I'll be honest with you. I was abused by a priest when I was an altar boy. It was an awful secret I kept from my family for years. I felt that if I said a word, God would strike me down. Doesn't that sound crazy, Father? The victim of the crime is made to feel like the guilty one."

His words stopped me short. "I am truly sorry that happened to you. I know the Church used to sweep crimes under the carpet. That was a tragedy."

"Since I'm off the case now, it doesn't really matter," he said. "My lieutenant worried that my experience biased my thinking. He's probably right. This isn't a child-abuse case, but I know exactly how manipulative priests can be."

"Good night, Detective Reed."

"Oh, I almost forgot. I brought you a present."

I eyed him warily. "Excuse me?"

Reed handed me an unsealed white envelope. There were two sheets of paper inside. The one on top looked like a photograph of a torn sheet of hotel stationary, only the gold griffin at the top of the page was severed in two. I could make out Abby's handwriting clearly. *Reasons I Will Never Go Back to Frank,* it read:

He made my life hell
He is crazy and violent
My mother has always hated him
He has a gambling addiction
He drinks too much
I don't love him anymore

"Hold on," Reed said, pulling that page out of my hands and gingerly folding it into thirds. "That wasn't supposed to be in there. The other page is for you." He took the envelope from me and replaced the note.

"That was a note Abby wrote," I said. "I recognize her handwriting."

"Yes, we found it in her suite. The bottom of the page was torn off."

I remembered exactly what Abby had written. The last line of that list was *Because I love you.* I tamped the memory down. The police would never find that slip of paper; it was already ash.

"Abby Killingsworth didn't have many paper books, but she had an electronic reader," Reed added. "That page you're holding has a list of the books she downloaded in the past six months."

I glanced at it, and my eye fell on a book entitled *Dilemma.* I couldn't help it; I flinched.

"She bought Father Cutié's book," Reed said quietly. "Isn't that interesting?"

Father Cutié was a cautionary tale in the priesthood. A rising star in the Church, he was photographed embracing a woman on a beach in Miami; he abandoned the Church for that woman, and married her. *Dilemma* bore the subtitle, *A Priest's Struggle With Faith and Love,* and it was popular, especially among those who believed that the Church needed reform. He had since become an Episcopalian priest, and a powerful advocate for allowing Catholic priests to marry.

As I stared at the page, I could hear Abby's voice in the back of my mind. *You could become an Anglican priest, Michael,* she had told me. *You would still have a parish. Think how wonderful it would be.* She had been such a little fool. She refused to understand that serving an audience of dull, careless Protestants had little allure next to the might and glamour of Rome. It wasn't even a consolation prize; after everything I'd sacrificed in my life, it would be a crushing failure. I had failed to live up to my vows a mere handful of times; I wasn't going to depart from the Church because of a rare misstep I'd made.

"Here's what I'm sure of," Reed said. "You weren't just Abby's priest. You ministered to her in other ways. Hell, you might even be the father of her child, Father." He leered at me. "Wouldn't that be a kick in the head? How about a DNA sample to prove me wrong?"

"I'm not going to listen to this nonsense," I said, but I felt faint. There was a pounding behind my eyes that wouldn't die down.

"I also know that it's not a coincidence that Frank DeSilva went to see you, then killed Abby that same day. What did you say to him that set him off, Father Byrne?"

I didn't answer him, stepping toward the front door, key in hand.

"Here's what I can't quite put together," Reed said. "If you told Frank DeSilva you were sleeping with his wife, he probably would've killed you. What did you say?"

"I'm not responsible for what Frank did," I said. "He made his own choices. If you were any sort of proper detective, you'd find him, instead of harassing me." I went into the parish house and locked the door. Reed finally walked away, but the pounding in my head remained.

I COULDN'T SLEEP THAT night. There was an echo of Abby's voice still in my head. *I have wonderful news, Michael,* she had told me. *Don't be upset. I'm pregnant.*

The news had run through my body like an electric current, paralyzing me, rooting me to the spot. It was as if the doors of paradise had suddenly swung closed in my face. I was a man, subject to weakness as any man might be, only the punishment for any transgression was so much worse.

All I'd been able to say to Abby in return had been, *Then you'll have to go back to Frank.* The look she gave me then was seared on my brain. It was a mix of fury and contempt.

I'll never go back to Frank, she insisted. *Never.*

Make a list of pros and cons, I had told her. *Truly think about it. Write it down.* I had handed her one of those notepads they left by the bedside in hotels, along with the ballpoint pen with the name of The Griffin embossed in silver on the side. *One page for reasons to leave Frank, one page for reasons to stay.*

This is ridiculous, Abby protested.

Try it, I insisted. *See what happens.*

No matter which way I tossed and turned, I couldn't find any peace. Finally, I gave up, getting out of bed while it was still dark out and reviewing the remarks I was going to make at Abby's funeral that day. I'd always been an early riser, but it was a habit the priesthood had enhanced and reinforced; you simply didn't rise in the Church if you had trouble getting up in the morning. There were all manner of difficulties one could have, but not that one. I had some tea and took a long, solitary walk around the neighborhood and to the park, determined to clear my mind. None of it really helped. No matter what I did, there was a heaviness in my chest when I thought of Abby.

Her funeral mass was at ten that morning. I arrived at the church at eight-thirty. Abby's parents walked in just before nine; Janet was ghostly pale, while Stewart's face was red. I embraced them each in turn, murmuring words of comfort.

"You'll say the Absolution?" Janet whispered to me, while her husband wandered up to his daughter's coffin. The polished mahogany box was closed. Flowers lined its surface and greenery cascaded down the sides, as if it were a garden in bloom.

"Of course," I promised her.

Waves of mourners flowed into the church as somber organ music played. The Killingsworths were a popular family, wealthy and attractive, the sort of people one never imagined tragedy befalling. There were friends and supporters who loved them, and loved Abby, but there were also vultures there to witness their sorrow. I noticed a lone police officer looking vaguely out of place in the sanctuary; presumably, he was there in case Frank made an appearance.

Just before the service was to begin, I noticed that Janet wasn't in the front pew. Her husband was slumped there, head bowed.

"Where's Janet?" I whispered to him.

Stewart barely lifted his head. "She went out for a smoke."

There was a small side door that led to the church offices, as well as a small, private garden. It was as far as one could get from the mourners, and I imagined that was where Janet had gone for privacy. I headed that way, the din of voices and organ music behind me. It was only when I opened the door that I saw there were two people in the garden. Frank was holding a knife against Janet's throat.

"You drove us apart!" Frank seethed.

They both turned to stare at me.

"Frank, my son," I said. "Please, put down that knife."

"She hated me, Father," Frank gulped. "You know she did. You saw the list."

Abby's list of reasons not to go back to him, he meant. Sandwiched between, *He is crazy and violent* and *He has a gambling addiction,* were the words, in Abby's loopy handwriting, *My mother has always hated him.*

"Frank, give me the knife," I pleaded. "You're a child of God, no matter what you've done. Let go of Janet."

"She broke us up," Frank was weeping now. "She made Abby leave me."

"You hurt Abby," I said, as gently as I could. "That's why she left, Frank. Not because of her mother. Because of what happened between the two of you."

"I love her," Frank wept brokenly. "I really did. I didn't mean to hurt her . . ."

"Then let go of her mother," I insisted. "Let me help you, Frank. Give me the knife."

He shoved Janet away, and I caught her, but he held fast to the knife. Once I made sure Janet was steady, I asked her to step back and turned my attention to Frank.

"Give me the knife," I said. "We don't want anyone else getting hurt."

"Abby was everything to me," Frank whispered. "I didn't mean to kill her. After you told me she was pregnant . . ."

"I know, Frank, I know," I said softly. "You'll be reunited with her one day, I promise you."

"But . . . she's dead."

"She's moved into the next life," I whispered. "One day, so will you."

"But I'll go to hell, Father," Frank whispered back.

"There is no hell, except the one we make for ourselves. Now give me that knife. I'm afraid you'll use it to see Abby right now."

Frank gazed at me like a child in wonderment, fully understanding what I meant. He held the tip of the blade against his abdomen, as if deciding how to proceed.

"Damn you," Janet hissed, stepping forward and plunging the knife into his bowels. "Damn you to hell."

THE HEADLINES DIED DOWN within a fortnight, but I kept a few of the best in my study. My favorite was *Hero Priest Saves Grieving Mother From*

Daughter's Killer, which was gloriously lurid. I sent it to my mother in Cork, expecting that she would be impressed, but her note of reply only mentioned that it should be *Heroic*. Hero or heroic, I would take it either way. Bishop Calton may not have cared much for me, but he'd had no choice but to nominate me for the title of monsignor. Rome no longer seemed like such a distant dream.

I attended Frank DeSilva's funeral, but no one else did. The police took no interest in his death. Janet and I both described it as a suicide, and they accepted that.

It was a surprise to have Detective Reed appear at my office at the church one morning, shortly after I arrived. He let out a low whistle at the sight of a framed cover from a local newspaper.

"My secretary insisted on doing that," I said, feeling my face redden.

"It's great publicity." He turned to face me. "But I wanted to give you a heads-up that you need to brace for some bad publicity."

"How's that?"

"I'd always wondered how you engineered everything," Reed said. "Abby's murder, specifically. It wasn't easy for me to piece it all together."

"Frank killed Abby. You know that. I had nothing to do with it."

"You had everything to do with it, Father," he said. "You had an affair with Abby. Please don't try to deny it. We know."

"Even if that were true—and it isn't—it has nothing to do with her death."

"It led directly to her death. You remember this piece of paper?" Reed pulled out the photocopy of Abby's list of reasons to leave Frank. "There are three sets of fingerprints on it. Abby's. Frank's. And yours."

"That proves nothing. I was the one who suggested to Abby that she write the list. I must've touched the page."

"You're the one who gave it to Frank," Reed said. "Because Frank had it after he left your office, when he hit the bar. The bartender remembers him mooning over it."

"You're suggesting I *gave* Frank that list. I didn't."

"Maybe you left it lying around your desk for him to find." Reed shrugged. "Maybe *that's* the reason you left him alone in your office. Give Frank some time to root around. How convenient that the name and address of the hotel Abby was staying in was at the top of the page."

"I can't believe you're spouting such nonsense." I tried to rise to my feet, but my legs were trembling. "You can't prove any of this."

"Here's something I can prove: the day Abby died, you called Frank and asked him to come to your office. We have the voicemail you left him."

I blinked at him silently. There was no answer for that.

"But you're right, it would be hard to prove all this in court," Reed said. "It's enough for me that I know the truth." He stepped toward to door. "And that Janet Killingsworth does too, of course."

"What are you doing? Filling Janet's head with lies?"

"Janet was deeply shaken by Frank's death at Abby's funeral. She had to be sedated for a few days. After that, we started talking. You know what she told me? Frank knew Abby was pregnant because *you* told him."

I swallowed hard. "What?"

"Janet remembers it very clearly. She was so upset at the time, with her daughter's funeral and thinking she was going to die herself, that she didn't put it all together. After we started comparing notes, she understood what had really happened to Abby. She knows you pulled Frank's strings. You gave him Abby's location."

"Frank made his own choices," I protested, but my voice was faint.

"You keep saying that," Reed observed. "But what I see, over and over, is you tempting others into sin, and evading consequences for it. But I don't think you'll be doing that much longer."

"Detective," I said urgently. "I have a confession to make. Frank didn't kill himself. Janet was the one who stabbed him."

Reed gazed at me, and his face cracked into a smile. "I know," he said.

I stared at him in astonishment. "Aren't you going to arrest her?"

"No, I'm not." Reed opened the door. "But I'd start making things right with my Maker, if I were you. I'd hate to guess how long you have to do it."

FAUN

BY JOE HILL

PART ONE: OUR SIDE OF THE DOOR

Fallows Gets His Cat

The first time Stockton spoke of the little door, Fallows was under a baobab tree, waiting on a lion.

"After this, if you're still looking for something to get your pulse going, give Mr. Charn a call. Edwin Charn in Maine. He'll show you the little door." Stockton sipped whiskey and laughed softly. "Bring your checkbook."

The baobab was old, nearly the size of a cottage, and had dry rot. The whole western face of the trunk was cored out. Hemingway Hunts had built the blind right into the ruin of the tree itself: a khaki tent, disguised by fans of tamarind. Inside were cots and a refrigerator with cold beer in it and a good wifi signal.

Stockton's son, Peter, was asleep in one of the cots, his back to them. He'd celebrated his high school graduation by killing a black rhinoceros, only the day before. Peter had brought along his best friend from boarding school, Christian Swift, but Christian didn't kill anything except time, sketching the animals.

Three slaughtered chickens hung upside down from the branch of a camel thorn, ten yards from the tent. A sticky puddle of blood pooled in the dust beneath. Fallows had an especially clear view of the birds on the night-vision monitors, where they looked like a mass of grotesque, bulging fruits.

The lion was taking his time finding the scent, but then he was elderly, a grandfather. He was the oldest cat Hemingway Hunts had on hand and the healthiest. Most of the other lions had canine distemper, were woozy and feverish, fur coming out in patches, flies at the corners of their eyes. The game master denied it, said they were fine, but Fallows could tell looking at them they were going down fast.

It had been a bad luck season on the preserve all around. It wasn't just sick lions. Only a few days before, poachers had rammed a dune buggy through the fence along the northwestern perimeter, took down a hundred feet of chain-link. They roared around, looking for rhino—the horn was worth more by weight than diamonds—but were chased out by private security without killing anything. That was the good news. The bad news was that most of the elephants and some of the giraffe had wandered off through the breach. Hunts had been cancelled, money refunded. There had been shouting matches in the lobby and red-faced men throwing suitcases into the backs of hired Land Rovers.

Fallows, though, was not sorry he had come. He had, in years before, killed his rhino, his elephant, his leopard, and buffalo. He would get the last of the big five tonight. And in the meantime there had been good company—Stockton and his boys—and better whiskey, Yamazaki when he wanted it, Laphroaig when he didn't.

Fallows had met Stockton and the boys only a week ago, on the night he arrived at Hosea Kutako International. The Stockton gang were fresh off a BA flight from Toronto. Fallows had flown private from Long Island in the Gulfstream. Fallows never bothered with public aircraft. He had an allergy to standing in line to take off his shoes, and he treated it with liberal applications of money. As they were all arriving in Windhoek at roughly the same time, the resort had sent a G-Class Mercedes to gather them up and bring them west across Namibia.

They had only been in the car for a few moments before Immanuel Stockton realized he was the very same Tip Fallows who operated the Fallows Fund, which held a heavy position in Stockton's own pharmaceutical firm.

"Before I was a shareholder, I was a client," Fallows explained. "I proudly served my nation by feeding myself into the woodchipper of a war I still don't understand. I crawled away in shreds and stayed high on your narcotic wonders for close to five years. Personal experience suggested it would be a good investment. No one knows better than me how much a person will pay to escape this shitty world for a while."

He was trying to sound wise, but Stockton gave him an odd, bright, fascinated look, and clapped him on the shoulder, and said, "I understand more than you might think. When it comes to the luxury goods—cigars, furs, whatever—nothing is worth more than an escape hatch."

By the time they spilled out of the big Mercedes, four hours later, they were all in a jolly mood, and after check-in, they took the conversation to the bar. After that, Stockton and Fallows drank together almost every single night, while Peter and Christian horsed around in the pool. When the boy, Christian—he was eighteen, but still a boy to Fallows—asked if they could come with him to see him bag his cat, it never even crossed his mind to say no.

"The little door?" Fallows asked now. "The hell's that? Private game reserve?"

"Yes," Stockton nodded sleepily. The smell of Laphroaig exuded from his pores and his eyes were bloodshot. He had had a lot to drink. "It's Mr. Charn's private game reserve. Invitation only. But also, the little door is . . . a little door." And he laughed again—almost giggled—very softly.

"Peter says its expensive," said Christian Swift.

"Ten thousand dollars to look through the door. Ten thousand more to walk on the other side. Two hundred and thirty to hunt there, and you only get the one day. You can bring a trophy back, but it stays with Mr. Charn, at the farmhouse. Those are the rules. And if you don't have your big five, don't even bother sending him an email. Charn doesn't have any patience for amateurs."

"For a quarter a million dollars, you better be hunting unicorn," Fallows said.

Stockton raised his eyebrows. "Close."

Fallows was still staring at him when Christian touched his knee with the knuckles of one hand. "Mr. Fallows. Your cat is here."

Christian was all alertness, down on one knee, close by the open flap, gently offering Fallows his big CZ 550. For a moment, Fallows had half-forgotten what he was doing there. The boy nodded at one of the night-vision monitors. The lion stared into the camera with radioactive green eyes as bright as new minted coins.

Fallows sank to one knee. The boy crouched beside him, their shoulders touching. They peered through the open flap. In the dark, the lion stood beneath the camel thorn. He had turned his great, magnificent head to look at the blind, with eyes that were intelligent and aloof and calmly forgiving. It was the gaze of a king bearing witness to an execution. His own, as the case happened to be.

Fallows had been closer to the old cat, just once, and at the time there had been a fence between the lion and him. He had studied the grandfather through the chicken wire, staring into those serene, golden eyes, and then told the game master he had chosen. Before he walked away, he made the lion a promise, which he now meant to keep.

Christian's breath was shallow and excited, close to Fallows' ear. "It's like he knows. It's like he's ready."

Fallows nodded, as if the boy had spoken some sacred truth, and gently squeezed the trigger.

At the rolling boom of the shot, Peter Stockton woke with a little scream, twisted in his tangle of sheets, and fell out of the cot.

Christian Tears His Shirt

Christian followed the man Fallows out of the tent. The killer crossed the ground in slow, careful steps, always planting his feet just so, like a pallbearer lugging one corner of an invisible coffin. He laughed and smiled easily, but he had attentive, chilly eyes, the color of lead. Those eyes made Christian think, randomly, of the moons around Saturn, airless places where the seas were acid. Peter and his father enjoyed a good shoot, would yell with pleasure when a bullet thwacked into the hide of a crocodile, or raised a puff of dust off a buffalo's flank. The way Fallows killed, it was as if he himself was the weapon, and the gun was only incidental. Pleasure didn't come into it.

The lion's tail lifted slowly and slapped the dust. Lifted—held in place—and thumped the dust again. The big cat lay toppled on its side.

For a time, Fallows sat alone with his lion and the others hung respectfully back. Fallows stroked its wet muzzle and stared into its patient, still face. Perhaps he spoke to it. Christian had overheard Fallows saying to Mr. Stockton that after he got his lion he might give up hunting, that there was nothing left to go after. Stockton had laughed and said, what about hunting a man? Fallows had looked at him with those chilly, distant eyes, and said, "Hunted them and been hunted by them and have the wounds to prove it." Peter and Christian had debated, ever since, how many men he had killed. It delighted Christian, to know a no-kidding agent of death.

Some San ranch hands materialized out of the night from their own hideaway and a cheer went up at the sight of the dead lion. One unzipped a canvas cooling bag and dug in the ice for beers. The tail struck the ground again, and Christian imagined he could feel the earth vibrating from the blow. But then Christian had a colorful imagination. Stockton helped Fallows to his feet and handed him an icy Urbock.

Peter pinched his nose. "God. Smells like shit. They ought to groom them before a hunt."

"That's the chickens, dumbass," Peter's father said.

The tail rose and fell with a whap.

"Should he shoot it again?" Christian asked. "Is it suffering?"

"No. That's one dead cat," Stockton said. "Nevermind the tail. They do that. It's a mindless post-mortem spasm."

Christian sank down by the lion's head, sketchpad in hand. He stroked the lion's vast, trembling mane, tentatively at first, then more firmly. He leaned close to one velvety ear, to whisper to it, before it was gone, all the way gone: to say fare-thee-well. He was only barely sensible of Peter hunkering down beside him, and the two older men talking behind them. For the moment he was alone with the lion in the profound stillness between life and death, a separate and solemn kingdom.

"Will you look at this paw?" Peter asked, drawing him back to the now. Peter lifted the lion's great limp foreleg, spreading the leathery pads with his thumb.

"Hey there," Fallows said, but Christian wasn't sure who he was talking to.

"Make a hell of a paperweight, wouldn't it?" Peter asked, and growled, and waved the paw at Christian in a lazy swipe.

The paw extruded smooth, sharp hooks of yellowing keratin. A tendon in the foreleg went taut. Christian sprang, throwing his shoulder into Peter's chest. He was fast. The lion was faster. Fallows was faster still. Old, and broken more than once, but fastest of them all.

Fallows hit Peter, who jolted into Christian, and all three of them slammed into the hardpan. Christian felt something snag his shirt, as if the fabric caught on a branch for a moment. Then he was flattened under the other two and all the breath smashed out of him. Fallows kicked, turning onto his side, and rolling the rifle down off his shoulder and into his hands in one fluid motion. The barrel settled into the soft underside of the lion's jaw. The gun went off with a shattering crack that made Christian's ears ring.

Stockton's beer slipped out of his hand and hit the dirt where it spouted foam. "Peter? *Peter!* The fuck is wrong with you?"

Peter was the first to struggle out from the pig pile. He left Christian and Fallows sprawled in the dirt, both of them panting for breath, as if they had collapsed together after a hard sprint. The old soldier groaned exquisitely. Peter stood over them, staring down at the lion in a dazed sort of way, and slapping his own bottom to get the dust off his shorts. He remained in a foggy-eyed trance until his father grabbed him by the shoulder and wrenched him around. Mr. Stockton's face was an alarming shade of red, except for a branch of arteries in his brow, which bulged, pale and shiny, in high relief.

"You fuckin' asshole," Peter's father said. "You know what you just did? You just wrecked his fucking trophy. Mr. Fallows paid thirty thousand for that cat, and now there's a hole the size of a golf ball in its face."

"Dad," Peter gasped. His eyes were shiny with shock and grief. "Dad."

"It's not ruined," Fallows said. "Easily fixed by the taxidermist." He stared up into the darkness. "I might be ready for the taxidermist myself."

Peter Stockton looked from Fallows to his father and back again with brimming eyes.

"How you like that, Pete?" Christian said. His own giddy voice was muffled and distant, as if he had cotton wadding stuffed in his ears. "Mr. Fallows just saved your ass. Lucky for you! That's your best feature."

The San ranch hands had gone still in the tense aftermath of the gunshot. Now, though, they roared with laughter, and erupted into cheers. One of them grabbed Peter by the hands and another shook a beer and let it foam over the teenager's head. In a moment, Peter went from close to tears to crying out in laughter. Stockton gave his son a resentful, furious look . . . and then his shoulders dropped and he laughed too.

Christian felt a cool trickle of air on bare skin, and peered down, and fingered two long slashes in his shirt. The very white chest beneath was unmarked. He laughed and looked at Fallows.

"I'm going to keep this shirt the rest of my life. That's all the trophy I need." He considered for a moment, then said, "Thanks for not letting me get clawed to bits."

"I didn't save anyone. You moved first. You jumped like a deer." Fallows was smiling . . . but his eyes were thoughtful.

"I don't think so, Mr. Fallows," Christian told him, modestly.

"We know what's what around here, Fallows," Stockton said, reaching down with his big hands to squeeze the little man's shoulder. "We know a man when we see one." And he turned his beer over and poured it on Fallows head, while the San whooped it up.

Christian gently collected up his drawing pad from the dust so no one could see what he had been drawing.

Stockton Repays a Debt

When the bell chimed, Stockton went to the door of the suite and opened it on a crack. Fallows was in the hall.

"Come in. Be careful, though. It's dark in here," Stockton warned him.

"What's with the lights?" Fallows asked, as he slipped into the room. "Are we attending a presentation or a séance?"

The lights were off and the curtains drawn in Mr. Charn's corner suite on the fourth floor of the Four Seasons, across from the Boston Common. A single lamp shone, on an end table, but the usual light bulb had been swapped out for one that was tinted red. Stockton had expected the red light. Stockton had seen the Edwin Charn show before.

He opened his mouth to explain—or try to explain—or at least press Fallows to be patient—but Charn spoke first.

"Get used to it, Tip Fallows," came the reedy voice, wavering with age. "If I offer you a spot on my next huntin' party, you'll need to get used to the half light. What's to be shot on the other side of the little door will be shot at dusk, or not a-t'all."

Charn sat in a striped easy chair, to the left of the loveseat. He wore a spritely yellow bow tie and suspenders that pulled his pants too high. Stockton thought he dressed like the benevolent host of a television program for small children, one where they practiced naming the colors and counting to five.

The boys sat together on the loveseat, Peter in a tailored Armani suit,

Christian in a blue blazer. Christian didn't come from money, had made it to private school on his wits. Stockton was proud of his son for looking past the other boy's second-hand wardrobe, and for quietly accepting Christian's broke, shy, strictly religious foster parents. Of course, Christian was probably the only reason Peter had himself graduated from private school—Stockton was sure Christian let him copy on exams, and he had probably written more than a few of Peter's papers. That pleased Stockton as well. You looked out for your friends and they looked out for you. That was the very reason why Stockton had insisted on introducing Fallows to Mr. Charn. Fallows had been looking out for Stockton's boy in Africa, three months ago; Stockton took a certain mellow satisfaction in knowing he could pay the man back with interest. To be honest, a trip through the little door was probably worth any number of overweight, intellectually lazy sons.

A birdcage sat on the coffee table, covered with a sheet of red linen. Or maybe it was white linen and only looked red in the horror-house light, Stockton wasn't sure. If Stockton was running the presentation, he would've started with the birdcage, but he wasn't, and Charn wouldn't.

"Thanks for agreeing to meet me, Mr. Charn," Fallows said. "I'm very interested to hear about the little door. Stockton tells me there's nothing like it anywhere in the world."

Charn said, "A-yuh. He's right enough. Thank you for comin' all t'way to Boston. I don't much care to leave Maine. I don't like to leave the door for long, and t'isn't necessary for me to travel widely to drum up business. Word passes around. The truly curious come to me. I only offer the two hunts a year, and next is on the twentieth of March. Small groups only. Price non-negotiable."

"I heard about the price. That's most of the reason I came . . . the sheer entertainment value of hearing what kind of hunt a person could get for quarter of a million dollars. I can't imagine. I spent forty thousand to kill an elephant and felt I overpaid."

Mr. Charn raised an eyebrow and cast a questioning look at Stockton. "If it's beyond your means, sir, then—"

"He's got the money," Stockton said. "He just needs to see what he'd get for it." He spoke with a certain smooth, confident humor. He had not forgotten how he himself felt when he was in Fallows's boots, recalled his own disgust at the price tag, and his icy unwillingness to be conned. The pitch had turned him around and it would turn Fallows around too.

"I'm just wondering what I could possibly shoot that would be worth that kind of bread. I hope it's a dinosaur. I read a Ray Bradbury story about that, when I was a kid. If that's what you're offering, I promise not to step on any butterflies." Fallows laughed.

Charn didn't. His calm was almost uncanny.

"And if I *do* shoot something—I understand I can't even keep the trophy? All that money and I bring home squat?"

"Your kill will be preserved, mounted and kept at my farmhouse. It may be viewed by appointment."

"For no additional fee? That's decent of you."

Stockton heard the edge in the old soldier's voice and fought down an urge to put a restraining, comforting hand on Fallows' arm. Charn wouldn't be offended by a brittle tone or a sarcastic implication. Charn had heard it all before. He had heard it from Stockton himself only three years before.

"Of course viewing is free, although should you like to take tea while you're visiting, there is a modest service charge," Charn said, in a blasé tone. "Now I should like to share a short video. It is not professionally produced. I made it myself, and some years ago. Still, I feel it is more than adequate to my needs. The video you are about to see has not been altered in any way. I don't expect you to believe that. In fact, I am sure you will not. That is no matter to me. I will establish its veracity beyond any doubt before you leave this room."

Charn pressed a button on the remote.

The video opened with a view of a white farmhouse against a blue sky on the edge of a field of straw. Titles whisked onto the screen, sliding from left to right.

Charn Estate, Rumford, Maine.

They were the sort of titles a person could create in-camera, if they didn't care that it made their video look like childish junk.

There was a cut to a second-floor bedroom, with homey New England touches. An urn, patterned with blue flowers, stood on the bedside table. A brass bed dressed with a handmade quilt took up most of the space. Stockton had slept in that very bed on his last trip to Rumford—well, not slept. He had lain awake the whole restless night, springs digging into his back through the thin mattress, field mice scuttling frantically in the ceiling. The thought of the day to come had put sleep well out of reach.

New titles swept in, chasing off the previous titles.

4 rustic bedrooms, shared bathroom facilities.

"Pretty sure 'rustic' means cold and uncomfortable," Stockton heard his son murmur to Christian. Good Christ, the kid was loud, even when he whispered.

Peter had been too young to go the last time. He wasn't much more mature now, but maybe Christian would keep him in line. Stockton had arranged this meeting to thank Fallows, for saving his son. Not for the first time, it crossed his mind he would be even more grateful to Fallows if he *hadn't* saved the fat little nose-picker.

The video jumped to a shot of a small, green door—a grown man would have to crawl through it—set at one end of a room on the third floor of the farmhouse. *The door!* Stockton thought, with the passion of a convert thoughtlessly crying out *hallelujah* at the sight of a holy relic. The sight of it inspired and delighted him in a way his son never had, not even on the day of his birth.

The ceiling was low on the top floor and at the far side of the room, opposite the camera, it banked steeply downward, so the far wall was only about three feet high. The room contained a single dusty window with a view of the field outside. A new title swept onto the screen:

the little door is opened for curated hunts twice a year.

Charn services cannot guarantee a kll and full payment is required regardless of outcome.

Stockton heard Fallows exhale, a brief hard snort of disquiet. The old soldier was frowning, three deep wrinkles in his brow, his body language stiff with unease. Up until now, Stockton thought, Fallows had assumed the little door was the name for a private compound. He had not expected an *actual* little door.

The titles zipped off the screen. Then the camera was outside, on a hillside, in the dusk—or the dawn, who knew? The sun was below the horizon, but only just. The sky was striated with thin, crimson clouds, and the rim of the earth was a copper line.

A flight of stone steps descended through high strands of pale, dead-looking grass and disappeared among bare, desolate trees. It didn't resemble the land around Charn's house, and it didn't look at all as if it had been shot at the same time of year. The earlier material had depicted high summer. This was Halloween country.

The next cut took the viewers inside a hunting blind, situated well off the ground, and placed them in the company of two hunters: hefty, silver-haired men dressed in camouflage. The one on the left was recognizable as the CEO of one of the biggest tech outfits. He had been on the cover of *Forbes* once. The other was a highly regarded lawyer who had defended two presidents. Fallows rocked back on his heels and some of the tension went out of his posture. There—he wasn't going to walk out of the room just yet. Nothing reassured a man about an investment like knowing richer and more powerful men had already gone first.

The CEO settled onto a knee, the butt of the gun against his shoulder and about an inch of barrel sticking out through the opening in the side of the blind. From here it was possible to see that staircase of rough stone blocks, descending into the valley below. The steps were no more than thirty yards away. At the bottom of the hill, through a screen of wretched trees, it was possible to detect a flash of dark moving waters.

"Hunting is not permitted on the other side of the river," Charn said. "Nor is exploration. Anyone discovered to have crossed the river will have their hunt terminated immediately and will not receive a refund."

"What's over there? State land?" Fallows asked.

"The dolmen," Stockton murmured. "And the sleeper." He spoke without meaning to, and his own tone—reverent, wistful—drew an irritable glance from the other man. Stockton paid him hardly any mind. He had seen her once, from across the water, and some part of him longed to see her again, and some part of him was afraid to go anywhere near.

A flickering light moved into the shot, climbing that distant, crude staircase. It was the figure of a man, holding a torch with a lurid blue flame. He was too far away to see clearly, but he appeared to be wearing baggy, furry pants.

They were coming to it now. The boys on the couch sensed it and leaned forward in anticipation.

The camera zoomed in. The CEO and the lawyer disappeared from the shot, and for a minute the figure on the stairs was an indistinct blot. Then the picture sprang into sharp focus.

Fallows stared at the TV for a long, silent moment and then said, "Who's the asshole in the costume?"

The figure on the steps was hoofed, his legs sleekly furred in a glossy brown coat. His ankles bent backward, close to the hoof, like the ankles of a goat. His torso rose from the flanks of a ram, but it was the bare, grizzled chest of a man. He was naked, except for a stiff looking vest, faded and worn, patterned in gold paisley. A pair of magnificent curling horns curved like conch shells from his curly hair. His torch was a bundle of sticks wired together.

"He's carrying a devil-thorn torch," said Charn. "It crackles and turns green in the presence of . . . menace. But fortunately for our purposes, its range is limited to just a few yards. A Zeiss Victory scope will put you well beyond its reach."

The camera zoomed back out, to include the shoulder and profile of the gunman in the frame.

"Shit," muttered the CEO. "I'm shaking. I'm actually shaking."

The bearded grotesque went still, froze in place on the faraway stone steps. He had the quick, almost instantaneous reactions of a gazelle.

The gun cracked. The faun's head snapped straight back. He tumbled bonelessly, end over end, down three steps, and wound up crumpled in the fetal position.

"Yeah, bitch!" the CEO shouted and turned and gave the famous lawyer a high-five. There was the sound of a beer can cracking and fizzing.

"Okay, kids," Fallows said. "This was fun. Stockton, my room cost, what, eight hundred? You might want to keep that as a down payment on your first therapy session."

He took one step toward the door and Stockton moved . . . not as fast as Fallows had moved in Africa, when he saved Peter from getting his face clawed off, but not too slow on the hoof for all that.

"Do you remember what you said, first time we ever sat down together? You told me no one knows better than you how much a person will pay to escape the world for a while. And I said I *knew*. And I do. Give him five more minutes. Please, Tip." And then Stockton nodded at the birdcage. "Besides. Don't you want to see what he's got there?"

Fallows stared at the hand on his arm until Stockton let go. Then he moved his gaze—that look of almost terrifying emptiness—upon Charn. Charn returned the look with a daydreaming calm. At last, Fallows shifted his attention back to the TV.

The video cut to a trophy room, back in Charn's Rumford farmhouse. It was decorated like a men's smoking club, with a deep leather couch, a couple of battered leather chairs, and a mahogany liquor cabinet. The wall was crowded with mounted trophies, and as Stockton watched the CEO—dressed now in flannel pajama bottoms and an ugly Christmas sweater—hung the latest head. The bearded faun gawped stupidly at the room. It joined a little over a dozen other bucks with glossy curving horns. There was also a trophy that looked, at first glance, like the head of a white rhino. On closer inspection, it more nearly resembled the face of a fat man, with four chins, and a single, stupid, piggy eye above the tusk of a nose.

"What's that?" Peter whispered.

"Cyclops," Stockton replied, softly.

Titles swept across the screen:

trophies are kept in a climate controlled room at Charn's.

Successful hunters may visit with 48hours advance ntice.

Tea and refreshments provided at small additional charge.

"Mister," Fallows said. "I don't know what kind of asshole you think I am—"

"The kind of asshole who has too much money and too little imagination," Charn said, mildly. "I am about to take some of the former and provide you with a bit of the latter, much to your benefit."

"Fuck this," Fallows said again, but Stockton squeezed his arm once more.

Peter looked around. "It wasn't faked. My Dad's been."

Christian nodded to the covered birdcage. "Go on and show us, Mr. Charn. You knew anyone who saw that video would figure it was a fake. But people have been paying you scads of money anyway. So there's *something* under that sheet that's worth quarter of a million dollars."

"Yes," Charn said. "Almost everyone who sees the video thinks of costumes and special effects. In an age of artifice, we only recognize reality when it shows us its claws and gives us a scratch. The whurls have sensitive eyes and ears and the electric lights of our world cause them exquisite pain . . . hence the red lightbulb. If you remove your smartphone from your pocket and attempt to video what you are about to see, I will ask you to leave. It wouldn't be worth the trouble anyway. No one will believe what you recorded, much as you do not believe my video . . . and you will *never* travel through the little door. Do you understand?"

Fallows didn't reply. Charn looked at him with bland, speculative eyes for a moment, then leaned forward and tugged the sheet off the birdcage.

They resembled chipmunks, or maybe very small skunks. They had black, silky fur, and brushy tails, with silver rings running up them. Their tiny hands were leathery and nimble. One wore a bonnet and sat on an overturned teacup, knitting with toothpicks. The other perched on a battered paperback by Paul Kavanagh, and was awkwardly reading one of the little comic strips that came in a roll of *Bazooka Joe* gum. The tiny square of waxed paper was as large, for the whurl, as a newspaper would've been for Stockton.

Both of the creatures went still as the sheet dropped away. The whurl with the comic strip slowly lowered it to look around.

"Hello, Mehitabel," said Mr. Charn. "Hello, Hutch. We have visitors."

Hutch, the one with the comic, lifted his head and his pink nose twitched, whiskers trembling.

"Won't you say hello?" Charn asked.

"If I doesn't, will you pokes my beloved with a cigarette again?" said Hutch, in a thin, wavering voice. He turned to address Stockton and Fallows. "He tortures us, you know. Charn. If one of us resists him, he tortures the other to force our obedience."

"This torturer," Charn said, "doesn't have to bring you picture stories to read, or yarn for your wife."

Hutch flung aside the *Bazooka Joe* strip and jumped to the bars. He looked through them at Christian, who shrank back into the couch. "You, sir! I sees shock in your eyes. Shock at the indecency and cruelty you sees before you! Two intelligent, feeling beings imprisoned by a brute who displays us to wring money out of his fellow sadists for a hunt with no honor! I pleads with you, *run*. Run now. Spread the word that the sleeper may yet awake! Someone may yet revive her with the breath of kings so she may lead us against the poisoner, General Gorm, and free the lands of Palinode at last! Find Slowfoot the faun, oh, I know he lives still, but has only lost his way home, or been bewitched to forget himself somewise, and tell him the sleeper still waits for him!"

Christian began to laugh, a little hysterically. "Wild! Oh, man. For a minute I didn't get it. It's, like, ventriloquism, right?"

Fallows glanced at the boy and exhaled: a long, slow deflation. "Sure. Pretty good. You've got a little amplifier in the base of the birdcage, and someone transmitting in the next room. You had me there for a minute, Mr. Charn."

"We only recognize reality when it shows us its claws and gives us a bite," Charn repeated. "Go on then. Put your finger in the cage, Mr. Fallows."

Fallows laughed without humor. "I'm not sure I'm up on my shots."

"The whurl is more likely to get sick from you than the other way around."

Fallows eyed Charn for a moment . . . and then poked a finger into the cage with a brusque, almost careless courage.

Hutch stared at it with golden, fascinated eyes, but it was Mehitabel who sprang, clutched the finger in both of her sinewy little hands, and cried, "For the sleeper! For the empress!" And fastened her teeth on Fallows's finger.

Fallows yanked his hand back with a shout. The sudden force of his reaction knocked Mehitabel onto her back. Hutch helped her up, muttering, "oh my dear, my love." She spat the blood on the ground and shook her fist at Fallows.

Fallows squeezed his hand closed. Blood dripped from between his fingers. He stared into the cage like a man who has been administered a powerful, numbing sedative . . . a Stockton Pharmaceutical special, perhaps.

"I felt her shouting into my hand," he muttered.

"It's all real, Fallows," Stockton said. "Real enough to sink its teeth into you."

Fallows nodded, once, in a dazed sort of way, without looking from the birdcage.

In a distracted tone, he said, "How much is the deposit again, Mr. Charn?"

Peter Feasts

THE MEN SAT UP front and Peter sat in back with Christian. The car glided through a deformed tunnel of whiteness, heavy flakes of snow falling into the headlights. Cell phone reception sucked. It was a rotten drive. There was nothing to do but talk.

“Tell me about the sleeper,” Christian said, like a child asking for a favorite bedtime story.

Peter could never decide if he loved Christian or secretly kind of despised him. There was something almost otherworldly about him, about his shining gold hair and shining joyful eyes, about the easy grace with which he carried himself, and the easy pleasure with which he attacked his studies, and the infuriating skill with which he drew. He even smelled good. They had shared a dorm room for the last four years, and the door was often open, and the room was frequently half full with honor roll kids and girls in pleated skirts on their way to Vassar, and when Peter stood next to Christian, he felt like a gnome lurking in the shadows a few steps from a blazing torch. Yet Christian adored him and Peter accepted this somewhat as his due. After all, no one else was going to take Christian to Milan or Athens or Africa . . . or through the little door.

“That’s the other side of the river,” Stockton said. “She stays on her side and we stay on ours.”

“But do you have any idea who—what—she is?”

Peter’s father unscrewed the cap on an airline size bottle of Jim Beam. He had cadged it off the flight attendant on the jump from Toronto to Portland, Maine, which was where they had met up with Fallows. He took a nip.

“You can see her if you go down to the riverbank. She’s in a clearing, beneath what you would call a dolmen, which is a little like a prehistoric . . . shed. A stone house with open walls. And there she is . . . this girl, holding a bouquet of flowers.”

Peter leaned forward and asked the question Christian wouldn’t. “What kind of girl, dad? The kind of girl who goes to third grade? Or the kind of girl who goes to third base?”

Christian laughed. That was something else Christian got out of his friendship with Peter. Peter got help with his history final; Christian had someone to say the things and do the things a polite boy wouldn’t say or do.

"What do you think would happen if someone crossed the river to look at her?" Fallows asked.

"Don't even joke. Remember your smart-ass line about going to shoot a dinosaur?"

"Sure. I said I'd be careful not to step on a butterfly. Because of the story, the Ray—"

"I know the story. Everyone knows the story. Walking across the river? That's stomping on the fucking butterfly. We stay in the hills. We stay on our side of the river."

Stockton abruptly switched on the radio and tuned it to a country and western station. Eric Church sang through a thin, grainy layer of static.

Fallows was his father's most interesting friend. Peter wanted to know how he had killed people in the war. He wanted to know what it was like to sink a knife into someone. Peter had read about soldiers who killed the enemy and then raped their wives and daughters. Peter thought that sounded like a pretty exciting reason to enlist.

He was daydreaming about soldiering when they slowed at a military style barrier, a mechanical arm lowered across the road at a gap in a ten-foot-high chain-link fence. Fallows rolled down the driver's side window. Peter's father leaned across him and saluted the fish eye lens of a security camera. The barrier went up. The car went on.

"Charn forgot to install a machine-gun nest," Fallows said.

Peter's father finished his bottle of Beam and let it drop on the floor of the car. He burped softly. "You just didn't see it."

They carried their own bags in across a wide porch that stretched around two sides of the house. There was a Mrs. Charn, it turned out: a short, heavy, shuffling woman who didn't make eye contact with them, but continuously looked at the floor. The coolest thing about her was the big gross red wart below her right eye. It was like a belly-button in her face.

She said Mr. Charn wouldn't be home until later, but that she would be glad to show them around. Peter hated the way the house smelled, of old paperbacks and dusty drapes and mildew. Some of the floorboards were loose. The door frames had settled over the centuries (centuries?) and some of them were crooked and all of them were too low for a 21st-century-sized man. The bedrooms were on the second floor: small, tidy rooms with lumpy single beds, Shaker furniture and ornamental chamberpots.

"You *hope* they're ornamental," Stockton said, as Peter nudged one with his foot.

"Good one, Mr. Stockton," Christian said.

The more he saw, the more depressed Peter got. The toilet in the upstairs bathroom had a pull chain and when he lifted the lid, a Daddy Long Legs crawled out.

"Dad," Peter whispered, in a voice that carried. "This place is a dump."

"You'd think with an income stream of a million dollars a year—" Fallows began.

"The house stays as it is," Mrs. Charn said from directly behind them. If she was disturbed to hear her farmhouse referred to as a dump, one couldn't tell from her voice. "Not a single crooked doorway to be straightened. Not one brick replaced. He doesn't know why the little door opens into t'other place and he won't change anything for fear t'won't open into t'other place again."

The Daddy Long Legs crawled across the floor, to the toe of one of Peter's Gucci sneakers. He squashed it.

But Peter cheered up when they arrived at the terminus of the tour. A grand table had been set up in the trophy room. The sight of all those decapitated heads gave Peter a funny tickle of sensation in the pit of his stomach. It was a little like the nervous pulse of desire that went through him whenever he was gearing himself up to kiss a girl.

Peter and Christian wandered down the length of one wall and along another, staring into shocked, wondering, dead faces. To a man, all of the bucks sported hipster beards; if you ignored the horns, it was possible to imagine Mr. Charn had massacred an artisanal chocolate company in Brooklyn. Peter paused at one, a blondie with elfin, feminine features, and reached up to ruffle his hair.

"Looks like we found your real dad, Christian," Peter said. Christian gave him the finger, but he was such a goody-goody, he hid the gesture behind his body, so no one else could see.

They studied the cyclops in mute, awed silence for a time, and then contemplated a pair of gray-skinned orcs, their ears studded with copper rings, their lolling tongues as purple as eggplants. One of the orc heads was at waist level and Peter surreptitiously mimed face-fucking it. Christian laughed . . . but he also wiped at a damp brow.

The first course was a pea soup. Even though it looked like something Regan barfed in *The Exorcist*, it was hot, and salty, and Peter finished his so quickly he felt cheated. The entrée was a leg of lamb, crispy and bubbling with liquid fats. Peter tore off pieces in long dripping strips—it was just about the best mutton he'd ever had—but Christian only poked at it with his fork. Peter knew from experience that Christian had a nervous, excitable stomach. He threw up easily, always on the first day of school, usually before a big exam.

Mrs. Charn noticed too. "There's some get that way. They get vertigo here. The more sensitive ones. Especially this close to an equinox."

"I feel like a fly on the edge of a drain," Christian said. He spoke with what sounded like a thickened tongue, sounded like a teenager who has found himself drunk for the first time in his life.

Across the table, Fallows held lamb under the table for Mrs. Charn's little dogs, three rat terriers who were scrabbling around his ankles. "You didn't say what Mr. Charn is up to."

"Taxidermist," she said. "Picking up his latest."

"Can I excuse myself?" Christian asked, already shoving back his chair.

He batted through a swinging door. Peter heard him retching in the kitchen. It used to be that the smell of vomit and the sound of someone puking turned his stomach, but after four years of sharing a room with Christian he was inured to it. He helped himself to a second buttery biscuit.

"I had a touchy stomach my first time here too," Peter's father confessed. He tapped Peter affectionately with one elbow. "He'll feel better after we get where we're going. When the waiting is over. By this time tomorrow he'll be famished." He looked to the head of the table. "Do save Christian some leftovers, won't you, Mrs. Charn? Even cold faun is better than no faun at all."

Charn Discovers a Snoop

Mr. Edwin Charn let himself in a little before eleven PM, carrying a bell jar under a sheet of white linen. He stomped his boots and cakes of snow fell off them and then a floorboard creaked somewhere above and he went still. He stood at the foot of the stairs and tuned his senses to the farmhouse. It was common to say that one knew a place like the back of one's hand, but in truth, Charn knew the Rumford farmhouse quite a bit better than the back of his own hand. He only needed to listen to the hush for a few moments to locate, with an uncanny degree of precision, everyone in the building.

The rackety snore in the rear of his house was the wife. He could picture the way she slept, with her head cocked back and her mouth open, a corner of the sheet bunched up in one fist. Springs creaked in a room on the second floor, off to the right side of the landing. From the heavy *sproing* of it, Charn guessed that would be Stockton. The pharmaceutical man was carrying about sixty pounds more than was healthy. His son, the boy Peter, farted and moaned in his sleep.

Charn cocked his head and thought he heard the soft, light pad of a foot on the staircase leading to the third floor. That couldn't be Fallows, the soldier, who had been torn apart and put back together in some war or another; Fallows was sinewy and hard, but moved with pain. The process of elimination left only Christian, the young man who so resembled an idealistic prince from an inspiring story for young boys.

Charn removed his own boots and climbed the stairs with far more care, bringing the bell jar with him.

Christian was in striped pajamas of a very old fashioned sort, the kind of thing one of the Darling children might've been wearing on a Christmas Eve in 1904. He was at the far end of the attic, a single long landing with gable windows. An old sewing table with an iron foot-pedal had a spot under the eaves. The moss colored rug on the floor was so old and dusty it was almost the exact shade of the floorboards it covered. The little door—it was like the door to a cupboard—waited at the far end of the room. Charn was silent while the boy turned the brass latch and drew a deep breath and threw it open.

"Just a crawlspace," Charn said.

The boy sprang partway up and clouted his head on the plaster ceiling: a satisfying reward for a snoop. He sank back to his knees and twisted around, clutching his head in his hands. Christian's face was flushed with embarrassment, as if Charn had discovered him looking at pornography.

Charn smiled to show the boy he wasn't in trouble. The ceiling was at its highest close to the stairs, but Charn still had to duck to move a few steps closer. He held the bell jar out in front of him with both hands, like a waiter from room service, carrying a bedtime snack on a tray.

"I never saw anything except the space behind the walls, until two-thirty am on the night of September twenty-third, nineteen eighty-two. I heard a sound like a goat loose on the third floor, the trip-trap of hooves across the planks. I made it into the hall just in time for something to come barreling into me. I thought it was a kid—not a child, you understand, but a baby goat. It struck me in the abdomen with its horns, knocked me down, and kept going. I heard it crash down the stairs and out the front door. Edna—my wife—was afraid to leave the bedroom. When I had my breath back I went down the stairs, doubled over in pain. The front door hung open on a splendid summer night. The high grass rolled like surf under a fat golden moon. Well. I thought p'raps a deer had got into the house somehow, terrified itself, and escaped. But then I was never one to leave the doors open at night and it struck me peculiar that one would've got all the way up to the third floor. I began to scale the stairs to the attic. I was halfway there when something flashed and caught my eye. A gold coin it was, with a stag engraven 'pon it. I have it still. Well, I climbed the rest of the way in a bemused, baffled, half-scairt state. The little door was shut and I don't know what impulse made me lift the latch. And there, on t'other side. The ruin! The murmur of another world's breeze! That dusk that I think may presage an eternal night. I opened the door every day after that. I kept a calendar. T'other place waited on equinoxes and solstices. On all other days there was nothing but crawlspace back there. I shot my first faun in the spring of nineteen eighty-four, and I brought my kill home with me and was pleased to discover it tasted better than mutton. In nineteen eighty-nine I began the hunts. Since then I've taken down everything from faun to orc, whurl to whizzle, and now my joy is giving other men the opportunity to kill fairy tales themselves, to slaughter the beasts of bedtime stories. Did you know if you eat the heart of a whurl, for a while you can understand the language of squirrels? Not that they have much to say. It's all nuts and fucking. I went bald in my thirties, but have recovered my youthful head of hair since I began eating faun. Though I never speak of it to Missus Churn, I fuck like a bull when I'm away. I get to Portland to see their ladies of leisure twice a month and I've left some walking bowed-legged. Powdered orc horn. Makes Viagra look like an aspirin." He winked. "Go to bed, young fellow. Tomorrow you will see your companions strike down daydreams in the flesh."

Christian nodded obediently and pushed the little door shut. He walked on bare feet, with head down, toward the stairs. But then, just as he crossed by Charn, he looked back, at the bell jar covered in the linen sheet, the same sheet that had previously covered the birdcage.

"Mr. Charn? What's that?" he asked.

Charn stepped forward into the moonlight, set the jar on the sewing desk. He slipped the linen cloth off it, folded the sheet over one arm. "This room is rather bare, isn't it? I thought it needed something to liven it up."

Christian bent to look into the jar. Two whurls had been stuffed and dramatically posed. One stood on an artfully positioned tree branch, holding a sword as long as Christian's pinkie and baring his teeth in a fanged roar. The other, in a green cape, huddled beneath the branch, eyes narrowed in sly thought: a conspirator preparing to spring.

"Good old Hutch," Charn said. "Good old Mehitabel."

PART TWO: *THEIR* SIDE OF THE DOOR

Stockton Wishes For Better Company

PETER WAS IN A pissy mood in the morning. He had forgotten to pack his tactical knife, an MTech with a pistol grip, and he bitched and moaned and stomped around in his bedroom, tossing the contents of his duffle, sure it had to be in there somewhere, until Stockton told him to give it a fucking rest or he could stay behind on earth with the old ladies.

When they assembled in the attic after coffee and pancakes, they were in autumnal camo, beiges and murky greens. They all had guns, except for Christian, who was armed only with his sketch pad. He was fully recovered from the previous evening's queasy spell and now his eyes shone with happiness. He looked from man to man as if it were Christmas morning and he was bursting with feelings of good fellowship. Stockton wondered if you could get a headache from spending too much time with someone so cheerful. Too much uncontrolled optimism ought to be prohibited; people needed to be protected from it, like second hand smoke. To soften the dull throb of pain behind his eyes, it was necessary to unscrew the lid of his thermos and have a sip of coffee, liberally punched up with some Irish Cream.

Charn was the last to join them, and today looked nothing like the host of a program for children on public television. With his Marlin 336 over his shoulder, he carried himself with the casually assertive bearing of the seasoned, lifelong hunter.

"One amongst you was too eager to wait for morning and tried the door last night," Charn said, looking around at them. Christian blushed and Charn smiled indulgently. "Would you care to give it another go, young Mr. Swift?"

Christian sank to one knee by the little door. He held the latch for a single dramatic moment—and then pulled it open.

Dead leaves blew across the wooden floor, carrying with them the scent of fall. Christian stared into the gloaming on the other side for the time it took to draw a single breath and then crawled through. The gay, bright, brass tinkle of his laughter echoed strangely from the far side. Stockton tipped back his thermos and had another swallow.

Peter Yearns For Action

Peter followed Christian through, across the dusty attic floorboards, onto bare, cold earth, and then out from under a low ledge of rock.

He rose and found himself in a clearing on the side of a hill, a natural amphitheater overgrown with pale grass. He turned in a complete circle, looking around. Boulders capped in moss had been scattered helter-skelter around the glade. It took a moment of study to recognize they had been deliberately positioned, creating a semi-circle, like teeth in the lower jaw of some enormous antediluvian brute. A single dead-looking tree, deformed and hunched, cast wild branches out over the ruin. Ruin of what? Some place of cruel worship, perhaps. Or maybe just the equivalent of a scenic turnoff. Who could say? Not Peter Stockton.

His father's hand fell on his shoulder. The wind hissed through the blades of the grass.

"Listen," his father said and Peter inclined his head. After a moment his eyes widened.

The grass whispered, "*poison, poison, poison, poison.*"

"It's murder-weed," his dad told him. "It says that whenever the wind blows and men are about."

The sky above them was the dull color of a bloodstained bedsheet.

Peter looked back at the door as Mr. Fallows pulled his way out of one world and into the other. On this side, the doorframe was made of rough stone and the door itself was built into the slope of the hill, which rose steeply away above that ledge of stone. Charn crawled through last and closed the door behind him.

"Regard your watches," Charn said. "I make it 5:40 am. By 5:40 pm we must be on our way back. If you open that door one minute after midnight, you will find naught but a slab of rock. Oh, and then you are in for it. In our world, the door opens every three months. But three months there is *nine* months *here*. You must wait the term of a woman's pregnancy before it will open again, on the summer solstice, June twenty-first. And in case you can't do the math . . . *yes.* It has been thirty-seven years since I first opened the door in our world. But it has been nine-hundred-and-ninety-*nine* years here."

"Number of the beast," Christian said.

"Number of the beast is six-six-six," Peter said. Peter knew a lot about Satan and the Inquisition and Tom Savini.

Christian said, "Yeah, but turn nine hundred and ninety-nine upside down."

Charn talked over them. "I speak from terrifying personal experience, you do not want to risk being caught here. I spent most of nineteen eighty-five in this world, was hunted by fauns, betrayed by whurls, and forced to strike a vile bargain with a golem in the service of General Gorm the Obese. It was always twilight; nine months of shadows fighting shadows. If we are separated and you do not find your way back here, you *will* be left."

God, he loved to talk, Peter thought. It seemed to Peter that Charn's true calling was not *hunting* but *lecturing*.

They followed Charn down the meandering flight of rough stone steps. The branches of dead trees creaked and rustled and ancient leaves blew around their ankles.

Once, they all stopped, at the sound of a great distant lowing.

"Ogre?" Peter's father asked.

Charn nodded. The groan came again, a sound of aching despair. "Mating season," Charn said and chuckled indulgently.

Peter's rifle thudded and banged against his back and once the barrel caught on a branch. Mr. Fallows offered to carry it for him. His voice did not quite disguise an edge. For himself, Peter was relieved to get it off his back. He felt he was already carrying too much. He hated hunting for the most part. There was too much waiting around and his father wouldn't let him bring his phone. Shooting things was fun but often hours went by and *nothiiiiiing* happened. He sent a mental prayer up to whatever barbaric gods ruled this world for a good quick piece of slaughter before he himself dropped dead, of boredom.

Christian Longs For Night

They went down and down. Christian heard the rushing of water in the distance and shivered with delight, as if he were already up to his waist in the frigid stream.

Charn led them off the steps and into the woods. A yard from the path, he touched a black silk ribbon hanging from a low branch. He nodded meaningfully and walked on into the poisoned forest. They followed a trail of the discreet ribbons for not quite half a mile and at last arrived upon the blind, set twenty feet off the ground. It was a shed resting on cross-planks in the boughs of a tree that resembled but was not an oak. A mossy rope ladder had been draped up out of reach on a high branch. Charn dropped it with the help of a long forked stick.

There were a couple camp chairs in the blind, and a wooden shelf holding some dusty glasses, and a dirty looking paperback called *$20 Lust* if someone wanted something to read. A wide slot, about a foot high and three feet across, faced downhill. Through the trees it was just possible to see the flash of black water below.

Charn was the last up the ladder, and he only stuck his head and shoulders through the trap.

"I built this blind in two thousand-five and haven't shot from here since two thousand-ten. As every year of ours is three of theirs, I think it safe to assume none of them will be on their guard should they pass near. From here you can sight on the stairs, and also pick off anyone moving along the footpath beside the river. I must be out to check the condition of my other blinds and to place a few snares for whurls. With luck I will have some new prizes to replace Mehitabel and Hatch before we exit this world. If I hear a shot I will return at a brisk pace, and you need have no fear of shooting me in the half-light. I know what you can see from this blind and have no intention of crossing into your field of fire. Watch for faun! They are plentiful and you are sure to see some before long. Remember, there are no laws here against taking down a doe or a young'un and the meat is just as tender . . . but we only mount the bucks as trophies!"

He lifted two fingers in a wry salute and descended, gently dropping the trap shut behind him.

Christian had settled in one of the camp chairs with his drawing pad, but leapt up to study a cobweb in a high shadowed corner. The spider had spun a few words into the web:

FREE BED FOR FLYS.

Christian whispered in a breathless voice for Peter to come look. Peter studied it for a moment, then said, "I don't think that's how you spell flies."

Stockton dropped into a camp chair, unbuttoned one of the snap pockets on the front of his camos, and produced a small canteen. He had a sip of coffee and sighed and offered it to Fallows. The other man shook his head.

"Hard to believe it's real," Christian said, turning his drawing pad to a new page and idly beginning to sketch. "That I'm not dreaming this."

"What time do you think it is? Almost night or almost day?" Stockton asked.

Christian said, "Maybe it hasn't made up its mind. Maybe it could still go either way."

"What do you want it to be?" Fallows asked.

"Night for sure! I bet the best things come out at night. The real monsters. Be great to bring back a werewolf head for the wall."

Peter guffawed. He took his rifle back from Fallows and flung himself on the floor.

"Let's hope we don't see a werewolf," Stockton said over the rim of his thermos. "After what we spent to get here, we didn't have much left over for silver bullets."

Fallows Prepares

One hour went by, then another. Christian and Peter ate sandwiches. Stockton sagged in his camp chair, drinking Irish coffee, looking sleepy and content. Fallows waited by the open window, staring into the night. His pulse beat rapidly and lightly, a feeling of anxiety and excitement in him that made him think of waiting in line for a rollercoaster. Fallows always felt this way before a kill.

"I'd like to see her," Christian said. "The sleeper. Hey, Mr. Stockton. You never said. Is she a *little* girl, or like, a grown-up girl?"

"Well, I've only seen her from a distance, but I'd say—"

Fallows reached back with one hand in a gesture that called for silence. Peter stiffened, staring through the slot that faced the slope below. Without looking back, Fallows beckoned Christian to join them at the window.

Three figures mounted the steps. One of them, the tallest, held a torch that blazed with blue fire. Ram's horns rose from either side of his skull and he walked with his hand on the shoulder of his kid, a child in a loose flapping vest, with fuzzed budding horns of his own. The doe was close behind them, carrying a basket.

"It's all yours, Peter," Fallows whispered. "I loaded your gun myself."

"Nail the big one," Stockton said.

Peter stared out at the targets with inquisitive, thoughtful eyes. He seemed to weigh the gun in his hands, as if he was going to throw it instead of shoot it. At last he said, "If I shoot the kid, they'll stop to look after him, and we can nail all three."

"Oh, that's thinking," Stockton said. "You got a good head on your shoulders. And in a minute you're going to have an even better one for Charn's wall."

"Do it," Christian said.

Peter pulled the trigger.

The Hunter Racks up His First Kills

THE GUN MADE AN unsatisfying clack.

Frustrated and confused, Peter threw back the bolt. The rifle was empty.

"Fucking thing," Peter said. Behind him, a chair fell over. "Mr. Fallows, this isn't loaded."

He looked back over his shoulder. His face darkened, then went pale, and Christian tore his gaze away from the fauns to look for himself.

Peter's father had toppled over in his chair, the black rubber handle of a combat knife in his chest. His red, heavy, souse's face was perplexed, a man reading a bank statement that suggests somehow, impossibly, his savings have been wiped out. Christian had a distant, distracted thought, that it was the knife Peter had been unable to find in the morning.

Peter stared at his father, "Dad?"

Fallows stood over Stockton, his back to the boys. He was tugging Stockton's rifle off the dying man's shoulder. Stockton didn't make a sound, didn't gasp, didn't cry out. His eyes strained from his head.

Peter lunged past Christian and grabbed for Fallows' big CZ 550, which was leaning against the wall. His fingers were stiff and clumsy with shock and he only knocked it over.

Fallows couldn't pull Stockton's rifle away from him. The strap was still snagged over his shoulder, and Stockton himself was clutching the butt, in a last, failing effort to resist.

Fallows glanced back at the boys.

"Don't, Peter," he said.

Peter finally grabbed the CZ. He slid open the bolt to make sure it was loaded. It was.

Fallows stepped over Stockton and turned to face them. Stockton still had the strap of the rifle over his shoulder and was clutching the butt, but Fallows had one hand under the muzzle and a finger on the trigger and the barrel pointed at Peter.

"Stop," he said again, his voice almost toneless.

Peter fired. From so close the *blam* of the gun was deafening, a great roar followed by a deadening whine. A chunk of blazing white wood exploded from the tree trunk to the right and just behind Fallows. As the splinters flew past him, Fallows slapped Stockton's hand away and squeezed the trigger of his gun. Peter's head snapped back and his mouth dropped open in an expression that had been common to him in life: a look of dim-witted bewilderment. The red-and-black hole above his left eyebrow was big enough to insert two fingers.

Christian heard someone screaming, but there was no one left alive in the blind except for Fallows and himself. After a few moments he realized he was the one making all the noise. He'd dropped his notepad and held up both hands to protect his face. He didn't know what he said or promised, couldn't hear himself through the ringing in his ears.

The trapdoor rose about a foot and Charn looked in on them. Fallows wrenched the rifle free from Stockton at last and turned the barrel around to point it at the old man. Charn fell, just as quickly, the trapdoor slamming behind him. Christian heard a leafy crunch as the tall man hit the ground below.

Without a look back, Fallows flung open the trapdoor, dropped through it, and was gone.

Christian in Flight

It was a long while before Christian moved. Or at least he felt it was a long while. In that half-lit world, the passage of minutes was difficult to judge. Christian did not own a watch and had left his phone, by command, in the other world. He only knew he'd had time to dampen his crotch, and then time for that dampness to grow cold.

He trembled in convulsive bursts. He lifted his head and peered through the lookout. The fauns had long disappeared from the steps. The hill was silent in the gloaming.

It came to him, with a sudden, sickened urgency, that he had to get back to the little door. He picked up his sketchbook, hardly thinking why—because it was his, because it had his drawings in it—and crawled across the plank floor of the blind. He hesitated beside the corpse of Mr. Stockton. The big man stared at the ceiling with wide, startled eyes. His thermos lay close to hand. The coffee had spilled out and soaked into the floorboards. Christian thought he should take the knife and he tried to pull it out of Stockton's chest, but it was buried too deeply, the blade jammed between two ribs. The effort made him sob. Then he thought he should crawl back to Peter and pull the CZ 550 out of his hands, but he couldn't bear to look at the hole in Peter's forehead. In the end he left the blind as he had come, unarmed.

He made his unsteady way down the rope ladder. It had been easy going up. It was much harder going down, because his legs were shaking.

When he was on the ground, Christian scanned the gloom and then began to move across the face of the hill, toward the flight of rough stone steps. A black silk ribbon caught his eye and he knew he was not turned around.

He had hiked far enough to work up a good sweat when he heard shouts, and a sound like a herd of ponies running through the trees. Not a dozen feet away he saw a pair of fauns dart through the shadows. One carried a curved blade. The other had what looked like a throwing bolas, a mass of hanging leather straps with stones tied at the end.

The one with the scimitar leapt a fallen trunk, scrambled with the vitality of a stag up the hill, and bounded out of sight. The one with the bolas followed for a few yards—then caught himself and looked down the hill, fixing his gaze on Christian. The faun's leathery, scarred face was set in an expression of haughty contempt. Christian screamed and fled down the hill.

The trunk of a tree rose out of the darkness and Christian slammed into it, was spun halfway around, lost his footing, and fell. He rolled. His shoulder struck a sharp stone and he was spun again, continuing to tumble down the hill, picking up speed. Once it seemed his whole body left the ground in a spray of dead leaves. At last, he struck hard against another tree and was jolted to a stop against it. He found himself in the bracken at the bottom of the hill. Just beyond the ferns was a mossy path and the river.

Christian was too afraid to pause and consider how badly he might've been hurt. He looked up the hill and saw the faun glaring down at him from fifty feet away. Or at least that's what he thought he saw. It might've been a gaunt and hunched tree, or a rock. He was mad with fear. He sprang to his feet and ran limping on, breath whining. His left side throbbed with pain and he had twisted his ankle coming down the hill. He had lost his sketchpad somewhere.

The lanky boy followed the path downstream. It was a wide river, as wide as a four-lane highway, but at a glance, not terribly deep. The water rushed and foamed over a bed of rock, spilling into dark basins before hurrying on. In the blind, their shared body heat had created a certain stuffy warmth, but down by the river it was cold enough for Christian to see his own breath.

A horn sounded somewhere far off, a hunting horn of some sort, a long bellowing cry. He cast a wild look back and staggered. Torches burned in the almost-night, a dozen distant blue flames flickering along the mazy staircases that climbed the hills. It came to Christian there might be dozens of parties of fauns in the hills, hunting the men. Hunting him.

He ran on.

A hundred yards along his right foot struck a stone and he went down on hands and knees, hard.

For a while he remained on all fours, gasping. Then, with a start of surprise, he saw a fox on the far side of the water, watching him with avid, humorous eyes. They gazed at each other for the length of time it took to draw a breath. Then the fox bayed at the night.

"Man!" The fox cried. "Man is here! A Son of Cain! Slay him! Come and slay him and I will lap his blood!"

Christian sobbed and scrambled away. He ran until he was dizzy and seeing lights, the world throbbing and fading, throbbing and fading. He slowed, his legs shaking, and then shouted in alarm. The light he had been seeing at the edge of his vision, a wavering blue glow, was a torch. A man stood on the hill, a black shape against a blacker background. He held the torch in his right hand. In his left was a gun.

He acted without thought. Because the man was on his right, Christian swerved to the left and crashed into the river. It was deeper than it looked. In three lunging steps he was up to his knees. In moments he had lost all sensation in his feet.

He ran on and the ground dropped away and he plunged in to his crotch and cried out at the shock of the cold. His breath was fast and short. A few desperate steps later he fell and all but went under. He struggled against the current, had not expected it to be so strong.

The boy was halfway across when he saw the dolmen. A plate of gray stone, as big as the roof of a garage, stood on six tilting, crooked rocks. Beneath the roof of gray stone, in the center of the covered area, was an ancient, uneven altar stone, with a girl in a white nightdress, sleeping peacefully upon it. The sight of her terrified him, but fear of his pursuers drove him on. Fallows had moved out from beneath the darkness of the trees. He was already up to his ankles in the river, having removed his shoes before stepping into the water. While the boy had stumbled, sunk, and half-drowned, somehow Fallows knew just where to step so he was never more than shin deep.

The water along the bank was hip high and Christian grabbed at handfuls of slippery grass to pull himself up. The murder-weed hissed "*poison, poison!*" at him and came out in clumps and dropped him back into the river and he went up to his neck and exploded into sobs of frustration. He threw himself at the bank again and kicked and squirmed in the dirt like an animal—a pig, trying to struggle out of a mire—and floundered onto dry land. He did not pause, but ran beneath the dolmen.

It was at the edge of a grassy meadow, the nearest line of trees hundreds of feet away, and Christian understood that if he tried to make it to the forest, Fallows would easily pick him off with the rifle. Also, he was shaking and exhausted. He thought desperately he might hide and reason with Fallows. He had never shot a thing. He was an innocent in this. He felt sure that Fallows had killed the others as much for what they had done as what they had intended to do. The unfairness of it raked at him. Fallows had killed too. The lion!

He ducked behind one of the standing stones and sat and hugged his knees to his chest and tried not to sob.

From his ridiculous hiding place Christian could see the child. Her golden hair was shoulder length and looked recently brushed. She held a bouquet of buttercups and Queen Anne's lace to her chest. Everything Christian had seen in this place was dead or dying, but those flowers looked as fresh as if they had just been picked. She might've been nine and had the sweet pink complexion of health.

Firelight cast a shifting blue glow across the dolmen as Fallows approached.

"Have you ever seen a more trusting face?" Fallows asked, softly.

He stepped into view, the gun in one hand, the torch in the other. He had collected Christian's drawing pad and carried it under one arm. He did not look at Christian but instead sat on the edge of the stone, beside the sleeper. He looked upon her like one inspired.

Fallows set down the sketchbook. From inside his camouflage coat he produced a small glass bottle, and another, and a third. There were five in all. He unscrewed the black top of the first and held it to the little girl's lips, although it was empty, or seemed empty.

"This world's been holding its breath for a long time, Christian," Fallows said. "But now it can breathe again." He unscrewed the next and raised it to her mouth.

"Breath?" the boy whispered.

"The breath of kings," Fallows agreed, with a mild nod. "Breath of the lion and the elephant, the leopard and the buffalo, and the great rhino. It will counteract the work of the poisoner, General Gorm, and wake her and wake the world with it."

When he had emptied all of the empty bottles, he sighed and stretched his legs. "How I hate shoes. God save my kind from shoes. And those awful prosthetic feet!"

Christian dropped his gaze to the black, shining, bony hooves at the end of Fallows's ankles. He tried to scream again but was all screamed out.

Fallows saw him recoil and the faintest smile twitched at his lips. "I had to shatter my own ankles—smash and reset them—you know. When I first came to your world. Later I had them broken and rebuilt again, by a doctor who was offered a million dollars to keep my secret, and was paid in lead to confirm his silence." Fallows brushed back his curly hair and touched the tip of one pink ear. "Thank goodness I am not a Mountain Faun, but only a mere faun of the plains! The Mountain Faun have ears just like the deer of your world, whereas we simple country faun have the ears of men. Though I would have gladly cut my ears off for her if it had been necessary. I would have cut my heart out and offered it to her slippery and red and beating in my own hands."

Fallows rose and took a step toward him. The torch, which he had never set aside, shifted from blue to a lurid, polluted emerald. Sparks began to fall from the flames.

"I don't need my torch," Fallows said, "to know what you are. And I didn't need to see your sketches to know your heart."

He tossed the sketchbook at Christian's feet.

Christian looked down at a drawing of severed heads on sticks: a lion, a zebra, a girl, a man, a child. The breeze caught the pages and leafed through them idly. Drawings of guns. Drawings of slaughter. Christian's stunned, frightened gaze shifted to the torch.

"Why is it changing color? I'm not a menace!"

"Charn doesn't know much about devil-thorn. It doesn't change color in the presence of *menace*, but of *wickedness*."

"I never killed anything!" Christian said.

"No. You only laughed while other men killed. Who is the worse, Christian, the sadist who serves his true nature honestly, or the ordinary man who does nothing to stop him?"

"*You* killed! You went to Africa to kill a lion!"

"I went to Africa to free as many of my empress's friends as I could, and so I did, after putting a little money in the right hands. A dozen elephants and two dozen giraffes. The lions, I infected with one of your unclean world's many diseases, to give them their dignity and release. As for the grandfather I shot, he was ready to hunt the tall grass in the savannah of ghosts. I asked his forgiveness the day before the hunt and he gave it. You spoke to him too . . . after I shot him. Do you remember what you said as he bled out?"

Christian's face shriveled with emotion and his eyes stung terribly.

"You asked him how it felt to die. He tried to show you, Christian, and he almost did it. How I wish you hadn't escaped him. It would've saved me an ugly bit of work here."

"I'm sorry!" Christian cried.

"Aye," Fallows said. "Aren't we both?"

He lowered the barrel of the gun. The steel kissed Christian's right temple.

"Wait, I—" Christian shrieked.

His voice was lost to the rolling sound of thunder.

The Sleeper Awakes

After, Fallows sat by the girl to wait. For a long time nothing happened. Fauns crept close to the dolmen, but stayed respectfully outside the circle, looking in. The oldest of them, Forgiveknot, an elderly faun with a rippling scar across his leathern face, began to sing. He sang Fallows' old name, the name he had left behind in this world when he fled through the little door with the last of the empress's treasures, to find the breath of kings, and return her to life.

The light had taken on a faint, pearly glow when the girl yawned, and rubbed one fist in a sleepy eye. She looked up, her eyes fogged with drowsiness, and her gaze found Fallows. For a moment she didn't recognize him, her brow creased with puzzlement. Then she did and she laughed.

"Oh, Slowfoot," she said. "You've gone and grown up without me! And you have lost your proud horns! Oh, my darling. Oh, my old playmate! I shall never forgive you."

By the time Fallows had shed his human clothes, and Forgiveknot was cutting his hair with a wide-bladed knife, she was sitting on the edge of the stone altar, swinging her feet above the grass, as the fauns formed a line, to kneel before her, and bow their heads, and receive her blessing.

A World Awakes with Her

For the third time, Charn gritted his teeth to keep from passing out. When the woozy feeling passed, he went on, crawling arm over arm, staying down. He went slowly, crossing no more than ten yards in a single hour. His left ankle was broken—badly. It shattered when he fell from the blind and it had been a narrow thing, giving Fallows the slip.

There were six fauns in the circle of worship, set there to cut off any escape through the little door. But Charn still had a gun. He had methodically worked his way higher, avoiding the murder-weed that would whisper if it saw him—*Poison! Poison!*—moving so slowly that the crackle of dead leaves beneath him was all but imperceptible, even to the sharp ears of the fauns. There was a shelf of rock, jutting out over the clearing. It was only accessible from one side, as the slope on the other side was too steep and the earth too loose. Nor could it easily be approached from the crag above. For an armed man on this outcropping, though, firing into the clearing would be like shooting faun in a barrel.

Whether he ought to open fire, well—that was another question. The faun war party might yet be led away. The boy Christian might yet make a convenient appearance and draw them off. On the other hand, if the numbers below swelled, perhaps it was best to simply slink away. He had survived in this world for nine months once before, and he knew a golem who would make a deal. General Gorm the Obese always had work for a bad man with a gun.

Charn pulled himself behind a rotting log and swiped the sweat from his brow. A single lightning-struck tree, like a beech, loomed over him, partially cored out. Below him, some brush rustled at the edge of the clearing, and the one named Forgiveknot slipped into the glade, bolas hanging from his belt. Charn knew him well. He'd misjudged a shot at the old faun years before, and given him that scar across the face. He smiled grimly. He so hated to miss.

The sight of him made up Charn's mind: kill them now, before anymore showed up. He slipped the Remington off his shoulder and rested the barrel on the log. He put the front sight on Forgiveknot.

Something clattered in the dead tree over him. There was a chittering and a rustle.

"Assassin!" cried a whurl gazing down at Charn from one branch of the blasted tree. "Save yourselves! A Son of Cain is here to kill you all!"

Charn rolled and swung the barrel up. His sights found the whurl and he pulled the trigger and the gun made a flat, tinny click. For a moment he just stared at the old Remington in a kind of blank bewilderment. It was loaded—he had put a fresh cartridge in himself only a few minutes before. A misfire? He didn't believe it. He cleaned and oiled the gun once a month, whether he used it or not.

He was still trying to come to grips with that awful, dead click when the loop of rope fell. It caught him around the face and Charn sat up, and as he did, it dropped around his neck and tightened. The lasso *yanked.* The rope choked off his air, and it jerked him back, over the rotten log and over the edge. He spun as he fell. He hit the earth with enough force to drive all the air out of him. Ribs broke. Pain screamed in his broken ankle. A thousand black specks wheeled around him, like midges, only they were in his head.

He sprawled on the ground, ten feet from his little door. As his vision cleared, it seemed the sky was lighter, almost lemon colored. He could see fair clouds in the distance.

His right hand fumbled for the rifle, but just as his shaking fingers scraped the butt, whoever held the other end dragged him away. Charn choked, tried to force his fingers under the rope, and couldn't. He rolled and kicked as he was dragged and wound up on his belly, beneath the single corrupted, dead tree that leaned out over the whole natural amphitheater.

"Rifle wouldn't do you any good anyway," Fallows said from above him. Charn stared at his black hooves. "I took the firing pin out last night, while you were upstairs with Christian."

The tension on the line slackened and Charn was able to loosen the noose a few centimeters and capture a breath. He stared up at Fallows. His skull was shaved clean to show the stumps of two horns, long since sawed off, and he was backlit by a sky the reddish-gold of new minted copper.

A little girl stood beside Fallows, holding his hand. She looked gravely down at Charn . . . the stern, cool, appraising look of a queen.

"It's come for you, Mr. Charn," the little girl said. "It's found you out at last."

"What?" Charn asked. "What's come?"

He was confused and frightened and desperately wanted to know.

Fallows cast one end of the rope over a bough of the overhanging tree.

"Daylight," the girl said, and with that, Fallows hoisted Charn kicking into the air.

About Our Contributors

N. J. Ayres has been a pioneer of the forensic mystery with her Smokey Brandon novels. But short stories are Noreen's favorite form; hers have been featured in many mystery and suspense anthologies, and earned her an Edgar Award nomination for "Delta Double Deal."

Laura Benedict is the Edgar- and ITW Thriller Award-nominated author of eight novels of mystery and suspense, including *The Stranger Inside* (February 2019). Her short fiction has appeared in *Ellery Queen's Mystery Magazine,* and in numerous anthologies.

A voracious reader, **Jill D. Block** is a partner at a global law firm, practicing real estate law. In between billable hours, she writes the kind of fiction she likes to read. Since 2015, Jill's stories have appeared in magazines (*EQMM*) and anthologies (*Dark City Lights*). She published her first novel, *The Truth About Parallel Lines*, in 2018, and is currently at work on her second. And she's still a lawyer, awaiting a sign from the universe.

Richard Chizmar is the co-author (with Stephen King) of the *New York Times* bestselling novella, *Gwendy's Button Box.* His latest book, *Widow's Point*, a tale about a haunted lighthouse written with his son, Billy Chizmar, is currently being filmed. *Ellery Queen's Mystery Magazine* and *The Year's 25 Finest Crime and Mystery Stories* are among the many publications in which his short fiction has appeared.

Hilary Davidson has won two Anthony Awards as well as the Derringer, Spinetingler, and Crimespree awards. She is the author of five novels; her latest is *One Small Sacrifice* (Thomas & Mercer, 2019). A Toronto-born journalist and the author of 18 nonfiction books, she has lived in New York City since October 2001.

Jim Fusilli is the author of eight novels including *Narrows Gate,* a World War II-era epic set in a gritty Italian-American community in the shadow of New York. His debut mystery novel *Closing Time* was the last work of fiction set in New York published prior to the 9/11 attacks. His short stories have been nominated for Edgar and Macavity awards. As a journalist, he served as the Rock-and-Pop Critic of the *Wall Street Journal.*

Joe Hill is the #1 *New York Times* Bestselling author of *The Fireman*, *NOS4A2*, and others.

Elaine Kagan is a Los Angeles based actress, journalist (*Los Angeles Magazine, Los Angeles Times*) and novelist (*The Girls, Losing Mr. North*). When she visits New York she always has a tuna melt at the Viand Coffee Shop on Madison Avenue. On rye.

Joe R. Lansdale is a novelist with over fifty novels to his credit, and over four hundred short stories and articles. His work has been filmed and made into the Sundance TV series, *Hap and Leonard.*

Warren Moore is Professor of English at Newberry College in Newberry, SC. He is the author of *Broken Glass Waltzes*, and a repeat offender in these anthologies, having appeared in *Dark City Lights, In Sunlight And In Shadow,* and *Alive In Shape And Color*. He has played drums in a variety of unsuccessful bands, and has the hearing loss to prove it.

Joyce Carol Oates is the author most recently of the story collections *Beautiful Days* and *Night-Gaunts* and the novel *Hazards of Time Travel.* Her story "The Woman in the Window," from Lawrence Block's *In Sunlight and in Shadow,* was reprinted in *The Best American Mystery Stories 2017*. She is the 2018 recipient of the Los Angeles Times Book Award for Mystery/Thriller Fiction.

Ed Park is the author of the novel *Personal Days* and the editor of *Buffalo Noir*. His stories have appeared in *The New Yorker*, *Vice*, and other places. He lives in Manhattan.

Nancy Pickard likes to read and write short stories because, she says, of the heat they generate from being compressed. She has recently moved from Kansas to South Carolina in search of heat, too.

Thomas Pluck has slung hash, worked on the docks, trained in martial arts in Japan, and even swept the Guggenheim museum (but not as part of a clever heist). His new collection, *Life During Wartime*, includes "Deadbeat," singled out as a Distinguished Mystery Story of 2017. *Library Journal* has called his stories "stunning," and Joyce Carol Oates says he's "a lovely kitty man."

A lifelong Texan, **James Reasoner** has been a professional writer for more than forty years. In that time, he has authored more than four hundred hundred novels and short stories in numerous genres.

Wallace Stroby is an award-winning journalist, and the author of eight novels, four of which feature professional thief Crissa Stone, whom Kirkus Reviews named "Crime fiction's best bad girl ever." A New Jersey native, for 13 years he was an editor at the Newark *Star-Ledger*, Tony Soprano's hometown newspaper.

Duane Swierczynski is the two-time Edgar-nominated author of ten novels including *Revolver*, *Canary*, and the Shamus Award-winning *Fun & Games*. He's also written over 250 comic books featuring such notable literary figures as Deadpool, The Punisher and Godzilla. He was born and raised in Philly and lives in Los Angeles with his wife and children.

Lawrence Block is the editor of *At Home in the Dark,* but evidently couldn't be bothered to write a story for it. He's been identified as a man who needs no introduction, and that's exactly what he's getting here.

Lawrence Block's Newsletter: I get out an email newsletter at unpredictable intervals, but rarely more often than every other week. I'll be happy to add you to the distribution list. A blank email to lawbloc@gmail.com with "newsletter" in the subject line will get you on the list, and a click of the "Unsubscribe" link will get you off it, should you ultimately decide you're happier without it.

Email: lawbloc@gmail.com
Twitter: @LawrenceBlock
Facebook: lawrence.block
Website: lawrenceblock.com

CPSIA information can be obtained
at www.ICGtesting.com
Printed in the USA
LVHW082257220422
716606LV00033B/337

9 781951 939892